Adameen

– DONALD MADGE –

An environmentally friendly book printed and bound in England by
www.printondemand-worldwide.com

Mixed Sources
Product group from well-managed
forests, and other controlled sources
www.fsc.org Cert no. TT-COC-002641
© 1996 Forest Stewardship Council

PEFC Certified
This product is
from sustainably
managed forests
and controlled
sources
www.pefc.org
PEFC/16-33-415

This book is made entirely of chain-of-custody materials

www.fast-print.net/store.php

Adameen
Copyright © Donald Madge 2011

ISBN 978-178035-023-3

First published 2011 by
FASTPRINT PUBLISHING
Peterborough, England.

One

Four years and an introduction: 1957 – Driscolls' farm at Three Crosses, my mother, my sisters and me. This year, realtime – a Connecticut connection. 1975 – a London wedding. Back to the dramatis personae and further back to 1956 – my father remembered.

Nine miles east of the massive, naked, mauve flank of Mount Slievegarriff, Kilcreggan hill likewise rose out of that gentle land. On Kilcreggan's southern slope, beneath the government conifer plantations, our fields began. The road itself did not begin on our side of the hill, but in Coole valley beyond to the north, where it had once served the Kilcreggan slate quarries. Straight and metalled, barely wide enough for a well-loaded hay-wagon, it ran down by our farm gate at Three Crosses, passing for the most part between low and ancient walls of slates and granite or hedges of elder, bramble, ferns and hawthorn.

In the 'fifties, the entrance to our farm, Driscolls', was guarded by a pair of maroon-painted, high, timber gates. Standing outside the gates with your back to the mountain, you looked south to see the road dip out of the sunlight into a tunnel-like avenue of mature horse chestnuts, wisps of hay dangling from their lower branches. After a couple of hundred yards, it turned sharp left and then took you away off past the field with the three Celtic crosses, a mile or two to the good farming land round the nearest village, Tourmahinch, and, beyond, Blanchardstown. In the other direction, the road toiled up the side of Kilcreggan hill and on past to Coole and the north.

Perched on the highest bar of the double gates and leaning out over the road, I saw my mother coming back up from Cullen's dairy, pushing a black Rudge bicycle with a brick of cheese in brown paper clamped on the carrier. I wanted to cry again when I saw her so lonely. Last summer she and my father would always go down to the dairy together. I dropped back into the farmyard and pretended to be playing in the stack of kindling wood. Mother came in, propped the bicycle against the pier, then shot the bolt and tied the gate-hasp with a shoelace-knot of clothes rope, to keep in my younger sisters. Emerging briefly from her preoccupations, she told me what a great man I was and went into the house through the green half-door. I clambered the six feet over the heavy gates and dropped down into the forbidden territory of the roadside. I knew the gates would be untied and swung open soon, so that Grandfather Thomas could drive in with the donkey and cart between the stuccoed, whitewashed gate piers and I would be able to slip back in too.

I looked left, up the hill towards the woods and then right, down the long sweep of the road towards the avenue. In those days it was a highway for ponies and traps, for wary, weary donkeys hauling farm carts; a high road for bicycles too, ticking loud like cicadas as they freewheeled down to the turn. You could hear motorcars from a mile or so off, a wheezing Ford Prefect, the whine of a side-valve Morris or the throb of one of the new, all-conquering Volkswagens. Like old ladies' shawls or telephones, motorcars were always black in those days. The verdant canopy of the avenue would muffle their sound for a few moments and then the motorcars would shoot up at you from out of the trees and pass with a whoosh and a glimpse of a driver saluting, scattering the debris of hay and seed and straw and capsized beetles in little eddies at the road edge.

I peered back into the yard through the crack between the gates. Mother was out in the yard again. The pump handle untethered, she was about to draw water for the potatoes. A few yards from mother, my sisters were playing - Lindie, in her plaits and lilac frock; Beebie and Kate, barefooted and a toddler, in their emerald dungarees and bobs, sitting over in the kindling stack, chattering. Beebie was knitting with two bits of twig and no wool.

'Show the big gallon', said Mother. Lindie, the eldest, got to her feet and skipped over, swinging the larger of two aluminium pails. Mother had not missed me at the maroon gates, assuming I had gone up into the orchard at the back of the house. I think I wanted her to find me outside, on our road, where I should not be. Needled by me, she might yet give away that she loved me. I had, you see, the beginning of a fear, a premonition: now that I had no father, I was losing my mother, too. The sting of her anger then might have persuaded me otherwise.

'Addie!' She called out twice and, through the crack between the planking of the gate, I searched for the expression on her face as she formed my name. 'Addie!' Mother went backwards into the house through the half-door with the big pail. 'Beebie!' She called again and this time she got an answer. Beebie put her two twig knitting-needles into the breast pocket of her dungarees and hopped and skipped into the house after mother. I was locked out.

*

Locked out? Perhaps I have said too much, too soon. Half a century on, my middle sister Beebie's eldest, Susie, has just married Todd Davern, a publisher from Grand Rapids. My niece's wedding was in Hartford, Connecticut on Saturday, real-time, and I got back yesterday. On Friday, the night before the wedding, over his second bourbon, Todd told me to put all of this down on paper and send it to his company's New York office. But it wasn't whisky that set me on this journey to the past in front of me. By God, I'm done of the drink. I went dry many years ago. Two things had me writing this.

One was Todd Davern's own surname; there used to be Daverns in Three Crosses, you see, but in the distant past. Todd said to me: 'Your story is one people will want to read.' It has to be one I want to write, is what I said. If I put words to realities, it's because I want messages for myself. Maybe there are meanings for others, too.

The second thing that made me begin the tale this morning is a 'thirty-nine Morris Eight handbrake-release. I keep it in the passport drawer in the bureau in front of me. Thirty years ago and more, when I was twenty-eight, this brake-release came back with me to London from another wedding, in Tourmahinch, and I made up my mind at the time I would turn it into a walking-cane handle. That is still an uncompleted project. The handle has a good feel; it has the look of the top end of a riding-crop, in nineteen-thirties, white Bakelite and a release button in grey plastic like a small octave key. I should get on and find someone to set it on a cane for me; then its role will be to take me out on my walks.

At this moment, where it takes me is three decades back to that wedding in the seventies in Tourmahinch, near Three Crosses. But we go back further, I and this piece of black-painted tube and early plastic, another twenty years, to when I am eight years old and I first set my child's hand on it, inside the bluebottle-coloured rotting shell of Great-Uncle Vance's Morris Eight, in our orchard at Three Crosses. Here are the tears of things; the dead-seeming past, that goes straight to the heart.

*

On our road, in the fifties, the older farmers delivering to the creamery drove unshod donkeys and flat, two-wheeled carts they called 'cars', freighted with churns. The first you heard was the grinding of the iron tyres on the road-chippings. The old fellows sat up front left, in greasy suits gone at the cuffs and elbows and collarless shirts, battered fedoras shading their eyes and their booted feet dangling over the side, inches from the nearside wheel. The younger men would take a pony and car and for them it was a point of honour always to stand as they drove. Facing down the road, you would hear the ponies' clip-clop borne up on the summer air for many minutes, before they and their drivers took form slowly from beneath the trees.

''Tis Jimmy Grehan, girl.'

'Arra, 'tisn't. He has an ass and car, girl.'

''Tis Peter Cody.'

'Faith and it isn't.'

'It is so. He've three churns.'

''Tis Panloaf.'

I stood listening to my two aunts as they leant out over the road from the bedroom window in the grey-washed gable end of the house, chattering and giggling. My Aunt Margaret, or Peggy, was eighteen then and Aunt Finola, or Feena, not much older. Peggy and Feena kept their printed frocks and new cardigans on, till all the lads from Three Crosses and Coole and Kilcreggan and Ballindarragh beyond were gone up from the creamery. I flattened back against the fuchsia hedge in case the aunts saw me and whisked me back into the yard. Aunt Feena would tell me I had no right to be out playing on the road. My gentle, beautiful Aunt Peggy, whose gaze was the warmth of the sun on me, wouldn't contradict Feena.

'You're a big old fuchsia yourself, Bozer', Aunt Peggy would say, 'so you are, hanging in the hedge there, with the pink shirt and them red britches; go in out of that!'

It was partly the danger from the occasional motorcar or the wool-factory lorry, but even more so the feeling that the road beyond the gate-piers was the world, and the world was not yet ready for me, nor I for it. I, Addie, at ten years old, was newly fatherless and so needed special protection. Aunt Peggy had a name for me, Bozer, that came on my ears like an arpeggio when she called me.

Panloaf was what everyone called Michael O'Donoghue behind his back because of the odd way he went hatless out of doors, though a grown man, with his fair hair smarmed down like a bread crust on either side of his oblong head. Panloaf had not been to the creamery and was driving a Shire horse and four-wheeled dray - both rarities in our parts. He had a dozen sacks of calf nuts. One sack was for us. He pulled up at our gate, his knowing and eager eyes seeking out Peggy or Feena. He unhitched the horse, though there was no need, then gave me a couple of empty potato sacks to drape over the wheels in case the heat of the sun loosened the iron tyres. Everyone knew why he liked to make himself useful to Grandfather Driscoll, but his interest in my aunts appeared not to be reciprocated and they slipped off up the road to Brittans', to borrow bread soda. So Panloaf supped away at his cup of tea for half an hour, but to no avail. 'Thank you Mrs Bennett, thank you Mrs', he said to my mother on his way out, just as he did when he took the collection in chapel.

My aunts reappeared soon enough. Behind them, a motorcar could be heard louder and louder coming down from Coole and the girls stepped carefully well back into the verge, knowing from the sound and hour who the driver was.

'Mind yourself, Bozer', said Peggy to me.

'Go back in out of that', added Feena, "tis Hughie Heaphy.'

'I know.'

'He has two working gears on that motorcar and no brake cables, only baling twine, and he the devil of a driver.'

Heaphy's motorcar, a Standard Ten, went by at a rate. I glimpsed a laughing, tousled, red head and an arm dangling from the car window in the heat. The tang of burnt petrol spread its taint.

I lingered outside the gates for the post-van, which had not yet gone up to Coole. Last year, I used to collect my father's letters to us at the gate. I heard from upstairs the sound of a sash window, the cords long rotted, being wedged open. My aunts were upstairs and had finished making the beds. They did all the rooms - my grandfather's, my mother's, the landing where I slept, Uncle Packie's and finally their own room. They shared this chamber for the summer with my sisters, Lindie and Beebie - the only bedroom at Three Crosses to be wallpapered, in a nineteenth-century design I saw years later in a Manchester museum where they had pattern-books for the Great Exhibition. The territory even Peggy and Feena were forbidden from entering was Great-Uncle Vance's bed-sitting-room off the kitchen on the ground floor.

Vance was a well-preserved and elegant bachelor and the oldest Driscoll in the house. Farm work had been a lifelong joy to him but, as such, to be partaken of sparingly. Rhyming couplets, delivered extempore, were a particular ornament of Vance's conversation. My father used to imitate them to me behind his back:

'Great uncle Vancey

Not milking, I fancy.

Could he still be abed

Reposing his head?'

Vance's younger brother was Thomas Driscoll, my grandfather and a widower. Grandfather Thomas' second son, Pascal, Uncle Packie, then in his mid-twenties, also resided with us, when not in a rooming-house near his work in Rossbeg. Packie's three sisters completed the ménage at Three Crosses Farm: Peggy, Feena and Geraldine Bennett, née Driscoll, my mother. My deceased grandmother Maeve Driscoll and her eldest son, Christie, had, each of them, died young and lay side by side in Ballinsaggart cemetery, eight miles away.

The other family that still dwelt in Three Crosses proper, in those days, were the Deegans. Forty yards up our road Liam Deegan and his two unmarried sisters, Josie and Mary, farmed above us, their back paddock adjoining our orchard. There was another brother, Ed, a priest in the U.S.A.

I had met Father Ed, (after a fashion) one Sunday in 'fifty-six, when he was at home in Three Crosses on summer furlough. That year, my English father was still in Liverpool, not yet on holiday with us; my mother was hustling me and Lindie and Beebie out through the maroon gates to walk down to the chapel. It felt cold for a June morning; but then perhaps the mass was at seven, that seems likely. Anyway, it was then that I made the acquaintance of the back of Father Deegan's head. Their smart trap passed us, very slow, a few yards down from our gates.

'When is Roy coming over on his holidays, Geraldine?' says Liam to my mother.'Next Saturday night, please God.' Liam doffed his hat to my mother, then, as an afterthought, tugged Father Ed's elbow to pull up after a few yards in the middle of the road. Liam looked back down at me over the great, black, polished wheel. Alice, their pony, piebald like an Apache's, had to swing her head right round, on account of the blinkers, to see why they had stopped. 'Will we give Addie a spin, Mrs?' Josie Deegan enquired from her high perch next to Liam on the oilcloth cushion. 'Sure, do.' Mother and I knew we would not face protests from Lindie or Beebie: they preferred motorcars to traps and hoped for a better offer.

I got a foot on the cast-iron step, then clambered up. Deegans had an elegant trap. The black coachwork shone with beeswax, but it had no back door and was thus a lesser vehicle than ours. I was bidden to sit opposite Josie, next to Mary, behind Father Ed, who liked to drive when he was home.

'Oh boys, will you look at the shine on those shoes!' Mary Deegan said, speaking from behind her hand. She did not need to with me; I knew what a harelip was. 'Spit and polish", I said, with a touch of pride. 'Oh yes', said Josie, with no idea what I meant.

'I polish everyone's shoes on Sunday.'

'Isn't he a great little fellow? God love him', said Mary.

'The business', said Liam, looking across at me.

'You spit into the polish then mix it and let it dry before you shine the leather with a different brush. Dad' - modesty reasserted itself – 'showed me.'

'Oh yes', said Josie and Mary, nodding.

Our driver was in his priest's collar and black suit. Though bald, he wore no hat. I assumed hats weren't the fashion any more in Sacramento. As he drove, he held his head slightly cocked to one side like a parrot considering a problem from a different angle. He had two folds in the skin of his neck at the back of his head, just above what should have been his hairline. They reminded me of the shape of a mouth, as if he were smiling out of the back of his head. As we clip-clopped under the horse-chestnuts down our road to the turn, I wondered if the creases were a family trait. What lay beneath Liam's hat and his sisters' abundant coifs and headscarves? At any rate, as I have said, my catching Father Deegan's eyeless retro-smile was the full extent of our acquaintanceship on that occasion.

It was just as well, perhaps. Only the Friday before, in that same June of 'fifty-six, trespassing into the Deegans' dairy, I had discovered a pile of farming publications dedicated to wool production. No-one reared sheep in our parts. But each dreary magazine seemed to have, as a saving feature, one article of general interest. Accordingly, I stole thirty or forty of the publications and concealed them in the derelict motorcar on our farm. Back in my own territory, I was absorbed on wet afternoons by stories of the lifecycles of fearsome insects like the ant-lion and the ichneumon fly, or by the heroism of Padraig Pearse, or by the loss of the Andrea Doria in Nantucket Sound. There were still a good few which I had not read and this year, 'fifty-seven, I had returned to find them undisturbed in their hiding place.

Great-Uncle Vance Driscoll had been the owner and driver, until a few years previously, of that 'thirty-nine Morris. When the time came, he rhymed:

'The grand old Morris Eight

That put me cursing there of late

Leave her reckon with her fate.'

Accordingly, he sold off its back axle, wheels and engine, but abandoned the remainder of the vehicle up in the haggard, in its own miniature grove, its canvas roof still waterproof, steering-wheel, windows and doors intact. The ryegrass and docks had grown high in the vacant wheel-wells, stinging nettles under the bumpers. The black paintwork, unpolished, had weathered to an inky, iridescent blue. Vance had locked the doors, somehow, to keep us children out. But I could get in through the boot, pulling the lid up after me and forcing down the back of the rear seat to clamber inside.

Thus I mused on that last year, the summer of 'fifty-six, the summer of my father, until finally, still out of bounds, on the road side of the maroon gates, I heard the post-van half a mile away changing gear for the last turn, below the avenue. Minutes later, it throbbed past me and all of Three Crosses, on up the hill to Coole. I slipped back inside. Our yard was deserted; I made for the orchard and the grove with the ash trees, where Vance's Morris Eight sat in hope of better things. This year, 'fifty-seven, I intended to secrete under the bonnet, in the engine bay, a few books along with the farming publications stolen from Deegans' last summer. I drew out the first of the unread magazines and sat back on the red oilcloth of the rear seat in comfort.

The Sheepman of Ireland had a photo of some kind of executive on the second page. His burnished, black hair and spectacles put me in mind again of my father. Put me in mind of my father? I closed my eyes to the damp interior of the Morris Eight and dream-drifted, once more, to a tiny dining-room in a terraced house in 44 Curzon Street, Liverpool.

★

The past we see ahead of us; it is, of course, the future which creeps up on us from behind. In the shell of old Vance's car, I envision the evening in Curzon Street, when my father begins to read to me from *King Arthur and the Table Round*. The book is a gift from my English grandmother. Father is sitting in the high-backed mahogany chair with the pineapple finials on either side of his head and I am at his feet on a hand-woven, semicircular hearth mat, my back to the coal fire and the steam behind me rising from drying laundry. My father sits bolt upright, dutiful. A dressing-gown over his demobilisation suit keeps the chill off his shoulders. He wears not slippers, but his working shoes with the leather soles he has cut and fitted himself. I can see that he has been miserly with the nails. His spectacles are tipped forward, the wings buried in the brilliantined hair above his ears. His reading voice is low, melodic, sweet; his accent south-eastern English.

'Queen Guinevere knew of the passing of noble King Arthur; she was filled with guilt and shame at her wickedness and entered a nunnery to do penance for the rest of her life. For his part, Sir Lancelot returned to the realm when he heard of the death of the King. It was six years before he found the Queen and when he came to the convent, she had already died.'

Father's words came back to me then, alone in that rotting, steel compartment. I hear the words now, as I write. Back home in Liverpool, after I had learned to read at Pius the Twelfth Primary, I would slip into the front room, into the world of *King Arthur and the Table Round*, at the half-round table of Roy and Geraldine Bennett, in the bay window, secreting myself behind a gold brocade curtain with a flock of embroidered birds-of-paradise strutting in appliquéd undergrowth along the bottom hem. 'That's it. Now then, it's up the wooden hill for thee, Beau Sir', Daddy would say to me when he was too tired to continue.

★

Sitting there in Vance's Morris Eight, on the first day of the holidays in July 'fifty-seven, it dawned on me then from where Aunt Peggy had got her nickname for me:

Beau Sir, Bozer.

With the passing, only four months previously, of my noble Father, as surely and finally as the passing of Arthur, hints of guilt and suggestions of betrayal had also entered and tinged my own consciousness; there, in Vance's car in our orchard, that picture of the bespectacled sheep executive who bore Daddy a faint resemblance, triggered in me a battle with feelings I could not understand.

My eye lighted on the Bakelite handle of the brake release under the Morris' dashboard. Tugging at it, I discovered the secret of the ratchet, rasping it up and down in its housing. It came out of the shaft and sat in my hand so that I could turn it this way and that, savouring its workmanship. In these avocations I blotted out a ten-year-old's sad reverie.

Two

In which my mother attends a christening and my Aunt Peggy takes a special interest in me. Am I godmother-less? Other cauchemars. Uncle Packie arrives. Two temporary losses – one witnessed, one recalled.

''Tis ten apast, Geraldine. We had right to be going', Aunt Feena said next day.

My mother was to attend the christening of the latest of the Brittans in Tourmahinch chapel at three that afternoon, the 27th June, 'fifty-seven. It was the second day of the holidays; she had been asked to stand for little Daniel on the day we arrived at Three Crosses. It was her first 'occasion' as a young widow. The Brittans, like us Driscolls and the Deegans, were farmers in Three Crosses. Strictly speaking, they lived above and outside the hamlet and had most of their thirty-five acres of fields below on the flatter land. There was a crowd of children in the family which, I believe, came to be complete at eleven boys and girls, some years later. Great breeders, said Father Haines of Rossbeg and Tourmahinch, speaking without malice, but I wonder if they were offended. No matter, I think I took offence on their account.

The christening was to be a quiet function without guests, as was the custom, if not the theology as well, in those days. My mother put on the A-line, belted, mauve dress she had brought for Sundays and walked on down to Tourmahinch chapel along with Aunt Feena. They took baby Kate in the pushchair. Lindie, Beebie and I were left to our own devices, with Aunt Peggy in charge.

That day after dinner, the grey cloud came down fast out of a summer sky, whether from west or east I could not see. The rain came out of the cloud, like sweat at first, then in suffocating sheets, closing down my world, isolating our house and its yards, where the gravel and cobbles swam with a dozen miniature watercourses stained olive-green by run-off from ordure. Under the lee of the henhouse, the downpour came off the thatch like a torrent, washing clean the long plank of slate where the thick porridge of slops for the chickens was doled out by Aunt Feena each morning. 'Chook, chook, chook', she would call, and the chookies would come running, seventeen white and a couple of brown hens. We had no cockerel ourselves; our neighbours did. I discovered early on that chickens could be hassled: I made the mistake once, on Brittans' farm, that cockerels, being of the same species, could be bullied too. I tossed a crab-apple at theirs. Once. Twice. The third time, the gaudy bird turned on me, flew up at my face and put me running. Its black and yellow eyes, full of an alien malice, gave me a fright as good as any on offer from one part of the animal kingdom to another.

I had made it into my snug in the Morris Eight. The tempest beat down on the black fabric over my head. The grey daylight outside flashed violet sporadically. It thundered; there was menace and unspeakable power in it and I was afraid. The drumming of the rain became a frantic tattoo, then back to a drumming; again, a capricious and violent hammering, with blasts of hailstones interspersed, so that I wondered if the canvas over my head would hold.

After a quarter of an hour, my Aunt Peg came up in her housecoat and wellingtons, with her oilskin over her head, and found me. I couldn't open the door of the Morris for her.

'Bozer, you're an omadhaun, so you are, you'll catch your death if you move. Stay there now for yourself until it stops', she shouted over the drumming of the rain. 'What about Mother and Feena and Kate?' They were my responsibility.

'They'll get a spin back with Frank Brittan.'

Peggy gave me a last look through the steamed-up car window. The water ran off her nose and her eyebrows furrowed as if she were worried about me. I couldn't let her go.

'Wait, wait', I wailed.

I dropped the copy of *The Sheepman of Ireland*, scrambled out of the car under the rear parcel shelf and through the boot. Peggy held out the oilskin for me like a tent and clasped me in to herself under it, enfolding me, uniting us. We splashed our way laughing down to the front yard and half door. I could not see where I was going, looking down into my wellingtons and into hers with the chafing rings red on her calves. I could hardly breathe with the heady warmth and the scent of her. At eighteen, Peggy had just begun to experiment with perfumes. What was that scent?

A thundercrack sounded, sharp and violent, close at hand. Her body shuddered with it.

'Jesus, Mary and Joseph!'

But we were at the porch. Peggy had rescued me, guided me, warmed me. It was exquisite, too beautiful to last.

She went up into the bedroom to Lindie and Beebie, I to the kitchen. I sat on a black, oak form in our dark hobgoblins' cavern of a chimney recess. My eyes followed the smoke upwards as I aired myself by the open hearth. Sometimes, when it rained hard, the drops would make it down the open chimney against the updraft of hot air and wood smoke. Then they would sizzle and sputter as they hit the embers. If it was a storm or a deluge, you could peer up into the chimney and see the water coming down the masonry in trickles, at the top of its black gorge.

*

The next week, Mrs Brittan came into the kitchen with a big Kodak envelope. Then she extracted half a dozen photographs and set them out on the table, aligning them geometrically with the squares of the tartan oilcloth as if she were dealing herself a hand at patience.

''Twas a mercy us to get any pictures at all outside the chapel with the storm we had that evening. But didn't they come out well?'

'Oh, stop', said Feena, 'will you look at the omlucht idiot there. Why didn't I wear the new blouse and skirt?'

'Go way, girl, you look real stylish in the gymslip.'

'Don't be blaggarding me!'

'Geraldine, you came out great too', said Mrs Brittan, and it was true.

It was true. Lonely, demure, beautiful, my mother, Geraldine, stood slightly apart from the little group. These were not snapshots, but well-composed pictures taken on the sward outside the chapel by a professional from the city of Comerford, with a camera the size of a breadbin slung from his neck. There was a close-up of Mr and Mrs Brittan with babby Daniel and two small groups, one with Father Haines. I studied them, kneeling on the long bench at the kitchen table, chin on my hands, for as long as the pictures lay out on the tartan oilcloth. I drank in deep the vision of my mother, still in her mantilla, shining out of those images. I sidled along the form on my knees to be closer to her as she sipped at her tea with Mrs Brittan.

Then the three women went out into the sunshine of our front yard where babby Daniel lay sleeping in a silver pram rocked by his dutiful seven-year-old sister, Ann.

Photographic activity would go in phases in those days. Before we went down to the maroon gates to say our goodbyes, my mother produced a box camera. There was a fillum in it - an unseen entity which, I assumed, by an erroneous etymology, was that with which the camera was filled. Mother took two pictures of us, along with babby Daniel, up against a sunny patch on the grey-rendered wall of our house. My head reached above the level of the kitchen windowsill. The copper kettle that sat inside in the window recess came out next to me in the photo. Empty vessels, said Aunt Feena, when she saw the snap.

★

We had three or four albums at home in 44 Curzon Street, Liverpool, kept with the Wedgwood tea service in our front-room sideboard. In the interminable months after my father's death in February 'fifty-seven, I would wake up at sunrise, frightened that I could no longer see his face in my mind's eye. So I would tiptoe downstairs to the photographs, to find him again. There were, strangely it seemed to me, no photographs of my christening, though I remembered the same photographer had attended for Beebie's and Kate's, the week after they were born.

★

After the Brittans went, Mother did not linger at the maroon gates; she always had work to do. Still affected, shaken by her beauty and dignity in the christening pictures, I tagged along in her wake back into the house. I nuzzled up to her in the kitchen, fitting my head into the curve of her side above her hip. She would not hug me; she drew back from me to search for something in the pocket of her housecoat. But I had the courage to say:

'Mummy, who is *my* godfather?'

'Sure Addie, why are you asking? You know as well as I do your godfather is your Grandaddy Driscoll. Grandfather Thomas.'

'Did he come to my christening?'

'No.'

'Well, my godmother, then?'

'Mrs Frowstie.' (This lady was the headmistress at my primary school in Liverpool - Pius the Twelfth.)

'But she's Beebie's. She can't be mine as well, can she?'

'She can, of course.'

'Well, is she?'

'I don't - Addie, don't be addling my poor head with your questions - couldn't you have asked your Dad and he still alive, God rest him? Lookit, did you brush your hair this week? Come here to me.' I stepped a pace closer. Mother whisked the children's hairbrush out of her navy housecoat pocket. She gripped my jaw in her left hand then plied the brush on me hard, as if she were buffing Father's suede shoes with a wire brush.

For those few seconds, I struggled against her grip to look up into her face; let me not indeed addle her poor head with questions about my godmother, because? Ah, because! Because, you see, in the play of Mother's lips over her teeth, in her dark-hazel eyes, in the set of her mouth, I saw the face my father would turn to on his pillow. I thought, too, that I saw the beginnings of a softening for me. A faint tide of anticipation rose in me; though my scalp hurt and my eyes watered, my mother was holding me and I hoped to be held closer. The hair-brushing treatment was what Lindie, Beebie and Kate received each morning to shrieks, pouts and joy when it was over. What my sisters were to my mother, I wanted to be. They, moreover, had godmothers - who was mine?

★

Clumps of honeysuckle in our yard, ammonites in its walls and the very ruts in Driscolls' lane I counted as daily acquaintances, that summer of 'fifty-seven, when I was ten. Our farm was a setting so intimate; yet my wider surroundings were monumental too: the rich fields of the Great Vale, the grey churches with their holy acres behind rendered walls, the farmhouses, grey- or white-washed, thatched or slated, our road that was made for horses and bicycles and the slow-walking countrymen with their gestures of salute; the green wastelands on the higher hills and the flanks of Slievegarriff; the bailey castles, the very Rock of Munster; Mount Slievegarriff above all. All were the elements of my dreamtime. An archetype, a map, was being drawn for me for the years to come. It entered my child's being as language does, once there incapable of being unlearned, a moment without an end where time, place and personhood are fused immutably; a moment to which (though we never leave it) we must return for the truth that sets us free.

My dreamtime I have called this moment and I have made myself re-enter it; ideal and idyllic, as it was and is, beautiful and beatific, pristine and primordial, reality and fantasy. All was, is, unspeakably sweet and poignant to me, for that I knew my revels now were ending; this dreamtime vision was dissolving and would be gone tomorrow, like the summer clouds massed high above Slievegarriff; I knew, in the marrowbone, that these few weeks of 'fifty-seven would be my last summer at Three Crosses.

★

My sleeping dreams, too, formed a seamless part of my world that summer. I seem to remember a nightmare of a kind others have had and which recurred then, and indeed afterwards; but there were other powerful and beautiful night-visions, vivid in their colours and backdrops and I will return to these later in my story.

I do not recall the first night of the cauchemars. Usually, I dreamt myself in the schoolyard at Pius Twelfth in Liverpool, playing with an Irish friend, Busty Heaphy of Coole, on the raised bank under the elms. I would see my incubus way off down on the tarmac, in the shape of a small, round, dark cloud, part-floating, part-bouncing at knee height amongst the other schoolchildren, like some malign tumbleweed. But there was method in its seemingly random movements. I knew it was present in the playground only because I was there. My father was there, too, at a distance. When I looked again, the incubus was nearer to me. In consternation, I would catch Daddy's eye - he must surely know my danger - but though he smiled back, he seemed unconscious of peril. I looked again at the incubus. I sensed it was watching me, eyeless and amoebic though it was, and disturbingly out of focus, so that I strained and dreaded to look, all in the same moment. Suddenly it was much larger, blacker and almost upon me, sucking me into itself. I could not move. As the thing descended on my shoulders to engulf me, I awoke. (It was with a certain familiarity that, at the grammar school in Liverpool, I later absorbed the scientific lore of black holes.) I was wet and palpitating, but I did not scream, as my sister Kate, who also got nightmares, was later to do. I knew it was over as soon as I awoke. I did not fear the dark, at least at Three Crosses, where my corner of the landing above the kitchen, my creaking camp-bed and my rough, woollen blankets without sheets provided a womb-like comfort.

A variant of this cauchemar had me going to school in humiliation and despair, naked from the waist down. Why couldn't my mother and father, who had more or less frogmarched me to the school gates, see my distress and embarrassment? Mrs Frowstie, the headmistress, Miss Pargeter, my teacher, the big boys at Pius Twelfth, others, of whom more in due course, all made their appearance to cluck or jeer. I was left to get over my shame and disgrace, fold down the bench-seat of my desk and sit there, bare-cheeked, for my lessons, with my tassel out for all to see as they walked between the rows of desks and looked down on me.

Through the Irish summer of 'fifty-seven, I kept my nightmares to myself, not sharing my experiences with my mother or sisters or Aunt Peggy. To have voiced that reality and named the fears would have been more painful than the comfort my mother might have given to me against those dark, inchoate terrors.

★

I was sitting in the chimney-corner about to spin the blower so as to bring on the fire for the tea-kettle. Fitted to the cement floor of our hearth, and to that of every other hearth in a farmhouse at Three Crosses, was a wheel-driven bellows which sent air up through the grate under the fire. The wheel, eighteen inches or so in diameter and mounted on a cast-iron housing, was turned by a horn-coloured handle at its edge. It was connected to a small pulley below, by means of a belt round its circumference. The pulley in turn drove the underfloor fan. When, in the course of time, the original belts snapped, their owners replaced them with strips of old tyre from cycles, recycled.

The blower in our hob was a most attractive toy to all of us children. Play was rigorously controlled by the adults. Indiscriminate use of the wheel burnt fuel too quickly. Too fast a rotation and the home-produced belt came off. Re-attaching it was a grimy business to be undertaken by Great-Uncle Vance or Uncle Packie, neither of whom was grateful for the imaginative opportunities the task presented.

The latter had cycled up that afternoon on his Raleigh from his job at the mart in our town of Rossbeg. He came into the kitchen from the dairy outhouse where he had left the bicycle. Packie was tall and spare with a good head of black hair. 'You sir', was his greeting to me; then he had some brotherly counsel for my aunt. 'Put out that fag, Peg, Daddy is coming in now.' Now I come to think of it, neither Packie nor my mother, Geraldine, smoked or drank. Aunt Peggy came over to the hob, giving the back of my neck a conspiratorial squeeze with her finger and thumb. She sat with me on the form. She took a last puff and jettisoned her cigarette into the fire.

Packie said what there was to be said about stock prices; in his hand, all the while he talked, was the front light from the bicycle. It was a seductive artefact, a huge, nickel-plated carbide lamp, a Lucas *King of the Road*. I could not take my eyes off it, coveting it, longing for the weight and feel and hit of it in my hand. I continued to hope but, for fear of a refusal, I wouldn't ask Packie to show me the lamp. When he disappeared upstairs to hide it, I went outside into the yard to play.

★

Ann of the Brittans was seven years old. That afternoon, along with her brother Desmond, she had been sent on an errand or 'message' to the store in Blanchardstown. On the way home, she felt tired and sat down to rest against the dry, grey, rotted wood and cast-iron frame of an old hay-turner in Dempseys' second field that had been mown around and had the yellow hay growing up through it. She fell asleep and no-one could see little Ann from the road.

I was digging with the beach spade in the half-swamp near the spring-water tap at the front of the yard, filling in time, in the knowledge that my mother would soon lean out over the green half-door to call me in for my tea. From the road outside, there came a rapping and shoving at the maroon gates. I drew back the huge, two-handed bolt, the size and shape of a sub-machine-gun, wrestling it with muddy hands. I hauled the left gate half-open. My mother had heard the squeak, squawk, squeak of the bolt from inside the kitchen and hurried down from the house behind me, addressing our two visitors over my head.

'Well, Mrs.'

'Oh God help me, it isn't well I am at all, Mrs.'

Mrs Brittan stood there in her housecoat with her boy, Desmond. She had a firm lock on his wrist. She had been crying and he had been crying.

'What?'

'Ann is gone.'

'What?'

'This little rip', (she gave Desmond a sharp yank to make sure he was aware he was being referred to), 'this little rip came home without her.'

'Well, Desmond'?' said my mother. I think he mumbled something.

Where we Driscolls favoured Tourmahinch, the Brittans, by family tradition, got their messages in Blanchardstown. On their return, Desmond and his sister had cut across the fields. Desmond had turned up at his home without the purse and the messages and without Ann, who had been carrying the string bag. His mother, speechless at first, had declined to accept his assurance that his sister would arrive any time now. She had marched him back the way he had come, shortcut and all, through Dempsey's second field, where they had missed Ann; then, panic mounting, they had dashed home again by our road.

No Ann.

The darling Ann in her new wellingtons that day and the crimson frock with the gold lamé threading she got in the post from her uncle in Killinunty.

Little Ann, the great girl that was the first to finish her spuds that dinner-time.

Little Ann, who was almost a wet-nurse to Babby Daniel, the latest of the Brittans.

Little Ann. Gone.

'What happened her, I wonder?' said Mother. Mrs Brittan burst into tears again, her sorrow made worse by the phrasing of Mother's enquiry. Desmond started to sob, softly. I had seen the faces of despair. I didn't want to meet Mrs Brittan's eyes in my gaze, because her pain was also anger and she frightened me; I knew even then, from my own repertoire of emotions, the enemy black thoughts and loss-misery that had poisoned the reservoir of Desmond's consciousness. I took in the shaken face of him, with its running nose, the raw and red skin over his upper lip and those parts of his eyes salmon-pink that should have been white.

My mother left us standing there and went up towards the house without a word. I rinsed out my hands and the tin spade under the spring-water tap. Mother came back with the beads. I knew they would say the *Fifth Joyful Mystery, The Finding of the Child Jesus in the Temple.* The women went back down our road, with Desmond still seized in the wrist-lock. I was told to bolt the gate after them. Poor, suffering Desmond.

★

One April evening in England after Dad died, I had lost my own sisters. I had thus trodden, a matter of a few months ago, where Desmond trod now. In Liverpool, we generally walked home with my mother from Pius the Twelfth after lessons, except when she was working. My father had always given me explicit instructions about which of the gravel paths through the park we were to follow on those days; we were to hold hands at all times; we were to walk unaccompanied by other children or adults with the exception of Mrs Frowstie or Miss Pargeter; we were not to dawdle, and so on.

We, (in the first person plural, as I thought at the time), had reached the homeward end of the park and, halfway to Curzon Street, had come out by the smut-blackened entrance piers. Waiting for the girls to catch up, I had begun to read the Cautionary Notices to Park Patrons. But Lindie and Beebie had not arrived. Ice-cold and clear, the truth had come upon me: I had lost my little sisters. Little Lindie and little Beebie, so precious to my mother, had been entrusted into my keeping, as my dead father's successor, and I had failed in my commission.

By what malign agency had this been visited upon me? Why had the last shred of my serenity been torn from me? Why had I to answer for a tragedy more monstrous than I could bear? I seemed to feel my mind disintegrating, my imagination playing havoc with powerful sensations of danger and images of Lindie in her pigtails and Beebie in her new knitted gloves, fixed on lengths of parcel-string to her school gaberdine, so that she could not lose them. Were they truly gone from me? Twice I had scurried back up the gravel walk, reenacting the last glance over my shoulder where, by this arbutus bush, I had seen my sisters. Or had it been by the bandstand? By the beds of narcissus? By the tall larches where, with my classmate Paul Sinkiewicz, once or twice I had catapulted gravel at starlings and pigeons? Why had I not held hands with my sisters as bidden? Distraught and utterly defeated, I had stood at the park gates weeping loudly.

'What is it, son?' The stranger had peered down at me from under his trilby.

'I've lost my family.'

'I've got a little boy just like you.'

The 'just like you' had made me give him my trust; I was not alone. I could be like the others - I could belong.

'And he's the world's worst for losing things. But they always turn up. Your family will be at home now wondering where you've been.'

The prospect that this might be true was inexpressibly exalting. I had hardly dared entertain it and began again to sob.

'Come on son, let's get you home. Your mum won't want to have to come out and look for you.' The Samaritan had looked at his wristwatch, then taken me by the hand and delivered me to 44 Curzon Street. My tears now dry through weariness, I had seemed to stand outside it all, behind myself and my kind-hearted friend, watching, as we had faced the shabby, yellow street-door. He had reached up for the lion's-mouth knocker, half-rusted in, and had forced a couple of raps out of it.

It had been Lindie who had opened and Beebie, puzzled, who had craned her head round the door. 'Where have you been?' she had asked. I remember no specific fear of my mother, only that foretaste of a vague terror, followed by the intense guilt of disobedience. It had not been my first disobedience. I have yet to describe the full fruits of that forbidden tree, whose mortal taste brought death into the world and all my woe.

★

By dint of searching more methodically in Dempseys' field, little Annie Brittan and the purse and the messages were discovered.

'A bold scut, so you are, not to obey poor Desmond, and that's all about it', Mrs Brittan told her.

'Don't give out to me again, Mammy', Ann bleated.

It was well that all was accomplished in a timely manner before Frank Brittan got home from Ballinsaggart that evening. He was known as a man with a temper on him, though not in the same choleric league as my elegant Great-Uncle Vance.

Three

*Aunt Peggy on Aunt Feena's plans. My mother; the question of exile.
Feena sings to the accordion, my life prefigured in her song.*

In the quiet of the mid-morning, the men were in the
kitchen reading the *Southern Express*. The women had
finished upstairs. Aunt Feena had fed the chickens and
started bread-making. My mother had taken my sisters
up with her to Brittans'. Aunt Peggy came looking for me
and I brightened. She had taken off her housecoat and
was wearing a beige cardigan over her shoulders and a
white blouse. She had a skirt on, somewhere between
pink and violet, and the look of her made me sad and
hopeful in the one moment. 'Will I smoke a cig before
Daddy comes out, will I, Bozer? What's that you are
building?'

I had been constructing a miniature road system in
the gravel and sawdust at the edge of the kindling stacks.
I thought wistfully of Medley's Toy Emporium in
Liverpool: how useful a couple of Dinky cars would have
been. In default of realistic model vehicles with which to

populate the roads, there was always the possibility of finishing with a war-game and, had Peggy not distracted me, I would have ended my solitary play with a different fantasy - a Second World War assault from behind the Pripet Marshes by the spring-water tap. I had brought with me the means to construct a catapult like the one owned by my classmate at Pius Twelfth in Liverpool, Paul Sinkiewicz: this would provide the artillery and its projectiles would thud, with satisfying little puffs of dust, into the infrastructure I had built up.

I was surfacing, with gravel, a delicate pinch at a time, a miniature bridge of red rowan twigs and looked up again at Peggy to take in her warmth and promise and beauty. We sat together on a spruce log with the springy kindling behind us to rest our backs. Across the yard, facing us, the green half-door of the kitchen porch was open and we heard Feena singing in Irish in the kitchen.

'Is Auntie Finola going to marry Jimmy Grehan?'

'Ask her, boy, why don't you?'

'She's your sister. Have you asked her?'

Peggy clucked with her tongue. 'Oh, I have.' She did not intend to deceive or throw me off the scent. But the intonation meant that she hadn't.

'Well?'

'I'd say she will, alright.'

'Jimmy wants to get married more than she does.'

'Is that a fact, B.?'

'Yes.'

'Who told you?'

'Anyone can see.'

I knew I was confirming as public knowledge what she knew for herself. I basked for some moments in my value to her, casting about in my mind for ways to prolong the moment.

'The thing is, Bozer, he could have to go to Dublin or Limerick or England for his work and I wonder would she folly him.'

'Why wouldn't she follow him?'

'Arra.'

'Why?'

'Because your Aunt Finola is not the emigrating kind. I'd say she'd nearly starve rather than go into exile. She could be wanting a fellow would stay on the land; a farmer, like our people. 'Twas the same with Geraldine.'

Peggy remembered too late that I was a child. She lost that easy mastery with which she had been responding to my questions.

'Geraldine?' I interrupted, thinking on to myself. Had my mother not wanted to live in Liverpool? Had she blamed my father, the father I idolised and idealised, for taking her there? Peggy read this sequence of thoughts in my face. 'Oh, Bozer, I wish to God you were a few years older, so I do. 'Tis very hard for you altogether. Be a great man now and stand by your mammy in her hour of need. Will you do that now for your poor Aunt Peg? Have you ever a fondie for me?'

Fear of my mother's indifference to me, fear to test out that indifference, conditioned my mood during this conversation. I knew my mother was stoical about her exile; not for her the romance of a new life in another country with new prospects, new faces: romance was what she had left behind. My father alone had been the reason for her life in Liverpool, as he had for mine. But I believed that her stoicism, her impassivity, might also encompass her feelings towards me. That was the thought I could not bear.

★

A heavy word, exile, Peggy had used. I told her the story of how, before Christmas, in Liverpool, at Pius the Twelfth, we had done the *Flight into Egypt*. Canon Grimble had come in to read a bit of Luke with us, and made us all stand up. In the afternoon, we coloured in cyclostyled drawings of the Holy Family and pasted them into Advent scrapbooks. Then Miss Pargeter had asked the class what an exile meant. I was the only one to know; my reward was to choose a book from the library shelf and sit with it on the easy-chair near the coke-stove until Mrs Frowstie, the headmistress, rang the last bell.

★

'There's no flies on you, Bozer', Peggy said, and got to her feet. She brushed off the bits of grass and twig that had stuck to the calves of her bare legs. Unlike me she took a good tan though, in those days, she did not care to. She stood there for a moment or two and I, glancing up at her out of the angle of my eye, imbibed all the loveliness and promise of her form; the melodic waves of her hair, glossy and chocolate-dark, so incomparably beautiful next to mine, which had the colour and consistency of last year's hay. I saw the play of the zephyrs on the wisps of hair over her ears; her bosom where I would have laid my head, the neat, sweet curve of her stomach and hips.

'Oh, here, lookit, I must be going, Bozer.'

'You haven't finished your cigarette.'

'I have enough of it smoked, boy.'

'Are you going to be a nurse next year?'

'I think I will, will I?'

'In Comerford?'

'Aye.'

'Not Dublin?'

'Aye. 'Tis Norses they call them in Dublin. You'd think you were in Oslo.'

'You're a gas woman! Not Liverpool, then?'

'Oh Bozer, you and your questions - you have my head addled with them!' The remark was careless and she was smiling. But I was an addler of heads - my mother's first and now hers.

'On your feet now, B., good man yourself.'

'Carry me!'

'Faith and I won't. I couldn't hoist you up - you're too heavy, so you are. Show me your hand.' I twined my arm around hers and we slipped back down the cow path and into the front yard.

Aunt Finola played the melodion or, more precisely, the melodions. There were two in my mother's family home. The better of these instruments was a huge and expensive-looking Hohner with the bellow-ends done in a cream-coloured plastic of a kind which is obsolete nowadays. The bellow edges were a handsome red and there were polished, hand-cut fretwork, metal panels on the plastic, with a two-octave keyboard at one end and an alarming number of round keys at the other. Silence would fall as Feena strapped it on and undid the tooled-leather clasps before breathing life into this Leviathan. The other melodion, my favourite, was half the size of the Hohner. Pre-war, pre-plastic, it was a cheap, boxwood model of uncertain lineage. Its end panels were varnished in a beautiful electric blue. I never discovered where these instruments were kept at Three Crosses, which was probably a blessing for their owner.

I rarely heard Feena play and would not like to say how good a musician she was. When, however, she buckled on the Hohner, she was an enchantress who transfixed me by the magical dance of her fingers over the buttons. When she played and sang to an audience Feena was somewhere we were not, though each siren note called to us. Feena, my corrector and scold, was transformed.

She had learned the accordion from her late Uncle Joseph who, in his turn, had inherited his talent from his mother, who would have been my great-grandmother of the O'Connors of Castlelaurence. Feena was thus recognised by all in our parts as, for good or ill, the carrier of a tradition. I do not suppose she had had a music lesson in her life. Though she had been well-educated at the convent in Rossbeg from the age of thirteen, music had not formed part of the formal curriculum there. Feena's gift, largely formed and developed even at that early age, would have been regarded as culshie, bumpkinish, and I felt she was slightly embarrassed to admit to it. Her repertoire was one of the old songs, some of them in Irish, some in English and some in the Hibernian patois of our parts. My favourite was a turn-of-the-century ballad, *'The Wild Colonial Boy'*. She also had a few from upcountry, like *'The Cliffs of Duneen'* and, from England, *'Geordie'*, I seem to remember as one, which she would have learned from the wireless or through her contacts with some of the showband crowd in Rossbeg. She also played what the showband and the wireless people were beginning to call instrumentals; I believe she had one or two of her own composition which she would render with improvisation. Her talent was, in sum, preliterate, bardic and, in its small way, of a piece with the gifts of an Ossian or a Homer.

One of the showband folk whom Feena liked in those days was Pad Dempsey. Pad's father was a publican in Rossbeg and a second cousin once removed of the Dempseys of Three Crosses. Pad wore silver rings on his fingers, was a little too stout for his twenty-five years and had smart, black hair, permanently wet-combed, which touched his collar at the back. He played the electric guitar in a seven-man showband in Comerford most weekends. Back in Rossbeg on weekdays, when not working in his father's bar, he was often out on Main Street wearing his emerald-green bandsman's jacket.

My aunts met Pad there after a visit in the trap to the farmers' Co-op. They had walked the length of the Main Street because the shoe and clothing emporia were at separate ends. 'The poor fellow', said Peggy to Phil after seeing him in the emerald jacket, and wearing a pair of sunglasses, 'I'd be kind of worried to see him in the black goggles. Be asking him now, Feena, are they something the matter with his eyes?'

'Arra, no, girl. That's the fashion in the showbands.'

'I'd no more wear dark glasses like them yokes than fly in the moon. Jimmy told me the work isn't in it for him in the bar. He said Pad Dempsey got very butty-looking with standing idle.'

''Tis easy known, girl.'

'Easy known what, Feena?'

'Sure Peggy, 'tis easy known what Jimmy would have to say to you about Paddy Dempsey.'

Reference to the encounter in Grandfather's presence was avoided in the trap on the return from Rossbeg. At the dinner-table I had heard Patrick Dempsey spoken of as disreputable - a caffler - in Grandfather Thomas's hearing, and he had given no sign that he disagreed as he speared a boiled potato from the communal dish with his table-fork and peeled it.

The evening of the feast of St Camillus, the patron of the chapel, the big Hohner came out and sat in readiness on the kitchen table, where I ogled it. We were already in semi-darkness in the kitchen, with the nights drawing in a little and Slievegarriff black as the hob of hell against the yellow, westering sky. The three childless Deegans came (Edward, the priest with the eyeless smile at the back of his head, was not at Three Crosses that summer) and the prolific Brittans with nearly a dozen children, including a couple of red-faced and recalcitrant babbies, clasped by their siblings, sitting on the stairs and peering down into the kitchen through the banister. There were two of the Heaphy girls. There was Panloaf's sister, Glory O'Donoghue, who had been visiting Reynoldses and had come across with old Agius Reynolds and his grandchildren, amongst them the eldest, PK. There was Vance, though not Packie. Vance had on a grin, or a gurn, which I think I only ever saw on musical occasions, though I include those when we were not in company and when the Ekco wireless and Radio Eireann provided the right kind of fare.

Feena sat next to her father on a parlour chair brought out in her honour, just outside the hob and facing into the kitchen. As she played her first piece, I studied her face above the accordion bellows: she was as if possessed by the Muses and drew all of us into her entrancement. Her face seemed childlike again, as mine was; her eyes were mostly closed as if in prayer. Her body seemed to embrace the Hohner and move at one with it in some sacred, ecstatic way.

Sometimes Feena opened her eyes and caught mine: her expression was as if the music made her see something else in me, something other than, beyond what I was. I think the first item was one of her improvisations, plangent, romantic and Gaelic, echoing, or of a piece with the dying sun outside in the west. I could hardly bear it and, at the same time, hardly bear for it to end.

Vance flicked on the forty-watt light-bulb, relieving the gloom in the outer kitchen, away from the hob. Currant bread, barmbrack, and tea and stout and whiskey all appeared. Agius Reynolds offered PK, his grandson, a boy of twelve, a cigarette, which even then I thought rather bold, and bolder still of PK to take it. On the stairs Ann of the Brittans, not more than seven years old herself, wrestled one of the babbies, now cantankerous, back onto her lap. The other Brittan girls and boys, along with PK's younger siblings and Grainne and Mercy Heaphy, sat, round-eyed, with their chins in their hands, waiting for the next number from Feena.

'Addie, Addie, sit up with us', they entreated, 'ah, come on.' I could have joined them, but PK was watching, so I preferred to maintain my dignity as one of the hosts. '*The Wild Colonial Boy*, now, let ye', commanded Grandfather. Finola began this ballad of an outsider.

'There was a wild colonial boy, Jack Duggan was his name

He was born and raised in Ireland, in a place called Castlemaine.'

She sang on of Jack's life as a rebel. I fancy the call of an American mockingbird came into one of the verses, though it was at the ends of the earth, in Australia, that, Ned Kelly-like, poor Jack met his violent end. Exile was in the minds of every singer in the room, apart from the babbies, all touched, perhaps scarred by it. Jack Duggan's iconic end, in a shootout in the outback, spoke to me. I could luxuriate in and identify with the hopelessness of his situation: somehow the spell Feena cast with her music made the poignancy bearable.

'He was his parents' only son, his father's pride and joy

And dearly did that father love the wild colonial boy.'

I knew with finality where my father was. Where was my mother? My eyes sought her out in the furthest, blackest corner of the hob, under the chimney, she mouthing sadly the words of the ballad, hunched forward on the form with Kate next to her and looking into the embers.

Later, Feena accompanied some of the great songs of our parts, *'Killinunty,'* which they all knew in Irish and *'Slievegarriff.'* She played other beauties from up country: *'The Coming of the Road'* and *'Galway Bay'*, songs that my English father knew and would sing in his vest in the chill of the bathroom in Curzon Street.

★

But it was the melancholy couplets of *The Wild Colonial Boy* that stayed with me. Jack Duggan was wild, and that went to the core of me, imprinted itself within me. I was later to spend several troubled, maverick and antisocial years at the grammar school, attracted by, yet simultaneously resisting, most influences for the good. At each moment of crisis, the thought would seep back that, like poor Jack, I had long been marked out for future wildness. And for the wilderness.

Donald Madge

Four

A dangerous brother, Hughie, and a safer one, Busty. Busty and I to school.
My mother loves me nearly, Aunt Peggy dearly.

Hughie Heaphy with his Standard Ten was a
dangerous man and unwelcome at Three Crosses from
the time, when I was small, he had cut the two fingers off
Great-Uncle Vance with his American chainsaw, the only
such instrument between Coole and Comerford and
shipped over to him by a second cousin in Pennsylvania.
Hughie used it to make a bit of money trimming fence-
stakes and the like.

One February, Vance had sold an ash tree in our
orchard for hurley sticks and gave Hughie the work of
cutting it down. The hurleys with the best grain came
from the base of the tree and there were sixteen or
seventeen good ones in it. Vance was showing Hughie
where to place the cut. Heaphy touched Vance's right
hand with the tip of the saw. One of the fingers flew off
into the air. Our Shep, stone deaf, but a lip-reader and
the sharpest collie there ever was, caught it in his mouth

only to vomit it up later. By means of the telephone in
Hassetts' bar at Tourmahinch, Doctor Gilbank was called
out from Rossbeg and sewed up Vance's hand there and
then in the parlour. The story made the Southern
Express and the news clipping was still in the parlour
behind the Cossor wireless; I think the Heaphys paid
Great-Uncle Vance something for the fingers.

Hughie had four or five sisters including Grainne and
Mercy, and a brother, Busty, who was a friend of mine
and at our house still persona grata, up to a point. I had
come to know Busty because last year, 'fifty-six, when
Dad was still alive, my mother, sisters and I had spent
eight months at Three Crosses from before the
Christmas of 'fifty-five right up to the summer break.
Then Daddy had come from Liverpool for his holiday
before the schools closed down for the summer. For the
first two weeks of his presence with us, I was to be sent
over to the National School with Busty as my companion
and amanuensis. I resented going, wanting to be with my
father and fearing my mother was the mover behind the
plan. 'Now, look at the beautiful satchel I have for your
copybook and sangwidges. That's your satchel, so it is',
mother had said. I did not want it to be my satchel; it was
not, in any case, a satchel, being of blue velvet; it smelt of
sour milk; I did not admire it and I said so.

'You'll be great company for Busty', she said, turning
out to be right on this point.

'Busty has his own friends.'

'Oh, come on now, you'll go, for Mammy and
Daddy, sure you will?'

'I don't want to, Mummy.'

'And Great-Aunt Stacey thrilled, thrilled out, with you coming to her school.'

'She doesn't know me.'

The first morning Mother and Father, in his clip-on sunglasses, holiday brown check shirt and buff oxford bags, stood outside the maroon gates with me, to await Busty. Thereafter, only my mother saw me off. For a few minutes each morning, our road gave off a strange hum and a buzz, like congregational prayer at a distance, as a hundred or so pupils from Coole and Kilcreggan and Three Crosses, in parties of three and four, marched down to the turn. Some were in silence. Others recited their lessons by rote, or declaimed their poems or their catechism. It was unlike the wild playground sounds I would begin to hear as I trod the pavements towards my real school, Pius the Twelfth, Carlisle Road, at home in Liverpool in the mornings.

Blanchardstown National School was a mile-and-a-half's walk from our farm in Three Crosses. You went down our road under the chestnut avenue to the first turn, where the land flattened out and the better grass began. A half-mile later, at the crossroads, you bore left. Right would have taken you to Tourmahinch and to the creamery beyond. Apart from the school, our family had never had business in Blanchardstown. The chapel, the shops and the two bars were in Tourmahinch. Traversing those roads, I always thought this was right, because we were what nowadays would be called hill-farmers, and Tourmahinch had mighty Slievegarriff as its backdrop. The schoolhouse, like most of the dwelling-houses in our parts, was a one-storey construction with a central porch, but longer and grander. It had three class-rooms, great dark sheds from within, with no ceilings and a timber-braced roof. From without, it was finished in grey-washed stucco with a roof in rippling sheets of galvanised.

Great-Aunt Stacey was a first cousin of my grandfather and I was put in her class. I was told later how impressed they were by my writing and spelling and by an account I had given the class of life in Liverpool. I was unconvinced by the praise; I was, after all, nine years of age at the time. But in any case, I can remember nothing of the experience, nor very much else of the school-room except the handing out of writing slates to be balanced on our knees, and the half-hour at the end of the day for Plasticine modelling, which we had in Liverpool too.

After the bell from Blanchardstown chapel and the noon angelus, we were turned out for an hour onto the grey gravel of the recreation patch and the wild hillside, into whose bracken, ferns and conifers we scampered with our sangwidges. These we augmented with wild strawberries and hawthorn leaves (which, Busty assured me, were nutritious). He and I would climb up high above the others and look down on the lads practising hurling shots with stones on one side of the bit of level ground behind the School. The girls played on the other side.

George Barrett, the schoolmaster and second-in-command, came out from time to time to pace the yard. He knew who I was, but had no words for me. I assumed this was because of the anti-English feelings for which he was known. He had once given out to my mother (a former pupil of his) to her face for not marrying an Irishman. With his Anglo-Saxon name par excellence, I suppose he had something to prove.

The friendship I formed then with Busty had lasted into the summer proper, once the National School had closed for the vacation. Busty had protected me from the inquisitive; he had sat companionably in class with me on the bench, whispering to me brief biographies of the bolder boys, when it was safe to do so; he had showed me how to roll my Plasticine between my hands, rather than one-handed on the slate, so as to make a truer sphere of it for collection at the end of the day. Back in Liverpool, I had even received a couple of letters from him, one-siders, in an Irish school hand quite different from my own. He remained mine sincerely. But the Blanchardstown National School experiment lasted only the first week: Great-Aunt Stacey told my mother I had pined too much for my father and that, for all the good her academy was doing me, I would be better off at Three Crosses in my parents' company.

★

Peggy and Feena had come down our road from Brittans after returning the loan of some bread soda. They met me on the roadside with the maroon gates ajar behind me. Feena came back to tie them again.

'Come in, Addie, you don't want to be out there now, with them motorcars and lorries', said my corrector. Our road was silent.

'I'm waiting for Busty.'

'Faith and you can wait away for Busty in the yard.'

Aunt Finola had me by the wrist and I submitted. She tied the gates behind us and shot home the massive bolt. I went at a trot to the back of the house to find Lindie and Beebie. At six and five years of age they were capable of inventing their own games and lore. I caught up with them chattering away to each other in their den. It was a patch of bare earth, bordered with stones, under one of the horse chestnuts.

'Oh, here's Mr Williams coming now', said Lindie, controlling the game and casting me into it.

'Good morning, Mr Williams', piped Beebie, in falsetto, 'this is our school.'

They had dressed their dollies and sat them out with their backs against the tree roots and a couple of my aunts' old textbooks open in front of them. I was offered, and drank, an empty cup of tea with my sisters and their pupils.

'Here's Mr Johnson', said Lindie. Busty had arrived.

Finding the maroon road gates shut, Busty had skirted around the house by way of Driscolls' lane which flanked it, and shinned down a dyke direct into the orchard from the neighbouring farm, Deegans', where there were no children and the yard gate was always open.

'How're you, anyway, boy?'

'How're you?'

'Liam Deegan was turning hay yesterday and caught four rabbits. Will we go look at them?'

Liam was the Deegan we saw most. He and his sisters, Mary and Josephine, farmed sixty acres. Edward, the other brother, the back of whose head I had met last year, was the priest in Sacramento who came home by way of New York and the Queen Mary once every five years.

'Where are they?'

'He have them up in a loft. Babbies. Orphans.'

It was prudent to make an appearance in the yard first, therefore Busty and I idled by the maroon pump for my mother or an aunt to register our presence. Aunt Finola looked out over the green half-door and saluted Busty. So we slipped away back to the orchard and up over the dyke into the lane out of sight of my sisters.

There was a stretch of Driscolls' lane, our lane, to cover before we reached the back approach to Deegans' paddock and outhouses. The powder-dry mud and embedded stones underfoot gave me a different sensation with every step. Joy surfaced from some deep well in me, pulling up in its train guilt, setting me thinking of my father, with whom I might have shared this walk and the discovery of the rabbits. We kept to the centre of the track in single file, my feet in their wellingtons too big now to walk, as once I had in sandals, inside the deep ruts. Granddad had chopped back the thorns and the brambles with a billhook, but still there was a proliferation of green berries on them, showing the first bloom of red. Horse ferns and cuckoo-pints, orchids, campion and loosestrife and patches of forget-me-not grown to the dimensions of small bushes, graced the banks. The high hedgerow parted for a few yards and, between the hazels and the whitethorns, the grand parabola of Slievegarriff appeared in the distant haze, far beyond the long perspective of fields and woods: Slievegarriff, blue and remembered; forget me not.

We were following where Shep and Vance had gone, earlier in the morning, with the cows to the fields after milking. A glassy rivulet trickled out from the interstices of the low, granite wall holding back the high, elder bank on this stretch of the lane, at the back approach to Deegans' paddock. Summer or winter there was always mire there. The ungulates had sucked and squelched their way through the glaucous mud and Shep's prints were there too. Busty hopped across to the spring from one dry stone to another, then cupped his hands in amongst the surface green scum and shamrocks, catching water from the meagre flow and sucking it noisily, like a tea-taster, off his palms.

'Spring water, drink your 'nough', said Busty and I copied him, all but for the noise.

We slipped in to Deegans' and went looking for Liam by their cowhouse, reckoning he would be back from the creamery. He was indeed there, cleaning out churns with a hose and brush. His jacket and hat were off. If not a retro-smile, like his brother, Father Ed, he certainly had eyes in the back of his head, for as we came near he tipped the churn towards himself, dipped the brush and deftly sluiced each of us with milky water by a backward flick of the wrist.

'Well, lads. Are ye going looking for rabbits?'

'Well, Mr Deegan. Can we look at the ones you found?' I wiped the milk-water out of my eyes.

'Oh ye can. Close up the door behind ye and come back to me, sure you will? I have a message for ye.' I knew the word 'message' meant an errand to Tourmahinch; Liam always paid top dollar, sixpence, three times the rate thought fair by my own circle of adults. But then, with no children of his own, he could afford to spoil other people's.

The loft was a long gallery above a tractor shed, with a steep ladder up to a door in the stone gable-end. It was wooden-floored, bare and, for some purpose, clean as a whistle inside, like the outhouse below on our farm that Great-Uncle Vance and I had scrubbed out ready for our barley. But in a corner was a deep crate with 'Finest Assam' stencilled on it. On the floor of the chest, nestling in hay, lay the four rabbits. Liam's sisters were feeding the creatures on sops of bread and milk. I stopped Busty lifting one out by the ears and, instead, scooped it up to my chest. In a long moment of rapture, I was oblivious of the world. The little creature's beauty had brought me ecstasy. Its twitching nose and perfect, brown eyes, the silk of its coat, its trembling form and body-heat close to mine. Its whole being and essence there in my hands, at my mercy.

'What's on you?' said Busty, scrutinising me.

'Dad had a prize rabbit in a hutch. It was called a chinchilla rabbit. When he was a boy. Before the War.'

'In a hutch. Oh yes.'

I do not think Busty had met the word 'hutch' before, for all the worldly wisdom of his eleven years.

★

There in the primordial land, at Deegans' farm above us in Three Crosses, would have been a moment to begin to tell him my story about Dad; our story. But I had neither the courage nor the right words to expose my three wounds, three sadnesses, Three Crosses: grief for my father, the light extinguished in my life, the pain of the unrequited love I had for my mother, my guilt and responsibility for the loss of my father and for what might happen to my family. No, these were crosses I would carry with me out of the dreamtime. I let out a long, deep breath, a sigh, I suppose. Then I took out each of the other rabbits in turn, to be stroked and privileged. And cherished equally.

★

'I could make them screech,' said Busty, eyeing the last little rabbit in my arms. He suddenly sickened and enraged me. I took stock of the two years and the two inches he had on me. But the situation, if there was one, was saved when we heard a foot on the creaking ladder and Josephine Deegan was silhouetted in the doorway.

'Well, boys?'

'How are you, Josephine?'

'Aren't they grand little fellows, God help them?'

'Oh they are', said Busty.

Josephine had come from their kitchen carrying an aluminium gallon, within all silvery burnish, but blackened with a greasy crust of soot and wood-tar without. She had a few scraps of bread and milk in the bottom of it, to see if they would eat.

'What's on you, boy?' said Busty to me when we were out of the loft.

'Nothing.'

'Don't be thinking I meant harm to them little yokes. I liked them, too, so I did. Why else would I tell you about them?'

'I hope she'll rear them and let them go.'

'If they were reared and growed, sure it would be a different thing', said Busty.

I knew that the Heaphys kept a gun and that Hughie, at least, regularly went out of an evening with his father lamping for rabbits in the fields. They ate some of the meat, but the rest went to a butchers' in Rossbeg at one-and-six a carcass.

We had promised to go back to Liamie, who had an errand for us, and we found him in their cowhouse. Like his sisters, he had a face ruddy, rather than tanned. It must have been a family thing. But Liam was fine-looking, kindly and blue-eyed, always with well-cut, steel-grey hair. He shaved himself every morning, unlike the men in our family who, for six days of the week at any rate, only did so after the midday meal. He still had good teeth and young, clean hands and nails. I wondered why he had never married.

Liam had a disappointment for us: 'No messages, now, lads, the weather is dirty-looking; go on home out of the rain, let ye. Good luck, now.'

The sky was still blue, but a cold wind had set in from the west. Thunderheads, maculate and ugly, were massing, as from nowhere, above and behind the horse chestnuts in Three Crosses and behind the Sitka spruces up by Kilcreggan. We left Deegans' by the shortest route out through their gate and onto the deserted road. Busty set off left at a trot and a skip for his home in Coole. Soon he would walk at a man's measured pace.

'Good luck, now', Busty said over his shoulder and it would be a week before he came back.

'Good luck', said I and turned right down the road in the direction of the avenue and the turn, for my gallop to the maroon gates. I ran in with spirit through the gates and up to our green half-door as the rain came down with a rush.

Mother was at the hob, putting on the potatoes. They would be boiled in their jackets in a cast-iron, black crock - it seemed a huge cauldron to me - which she struggled to position on a wrought-iron trivet over the fire. The spuds began to bubble and something like joy effervesced in me, too, to find her alone. But I cannot explain why I could not embrace her, nor she me. When she had put down the rag she had used to manoeuvre the crock's handle, I clutched at her overall and nuzzled it. It was a navy-blue cotton print with tiny, white flowers, and smelt of wood-smoke and clothes soap. I pressed my head into her, over the curve of her waist, without letting go my grip. The hug would not come. I looked up for her expression. Her sadness had lifted a little and for a moment she caught my eyes in her gaze. She said, without managing to smile: 'Well, boy. Is Busty gone home out of it?' I feasted on the words, hearing them as if coming on wings of kindness for me. I nodded.

'Deegans have got baby rabbits. Can I look after one? Lindie and Beebie could help. It could go in the dairy.'

'I'll have to ask' - she redirected her thoughts - 'your grandfather. Be a good boy now and pick up your sisters' truckall.'

The clutter she meant was dollies' tea-sets and old cutlery and beads and the like, scattered out on the floor. I went down on my hands and knees on the kitchen floor and gathered in the toys. It was a dark, smooth, cement floor with a waxy patina, dust-free. It had invisible undulations and a visible slope towards the hob and the hearth surrounding it, which was red-tiled. If you rolled a glass marble across it from end to end, the ball would never travel straight but was pulled this way and that by strange forces. When, later, we did something called Brownian motion in a physics lesson at the grammar school, it was to the image of marbles on our farmhouse floor at Three Crosses that I recurred.

The walls of our kitchen, the core and oldest part of the house, were of undressed slate and granite boulders with a bit of mortar and a great deal of clay, rendered outside and plastered within. They were thus a couple of feet thick, with the ground-floor windows in deep recesses. In the kitchen, the walls were distempered in pea-green. Looking up at the ceiling, you saw brown pine planking, long kippered with the wood-smoke from the hob and the sticky patches where the timber had wept resin. In one of the two windows at either end of the room stood the Ekco wireless, blocking out most of the daylight and, in the other, the copper, electric kettle. (Grandfather Thomas had another wireless of his own, a Cossor, which he kept in the parlour). I had not noticed him that morning, sitting in his place on the form at the dinner table by the copper-kettle window so as to be able to read the Southern Express. As he read, he whispered the words occasionally and, when not whispering the text, he was humming a little song to himself.

Great-Uncle Vance came out of his room, looking friendly and scrabbling with his bad hand to claw the door shut behind him. You would not have said Vance was my grandfather's elder brother. He had a full head of silver hair and, evidently, a good barber somewhere. He was stocky where Grandfather Thomas was lithe; he dressed like a gentleman, where Grandfather dressed as he pleased.

I gazed out of the back window by the wireless and then across the table out into the yard, missing the familiar landmarks that comforted. But there was no Slievegarriff, no more Coole hill, no more avenue, no more sky, only a hard fall and a choking, grey mist of rain. It belted down on the slates over the cowhouse, throwing over it a misty halo from a thousand exploding drops. I could hardly read the date graven on the keystone. Our ass, Thady, and our horse, Jellico, were tethered temporarily in the cowhouse. I was told they were great company for each other; in the fields they kept away from our cows and at home thought themselves too grand for the cowhouse, even when it rained. That was strange, for the cowhouse, with its dressed-stone walls and regular slate roof and its 'Anno Domini 1869' over the arch, it was clear to me even then, was a handsomer building than our rendered and thatched house or indeed the construction, in larch poles and galvanised, which Jellico and Thady normally shared with the carts and churns.

'Look at the rain,' I said to anyone who would listen. 'You can't see Mount Slievegarriff.'

'By hell a man,

Said Judy McCann',

responded Great-Uncle Vance from the darkness of the chimney hob,

'When the 'Garriff is gone,

Can mankind go on?'

For one who only put his teeth in when he had to eat, Vance articulated well. Habitual toothlessness was one of the few points in which he fell short of gentlemanly aplomb.

Aunt Peg came in by the green half-door and took off her hood and black oilskin, streaming water onto the floor. She walked over and inspected the bread in the Valor oven somehow, through the greasy mica window, without opening the oven door. She always made that check but I could never see anything inside. Then she turned down the oil. There was the sweet scent of soap off her. She gave me a smile as I turned from the window.

'Where's your Mammy, B.?'

'Gone upstairs to the girls.'

'Have you ever a fondie for me?' I said I had and so she hoisted me up for the kiss. I delivered it under her ear, her black hair enveloping me for a moment so headily that my breath caught.

'Bozer, you're a fierce weight altogether. I can't hold you.'

She pinched my cheek then she took the rag from the stone shelf at the back of the fire and raised the black crock and its bubbling spuds off the trivet and above the fire, onto a long, adjustable, wrought-iron hook with its root somewhere up in the soot of the chimney.

Donald Madge

Five

Making hay in 1956 and how it led to a trial for me.

In former years, our summers at Three Crosses had begun after the hay was cut and, mostly, saved. Last year, the summer of 'fifty-six, had been an exception. Living there for the best part of eight months while my mother nursed my grandfather, we had helped out from the first cut in June. 'Fifty-six, like this year, had been a good one for the hay.

We had two barns: a long, low, home-built lean-to, in split timber and recycled galvanised, put up before the War, against the back concrete wall of the calf pens, by Grandfather Thomas and Great-Uncle Joseph, before he went away. There was also a new, two-span Dutch barn with a silver half-barrel of a roof on six uprights of telegraph pine and the roof-trusses in machined timber. The latter was a good way from the house in our nearest field off Driscolls' lane.

Each barn occupied its own place in my child's fantasies: the old lean-to had a nautical feel to it and was a redoubt to defend against imaginary enemies: holes where the knots had fallen out of the split-pine planking provided squints for cow-sticks, imagined as rifles; an unglazed window, aperture is a better noun, gave onto a southern vista through a gap in the chestnuts across flat and empty pasture which did service for sea; when I would come to read in Robert Louis Stevenson of Stuart Breck's stand in the roundhouse of the brig *Dysart* or of Long John Silver's attack on the wheelhouse of the *Hispaniola*, that barn would be the blueprint on which, willy-nilly, I would superimpose the novelist's descriptions. On the other hand, the Dutch barn (the Kanturk we called it, after the roofers' plate on its semicircular gable) supplied the locale for other kinds of fantasy, as will become clear.

This year, 'fifty-seven, this last year of the dreamtime, given the abundance, the old hay, which was still yellow, glossy, wholesome and dust-free, was going for bedding and we were already feeding the new. When the straw came in later, there would be the chance of selling it.

In 'fifty-six, I had gone out most days with the men for haymaking - I was of limited use, not being able to handle a sprong or a scythe properly, on account of my height. I was deemed capable of tidying with a rake around the haycocks, or of pouring the tea (made up with milk and sugar in enamel jugs - I have never tasted a finer liquor, though every liquid comfort of man's devising has passed my lips since) and of leading on Thady, our donkey, or our bay, Jellico, from haycock to haycock while the men lit up for a smoke from time to time.

We had no haywains as such, nor did I ever see such a vehicle in our parts. We and our neighbours gathered hay on the same general-purpose, two-wheeled carts, cars as they called them, that were used to take the milk down to the creameries in the mornings. One or two upgraded versions of these conveyances had had their traditional axletrees replaced by recycled back axles and wheels from motorcars and thus ran on rubber but, in the mid-fifties, the iron-tyred cartwheel or, indeed, the bicycle wheel and Dunlop tyre, was still king of our road.

For saving hay, the carts, cars, would be adapted by the fitting of simple, wooden mudguards and high, spruce poles at each corner. Both sets of accessories were butted into special slots between the bottom boards, the poles being secured in position by scrapwood wedges and a couple of taps from the lump hammer. The modification took only a few minutes.

We had two such cars, the smaller of which was Thady's. The coach house, if that is the correct term, where these were kept, was a square hard-standing in slate flags, surmounted by a galvanised roof and abutting a high stretch of good sandstone wall, a relic of a grander building, who knows now what it had been, separating us from our lane. Our trap lived here too, and a third car, whose two wheels had once been orange, with high-boarded sides and a faded blue paint finish on the upper coachwork. I only once saw it in action, hauling mangolds, and its tyres had a patina of rust. All the cars were chocked at the wheels, with their shafts pointing heavenwards and lashed to the roof trusses by lengths of hand-braided rope which hung down for that purpose. Next to the faded blue wagon we kept a single-share plough and a harrow. A '47 Ford Anglia van, the successor to Vance's old Morris Eight, was domiciled there too. The van was nominally the property of my grandfather Thomas, who never used it. On the rare occasions when it was fuelled and well enough to be driven, it was Uncle Packie who took the wheel.

On the last day of hay-saving the year before, in 'fifty-six, I remember us in the high field up against Kilcreggan woods, the same field where this year I was to have a bruising experience with our donkey, Thady. That day, I stood next to Grandfather. I asked him what he thought of the hay and he said it was good enough alright but with a few too many thistles and docks. I wanted to ride home on the top of the load like some maharajah in his howdah. Whether I would do so, I calculated, would depend on my grandfather's advocacy and on whether Uncle Packie would lead Jellico home by the bit or drive him by the rein from the top of the load. If the latter, I could sit up with him to hold down the sprongs and my rake.

This was our last load. In one consummate, seamless stroke, Grandfather skimmed a few wisps off the surface of the grass with one tine of his sprong, then scooped up a heavy swathe from the cock, then launched the forkful up to the top of the wagon, the polished handle of the sprong slipping up through his hands. He walked around the load, whose level had now reached the top of the four poles, preening and combing it with his sprong and pulling out weeds when he saw them. Grandfather Thomas was a canny worker, always looking for the shade; he would have the brim of his boater well down over his forehead, like a silent-movie comedian, to keep the sun and the hayseed out of his eyes. Packie, building up the load atop the wagon and Vance, breaking down the haycocks with his pitchfork for Grandfather, sweated into their vests, as I did, the seed and the dust sticking to their forearms and damp fedoras. Grandfather kept as dry as a bone.

I was hungry, thirsty, hot. In childhood, these afflictions have a memorable intensity. Packie, Vance and Grandad were doubtless as ready for tea as I was. But an adult, except in time of want or war, knows when his needs will be met. Vance flung up the first of the two ropes to Packie, who positioned it diagonally across the top of the load. Grandad took hold of it near the pole at the opposite corner and hauled and dragged on it, putting his whole weight into the struggle. At seventy-one years of age, he was hanging from the wagon, horizontal, with his feet planted in the back of the hay-load like an abseiler.

'Good man yourself', said Grandad, as I tugged on the last rope. 'Hoist up them sprongs now to Pascal then shin up for yourself, let you.' I needed no second bidding.

Packie led Jellico off by the bit, Grandad and Vance followed the wagon carrying the sprongs and rake over their shoulders, and I sat alone atop the load, out of sight to all. The vehicle swayed and lurched in the field as the horse followed the yellow clay cow-path down to our lane. I was flung left and right but gripped the stay-ropes at their crossing point. It was exhilarating and, at times, frightening. When we got to Driscolls' lane it would be worse. Images of toppled hay-wagons began to form in my mind and I replayed there all the farming conversations I had ever heard for hints about the inherent stability of the hay-wagon. The experience was archetypal for the countless hours I have spent on aircraft, journeying to the US in my later life. I loved flying, period. Nevertheless, any prolonged episode of turbulence in mid-Atlantic would lead, willy-nilly, to questions of the same order. How much more bouncing and jolting does it take for this to become really dangerous? What price the Comet disasters? And, finally, what in God's name am I doing up here?

The vehicle made its way out into Driscolls' lane and back homewards to the Kanturk. Though the jolts and judders were sharper, even through fifteen feet of hay, the lateral swaying was less violent and I felt safer, needing only to avoid overhanging branches as I slid secretly through a new world, the tree-canopy, twenty feet above our lane. I slithered down from the top of the load when we got to the house. I had had enough. The men went on to unload at the Kanturk for the last time before they ate their tea.

That evening after the meal, the maroon road gates at the bottom of the yard were open. No-one was there to see me, so, Gene Autry now, I spurred on my palomino and galloped down to the Kanturk. The evening air around the barn and by the horse-chestnuts filled with exquisite little sparks of sound, here, on my left, overhead, back here, up there, everywhere. My eyes found their originators: two bats.

The new hay almost reached to the rafters under the first of the spans. In the second span last year's crop was now reduced to a height of three or four feet. There was a twenty-foot drop between the levels. Thus, last year, the Kanturk had offered me and my sisters two imaginative possibilities, the first of which was parachuting and the second tunnelling. When, at the age of fifty, I parachuted for the first time from an aircraft, it was not my life that flashed before me in the few seconds before despatch, but a memory of the itch of hayseed down my back, the panic before I launched myself into the twenty-foot void. Geronimo!

I had read *Wind in the Willows* earlier that year and become imprinted with the pictures in the edition my English grandmother had given me. I was affected by the womb-like intimacy and cosiness conjured up by these sub-Beatrix Potter illustrations of the animals' underground abodes, and especially by the painted evocations of old Badger's set. At the Kanturk, I discovered that there were gaps, or fault-lines, in the strata of hay laid down, swathe by swathe, under the first span, by Packie and Vance. Before long, I had tunnelled head first into the hay to a distance of fifteen feet or more. The gallery which I made kept its shape and diameter, more or less, and at its end, in the centre of the stack where I had chanced upon another area of less-densely-packed hay, I had a kind of cocoon. This I hollowed out and, by stuffing back the hanks of hay into its walls, enlarged into a chamber where I could sit upright, perspiring in the womb-warmth of the hay, in the pitch darkness.

No sense of claustrophobia oppressed me in that Dutch barn snug; a short-lived hiatus in time and place, I enjoyed it alone for two or three occasions, running with my thoughts and fantasies: old Badger *contra mundum*. I would, even so, soon leave waistcoated rabbits, boatered frogs and badgers with reading-glasses behind. Though it was with empathy that, years later, I encountered, through my reading at the grammar school, the semi-troglodyte hobbits of Middle Earth.

My chamber must have been in the centre of the stack, with twenty feet of hay above me. When I felt the need to get back to the fresh air, I could turn in my cocoon, feel for the exit and, head-first, slither back the way I had come. For a few days I kept the tunnel to myself, disguising its entrance a couple of feet above the ground by arranging hanks of the outer, overhanging thatch of hay.

My sister Lindie was unusual, indeed all three of my sisters were, in that they were not curious about me and did not know the chapter and verse of my comings and goings, as did other sisters in other families, Busty's, for example. Eventually, I divulged my secret to her at the wash-up under the rain butt near the back gable-end of the house.

'It's like - like Beatrix Potter. You know, in *Benjamin Bunny*.' I knew she had not read *Wind in the Willows*.

'That wood was full of rabbit-holes; and in the neatest sandiest hole of all lived Benjamin's aunt and his cousins - Flopsy, Mopsy, Cotton-tail and Peter.'

'Yes, but where is the tunnel? Where?'

'In the Kanturk barn.'

'Why?'

'Because it's a special hay-tunnel.'

'I'll come if it's not more than this long.' She measured out with her arms a span of six feet on the dairy wall.

'You could be Flopsy. Or Old Mrs Rabbit. I'd have to be Peter.'

'I don't want to be either of them. They're useless. I'd be Mrs Tiggywinkle because that's the best story. Anyway, let me have a look first, before I say yes.'

We took my blue velvet bag, together with a jam-jar full of water.

'I'll go first. Close your eyes in the tunnel, you'll get hayseed in them.'

I squirmed in and Lindie followed. Sharing my cocoon with Lindie did not offer the exhilaration I had expected. Neither of us was in the mood to enter a Beatrix Potter fantasy so we sat there for a moment, cheek by jowl, listening to the silence. Unexalted by this experience, Lindie began to gossip away about the school game she was playing in her den in the haggard behind the house with Beebie and two of the Brittan girls, Ann (she that was lost and then found) and Alice. The Brittans were coming back after their dinner and she did not want to miss them. We drank half of the water.

The tunnel in the hay was discovered a few days later, and duly crimed, by Uncle Packie. I stood accused. In the kitchen with the other adults, Feena said 'Yeugh' and hugged Lindie to herself, in order, I later thought, to whip up emotions and fan the flames. Then she took my Aunt Peggy aside and upbraided me to her, out of the earshot, as she thought, of us children.

'Yeugh! He have the ringworm in him. Lookit. 'Tis a fright to God. 'Tis a little rip he is, and nothing else.'

'Arra whisht', said Peggy, 'don't be giving out to Adameen all the time. Did you never put a foot wrong and you ten or eleven?'

'Go away, girl, I had regard for my mother, the Lord have mercy on her.'

'Well have a bit of regard for Geraldine, now, and don't be adding to her tribulations.'

I knew enough of gender differences to be aware that mine was a boy's crime. A young Feena could never, I thought, have perpetrated a tunnel even if she had had the imagination to conceive it. But the implied charge of lack of regard for my mother cut me very deep.

My father had been reading at the kitchen table waiting for me to appear. He had gazed across at me from where he was sitting. He had been unwell-looking with the worry of it, along with the pressure from the other adults (it seemed to me) to hold a tribunal and to be seen to disapprove. He had remonstrated with me quietly but in open court.

'Highly dangerous. You and Lindie could have been buried alive. Do you know what that means? What possessed you, son?'

'We were playing a game. I was Badger in his set. You know in *Wind in the Willows*?

'The wind in the willows

The wind from the bellows

The wind on the billows

The poor drownded fellow

And his tiny sister

How they missed her',

Great-Uncle Vance had intoned, with his back to us, looking out at the sky from the Ekco wireless window. He had got away with it without criticism from the other adults, on account of his seniority.

Uncle Packie and my two aunts had stood behind me. 'Tis all a matter, now', Packie had said, knowing well that it was not, but dropping the prison guard approach to simulate kindness to me. With the blue velvet bag and jam-jar he had removed from the chamber in the hay, he held the evidence in each hand like a clerk to the court. Trapped, I had not wanted to look over my shoulder for him to see my humiliation.

'That burrow you had there, Addie, wouldn't be safe at all. You could suffocate there at the end of it in the blink of an eyelid.'

'The blink of an eyelid, boy', Grandad had said from his captain's chair at the hob.

There I had stood on the patinated cement floor, hardly daring to look up at the adults in a semicircle around me, except for Daddy and Grandad who were seated on a form at the kitchen table. My father's eyes at the level of my own had disturbed me most.

'Show me them, Pascal', said Peggy, and Packie handed over the blue velvet bag and the jam-jar.

Daddy's face had been the colour of putty, with my mother looking on beside him and Kate on her hip.

I had deserved to be chastised. I knew it and I had hoped, pointlessly, for my mother to walk across from their side of the table to me to cuff me or give me the flat of her hand across the back of my legs. But she had stood with her left arm around my father's shoulder, as if defending him.

'Look at your father, Addie. He is trying to speak to you.' Her words had not quite corresponded to the facts. I had hardly taken my eyes off my father and I knew my father had said his piece to me.

Dad had sat hunched forward. He had joined his hands in front of his face as if in prayer and kept talking to himself under his breath through the tips of his fingers, as if he were ruminating, hardly addressing me at all. He removed his glasses wearily and Mother said something in his ear.

'Highly dangerous. Highly dangerous. I know, Geraldine. You and your own little sister, Addie. You could both be dead.'

Then, for the only time in his life, my father had frightened me, when he had added: 'But pull a stunt like that again, my son, and you'll be the death of me. Do you hear me?'

I hear him, God help us. I hear him.

★

In Liverpool, one Saturday four years later, I was to relive the whole wretched hay-tunnel trial again in a city art gallery. The guide, a French student, took a reverent stance in front of the nineteenth-century canvas which was the gallery's particular treasure. Perhaps you know the picture. An eight-year-old Royalist child stands in the midst of a squad of Roundheads who have taken over his home. The boy faces a military inquisitor seated behind a table. The Frenchman was earnest about the moral dilemma faced by the child in the painting. The Victorians, he told us, saw children as ideals of truth and honesty. How to honour the truth and yet not betray another? The Royalist boy was *tout seul*. I stood at the back of the little group of visitors, lest I be seen too moved by the pathos of the scene and the turmoil of emotions I felt when I learnt the title of the painting. It was Yeames' *And when did you last see your Father?* Déjà veçu.

Six

*What happened at home in Liverpool at the beginning of 1957, the last
year of my dreamtime.*

'Go up and lie down again, Daddy', Mother had said
on the morning of February 19th.

I had been sitting in the front room in 44 Curzon
Street, at the window, with the brocade curtains drawn
back. I had my head under the net curtains with their
pattern of tricorn hats and up against the window pane,
so that I could watch the street. At the same time, my
grandmother's present to me, *King Arthur and the Table
Round*, lay open on the half-moon walnut table in the
bay. I had heard my mother's voice from the kitchen
through the open door. My sisters were still at the
breakfast table, arguing.

'I have no aspirin, Daddy.' Again my mother's words
had seeped in, subliminally, but by then I had started a
fresh chapter in Grandmother's book.

'When Queen Morgan le Fay heard that King Arthur had his sword Excalibur and the scabbard again, she was very sorrowful and more than a little afraid.'

I had heard Daddy speak softly to my sisters at the table. Their bickering had stopped, quite suddenly. But I had turned the page.

Nor had I looked up from my book at the window when Mother came in to the front room.

'Adam, I have no aspirin. Go down to Blacks now and bring home a bottle. If Blacks are closed get it from the Post Office. Daddy's not going to work today.' I had brightened up. It had, after all, been Saturday.

'Can I go on the scooter? I'll be quicker.'

'Ten minutes, now, mind, Adam. Daddy said he's waiting and don't be long.' She had vanished to the kitchen and I had heard the muted screech of the dresser-drawer hinge as she extracted her purse. She had darted down the tiled hallway to bring in the milk with an urgent little adjustment of her step. It was Mother's correction of pace with the half-skip that had been the beginning of my awareness. I abandoned Morgan le Fay at the Castle of Joyous Gard.

Daddy was not alright.

'Is Daddy alright?' I had said when she came down.

She had left the street door wide open for me. Then she had gone back to make more tea, and slipped back upstairs after my father.

'He's better now, but bring back the aspirins quickly, boy.' My mother had led me out to the hallway by the wrist and opened the stair cupboard. I had wheeled out the scooter and ridden straight down the hall and onto the street.

The pavements of Curzon Street provided several kinds of challenges for the child scooterist. Outside our house, the pavement presented an irregular surface, Victorian granite flags, finished with dressed kerbstones. Here the trick was to scoot along the kerbstones, a somewhat dangerous practice requiring the skills of a tight-rope artist. Next, where the German bombs intended for the marshalling yards had pounded the area, the road had been rebuilt, the bombed-out houses demolished to their foundations and a splendid new section of pavement in well-laid concrete slabs as smooth as a runway, which allowed a decent speed and a clean line with long swoops. Unaccountably, this section gave way to a puddled, pot-holed stretch of several hundred yards which had not been adopted by the council. Here, little more than walking pace could be maintained, with an ever-present danger of encountering a brick or a deep pothole and going over the handlebars. At the end of this third section Curzon Street finished, opening onto the High Street of what was still referred to locally as the village, some hundred years after it ceased to be such a thing.

I had scooted along the kerbstone surface to the accompaniment of the swansong of hoots, judderings and metallic screams from the marshalling yards in those last days of the age of steam. Bursts of chugging near at hand, rhythmic and sudden, would send up dirty vapour in packets, like smoke signals in Arizona. Through the pewter-coloured miasma, above and behind the terraced roofs on my right, the heavy skies had begun to sweat rain, mist at first, then spots on the damp paving- stones.

Blacks the Chemists was owned by an Ulsterman whose first name was Calvin. Mr Black smiled perfectly, like an American politician, whatever the occasion. His manner nevertheless left me with a permanent sympathy for his sixteenth-century namesake, whom I could never quite place in the same category with the other ogres of the protestant reformation against whom we were later proofed at confirmation class. In his elegant shop-window, with its narrow panes and simple, white-painted tracery, Mr Black displayed all the achievements of the glass-blower's art, from alembics to breast-milk extractors, keeping his stock of machine-made bottles for the inside shelves. On the window-sill inside, he kept a range of mysterious appliances, all dials and stainless steel and red and black rubber tubing.

'I'll have a bottle of aspirins, please.'

'Who's got the 'flu, then, Addie?' He had decanted the pills into a bottle.

'Dad, I think.'

'High is he?' (He meant 'How is he?')

'Better, thank you.'

'I see', he had chuckled. 'Give these straight to your mother, along with my respects.' I had handed over the half-crown and pocketed the bottle.

The drizzle had hardened to a firm rain as I came down Black's steps on to the High Street. Over the road, I saw that Medleys' General Toys had their blue awning out. If I crossed the High Street by the Belisha beacon, I could wait out the downpour for five minutes. Medleys' sold every kind of toy but since the old man, Sod Medley, was a model-railway enthusiast, there was, contrary to the practice in the department stores, a display where different trains ran daily, where the points were switched periodically and the rolling stock and model passengers were moved frequently. Only Sod Medley dealt with model trains. His brother Grenville, despite the loss of an arm in the War, seemed content to manage all the rest of the toy stock.

I had stood my scooter on its stand and gazed at the miniature England laid out before me. Four-coached passenger expresses, in blood-and-custard livery, raced around improbably tight curves on the three-railed permanent way. They flashed through little groves of moss-trees, reaching alpine heights in a matter of a couple of feet. Logging trains hurtled from short tunnels to pass through stations under the impassive gaze of early morning travellers. Plastic porters rested on their trolleys. A tinplate level-crossing held up a three-wheeled lorry and half a dozen cars. They would have a long wait. The rhythmic passage of the trains was mesmeric and put me into a long, exalted reverie. Yet I needed to hear more loudly and to sate myself with the whirr and the squeaks of the locomotives and the miniature clackety-click of the diecast wheels over the fishplates, so, gradually, I insinuated myself across old Medley's threshold and edged into the shop...

Later, when the last terraces of Curzon Street, where number 44 was situated, had come into view over my handlebars, there had been a dark-green Vauxhall parked in the road. As I had swooped nearer home, a train-driver now, on the kerbstone permanent way, I had seen that the car was standing outside our house. I had reached the front door and pushed it open, leaving the scooter outside under the front-room window.

Thinking to please, I had dried my shoes energetically on the doormat, then marched straight up the corridor towards the light of the kitchen. My mother had been sitting in her chair at the fireplace, looking into yesterday's embers. Lindie and Beebie, one on each side, had their arms around her. All three had been aware of my presence in the doorway, but none had moved her head.

I had heard a creak behind and above me and Doctor Oliphant came down the stairs, thinking deeply, it seemed, before each step. What, for my part, I had been contemplating, as the doctor prepared himself to address me, was the accusatory pressure of the brown aspirin-bottle up against my backside in the pocket of my school trousers.

Now the first, unspeakably catastrophic, consequence of my disobedience that morning would become manifest; indeed, I already knew what the substance of Dr Oliphant's words to me would be.

'Be a strong and brave lad, now, Adam', said he, looking down at me over the banister. 'Your dear father has died.'

Seven

In which it is suggested that there is a simpatia, between my Aunt Peggy and one Peter Cody. My companion Busty is curious about my father's funeral. I am curious about one person who attended it.

At Three Crosses on the Tuesday morning in the week after Feena's kitchen concert for St Camillus' day, I scaled the maroon gate from the inside and then heaved myself across and up onto the high, flat-capped left pier. Slowly I got to my feet. My head wanted to spin with the height but I kept my balance and looked out over my world. Slievegarriff was there again, very near, her breast-like profile and cairn, like a nipple, all crisp in the morning air. Her lower reaches were patched with the green fields of a few hardy farms. Higher up, she was like a royal woman in purple and undertones of gold, yet naked.

From down the road came the sounds of a shod pony and the crunch of iron-rimmed wheels on road metal chippings. Below and behind me, our milking was over and I heard the clink of the chains as Peggy and Feena loosed our eight cows. I clambered off the white pier and planted my feet on the uppermost rail of the gate, and leant over to look out, half hanging on my ribcage. To occupy this perch was a transgression, albeit a lesser one than to be found on the top of the pier. But when the aunts came out, they let me be. Then they swung open the other gate, for no good reason, it seemed, for the moment.

Peter Cody drove his fine, glossy tan pony up past our farm, three tall, silver churns swaying behind him. He slowed from a trot to walking pace. He stood foursquare on the boards of the car like some hero of the south, with his jet-black hair and bronzed young face - a handsome Achilles in his chariot, I often thought later, or a Galahad. The rope reins curved up from the collar guides to his right hand. In his left, he held his crop like a sceptre and the excess length of rein in a neat coil. A half-smoked Sweet Afton adhered to his bottom lip, its successor in reserve between his ear and his peaked cap. Tieless he was, yet he looked almost urbane in an elegant, brown pinstriped suit, far too good for farm work. Folded in his pocket was his *Southern Express*. He shot me a sombre glance from under dark brows, then acknowledged my aunts with a tiny upward jerk of the head. They had had a good view of him as they moved nearer the open maroon gates, ostensibly to collect kindling.

'Would you marry Peter?' said Aunt Feena at the gate, when he had passed on out of earshot.

'He has only thirteen or fourteen acres, girl', said Peggy.

'He has more. There is, I think, a cousin farming in a big way, around our parts. A powerful man altogether. Don't be asking me who, for I couldn't tell you. But 'twas this fellow put Peter's mother Agnes in the way of buying Walsh's fields, there, after his father dying.'

'Go away, girl. He's renting Walsh's land.'

'No, girl. Agnes got a power of money from the cousin or a godfather or someone for that land', said Feena.

'Agnes who?'

'Arra, Agnes, Peter's mother, who else? Will you listen?' said Feena and went on: 'Would you go dancing with him?'

'He's drinking the farm, girl', whispered Peggy.

'Peter is a bitter man, after his father dying. He speaks to no-one now', said Feena, after a pause.

'Oh, sure Peter used to be a grand fellow ...before he got his crosses', Peggy said.

'Would you have married him then?'

'God knows...you're full of talk, Finola.' And Peggy's beautiful eyes darted away.

Hughie Heaphy came down in his Standard from Coole on the Wednesday morning after creamery, towing a small trailer, with a Hereford calf spancelled to the uprights. He had Mercy, a sister of his, with him in the back of the car to take to Rossbeg on her messages. Busty was sitting on the floor of the car where the front passenger seat had been removed. Apart from the sparking-plug circuitry, the only other working component of the electrical system on the Standard was the horn. This did not deter Hughie, a dangerous man, from night-time driving as long as the moon was up. Hughie brought the car to a halt at our gate as I looked out over our road, balancing precariously on my ribcage. Busty deftly opened his door with the outside handle and alighted. The Standard, with its trailer, ground away in second gear, assisted by the slope of the road down towards the avenue.

'How're you?'

'How're you?'

I took Busty behind the house to our dairy. This was a gloomy prison-cell of a room forming one end of a long outhouse, built in the vernacular style with rendered walls of boulders and clay which had once been whitewashed. There was a rumour that the building was older than our house and indeed that it had once been the principal dwelling. Two unglazed windows, protected by chicken wire and iron bars, afforded minimal illumination. A rusted, galvanised roof with long eaves kept the rain out of the walls. No cheese or butter had been made in the dairy since before the War; now it was rarely visited and housed a few mice, bicycles and bits of timber standing on end on its ancient clay floor.

In the gloom behind its closed door, painted in the same grass-green as the half-door to the house, I had been working away to build myself a little handcart. The chassis was a wooden butter-preserver about the size of a shoebox. To the cart I had fitted four wheels, secured on axles I had whittled out of ash canes. The bearings for the axles were loops of wire attached at right angles to a couple of springy osiers from which the chassis was suspended. The wheels were fashioned from discarded shoe polish tins and trundled over the grey gravel of the yard in a very satisfying way, leaving discernible tracks. One of the sets of wheels I had long hoarded under my bed on the landing, the second I had triumphantly removed from the shoe-shelf in the kitchen press on Sunday, having consumed the last crust of black polish in a tour de force of spit-and-polish lavished upon seven pairs of shoes. A characteristic of the wheels was that they gradually loosened on their axles, especially under load conditions. This required further fulfilling play, in that they had to be adjusted and tightened. The toy was drawn by a piece of string and I had used it the day before for deliveries to the girls' den, up in the orchard where the school game under the horse-chestnuts still captured Lindie's and Beebie's imaginations. I suppose it is no coincidence that both my sisters would turn out to be teachers later in life.

I had harboured, but not implemented, a plan to fit the box, or perhaps the undercarriage, with shafts and to devise a harness for one of the three or four half-feral cats which lived in Three Crosses. A dog would have been better but our own mongrel, Shep, was simply too big. The only suitably-proportioned canine candidate was Dempseys' Punch, a Jack Russell type, as I remember, but Punch spent most of his day tethered and, besides, I was not on speaking terms with him. One of the feline possibles, a black tom we had named Zulu, was a creature of equable disposition who would sometimes come when called. Zulu had a mainly-ginger half-sister, Thpoth, who was a rare visitor. I saw Zulu as a potential draft animal, but this game would need to await a day when I was not with Busty.

My efforts to construct the handcart were aided by the discovery of a pair of pincers during one of my many solitary forays amongst the outhouses. I removed them to the dairy and kept them hidden in a dark corner, with all the care and skill of a prisoner secreting escape equipment in his cell. The matter of their disappearance never arose in conversation with Vance or Grandfather or Packie; perhaps they had belonged to my late Great-Uncle Joseph, the second of my grandfather's brothers.

'Will I pull it now?' said Busty, as I rolled out the vehicle into the sunlight. I handed him the string. I was happy for Busty to take the cart for a tour of the yard, but disappointed in his inability to enter into the spirit of the game. He pulled away looking straight ahead, unfascinated by the little cart's swaying motion over the irregularities of the ground, uninterested in the marks of wear appearing on the wheel rims, deaf to the intriguing squeakings and scratchings as the vehicle I had built forged on in his wake.

'It's grand', he pronounced, the circuit complete. But now I longed to take the handcart out for myself. I therefore set out on the same course with Busty accompanying me.

'Well, Busty', said my mother as we passed.

'Well, Mrs', said Busty.

She was washing clothes at the rainwater butt. I liked to see her without her housecoat, with her brown arms and her orange floral-print shift dress rucked up above her knees. She wrung the water out of a shirt and twisted it into a white sausage, which she added to a heap on the concrete drainer. The next shirt got a dusting of Lux flakes and mother began to scrub at it. Over her shoulder, she asked:

'Are ye all in good form above, Busty?'

'Ah we are, only Mammy have the shingles.'

'Did Doctor Gilbank look at her?'

'He did.'

'And what did he say?' She turned to face Busty. I moved nearer to my friend, so that my mother might take me, too, into her gaze and confidence.

'He said he could give her some medicine that would be a good friend to her alright, but Cleary's blood would be a better one.'

'And did she get Cleary's blood?'

'Oh, she did, Mrs.'

'Where?'

'From Breda Cleary of Borrisrobbard.'

'With all those Cleary ones gone out of Borrisrobbard and Killinunty to the nursing in London and Coventry, I'm glad Breda is still in it giving the blood. Well, your Mammy won't be long getting better. Faith she won't.'

As Busty and I convoyed on down the yard to the maroon gates and the spring-water tap, he told me what the shingles was, although he couldn't satisfy my curiosity further on the matter of Cleary's blood. With her blood that would cure shingles, Breda was the carrier of a tradition, rather like Aunt Feena with her music.

I stopped to load my toy cart with pebbles from the miniature wetland below the leaking spring-water tap. The last stage of the play-journey would take us back by way of the kindling stacks and the granite-arched cowshed up to the long, white outhouse dairy. I was John Chisholm at Council Bluffs or on the Oregon Trail; Paul Kruger and the Great Trekkers were in there, somewhere, in my fantasy. Perhaps, too, I was Peter Cody, the striking hero of our road that morning, the brooding Achilles, the Galahad, preoccupied with his crosses and compulsions.

'Do there be any of your aunts sleeping with your mother?' asked Busty impertinently, but I answered nonetheless:

'I think Auntie Finola sleeps with her some nights.'

'It's lonesome for her. Your Da was great crack', he murmured. 'Do you remember the show-jumping last year?'

Pangs of sadness assailed me; why had Busty felt it necessary to remind me? Yet, confusedly, I was grateful to go to the memory of that game of my father's devising which we had played over makeshift hurdles in the orchard with Busty, his sisters and PK and the other

Reynoldses and Brittans. He pursued the topic of my father.

'Was there a good few at the funeral over there in Liverpool? I'd say there was?'

'No. Mum said we had only a dozen in the Hall afterwards.'

'Why?'

'How should I know, Busty?'

'Who out of the Driscolls came? Not Vance, I'd say?'

'Grandfather came with Aunt Finola and Aunt Peg. So did Josie Deegan.'

'That was good out of Josie, so it was.'

'And who else? Your English relations?' He had a whimsical, slightly mad, way of posing his questions.

'My granny and my two uncles.'

'And, without ever a cod, now, whobody else?'

I could not open the secret recesses of my unhappiness to Busty, but I did not want to cod him either. Why was he so keen to know who had attended Daddy's funeral?

'There was a lady called Greta from the company, with a small baby in a pushchair, that none of us knew. She told my mother she was a golden friend of Dad's, but I heard Mum say to Aunt Finola afterwards that she had no idea why the woman was there.'

At that point, the cart behind me toppled over on a rock and shed its pebbles. We stopped so that I could rectify matters, with Busty looking over my shoulder, arms akimbo and very bemused. One of the tin wheels had loosened. But we had reached the end of the cowshed wall and we finished the home run to the dairy door without further mishap.

'Wouldn't it be great now', said Busty, innocent of my intention to adapt the little cart for haulage by the black cat Zulu, 'if you had a small engine to pull the car?'

I wondered what he meant. A toy engine? Not only did I know Busty had no toys but I didn't think he knew anyone who did. The concept was quite beyond his experience; there were no toyshops in Rossbeg. Now we were sitting up in the orchard near the girls' den. I had carried up the cart, which was not such a good performer in the grass.

In one of the *Sheepman of Ireland* magazines I had lifted from Deegans' and secreted under cover in the shell of Vance's old Morris Eight, I had recently read an inspiring piece, *Steam Power from Hiero of Alexandria to James Watt*.

While I had all the confidence of a Victorian engineer, I could not be absolutely certain of my ability to construct, from the tooling and material available to me, a device that would serve as a source of motive power for the cart. I told Busty I thought we could build a demonstration model steam-engine. He would have to find us a good-sized tin for a boiler. Busty became very interested, at first, and promised to bring a cocoa-tin the next time he came down to Driscolls'.

But he also had the hunger on him and the Heaphys were getting boiled bacon and cabbage for their dinner. He hooked his jacket over his shoulder and slipped out of our yard by the maroon gate. He headed uphill, north, to Coole. Busty was outgrowing his childhood by the week: after his last visit, the time we saw Deegans' rabbits, he had run home; today he adopted the spare gait of his father and forefathers, men who knew how to walk, because walk they must.

As my eyes followed him, I wondered again why my father's funeral was of such interest to him. Busty was a proficient fisherman, as I discovered later. Because his mother had it as a principle never to trade in the intimacies of her neighbours' lives from a position of lack of knowledge, she had Busty well-trained for fishing expeditions of another kind.

★

Daddy's obsequies in February had been by no means the first I had attended. I was no stranger to a requiem or an interment: I was already an altar-server, had passed the holy water to the priest, had held up his black chasuble as he blessed the coffin, had lit the orange candles, four or six, depending, around the bier, had remembered to carry the Latin response cards to the cemetery. On days when a parish funeral was due, the priest would come in to Miss Pargeter's classroom asking for me and conversing with her in hoarse whispers at her desk. I would try to pick up their conversation: if the funeral was after dinnertime and I was wanted for the interment as well for the mass, I would conceal an improper pleasure: it was the end of school for me that day. The odds were that I might pocket a threepenny bit or even a sixpence for my services.

Father had been buried on Tuesday February 26th, 1957. Lindie and I went into the church holding hands. It was a different church from our own. Unaccountably, we lagged behind my mother and Beebie.

'Are you C of E or RC?' asked the sexton, in a navy-blue soutane, rounding us up, 'Church of England?'

'Oh yes.' I answered for both of us. (I knew we weren't protestants.)

In our pew at the front of the nave, I was comforted to catch their altar-boys' eyes seeking me out from the choir stalls; it was the same heartless urge I had often felt to stare from the altar at the faces of the newly- and closely-bereaved.

I held up well until I witnessed an unconscious gesture on Mother's part in the last minutes of the service. At home, my father would always help Mother on with her coat and I would stop on the angle of the stairs to watch them in the hallway below. This intimate action would often end with a straightening of the wide collar, a dusting-off of each shoulder and a couple of pats on each side. As we sang *Abide with Me*, and the attendants turned my father's coffin for his last earthly journey, Mother reached back to ascertain that her collar was sitting straight. It was when I could not reach her to help with the collar, that I became distressed. I pictured, under the mahogany coffin-lid, Daddy's bloodless hands, that should have adjusted her collar, folded over his chest, dead cold. In that moment, I was proffered the foretaste, the focus, the horror I feared might envelop me. The loss of my father was not to be remedied the way the loss of my sisters in the Park had been, by the intervention of a kind stranger. My disobedience over the aspirins had led to my irrecuperable fall.

Mrs Frowstie took me out of the church. I made no protest although I was ashamed of myself and Lindie peered round Mother's front at me, shocked. I sat down in the lych-gate in February sunshine. Mrs Frowstie made me drink a beaker of water from the dusty decanter they kept at the back for old ladies who got fainting fits.

'He's been a brave boy. He felt a bit sick with the smell of all the incense, didn't he, Addie?' Mrs Frowstie seemed to be talking to me, but in some form of the polite third person. I remember, as well, that she administered a verbal sedative I have not encountered since, except in literature. 'There, there', she kept saying. 'There, there.'

Greta, the mysterious woman from the foundry where Daddy had worked, came out at the end of the cortege, pushing a tubby infant in a perambulator. Mrs Frowstie wouldn't let her or any of the other mourners near me. For many years thereafter, I conserved the hope that Greta might be the godmother I was unaccountably missing. As I say, I received no intimations of condolence from her, or from any other mourner, until I was back in the schoolyard at Pius the Twelfth that afternoon, in time for the last playtime of the day.

I found myself separated from the main pack in the playground, shivering. Another little knot of classmates was looking across at me. Their expressions were shocked and strange, yet kind. Paul Sinkiewicz, I knew, was telling them my father had died suddenly. I have never met, in a hundred books, the adjective 'sheepish' except it was followed by the noun 'grin'. It is a cliché, but a good one. My grin, sheepish, was to say it was all right, but it wasn't. I appreciated my classmates' wordless sympathy. It angered and confused me that my father, head and shoulders above their fathers, the best man I would ever meet, was gone. All I could do was grin like a sheep. It was myself I hated.

★

In the warm noontide at Three Crosses, after the midday meal, I lay outstretched on a slate churn-stand. Busty had long departed for home above in Coole; I had put away my toy cart and was idly scratching at the slate with my knife.

Uncle Packie had long admired my penknife. It was one I had chosen with my father, who had then arranged for Santa Claus to present it to me for Christmas when I was seven. It had one folding Sheffield blade and a handle in real grey horn with a grain. It was as smooth in my hand as a fish. I have lost that knife, yet I now see it in front of me in every detail as plain as day, and I mourn it.

That summer, because I had discovered a businesslike black clasp-knife that had belonged to the deceased Great-Uncle Joseph, who had lived out his exile in the States, my own knife got little use and I kept it hidden in my britches. Packie knew quality when he saw it and coveted my possession. I nearly gave in to a proposed exchange when he offered me for it a gaudier pocket-knife with a painted tinplate handle.

'This one have a grand little picture of Montallond Castle, lookit', said Packie, 'and you'd have the second blade handy, fearing the first one needed edging.'

I refused and, in any case, had I given in, my mother would not have permitted the trade to stand.

The need for treasures in the form of the works of the hand of man expressed itself in strange ways. Mother would listen to the *Barrys of Ballyfergus*, a serialised farm soap-opera, in the kitchen on the Ekco wireless, big, black and Bakelite. The receiver, with its veiled round oracle-mouth of a speaker, stood taller than me at the back window. But she also had, and I treasured, my father's last gift to her - a handsome little portable set, called a Perfectone, housed in a kind of vanity case in grey and red oilcloth. I sometimes heard the Perfectone in her bedroom in the small hours. I loved to flip open its chrome-plate catches and practise changing the green, cardboard-encased Exide battery. I had read 'Perfectone' as 'Perfect One' when I first saw the receiver, but my child's mistake betokened a truth. To my small fingers, the feel of the ivory-look knurled knobs, made so exquisitely by man for man, gave a sensual delight which, time and again, never failed me. With the battery back in, I would click the set on and wait for the soft Dublin tones of the man from Radio Eireann to fade in. The tuner dial, massy, fat, yet so gently responsive, elicited wafts of music and strange tongues. Mysterious place-names too, Hilversum, Daventry, Tirana, Kalundborg, asserted themselves in red and black print over a dim, religious light.

Uncle Packie walked up to me to see what was commanding my attention there in the long grass of the orchard, near the shell of Vance's Morris Eight.

'Who gave you that?'

'It's Mum's.'

'Oh yes.'

'It's Dad's Christmas present to her.'

'What would one of them cost now in Liverpool?'

I knew, so I told him. 'Two pounds seventeen-and-six.'

'Oh yes.'

A sixth sense told me why he was interested.

'But you can get them second-hand.'

Packie gave me a straight look, ill-concealing the offence taken. 'Oh, no. I wouldn't be buying one second-hand at all. Oh, no. Sure what good would one of them yokes be to me?'

A couple of days later - it was the third week in July - Skellymoher Races week - I watched Packie harnessing Thady the donkey. From a vantage point where he couldn't see me, in my favourite horse-chestnut, I spied Mother's Perfectone, half covered in sacking, on Packie's cart. He would get the Races as he thinned spuds that long and hot afternoon, on his knees astride the drills in Sheehans' field. I did not call out to him about the wireless, nor did I later mention it to my mother. I didn't want to go with Packie and now, with the portable wireless set, he wouldn't need my company. But I feared the adults' wrath if the set were to suffer that afternoon. Perhaps the battery would run down. The crime would somehow come home to roost with me, I was sure.

Eight

In which I discover an affinity between Peter Cody and me. Peggy confides a dark family tale to me which may presage ill for my future. An inkling of my mother's love proves delusory.

I heard a pony-and-car approaching at a fast trot from Tourmahinch in the south, outside on our road, and I shinned up our gate. I was in time to see Peter Cody sweep past, stern-looking, be-suited Achilles, on his way up the hill to Kilcreggan; he was in his own world and did not notice me. I squinted down the avenue through the summer morning haze. I saw Grandfather's ass-and-car take distant shape out from under the trees, before my aunts noticed his approach. I dropped down over the gate on the road side and ran off down the road in delight.

'Bozer, Bozer, come here, I want you!'

'Come back in out of that!'

'Your mammy will give out to you!'

'I'm telling you now, Addie, you're a bold boy, so you are.'

I ignored Peggy's and Finola's shrieks. I knew they wouldn't come out after me on the road in front of Grandfather, without wearing their dark cotton-print housecoats on a weekday morning. Slapping my thighs, I became Peter Cody's fine tan pony, Diamond. I galloped and pranced towards the avenue, down the trail of sun-dried ordure which stretched in a khaki felt, along the crown of the road. As I cantered past the three old crosses, I changed persona and fired off a couple of pretend rounds at them as if I were now Gene Autry and they were saguaro cactuses.

Our donkey, Thady, looked up from his task of breasting the slope and cocked an ear in my direction. Grandad pulled over and began to light his pipe. He never took off his cap except for meals or to get at his tobacco. I was fascinated by his baldness - the pink of that naked, warm dome against the tan of his soft face, a dome dimpled and buffed to a wondrous lustre.

'Come up, Thady', said Grandfather, 'you jennet, and you're nothing else. Now, Addie, climb up in there for yourself, let you. Good man yourself.'

Grandad hoisted me up off the road and sat me down on a jacket ancient of cloth and cut. He gave me Thady's reins and eased himself down from the car, to walk alongside the great wheel as it ground its inexorable way over the tar and chippings.

I caught hold of Thady's tail but he was not to be trifled with. He whipped it from my grasp, and flicked it across my face. While I smarted, Grandad was laughing fit to burst.

'Thady' - he finally expelled the words between wheezes - 'taught you a good lesson there, - heh heh - so he did. A poor ass needs his tail with the horseflies at him.'

'The flies don't do any harm.'

'Oh as sure as God they do, boy', said Grandad. 'Did you see Peter Cody go up five minutes ago?'

'I did.'

'You did. And did you see the hard face and bitter look on him?'

'I did.'

'T was flies put it there, boy.'

We were coming up to Dempseys' long fence at the bottom end of Three Crosses. Behind the chestnut trees on Dempseys' side was their orchard. A hundred yards of green-painted fence and a ditch separated the Worcester Pearmains and Beauties of Bath from all comers. Last summer, in 'fifty-six, Busty Heaphy and I had found our way into that garden of delights. Once inside, you had twenty seconds or so to raid the old trees, before Punch started yapping. If he didn't yap, it was worse, because it meant he was off his tether. If Punch was off his tether, you were far safer out of it.

'Peter Cody's poor old father, Denny,' - continued Grandad - 'was five weeks in the Sancta Corona and he dying. He got a puck, so he did, from Andersons' bull. Sure, the flies were fierce at the poor bull and he swung up his old head, a kind of sudden, as Denny was tethering him and the horn, as sharp as a sprong, caught old Denny in the eye. The devil of it was, the bull was an easygoing poor creature. A show bull, reared real tame. Denny had the loan of him from Wesley Anderson of Tize Court. They say Miss Phoebe Anderson was in an awful way. And sure, poor Peter's mother was destroyed with the grief of it, after she finding him in the cowhouse unconscious and the old bull nuzzling Denny's face and he only forty-nine. The poor bull was rolling his eyes, so he was, and kind of yowling, because he could smell the blood on his horn and knew something was wrong. Listen.'

Grandad stopped and took hold of Thady by the bit. The creaking and grinding of the wheels ceased. Sure enough, I heard a bull's bellowing call at a distance of a mile or so. Perhaps I imagined a note of elegy and mourning.

'That's the very bull, now, Addie.'

Then after a few moments Grandad walked on, intoning a tune known only to himself. 'Dallydee, dally dah, dally dandy...', he sang, tapping out the beat with his pipe on the old wooden box that he used to bring the butter up from the creamery.

So Cody the Achilles, Cody the Galahad, had become suddenly fatherless, as I had. It was then, as I mused on Grandad's story, that something was born between Peter Cody and me.

The next morning, a Wednesday, I was sitting on the oaken form under the chimney, a piece of soda bread and butter in my hand. I looked out from under the hob into the kitchen when I heard the sound of a latch being turned. Vance stalked into the kitchen from his bed-sitting-room. I think I entered that room once only in all the time I lived at Three Crosses and this was a mark of special favour. I remember an art-deco washstand and a mahogany headboard to the bed, where the rest of the bedrooms had cast-iron-and-brass bedsteads. There was a black lacquered escritoire in which Vance was rumoured to keep twenty or twenty-five pounds in cash. As far as I knew, Vance's room was out of bounds to every other member of the family.

He laid his fedora on the kitchen table by the kettle window.

'Life is no caper,

When there do be never a paper.

Truly, indeed,

Life can hardly proceed

With no Southern to read.

You, sir?'

He gave a look across at me because I had been known to collect the *Southern Express* when the post van stopped at our gates and, a serious offence, read it myself before he came out of his room. But he drew a blank with me this time. He shuffled over to the wireless window and got out last year's creamery book from behind the Ekco. Then, since he had his reading-glasses on, he sat down with this document at the copper-kettle window (which got the best of the daylight), to await the newspaper, which would now be coming up from Hassetts' in Tourmahinch with my grandfather.

Vance's requirement for the printed word fascinated me in one so advanced in years. But I assumed it was a natural condition for one of my age and, in those days, I thirsted to read. Before we had left Liverpool, my English grandmother had sent up from London for me a turn-of-the-century copy of *Robinson Crusoe*; my mother had packed it for Ireland, being of the opinion that it would cover my summer needs. I saved Robinson for the evenings in the dim electric light of the landing where I slept. I was consuming the book at a rate. The one constraint upon my nightly journeys to Crusoe's island was Feena, who shared a bedroom with Peg. Sometimes Feena would see the glow of the electric bulb from under their door.

'Quench that light. Addie. Do you hear me? Put out that light.'

'Arra leave him, girl. Put it out when you are ready, Bozer, now and be sure. Sure you will? You're a great fellow. I'll have a fondie for you tomorrow.'

So for Peg, I would finish my chapter in a minute or two. The tale of Robinson's Adam-like first disobedience, in the matter of going to sea against his father's wishes, tweaked at the hook deep in me upon which, reader, I must writhe; in Robinson's case it had led, ineluctably, to half a lifetime of literal isolation without the possibility of a prodigal's return. Robinson spoke from his own deep loneliness to me in mine:

'I looked up with the utmost affection of my soul, and with a flood of tears in my eyes gave God thanks that, though I had esteemed my present condition very miserable, he had yet given me so many comforts in it...'

Yet those 'comforts', I knew, were distractions from his real problem. How, I asked myself, could he live with himself, after his premeditated rejection of poor Crusoe the elder, the only father he had?

When I finished the Defoe, little else was available to me until, later in that dreamtime summer, I discovered a collection of Celtic tales in our parlour at Three Crosses. The stories about Camelot in it duplicated some of the material from *King Arthur and the Table Round* which I had first listened to at my father's knee, in Curzon Street, before I could read. That only enhanced my appetite for them.

Peggy came in. She knew by the day, Wednesday, what time Grandfather was expected back from the creamery. She made his tea, drawing the water off from the cast-iron kettle over the fire. I finished the soda bread and helped Peg replenish the paraffin in the bread oven. Grandfather appeared in the kitchen and shuffled to the hob. The blackened aluminium teapot, with its heavy, dark brew, sat in a nest of embers at the side of the fire.

'Have you the Southern, Thomas?' asked Vance, looking up from the rows of longhand additions and subtractions in the creamery book.

'Faith and I have not. It came up with the post van', said Grandad.

'Feck it and it did not', said old Vance, white and shaking, maybe with frustration.

'Please mind the child, Vance', said Aunt Peggy.

Vance stalked back to his room, scrabbling the door shut behind him with his bad hand. We heard him muttering angrily and the sound of something slammed on the washstand or on the escritoire.

Peggy took the milk across to the dinner-table where Grandfather sat placidly, about to sip his tea. He drank, as always, from the saucer, decanting successfully from the cup. He had a flat, buttered slice of soda bread and cut it up into four pieces as if he were preparing it for a child. The table-knife he used was razor-sharp and worn as thin as a stiletto from constant edging: no-one in Three Crosses saw the point of a blunt knife.

Peg went outside to the rain-butt with a washbag so that she could rinse off the taint of the paraffin from her hands. She took me with her. We sat together on the stone drainer, looking down the yard towards the maroon gates.

'Vance have a fiery temper on him', said Peg, patting her hands dry and putting her soap away. Then she took my hands in hers onto her lap. 'Mind him, now, won't you Bozer? And Uncle Pascal too. You wouldn't know how they might take something.'

'I've never heard Grandfather swear.'

'No more did I, boy. Your grandfather is the gentlest of men. He got that from his mother. But Vance and Packie took from your greatgrandfather, that you didn't know. Sure my mammy too, the Lord have mercy on her, would get real mad. She wouldn't know what she would be saying. She was well able for a fight with Vance, all right.'

'Why?'

'Arra, Vance never took to her. Show me your face. Look up at me, till I find your parting.' She moved my head gently with the cool palm of her hand.

'I have my parting on the right, please, Peggy.'

'No, boy, on the left.' She took her own hairbrush out of the soap-bag. 'You have a grand little cow's lick to show off to the girls, Bozer, so you have.'

'Why didn't Vance like her? Your mother?'

Peg peeped around towards the porch. All was quiet. Even so, her voice lowered.

'Poor fellow, I'd say he was jealous of Grandfather. Vance was now the older brother, with Joseph gone away. Vance didn't like a woman coming into Three Crosses laying down the law. My mother - your grandmother Maeve that you never saw - came here to work, boy, and no mistake. She worked the way your mother Geraldine does, morning, noon and night. Now, when Vance was younger, he was no great shakes for the farming. 'Daddy would never say a word. But I often heard Mammy calling him to get up out of bed and bring over the spuds for her. And sure, wasn't she right to be at him, with the royal treatment she gave him while she was alive.'

'Well, why did Grandmother treat him so well?'

'Sure it was her duty. He was her father's brother. She washed and ironed for him and ran his messages. She had the dinner on the table for him. A Sunday, she could be out in the rain breaking her back to start his old car for him. I'd often see her at the kindling stack. '

I looked up and Peggy's eyes were full. She put her comb back into her overall pocket and lifted the hem to cover her face.

'One time, your Granny was out with Vance, with a good while, cutting timber over there by the stack. She hadn't the chickens or the calves fed and she told him she would go in when they had the last big log cut and then he could shift for himself with the small saw. Maybe she didn't mince her words. Anyway, when the log was done she left off her end of the saw and she upped and walked.'

'The two-man saw I help Vance with?'

'The very same one.'

Peg put her arm around my shoulder and began to whisper.

'Well, Vance had the lump hammer there with him to tap in the handles on the saw. He caught hold of the hammer, he stood up and he flung it at her. She got a hell of a blow on the hip from it, so she did, and I wonder was the bone chipped or cracked. But she kept going and she kept her mouth shut too.'

My aunt looked into my face, her brow cloudy. She kissed me, into my cow's lick. I felt her fingers settling the parting again.

'Faith and he never did it again, boy.'

'Why?'

'Your grandfather found Grandmother's bruise after a fortnight and got the story out of her. But Daddy is very cute. He bided his time until we had the priest here on the Lent visitations. Your grandfather brought Vance into the parlour and there he told him, over-right the priest, that he knew what Vance was after doing. When Vance said he knew nothing, Daddy asked him would he send for my mother. Vance said no, so Daddy told him he would put him out of the house if ever he touched Mammy again.'

Peg's tale, spiced with violence, gave me an initial frisson of enjoyment, but this was soon transformed into a deep unease.

'Vance must have gone berserk when Hughie Heaphy cut off his fingers with the chainsaw.'

'Well now, that's the thing, Bozer. He never said as much as a word to Hughie that morning. He stayed real quiet and was good as gold with Doctor Gilbank. Vance has a slow fuse, so he has. You wouldn't know what he might be thinking.'

My great-uncle had never been other than kind to me; at the time, however, I could not separate his ancient transgression and subsequent humiliation from my own story. It left me more in fear of what propensities for violence I might harbour within myself when I grew up, than of what I might provoke in Vance. Peg gave me a cuddle and left me.

I headed up behind the house and yard to the back outhouses where my mother would be feeding the pigs and calves. She was already at the second outhouse with the yearling Herefords. My sisters formed her entourage. Lindie had Kate by the hand. Beebie, who was too small to keep baby Kate under control, had therefore taken charge of my mother's stirring-stick. She also carried a tinplate scoop and the yellow-powdered worming compound in a cardboard box that had to be mixed into the milk before each creature was fed. A bolder calf forgot its manners and approached the wrong bucket. Beebie used the stirring-stick on the creature with gusto. I remembered how, last year, all the calves would surge forward when my mother swung back the wooden gate to the pen. It had been my role to single out the right creature to feed. Now Beebie had assumed that responsibility, with my mother behind her to guard her from being knocked over by the thirsty calves.

I stood close to Mother. I had not seen her yet that morning. I tried to be something to her, the way I had been briefly a week ago in the kitchen, during the downpour, after Busty had gone back up to Coole. I looked for some special sign in her face but she was intent on the calves. I offered to take over from Beebie, making to relieve my sister of the stirring-stick, at which Beebie squealed.

'No, Addie, let Beebie carry on', said Mother. 'You didn't come when I called you, boy.'

It was spoken without reproof, in a deadly, matter-of-fact way. I had not been there when I was needed. If only she had shown a little temper then, signalled anger. Yet I feared to provoke her to a different kind of wrath.

'Can I go up to Coole to play with Busty?' Coole was a mile away up the road and I knew perfectly well that this proposal would not receive sanction.

'No.' Mother manhandled the churn, tipping it forward to refill the two buckets with milk.

'You're not allowed', explained Lindie.

'Addie can't go, can he, Mummy?' said Kate, while Beebie held her peace and plied the stirring-stick about the ears of a Hereford steer. The beast took its head out of the bucket and looked at Beebie, aggrieved, its front legs splayed. It flicked its tongue into each nostril in search of the last drops of sustenance.

'Yeugh', said Beebie, 'what dirty habits he has! Will I give him another tip with the stick? For his dirty habits?'

'Can I get on with repairing my cart?'

'You can, boy.' There was a relenting there and a smile. But in its purposefulness and completeness, the little community that was my mother and sisters saw no reason further to trouble me. This troubled me, deeply.

Nine

A gentleman of the road foresees unhappiness for Aunt Peggy. A gift of my father's leads me to recall his arrival a year ago in 1956 for his last holiday on our farm at Three Crosses. A mysterious remark my father made about me to my grandfather.

I slipped away from my mother, the girls and the yearling calves in the outhouse. The previous night's reading surfaced in my mind and the persona of Robinson Crusoe took hold. I, Robinson, cast my mother and sisters as a party of natives whom I had wanted to befriend, along with the strange, wildebeest-like creatures they were tending. I took the winding orchard path back to the front of the farm and to my imaginary redoubt, the dairy. I sought out the little cart I had secreted there, behind the baulks of scrap timber, after Busty's visit last Wednesday. I would attach shafts to my cart. I would devise a suitable harness. Then I would search my island for a wild beast I might capture and train to draw the cart.

My efforts to whittle a couple of shafts from saplings and nail them to the cart's chassis only proved successful after much trial and error. Each shaft split as I attempted to nail it to the chassis, until I discovered the awl attachment on the black clasp-knife that had once been Great-Uncle Joseph's. Using this, I bored out holes in the shafts. The four precious nails I needed were pincered out from the wooden perches in our henhouse without, I thought, compromising unduly the guano-encrusted structures. I hammered the nails with a large stone, behind the dairy door, in semidarkness, with irregular, sporadic blows, in case Packie or Vance heard, investigated and put a stop to proceedings. Only my father would have understood why I needed to play out the game: now he was gone; I was without advocate and protector.

The solitary search for a suitable beast of burden was fruitless. It was Zulu, one of only two local cats with names, whom I had hoped to find. But he was not in any of his favourite haunts. I checked Vance's cabbage patch and raspberry canes. A large, cat-sized opening between the boulders of the granite wall at the top of our orchard was the focus for my search. It led to Deegans' back paddock and all the local felines used it. But though I sat, catlike in my turn, for half an hour in our orchard, watching the aperture as if it were a mouse hole, it was in vain. I clambered across the dyke into Deegans' territory to spy out the northern part of my island; this foray was, equally, of little avail.

Into this Robinson Crusoe reverie, as I heard the midday angelus bell from Tourmahinch Chapel, obtruded the pangs of hunger. When the bell stopped, the land was silent. Our road was still. Almost too hot the eye of heaven shone. The very birds were quiet, the sparrows, the linnets, the warblers, even our chickens and the turkeys at Reynoldses'. I listened in vain for the prize bull at Tize Court.

There was no one to be seen at Deegans', so I left their farmyard by way of its front gate and set off down the forty yards of our road to Driscolls' maroon gates. Though shut, our gates were not, as I had feared they might be, barred against me. I sidled back into our yard, into the more intimate world for which I so yearned, divesting myself of the Robinson persona and casting it off in the road behind me.

There was a stranger, sitting like a sentinel outside our porch, in the part-shade by the green half-door. One of our good dinner plates lay on the ground beside him, with the knife and fork he had been using placed neatly on it and a little pyramid of empty spud jackets next to that on a fold of newspaper. On the other side of the chair stood a khaki haversack with leather webbing and a japanned-steel frame. It was one of the parlour chairs that they had brought out for him - apart from Grandfather's captain's chair and Vance's car seat, our kitchen only had black oak forms. The stranger did not greet me as he watched me walk up the yard towards him.

Not wanting yet to pass him at close quarters on my way indoors to my dinner, partly through fear of him, I went to climb the drinking-water pump, as a pretence at play, to give myself a vantage point from which to observe him. He seemed of a generation even more ancient than that of my grandfather and Great-Uncle Vance: he wore brown leather, laced boots with spats; in those days, apart from on Sundays and holy days, black rubber wellingtons, like my own, were universal for walking males of any age in our parts. What also took me aback was his long hair, but thin and etiolated, like the aged Sir Bedivere's picture in *King Arthur and the Table Round*. His nails, grown out about an inch beyond the tips of his fingers, brownish and faintly corrugated, had begun to curve in on themselves. He had a gaunt face with the skin tight-stretched so that his skull and jawbone showed through. His eyes dark, bright and wary, glittered under abundant eyebrows that were fair but not so yellow as his moustache. He had a watch on a chain like Panloaf's.

Aunt Feena came out with a tray.

'Now', she said, collecting the plate and handing him a cup of tea and two slices of soda bread and butter with raspberry jam.

'Thank you, my dear.'

He spoke in a clipped, 'fifties English prestige accent, a form of locution I would not hear again until broadcasting entered my life and it went with talks on the Third Programme and television newsreaders in dinner-jackets. He cut the flat slices first with a clasp-knife of his own and sipped his tea out of the cup, rather than from the saucer, as did Vance and my grandfather and, I had presumed hitherto, all older folk. Without preamble, he fired off a question at me:

'Who is the good lady who has been looking after me? Your aunt, perhaps?'

'Yes. She lives here', I said jejunely. 'I don't live here. I'm English.'

'I see that. And in which part of the, ah, North Country do you live?'

'Liverpool.'

'Whereas, you see, I have come from London, by way of the principality of Wales and the port of Comerford. I spend my year mainly in London, being a native of that city.'

I considered these statements. Perhaps the stranger had sailed to Ireland on the *Western Warrior*, as my father used to do before his Liverpool days. In those days, the southern route passenger ferry service took you a good way inland up the River Glas to Comerford; it was more a voyage than a crossing.

'Do you believe in God, my friend?'

'Yes', said I, uncomfortably astride the spout of the pump.

'I believe in a Force. You have another aunt, I think, who is a great beauty?'

'Yes.'

'You must pray to your God, for all mankind of course, lest we roast, but in particular for this other aunt.'

'Why?'

'Because', he said suavely, finishing the last slice of soda bread and folding away his clasp knife, 'she is destined to suffer. Like Helen's, her beauty may undo her. But what may save her is her goodness. What is her name?'

'Peggy.'

'Peggy?'

'Margaret.'

'Margaret? Margaret the Pearl. By name and by nature', he said.

Every word of that conversation went to the core of me as into an echoing well where, deep below, it resonated for days, creating a mood of foreboding that I could neither understand nor shake off. Peggy to suffer? Us to roast? I thought he meant Hell; perhaps he did, but, in those weeks, I had gleaned from the Dublin man on the Perfectone, as I played with the tuning dial, that, in another world less remote than I would have liked, the wise men of science were at play, too, with fat black canisters on atolls and in deserts: man-made hells for the rest of us.

'As you see, I am a guest of the people of Ireland, your own family included, and I must neither outstay my welcome nor disturb further. Will you now be kind enough to pass on my appreciation for the excellent lunch?'

I nodded, but had to think about what he meant, since it was his dinner that I had seen him eating. It was out of that conversation that the word 'lunch' became part of my passive vocabulary.

'I don't want my Aunt Margaret to be unhappy.'

'Because you are a sad young man yourself?'

'I'm happy. I'm very happy indeed.'

'Ah, happiness. Happiness is but the occasional episode in a general drama of pain. You will have a long road to the uplands.'

'What about you? Where are you going next?' said I rudely, clamping both feet on the cast-iron bulb at the end of the pump-handle.

'To the Three Crosses; thence to Clarepoint, then True Cross Abbey and the very Rock of the Kings of Munster.'

He took out two pennies, an English and an Irish, from a purse in a pocket of the haversack and gave them to me. I walked down to the gate with him. There he got out a pipe and a lighter from the other pocket, and lit up, jetting the smoke down through his nostrils into his yellow moustache. He shouldered the rucksack and slipped away down our road towards the field with the three crosses.

I went back into the house to my dinner and caught up with Peggy behind the door of the porch. There was a shaving-mirror hanging there and she was examining her *maquillage* in it.

'Is the poor old fellow gone, Bozer? A kind of shook-looking he was, wasn't he?' said she, without taking her beautiful eyes from the mirror.

'Who was he?'

'Some class of a tinker, I suppose. But he was the quality, one time. I think he was at Three Crosses years ago and I a one of seven or eight. ''Twas your grandmother fed him then, the Lord have mercy on her.'

★

Uncle Packie handed me a long package in brown paper.

'That's yours, now', he said to me. 'Put it away under your bed.' I immediately recognised the package as one my father had brought to us from England the summer before. But I thought it polite to ask Packie all the same.

'What's in it?'

'You'll see tomorrow, Addie.' At first, I thought this a capricious response of the kind you got from adults. Later, I was not so sure. I had noticed that Packie, in particular, could not talk about my father to me; he, Daddy, had entered the same undiscovered country as Packie's eldest brother, Christie Driscoll. Uncle Christie was dead of a blood disease by the time I was a year old. 'He was the best of us', was the only comment on Christie I had ever heard on the lips of another Driscoll. I think it was Feena who said it. Had I become upset to see again my father's last holiday gift to us, poor Packie would have found me hard to deal with.

The present had been rewrapped exactly as it was when I had first seen it strapped to the side of my father's suitcase last summer. In that year of 'fifty-six, he had come to Ireland from London by Cardiff and Pembroke Haven, on the twelve-hour crossing, sailing up the Glas estuary on the *Western Warrior* to the docks at Comerford. Mother had taken me to meet him off the boat for a surprise. It had been my second Irish train journey that year of 'fifty-six, and Lindie and Beebie were jealous.

Rossbeg Railway Station was gateway to another reign and jurisdiction, steamland, with its own lore and laws, its own sounds, its own uniformed functionaries and its special vocabulary of excursions and alighting, corridors, compartments, tender, platform and sleeper - words which were railway-coloured long before they acquired other associations for me. Irish steamland was in our parts, but not of them. Though related to the iron fields of the Madras Street Marshalling Yards near Curzon Street, Liverpool, Irish steamland was, nonetheless, *sui generis*. The Irish railway gauge, I knew, was six and a half inches wider than in England and the rest of the world - something private and special, like an Irish gallon, an Irish mile, an Irish whiskey.

Mother had agreed with me when I told her the wider loading-gauge produced more generous proportions in our compartment than in an English train. She had patted me on my bare knee, and I had read the gesture as one of pride that she had such an observant son. She removed her straw hat, spread out her floral frock on either side of her, and got out her Southern to read for twenty minutes. The boat was late and we had to wait at Comerford Dock. A couple of emigrant families had boarded the train at a halt after Rossbeg. They did not know each other and sat silently on the pre-1920 Great Southern Railway benches with impossible piles of luggage around their feet, impedimenta, literally, of every kind. There was something exquisite in the misery of the young mothers, too sad to speak to their children, fidgeting and subdued. Their menfolk, hatted and dressed for the journey in suits, collars and ties, stood and smoked impassively. So the exiles waited quietly, bravely, opposite us, different from the other travellers.

From a mile or two to the east down the Glas, came the double hoot of the *Western Warrior*; a quarter of an hour later, the steamer docked. The gangplank was swung into position by crane. Once it was lashed into place, my mother could not restrain me and I wrested my hand free of her grip to rush up the steep, battened, wooden bridge from Ireland to the black hull and orange-streaked white superstructure of the *Western Warrior*. I had seen my wonderful father edging towards us in the crush. I dodged in and out under the arms of other travellers. In bliss, I looked up into Dad's face. Children's hearts are made for joy. 'Beau Sir! That's my boy,' Daddy said, and his face creased into one of the smiles I knew. But I couldn't find space to stand at his side and hold his hand in the press of bodies. So I took a small suitcase from him and struggled back down the gangplank ahead of him. Daddy said we would not have made it to the last train if I had not been there to help with the luggage. As we clattered back in the train along the single-track valley line from Comerford to Rossbeg, I eyed the oblong package, so carefully encased, with the grain of the brown paper running lengthwise. Daddy would not say what it was. I was to open it with my sisters.

At Three Crosses that evening, I was not allowed further access to my father as he took high tea with the adults. I was, instead, sent outside into the gloaming with Lindie and Beebie; we were instructed to shift for ourselves until bedtime.

I followed my sisters up to their den in the orchard. They showed a jam-jar which they had filled with pretend tea, having run the brown stalks of dock through their fingers to collect the tiny, sun-dried leaves. The Brittans' great-aunt, who was ninety, used to amuse herself likewise as a girl and had learned to do so from her grandmother before her. So she told Lindie. Before that, I supposed, there was no tea drunk in Ireland. Doubtless, dock-leaf dust would have served some other play-purpose in those olden times.

Once, sitting with Grandfather Thomas, I had broken off a dry, hollow stalk of cow-parsley and had blown through it at his face. Grandfather Thomas had chuckled. 'I used take my father's black tobacco unknownst to him and smoke it in them yokes and I a lad of your age. I'd be retching.'

'But it doesn't make you sick now, Grandad?'

'I'd be sicker without it, now, boy, God help me, so I would. But I wouldn't bother my head with it, Addie, had I my time again.'

His weakness on this point had looked out at me from his grey eyes. As he put his fedora back on that polished, baby's head of his and shaded those eyes, it was as if he was protecting that weakness. And yet he had reached out to my own vulnerability, I at the beginning and he at the end of our lives; sixty years, sixty seconds' worth of distance run: sometimes there was little between us.

My sisters and I were called in out of the dark when the time came. With the kitchen table indoors still set for the meal, we were washed for bed by Aunt Finola in the gloom at the rain-butt. She whisked us inside and upstairs without much ceremony, past the adults and the honoured new arrival who were all still at conversation in the kitchen. The prayers said, Feena took the landing light-bulb out of its socket. This was a favour to me, she explained, adding, when I remonstrated, that I was too young to understand. I could therefore neither read nor sleep. Tides of chatter, laughter, anecdote and the capping of stories surged from the fireside. There was the hint of a glow from the kitchen. All I could do was listen, in the near-darkness, and ache with longing, seemingly unrequited, for my father, sat at the hob a few feet below me and, all the while, the rattle of the train back from Comerford reverberated in my head. I rolled out of my boxwood camp-bed as quietly as I could - it creaked at the slightest movement - and edged to the banister. I manoeuvred myself to a position where I could peep around it at the angle of the stairs and see down into the kitchen.

My eyes lit upon my father, seated in state, though not, I suspected, in comfort, in front of the fire on a parlour chair brought down for the purpose.

'Will you smoke a Players with me, Roy?' Grandad had asked. (No one had the heart to remonstrate with him that Doctor Gilbanks had told him to stick to the pipe.)

Father accepted the cigarette and, with some difficulty, lit up, picking out a glowing twig from the fire. He had told me that the cigarettes he smoked there in the hob tasted different from any others, with the wood-smoke.

Mother had come to join my father and had sat on the end of the form up against the parlour chair. They held hands there; Grandad looked surreptitiously across the embers at them from his high seat in the captain's chair. Great-Uncle Vance had smoked away at his Sweet Afton on his own fireside chair, the leather-upholstered passenger seat from the pre-war Morris now sitting out the last of its seven ages, sans wheels, sans engine, in its grove in our haggard.

'Your old self again, Dad' - my father, to his host.

'Thanks to you, Roy, and to Geraldine. 'Twas she put me on the good road, alright.'

'Go away with yourself, Daddy', my mother had said, 'didn't every one of us help where we could?'

'And it was good out of you, Roy, to let her go. And won't be forgotten, boy. Won't be forgotten.'

'I've done nothing to compare with what you and your family did for me, taking Adameen to yourselves the way you did.'

This was the first occasion on which I had heard mention of one Adameen. I confronted a riddle. Which relation of mine was this Adameen? I half-formed a resolution that I would ask one or other of them the next day but, in the event, I never did. There had been, I thought at the time, a strained formality about this exchange, and both contributors were glad to move the conversation on.

'You had a good crossing, then, Roy?' Grandad had said, after a few moments. He had already put the question that evening, but courtesy required that he should offer my father this moment to enjoy contributing some further anecdote of his own.

'Flat as a millpond. But the boat was in late. They were held up loading cattle in Comerford.'

'The boat was in late,

Says Emily Kate.

What kept ye at all

Asks Henry McCall

'Twas a toot on the funnel

Says Daniel O'Connell.'

Our Greek chorus took his due place in the conversation.

Grandad cackled, but not at Vance. 'Heh, heh. Oh, there could have been a few of our steers on that boat. We sold four last week and half the herd there was for Smithfield. They do be taking everything we can send. Next year, in 'fifty-seven, it won't be so great. Now, Roy, at this hour, I'm in the habit of a bit of medicine. Will you take a sup too?' Vance had got up from his car-seat and scrabbled with his bad hand in a black corner of the hob. He had retrieved a Paddy's bottle. While my mother was in the parlour searching for glasses, my father had adjusted his spectacles and peered at the bottle in Grandfather's hand. It had appeared to be half-full of water.

'Oh this is not whiskey at all, Roy. I got this' (neither Vance nor my grandfather seemed prepared to let the word poteen fall from their lips) 'from Detta Hassett.'

Detta and her sister, Maud Hassett, ran one of the two bars in Tourmahinch. Hassetts' was the senior establishment to its competitor, Crealeys', because Hassetts' had its own telephone. The main point of the telephone was to assist trade: the Guards in Rossbeg would always pay Detta the prior courtesy of a telephone call of a Sunday when they were going to do a random check on her timekeeping.

Maudie, who was able for driving a car, had set out to meet a local supplier and take secret delivery of four bottles of illegal poteen liquor. It was a good eleven miles to the still on Slievegarriff, but no-one in Tourmahinch, apart from Detta and Maudie, knew exactly where. While Maudie was away, the Guards arrived, without the customary niceties, to set a little trap. Detta knew full well why they were there. No amount of sweet talk from her would send them on their way and she was scalded at the prospect of a summons. The coming anecdote was one I had already had from Grandfather.

'Well,' he had said to my father, as four glasses were filled, 'when Maudie pulled up, bold as brass, outside the door of the bar there in Tourmahinch, poor Detta thought she was done for. But, Roy, the Guards never found a drop on her or in the car. And how was that?'

'I don't know. She didn't get the poteen?'

'Oh, Maudie took delivery right enough. So how was the meaning of that?'

'I couldn't tell you, Dad.'

'Sure, didn't the old Austin run out of petrol there at Carty's Bridge? There are no flies on Maudie. She knew what she gave for the medicine there at the still and I'd swear 'twas less than for a half a gallon of petrol. So she poured them four pints into the tank and thrung the bottles out in the ditch. The Austin started first pull. The only lads to suffer were the Guards with embarrassment and Detta's few private customers going away dry for their sup!'

Grandfather began to wheeze and splutter as he laughed with the memory of it. His face reddened under his hat and his nostrils trembled. My mother withheld the poteen and looked across at him as the laughter transmuted to a long paroxysm of coughing. His hand shook so that I thought he would drop his cigarette, until he steadied it on the arm of the chair.

'You hadn't right to be smoking them yokes, Daddy', said my mother. 'Will I get your pipe?'

'No, girl', he spluttered.

'Will I make another cup of tea then?' she said and he nodded, with the tears streaming down his cheeks, as the bout subsided. That coughing attack was serious matter. It brought back fears from the months preceding my father's last arrival at Three Crosses that summer evening in the June of 'fifty-six.

Ten

*A sea and railway journey from Liverpool to Three Crosses in January
1956; my Aunt Peggy destined for a nursing career.*

At this point in the story, we should return to the
January of 'fifty-six and to 44 Curzon Street.

During the autumn, a series of bronchial attacks had
left Grandfather bedridden at Three Crosses. Dr Gilbank
had been summoned.

At home in Liverpool, I was aware of an exchange of
telegrams between Three Crosses and Curzon Street on
New Year's Day, the day before Lindie's birthday; I recall
my mother and father talking in bed in the small hours,
to the occasional faint accompaniment of ribald singing
and drink-fuelled squabbling from the street outside. I
did not hear what had been said. The next day, there was
no talk of any kind at breakfast, which was also ominous.
When Lindie and I got back from school in the evening,
letting ourselves in by the back yard into the scullery, we
discovered not our mother, but the holiday luggage,
including our second-hand pre-war suitcases with the

red and blue Cunard stickers, stacked in the dim hallway. My mother was plying the vacuum cleaner upstairs. When she came down, she began to move the luggage through to the gloom of the hallway. We helped without speaking. From upstairs, baby Kate began to bawl. The Electrolux vacuum fell silent. Mother despatched Beebie to comfort Kate.

'We're all going off to Three Crosses a Thursday, won't that be grand? You'll wear your new Sunday shoes on Thursday, Adam.'

'Why?'

'Poor Grandaddy has the bronchitis.' I already knew what that meant.

'I'm going to be nursing him, boy.'

'Is he in bed?'

'He is. We'll all be helping Vance and Uncle Packie and Aunt Feena.'

'Will Daddy go to the creamery in the mornings? For Grandad? I could go with Daddy. I know the way. Lindie doesn't. But she could help me harness Thady.'

'No; Vance will. Or Liam Deegan. Daddy won't be coming to Ireland for the time being.'

'Why?'

'Because he has to work and find us a new house.'

At the outset, the plan had been that, God willing, once my mother had nursed Grandad through his early convalescence, we would stay for at least six months until the summer of 1956. Our schooling was to be left in the air; the position (as my parents put it to Lindie and me) was that little would be lost by our non-attendance at Pius the Twelfth for the next two terms since I, and then Lindie, had been admitted early in any case. This logic was suspect to me even then, as a seven-year-old; but my experience of primary school was not one of unalloyed pleasure. It would have been then that Mother conceived the notion of a possible involvement, on the part of Great-Aunt Stacey at the National School in Blanchardstown, in our continuing education once we were back at Three Crosses.

Later, I discovered how money came into the decision. There was the prospect of six months' rent to be saved, because Father would live with my English grandmother. At work, he would take advantage of the abundant overtime and, they hoped, put together enough for a deposit to purchase a house in the autumn.

After these developments, and two days on from New Year's Day, 1956, a Tuesday, we sailed on a winter crossing to Dublin from Holyhead; against all my expectations, it was calm: the weather out on deck almost mild. Mother and the girls sat on a green leather sofa next to a mock fireplace in second-class. Screwed to the wall above the mantelpiece was a vivid, gothic sea-painting of a paddle-steamer in distress in mid-Atlantic. In the hot fug of the saloon, Mother, her eyes wet from the fresh parting with my father, knitted a cardigan for him. My elder sisters slept in their miniature purple overcoats, clutching tiny raffia baskets containing their luggage, their eyelashes so perfect and set off by little flushed patches on their cheeks.

We docked on a gloomy afternoon on one of those days which didn't seem to have broken. There was not the crush of passengers we experienced on a summer crossing and I was first down the gangplank with one of the Cunard suitcases. Waiting on the rust-stained concrete of the dockside for mother and my sisters, I watched horses and motorcars unloaded in gigantic nets as if trawled up from some surreal fishing expedition. I looked down at my new black brogues to make sure I had not scuffed them. A manhole cover under my feet bore the name of the Liverpool foundry for which my father worked.

We had reservations in a malachite-green coach on the steam train from Dublin to Limerick; the carriage was half empty; I did not sit with Mother and Lindie and Beebie in the compartment, but remained on my own out in the corridor.

That railway journey in 1956 is part of a reverie, part of my dreamtime now. But as I, Addie, write this at sixty-plus years of age, I half-believe, half-doubt myself. Is it likely that the weather lightened as the train hauled out of Heuston Station and the Dublin suburbs? Did this happen to me? What is it to truth, that the boundary between dream and dreamtime seems so mysterious, so blurred? Am I, after all, the same person I now describe?

It had been only a couple of months since summer, since I had bidden my goodbyes, and now would come the unmerited joy of a January reunion, especially with Aunt Peggy. That afternoon, the train beat down south through the early winter countryside. After Castlecomer station the last stretch was flat, even boggy but with the southern hills imminent, I began to look out for Slievegarriff, as my father had taught me, preparing me, when we pored over railway maps together, on the half-moon table in our front room in Curzon Street, for a journey I had never made, nor would now ever make, in his company.

A seminarian in a black soutane extinguished his cigarette and moved back into a compartment to join his companions. I now had the corridor to myself, so I let a window down and had no difficulty descrying Slievegarriff, grey, dominant, to be sure and snow-capped like Fuji or Kilimanjaro, yet rounded, womanly, like the mother she was, the she-mountain that faced, across the Great Vale, the angular masculine sierra of the Lackendarraghs further south. I was suffused with a rare and pure happiness. Once I had wanted to know from my mother the meaning of the name Slievegarriff. She knew the land and its old lore. I could see what she had studied when, at Three Crosses, I read the school textbooks she had saved from the convent, full of Irish history and ink underlinings and stacked in the bottom drawer of the dresser in the parlour.

'The Dark Mountain, boy.'

'Why?'

'When the Tuatha de Danaan came down to settle the Great Vale of south Toberenagh they got a shock with it, thinking 'twas awful black-looking from the northern side.'

I saw nothing of that, as the mountain's outline became clearer. At the very moment Mother was in my thoughts, she came up behind me and, with her free hand, grasped my wrist, but gently. Her voice was soft. I think it was as an intimation of her love that she said:

'For the love of God, child, close that window. 'Tisn't two of ye I want to be nursing next week.'

Where my mother was coldblooded was in her attitude to trains. Everywhere, of course, steam was king and steam trains entailed dirt. To run a hand across a misted compartment window put grime on fingers and clothing and a quantifiable addition to Mother's long list of daily chores. Both my sisters had a fascination with ashtrays, which they usually contrived to flip open and empty onto their clothing. Given the choice, they eschewed the compartment seating in favour of the filthy linoleum floor. At home, Mother's most visceral dislike was reserved for the railway smuts which blackened the Liverpool rain: the home we had just left, 44 Curzon Street, was a stone's throw from the flat acres of iron fields that constituted Madras Street Marshalling Yards. Screeching and hooting, spasms of chugging, the tinkling of strings of empty goods wagons shunted, were the music which, *con brio ma non troppo*, accompanied every step she took, whether into her backyard or along Curzon Street. Railways meant grime. Any kind of enchantment with the iron horse was for primitives, she considered. *Nostalgie de la boue.*

We made our connection at Limerick in the twilight and were met at Rossbeg Station in the dark of the evening by Tony Drennan who, that year, had an Austin of England motor taxi. He filled the twenty-minute drive to our farm with his talk, seeming to know all about us and everyone else in Three Crosses.

During those months of Grandfather Thomas's convalescence from the January to the summer of 'fifty-six, when my father rejoined the family for his last summer holiday with us, a division of labour of a kind set in, unplanned and informal. My mother nursed Grandad less as the time went on and gave more time to the running of the home and to farm work; in this she was assisted by Aunt Finola. Aunt Peggy was studying hard for her Leaving Certificate at the convent in Rossbeg, where the nuns let her board free of charge sometimes, on account of the difficulties at home; when she was with us, however, she took on more of the nursing of Grandfather. At nights, when his wheezing and coughing woke me up on the landing, it was Peggy, barefoot, who slipped past my camp-bed to his room to help him take his medicine. So Peg proved herself a natural nurse and, though I never heard any discussion of the matter, a general assumption took shape that, when the time came, she would follow my mother into that profession.

Eleven

A walk in the woods. Who is Adameen? My disobedience again.

The men were out, Vance to help save hay at the Reynoldses, Packie on his bicycle heading off with Jellico on a long rein for Dwyer the blacksmith in Killinunty, Grandfather Thomas to Doctor Gilbank. Feena and Peggy came in from the yard in their overalls. My mother had stripped the oilcloth from the kitchen table and had brought out from the press a great, white enamel basin in which she would knead the flour for the soda bread. Peggy observed for a moment, then said:

'You're very tired, Geraldine. Go over there to the fire and sit down. We have enough bread made. Will I take out the children for you, Geraldine? Will I go off up to Kilcreggan with them after our dinner?'

'You're a brick, Peggy. You'll have to push Kate.'

'That's no hardship, Geraldine. Addie is well able to push the pram, too. Isn't that right, Bozer?'

The folding perambulator was an attractive but forbidden toy. I volunteered my assistance with what I judged just the right degree of enthusiasm. A too-obvious delight on my part could be taken as evidence of my unsuitability.

'You could sit down then after your dinner, Geraldine, and get *The Barrys of Ballyfergus* on the wireless.'

'I could.'

'Or you can come in to Rossbeg with me and Liam and Josie Deegan after dinner', Feena said. 'Wouldn't the spin and the fresh air do you good?'

'It would.'

'Now, Peggy', said my mother from the fireside, 'mind the roads in the woods. Any of them to the right comes out at the quarries. Don't go that way, pet, sure you won't?'

'Not at all', said Peggy.

'What'll we wear, Mum?' asked Lindie and Beebie.

'What'll we wear?' asked Kate.

The idea of a holiday in the sense of complete repose from work was foreign to Geraldine and indeed to the other adults in my Three Crosses world. For my expatriate mother, holiday meant time available for the fulfilment of her filial duty to her family. It was acknowledged, on the other hand, that we children were 'on holiday'. Little was therefore demanded of us and in varying degrees we were left to our own devices. My urban English father, of course, had understood the notion of holiday as recreation and had favoured afternoon walks or outings during the summer fortnights he spent at Three Crosses. Needless to say, Mother would happily accompany us then, sauntering behind the rest, in a re-evocation of their courtship.

Peg opened the maroon gates and we turned left up the road. Kilcreggan Woods, with its two hundred acres of Sitkas and telegraph-pole pines, was about a mile away to the north on the left-hand side of our road. On the right, the terrain fell away to the valley of the river Shanaun, the county boundary; then the land rose up yet again and became the scrub- and furze-clad hill of Mickeleen. That territory of Shanaun and Mickeleen two miles to the east was not of our parts: we knew no-one there and it was as foreign to us as Borneo. After Kilcreggan, our road led on to Coole and the quarries on the northern side of Kilcreggan Woods. The road climbed the western side of the gap in a series of gradients. As you got near the woods, our great mountain Slievegarriff disappeared behind Kilcreggan, but, if you stopped and faced back the way you had come, the vistas opened up to the south, out across the Great Vale to Rossbeg and the Lackendarraghs, to the silver thread of the Glas and to Comerford; on a specially clear day to the very Rock of Kings in the west.

Lindie and Beebie skipped and trotted ahead, immersed in their chatter and lore.

'Hold hands', I said. 'Be careful.'

We passed Deegans on the left and, a little later, Brittans on the right. Brittans' farmhouse was built on such a steeply-sloping plot up against the roadside hedge that we could see across the thatched roofline to Shanaun. With the slope of their yard, it was a wonder that a trap could stand upright at their porch; a loaded hay wagon could not safely be brought to their barn through their front gates. They had a bit of land up by their house but most of their fields were below us, at the bottom end of Three Crosses.

Peg pushed Kate, keeping to the left of the roadside, while I marched along the grass verge in the shade, hacking at the ferns and feather-moss and the liverworts with my switch. From the bushes, blackthorns, whitethorns, hollies, or from Irish oaks and ashes and chestnuts, sang the linnets and warblers; as we wound our way up the hill, the birds fell silent with our approach. A yard or two ahead, to my consternation, a great bumblebee kept us company for a time. Small rustlings and scuttlings at the roadside betokened other unseen presences: voles, shrews, black rats, or stoats, maybe.

A rain began to fall out of the blue sky but we would soon be able to shelter in the woods. It was not a wetting rain and the sun still shone. Peg told us all to look out for a rainbow.

'Well, Adameen', said Peg. 'Is it tired you are?' when she saw me seeming to lag.

'Adameen? Why are you calling me Adameen, now? I like it when you call me Bozer.'

'All right, so. Bozer.'

'Yes, but why did you call me Adameen? Daddy - Daddy knew someone called Adameen. I heard him talking to Grandad about Adameen last summer.'

'Arra -'

I took over pushing Kate's pram and Peggy could now walk upright against the gradient. The entrance to the forestry woods came up on our left. There was a Government notice in English and Irish and a commercially-made wooden five-barred gate with a stile on the right-hand side. We left the pushchair at the gate.

'Is there another boy we know called Adameen?'

'No', said Peggy. 'Why should there be?'

'No reason', I said, crunching on up the slate gravel track in the wake of my sisters. But I was thinking back a year to when I had eavesdropped on my father's conversation with Grandfather, the night of his arrival after his last voyage on the *Western Warrior*. Of course. *I was Adameen.* Then why was it that my father had thanked Grandfather Thomas for accepting me, Adameen? Had he not accepted my sisters Lindie and Beebie under his roof without the need for thanks?

There were no blackberries yet. But there were still strawberries if you knew where to look in the scrub and undergrowth at the foot of the trees. Lindie and Beebie would squeal delightedly when they found them and scamper back along the trail to us. Peggy accepted graciously when they shared these sweet treasures with her. When the girls skipped off, Peggy held out her hand to me and I picked the fruit from it, tiny scarlet and green eggs in a warm pink nest.

'Don't go out of sight again', I said to Lindie, 'and hold hands with Beebie.' Baby Kate now wanted to be carried. I brought her across to my aunt. In the pellucid forest light, Peg had sat down on a log by the side of the cart track for a cigarette.

I spotted a path off to the right. I knew it would lead to the quarries and was thus forbidden to us, but decided to take a look. If I could get a glimpse of the quarry, I would at least know what the adults at Three Crosses meant when they warned of the dangers. The path began innocently and safely enough, taking me out of the trees into high undergrowth and banks of brambles and horse-ferns, glistening with the recent rain. After thirty yards or so, I came to a stake-and-barbed-wire fence across my way. The track seemed no different on the other side, so I shinned over the fence. Another turn and then the topsoil thinned and the path dropped away over a series of natural steps in the naked slate rock. Five yards ahead, the land underfoot came to a dead end. Giddy, I sensed an abyss. All further wish to see the Kilcreggan quarries vanished with my acrophobia.

Turning back abruptly, I missed my footing on the slippery bare rock. I fell backwards on the path. The slope was, in fact, not steep enough for me to have slid down the last few yards and over the edge. But I was badly scared and crawled back up the muddy path to the barbed-wire fence, not daring to stand upright, for fear of losing my balance. My shins took a couple of long deep scratches from the barbs as I climbed back to safety. I regained the woods. Peggy, now standing with Kate in her arms, saw me emerge from the fateful path on the right. She sat Kate on the log and came across to me, studying me, and, I think, perhaps, taking in everything: my pallor, my guilt, my dirty knees and bleeding shins. I searched into her face for a sign that my transgression would be forgiven.

'Oh, Bozer, boy, what did you do that you were told not to - and you such a good boy trying to give great example to your sisters.' She read me easily.

'I didn't mean it. I forgot about the paths.'

'You gave me a fierce fright, boy, so you did.'

'Can I push the pram again for you on the way home?'

'No.'

'Please, Peggy.'

'No.'

'Will you tell Mum?' I said aloud, with two thoughts in my mind: for my aunt to delate me would make reconciliation with my mother even more difficult. It would be proof that I was not fit for the responsibilities I had inherited from my father. But it would also show what I couldn't bear, that through my habit of disobedience I had diminished in Peggy's affections.

'Will I tell your mother?' Peggy echoed me but left the question hanging.

Pushing Katie in her pram on the downhill walk back to Three Crosses was no hardship. Peggy relented somewhat and, though she would not let me take over, she allowed me to ride the vehicle. So I stood upright on the back axle facing forward, behind the somnolent Kate, and hanging on inside the handlebar.

At the last bend in our road, with the maroon gates below on the right, I hopped off. Aunt Peggy and I looked at each other. My additional weight had bent the back axle. The rear wheels, in consequence, evinced a definite splay.

My mortification returned, but my aunt said: 'Packie can put that right. Your Mammy won't be any the wiser.'

'Yes, but will you tell her I went where I shouldn't have?'

Had I slithered over the edge there at the quarry and my mother been confronted with my loss, I imagined myself at last feeling the sweetness of her love, somehow, somewhere between limbo and reunion with my father. In the moment between two heartbeats, the path out of the forest might have opened and everything been completed, there and then. For all I knew, my aunt read my thoughts, for she said:'You are real precious - to your mother, now. Do you understand?' I nodded, to signify that I took her words at face value. But there was another message there: to Peggy, at least, I would have been a loss: oblivion would not, after all, have been my fate.

Lindie and Beebie ran to the gates. Kate slept on in the pram. Peggy and I were alone on our road. She cupped my face in her hands. She looked pale, too. I caught the scent of her soap. Years on, I recognised it as lily of the valley.

Twelve

The fly-hunt, Aunt Finola, Jimmy the hopeless.

For three seasons of the year, where you have livestock, especially cows and horses, you have flies, though we seemed to suffer less from their molestations than did some of our neighbours. The Reynoldses, the Deegans, the Brittans all used the sticky fly-papers in their kitchens. We did not, because our women objected to them and Aunt Feena told me once that the sight of the dead flies on the strips only drew more into the house.

So houseflies were reluctantly tolerated. The occasional sight of a bluebottle indoors provoked a panic of flapping and strapping with whatever cloth came to hand. I participated with zest on these drives. It was relatively easy thus to encourage these slow aerial movers to head back out of the half-light of the kitchen towards the dazzling daylight over the half-door. Otherwise they paid the ultimate price for their intrusion. The chimney hob was naturally an insect-free zone: therefore, in summer especially, it was the place of choice to sit, unless you wanted to read.

Horseflies and hornets, midges, bees and wasps, I knew about and had been bitten or stung by all of them apart from the hornet. Of bumblebees I was particularly afraid. Some years previously, I must have been five or six, I had been following Great-Uncle Vance along a potato drill in one of our fields, hand-weeding to the left as he did to the right. Vance, on his knees, with his trousers protected from the yellow dirt by hessian sacks tied on with twine, was dispiritingly adroit and I had fallen a good way behind. A bumblebee of massive proportions got between us, droning from haulm to haulm at head height. I dared not call out. Vance went further and further ahead. Even when I moved sideways to another drill, that black-and-orange aviator, furred and menacing, moved too. A moment; a minute; ten? I cannot say how long the terror lasted.

There was another insect, a bloodsucker called a skerthaun, which dwelt in dry grass. This creature aroused particular disgust in my mother and aunts, though no fear in me. It would bury its head painlessly in your skin. Attempts to dislodge it by squeezing it like a zit would, apparently, result in its decapitation and an infection. The correct procedure, to which I was subjected on several occasions without ill-effect of any kind, was to heat the skerthaun's backside with the red end of a cigarette, whereupon it discontinued its meal and released its grip.

I sat out on the drystone drainer under the water-butt on the Saturday afternoon with Lindie and Beebie. The smell of the soakaway under the slate at our feet seemed to draw the flies and Beebie swiped at them with her schoolmistress's cane. I told my sisters Grandfather's story of the fatal injury to Peter Cody's father, Denny, and its consequences, and how Andersons' bull would have done no-one any harm had he not been exasperated by the flies.

'How long was the horn?'

'Was it sharp?'

'Did his eye bleed?'

'The brown bit or the white bit?'

'The white, I think.'

'Did the white bit bleed?'

'It must have.'

'Did the horn break off in his eye?'

'Could he still see?'

My sisters being in agreement with me that reprisals were in order and that houseflies everywhere should be challenged and combated, we devised a game for hunting the arthropods.

It was necessary to procure suitable swats: I had discovered that, when stripped from an ash sapling, the bark produced a most satisfactory leather with the inner skin darkening from white to a convincing mahogany hue. The leather could, when part-dry, be prevented from hardening and cracking completely by the application of shoe-polish. So, with my beloved penknife,

I cut three swats or straps, one for each of us in suitable sizes. Lindie and Beebie gave advice.

We galloped down from the orchard behind the house and set to the hunt in the yard. We soon discovered that there were two places that the flies liked to pitch. They seemed to eschew natural surfaces, preferring the freshly-painted doors of the dairy, the barn and the maroon gates. They also had a predilection for the black coachwork of our trap and the sun-warmed metal panels of Grandfather Thomas' Ford Anglia van and Jimmy Grehan's Vauxhall, all three of which stood in the yard that afternoon. Jimmy had a good job, which meant that he didn't work Saturdays or Sundays and he was here, courting Aunt Finola.

The design of our flyswats meant that it was almost impossible to hit our targets on the wing; they had to be attacked when they had settled on a surface. By the late afternoon, we had a tally of kills between us of over three hundred insects; Beebie led the lists with a hundred and forty-three, including eight wasps. In the yard, the doors, the cars and the trap, and, further afield, the corrugated roofs of the calf pens, Great-Uncle Vance's derelict Morris in the orchard grove, all evidenced the smashed bodies of *musca domestica*, their remains appliqued to paintwork in interesting little knots of yellow and red and black, in the manner, as it were, of studies for a Jackson Pollock painting. With one final satisfying whang on the bonnet of Grehan's Vauxhall, Beebie announced that she had won the game and was quitting. Her leather swat was on the point of disintegration, but it had done its job well.

Jimmy came out of the kitchen with Aunt Finola.

'Good God, what happened the car?' wondered Feena. 'They have it destroyed! Jimmy!'

Jimmy Grehan's eye caught mine and he said 'By Gorr, lads! Ye gave Beelzebub and his angels a power of a fright today!'

'What?' said Feena, then, 'Show me them straps!' She collected our swats, wrenching one ostentatiously from each of us in turn. 'Yeugh. Look at the dirt on them. Is it the diphtheria you want your sisters to catch?' she said to me, well aware I was the originator of the game.

I supposed at the time that this must be a reasonable question, since it was posed by an adult and sister of the mother who loved me. Through my selfish action, in spite of myself, I must, indeed, have wanted my two sisters to suffer. It was, accordingly, with a deep ineffable relief that, many years later at the grammar school, I contemplated those two attractive propositions of Socrates, that sin is ignorance and that no man errs voluntarily.

Jimmy Grehan endeared himself further to me by affecting to an interest in the abattoir for arthropods to which we had reduced his Vauxhall.

'Ye did great work catching horseflies, lads, that's for sure anyway.'

His Vauxhall was brand-new, the property of the agricultural machinery company for which he worked. He cleaned the motorcar of a Sunday each week, a practice foreign to everyone else in our parts. English owners, of course, looked after their cars, which gave me a motive for liking Jimmy.

I warmed to him, too, for another reason: he was, I believed, devoted to Feena, lured, beguiled and smitten by that part of her being that dwelled in a secret world of muse and minstrel. But his suit to my aunt was doomed; I knew that, yet he did not; my knowledge against his ignorance produced in me a sympathy which, even though it was quite without smugness, had I been Jimmy, I should have resented utterly.

Tossing the makeshift swats onto the kindling stack, Feena ostentatiously rinsed her hands off under the hissing hard-water tap by the road gates. She dried them with the handkerchief Jimmy proffered. Then he put his arm around her waist and the two headed out onto the road for a stroll up towards Coole and a postprandial Sweet Afton, out of the sight of my grandfather or Vance.

Finola looked back at me once, rolling her eyes to heaven. All too often, it appeared to fall more to her than to my mother to have to point out my shortcomings to me. I could forgive her because of the way she spoke to me through her music. And was she not the sister and confidante of Aunt Peggy, my treasure and delight? It was Peggy, Peggy, who redeemed them all.

Thirteen

Rossbeg, East of Eden; things, playthings, other things; reports of the gentleman of the road again and an enigmatic remark of his.

Vance came out of the dairy, wheeling the Sunbeam. He was heading for Rossbeg, an hour's journey for an old-timer conserving energy.

Shep was going, too. Our collie-dog had no owner, but his core relationship was with Vance, who often fed him the vegetarian diet upon which he had been brought up; even so, reader, that Shep was a carnivore *manqué* is, as you know, proven by the fact he had once attempted to consume one of Vance's fingers, though after it had become detached from his hand. What I had seen Shep eat, in some instances, apart from his main collation of boiled potato peelings and half-fermented milk, is unprintable. I was also aware of a predilection on Shep's part for seasoning, which Vance encouraged. 'He would come at me to put the few pinches of pepper on his dinner. He'd be looking crooked at the pan there until he saw the pepper-pot. Then he'd wait for the dust to settle...'

'...Bite the dust, boy

On your crust, boy

If you must, boy',

you would hear Vance at the far gable-end of the house at feeding time. I was never to discover whether Shep enjoyed poetry; but then, he was thought to be deaf.

I watched Vance cycle off down the road towards the avenue. Considering how slowly he went, it was a masterly and stylish achievement on his part to stay balanced on the Sunbeam at all; it would be a hundred yards before he would even contemplate cranking the pedals. Shep followed.

There is a vulgarity about towns that bustle; Rossbeg, I am glad to say, did not bustle, whatever its other shortcomings. Neither did the opposite cliché, sleepy, describe it. It had a castle and a medieval bridge, a wool-processing plant and a market, a monastery and two convents, a railway station. Two thousand citizens and their concerns made it another world: a nexus of all trades, their gear and tackle and trim; an idyll fertile with human opportunity, when set against the simple paucities of our road and my Eden at Three Crosses. Even in Eden, I craved for art and artefact, and was thus always attracted by the chance of a trip to the town which I associated with such productions of the human spirit. An opportunity would present itself within the next couple of weeks.

In the meantime, a few feet of chicken-wire, a penknife, a tin can or a shoe-box represented untold possibilities to modify and model; in short, to play. The mass and feel of any carpenter's tool in my small hand gave a sensual delight. I had discovered in the darkest and driest corner of the clay-floored dairy, behind Packie's gleaming black Raleigh, a beautiful, unused pein hammer, a hammer in miniature, half-buried under a few bits of chain and half-a-dozen pipe tobacco tins of a pre-war pattern. The pein hammer had been another of Great-Uncle Joseph's tools and appeared to have been bought new. It seemed made for me, a child, and for a few days I carried it concealed inside my britches.

The hammer disappeared from amongst the accoutrements I kept under my camp-bed one morning after breakfast. I later spotted it, with the edging stones and Grandaddy's good blackthorn cow-stick, above the kitchen ceiling, in the secret recesses between the rafters: to have quietly placed it in a place of safety, without public comment or remonstration, was the kind of thing Peggy would do when she made our beds.

But for a few days last summer, I had the use of that hammer. I hammered in the morning. I hammered in the evening, all over that world. I hammered out three bright quartz crystals, the size of barley-grains, from the exposed slates of the henhouse wall. These I tapped into the softwood planks of the dairy door to mark our heights, mine, Lindie's and Beebie's, setting them like gems. This year, Packie had given the doors a new spring coat of green paint but hadn't dug out the jewels. Under the paint, they continued to signal last year's human growth.

I hammered, savouring all the sounds which that tool made: the bright clink of impact on cast-iron, as I played the railwayman testing carriage wheels for cracks; or, tapping bluntly at the slates and granite of the dyke - the geologist. Or an apothecary with a pestle, as I ground up slate powders or fragments of brick to make pigments. Or, as I despatched woodlice and the brilliant scarab-emerald dung flies that pitched on warm stones, glittering, the hammer of God.

Uncle Packie was back from that other world of Rossbeg on his holidays for a few days to help with saving our barley. Like me, Packie had an enthusiasm for the well-crafted object. He knew good steel from bad in a sprong or a shovel and what counted when it came to perfect balance in an implement. He could sharpen a scythe to perfection with loving and mysterious strokes and taps of the edging-stone, all the time turning and swinging and sweeping the tool with the grace of a fencer or a golfer, savouring its feel and its virtue.

He, like Vance, kept his bicycle in the dairy. Packie's was a Raleigh upright with a huge, shiny, Brooks leather saddle, the old rod-brake system, Sturmey-Archer hub gears and an oil-bath chaincase. Hand-painted coach lines set off its glossy black frame. The Raleigh was tended as well as any pony. Once, he wheeled it out and set it up on its back stand in front of the green half-door, to contemplate it like the work of art it surely was. It gleamed and it glowed. On the road, it ran like the proverbial sewing-machine, like a song, like a Singer. We sat together on the cement step and took in its being.

'You'll have a bicycle like her from Nottingham one day, Addie, boy.'

'Can I go for a ride?'

'I couldn't leave you out on the road, fearing a car could hit you, like.'

'Can I have a spin with you?' The bicycle had a sturdy carrier.

'Maybe you could. Maybe you couldn't. But isn't she a dinger?'

I found Packie ambivalent in his affections for me. At times, he treated me rather as Finola did, as wilfully wayward and in need of constant adult correction. At others, I was to him the younger brother he had never had and perhaps he saw in me something of Christie, the lost elder brother of the Driscolls. He wanted to privilege me with secrets and relive parts of his boyhood, at that moment of truth in our twenties, which comes on us when we take stock that our dreamtime is consigned to the shimmering realms of memory and that we will not be young again.

Packie saw he had disappointed me. He wheeled the Raleigh back to the dairy, then beckoned to me to follow him in to the house. We went up to the landing above the kitchen where I slept. Unknown to me, Packie had a hiding-place for his childhood treasures very near my camp-bed, where the round log-ends of the rafters were exposed between the joists under the landing. Standing halfway up the stairs, he reached into the space at shoulder height, something I could not do, and extracted an old cardboard box held in shape by rusted staples. We took it into Feena's bedroom where there was daylight and he opened it up on the floor.

The first thing he drew out of the box was the Lucas carbide bicycle lamp. He passed it to me. The *King of the Road* was a seductively beautiful artefact. In shiny nickel plate, with its sprung miniature suspension bracket, and huge jewel of a lens that refracted gorgeously at the edges, I had coveted it the first moment I had seen it. I turned it this way and that in my hands. I longed to ride out with it one gloaming, and saw it in my mind's eye carving out the midnight pitch dark of our road, dazzling rabbits and catching owls as they flitted between fields. Packie did not keep it on his Raleigh, out in the dairy; I fancy he used a battery headlight for that bicycle, for fear the carbide lamp might be stolen by a caffler in Rossbeg, but he always averred that the Lucas belonged to the Raleigh.

'Twould give a grand light', he said, then replaced the lamp in its box in the place of concealment, dusting off the sleeve of his jacket. He paused and thought for a moment. 'I've something else for you to see. Only, you mustn't be telling anyone at all you saw it.'

'Cross my heart.'

'Anyone at all, now, Addie?'

'No.'

He reached back into the box and drew out a small parcel of waxed brown paper. He removed the twine and unwrapped it precisely so that the folds opened out like a calyx of huge petals. When he had finished, a pistol lay there at the centre of the flower.

'Whose is it?'

'It belongs, belonged to Christie. Before him, it belonged to my Uncle Joseph and before that to another fellow, Hourihane. Before Hourihane owning it, I'd say it belonged to an Englishman like yourself.'

'Why?'

'Because it is a Webley, an English gun.' It would, I think now, have been a Mark IV.

'Why did the Englishman give it to Hourihane?'

'The poor man didn't give it to him at all. 'Twas robbed from him.'

'Why?'

'Because he was a Black and Tan. Forty years ago in the Troubles the poor devil was in a patrol that got cornered in the handball alley at Carty's Bridge.'

I knew that handball alley. It was a sombre place now, ivy-covered within and without, and a concrete floor you couldn't walk on for cow dung.

'Did Hourihane shoot the man?'

'I'd say he didn't, anyway.'

'Why?'

'Sure in our parts we were all Fine Gael. If it wasn't for the English, who'd buy our cattle? But he could have had to hide the gun up here with Joseph. You wouldn't know. 'Tis all a matter now.'

'What happened to Uncle Joseph? What did he die of?'

'I don't rightly know. Old age, sure. I wasn't there when he died.'

'Where did he die?'

'He died in Cheeseburg, Michigan, in the U.S.A. With Vance and your grandfather, there wasn't the work for him here, like. He trained as a cheese-maker but there was no cheese made in our parts before the creamery came in. There don't be many of us would eat it today, sure. He did well for himself in the United States. Jellico was bought and the Kanturk was built and your grandmother's headstone paid for with the dollars he sent home to your grandfather.'

'Why didn't he come home when he had enough money?'

'Uncle Joseph was always coming home, like, but the sands ran out for him, so they did. When he would write, it was always 'Have you the room ready for me? I won't be long coming now.' In the heel of the hunt, there was a room ready for him, alright, in another place and that's where he got his call.'

'And Christie?'

Pascal clucked his tongue.

'Ah sure, poor Christie, God help him.' He did not look at me nor say more.

The brutal, diamond-hard mass of the gun was a lure to my eyes. I took in every screw, every precise, unforgiving edge, every bluish, satanic curve. Packie drew back the hammer two clicks and that wicked beak was poised to strike. He released the hammer gently with his thumb. It took a certain effort for me to cock the piece and a good deal of pressure from my child's finger to release the trigger. When I did, the predatory beak snapped home with malevolence. I relished the fantasies I played out with my toy rifle, but this Webley was a weapon, perhaps once the instrument of a killing, which I was glad to hand back, even though there were no shells in it. Go, go, go, said the bird: humankind cannot bear very much reality.

Packie went. He put away his treasures in the old cardboard box between the rafters of the landing under my camp-bed. I thus carried on sleeping with a gun at my head.

Vance pushed his Sunbeam up the yard and propped it against the pump. He had returned from the Auction and had brought back the catalogue. He came into the kitchen behind Feena, who had the milk gallon. She was talking to Vance over her shoulder: 'I was gassing with the tinker fellow there a good while in the Toberenagh Tea Room', she said.

'That's no surprise', said Vance, 'Because any time he do be passing by Sheehys, old man Sheehy would put him in the Tea Room for his dinner with his beard and his yellow nails and all.'

'Yeugh', said Aunt Feena.

'And by God there's no yeugh about it. That tinker fellow was quality, one time, girl.'

'Why?'

'Old man Sheehy always got the tip from him, like.'

'For the Races?'

'Arra no. For the Mart. For the business, girl. He used be telling the old man where the bloodstock prices would be going.'

'How would he know?' Peg raised an eyebrow.

'Maybe he have the gift', said Feena.

'The gift of the gab, is it?' asked Packie.

'The gift, boy, the gift - and that's all about it. That fellow do be seeing more than the most of us knows.'

'He do, I'm sure', Packie snorted.

'Faith and he knew who we were, right enough', said Vance. ''Twas Peg I think gave him the bite of dinner a Sunday. Is that right, Peggy?'

'It is. And Addie gave a while there talking to him. He was great company for him.'

'By God and he knew all about Adameen', said Feena.

Adameen! I knew I was an Adameen to some because Peggy had confirmed it the day I had disobeyed and nearly gone over the edge at Kilcreggan quarry. Vance's remark carried the troubling implication that there was something else to be known about me. On the other hand, perhaps he had in mind another, more hapless, bearer of the name Adameen. I preferred to believe that.

Ominously, this was not a public conversation: Vance had lowered his voice the way you did if you were an adult with a bit of gossip not for the children's ears.

'What?' said Peggy, moving to stand between me and Vance with her back to me.

'He told me', Vance went on, 'there's not a drop of Irish blood in that little gentleman.'

(Which little gentleman, I wondered. Did he mean Adameen? Which Adameen?)

'Well, honest to God and Janey Mac!' said Peggy.

'How in the name of God would he know that and he hadn't the gift, poor fellow?' asked Feena in triumph.

'Will ye stop!' said Packie to my aunts, after shooting a worried glance at me. 'What's poor about that malfoosterer, in the name of God? What's on him, that he could not go back to his own people in London and mind his own business there, along of the rest of the quality?'

Fourteen

An afternoon at the river with Busty; my late father's presence with me that day; yet who was he? Why had he been taken from me?

Grandfather Thomas reported that he had met Hughie Heaphy of Coole at the creamery that morning and that he had given Hughie a message to tell Busty to come down to Three Crosses to play after his dinner. Grandad did not use the expression 'to play', but that was the sense of it. In our parts and parlance, the logic of the verb 'to play' was that it was always transitive, taking as an object some sport or accomplishment such as hurling, or patience, the melodion, the fiddle, or the fool. Play in a non-specific or abstract sense was a concept not often deployed.

After dinner, I lay out in the sun on the concrete footing under the water pump. I had with me the June sheet from the Caltex calendar which hung in the copper- kettle window. Upon the back of this sheet I had done a preliminary sketch for the tin-can steam-engine and was intent upon refining the blueprint. Busty arrived, sat down next to me, scrutinised my sketch over my shoulder and handed over the key component, a cocoa-tin, which his mother had released that morning.

I knew I could make a suitable burner or firebox for the engine and that the cocoa-tin would be the boiler. The blueprint envisaged adapting the cocoa-tin lid into a piston-cum-sleeve-valve. The feasibility of the design had, naturally, depended on the kind of tin-can Busty would bring. As a fall-back position we could, I felt sure, produce a different engine which would turn a turbine.

According to the article in *Sheepman of Ireland*, James Watt had been inspired by the power of steam when watching a pot boil over the fire, its cast-iron lid vibrating loudly as the pressure rose and the steam forced its way out. I had seen the very same thing at our hob. Busty studied the drawing on the Caltex calendar, then watched me turn the cocoa-tin this way and that in my hands. Could the cocoa-tin lid, with its long, close-fitting exterior lip, be adapted to slide up and down under steam pressure? I decided that the modifications to the lid which would be required would be too complex for the tools and techniques at my disposal. It was too tight a fit, its lip too short to provide a long enough stroke.

I told Busty.

'Right, so', said Busty. Fascinated by the prospect of fire, my Prometheus had brought down from Coole a box of matches and I could see his imagination turning to other uses for them. The cocoa-can was too valuable a resource or toy to jettison, so I explained to Busty my idea for a turbine.

'A yoke like that wouldn't pull skin off of milk, don't mind your cart.'

He was right; all the same, I felt sure it was possible to demonstrate a principle by means of a stationary engine: in my mind's eye, I saw steam jetting out from a pinhole in the boiler and onto some kind of miniature fan, in tinplate or foil, which, I thought, would whirr away edifyingly while the water boiled. I painted a word-picture for Busty.

'Oh yes', he said, politely enough, 'but what would be the use of that?'

'So that we could see how it works.'

'Oh yes.' Busty understood the principle fine. He didn't need it demonstrated.

My imagination leapt ahead: we could dispense with a turbine wheel. The jet of steam from the boiler could vent to the open air. If the boiler were mounted on a little boat, the jet should be enough to power it. We could take the model steamer down for trials to a pool in the river Shanaun, the Dogs' Hole.

Busty had told me he had been lent the cocoa-tin on an agreement to return it intact to his mother for further domestic use. There would, thus, have to be a good reason, from his point of view, to vary the contract. An afternoon by the Shanaun might provide such justification, because the Heaphys were great fish-eaters and amongst Busty's gifts was the knack of tickling for trout.

Busty used a table knife (ours, as I have said, were viciously sharp) to whittle out a boat's keel from a foot length of four-by-two which we found in the cart shed, where it had been a wheel-chock. We used the halves of an empty shoe-polish tin as a couple of burners; the fuel was pigs' dripping with dried moss for a wick. I punctured the cocoa tin with a thin shoe-nail for the steam vent and we rigged the boiler over the burners with wire. A bit of tinplate for a rudder completed the construction.

The Dogs' Hole was black and mysterious, thirty or forty feet in diameter, at a bend in the Shanaun. Not many of the children in our parts swam for recreation and, of those that did, most preferred other reaches of the river. The Hole was a couple of miles from us to the east and approached from the Slievegarriff side across a trackless cornfield. Rumoured to be thirty feet deep, its edges were sheer on our side; it was deeply shaded on the opposite bank by alders and willows.

Some were said to have drowned farm-dogs in it, luckless creatures that had bitten or got the mange. There were those in our parts who called it the Lacks' (or girlfriends') Pool, which raised an interesting, if macabre, question or two. I think the farmers on the other bank, in the next county, had another name for it. My mother said there might be gold at the bottom of it from the rites of the Fir Bolg or the Tuatha de Danann, in the times before Saint Patrick. Upstream and downstream from this Celtic Titicaca, where usually the Shanaun ran limpid and shallow, Busty could ease himself into the water and feel there for trout in the lee of the boulders. Sometimes, when the rain had fallen further up the gap, you could find the river in spate, the colour of weak tea and the Dogs' Hole disturbed by sinister little whirlpools and strange eddies.

With our boat in my lap, I sat in the rich grass and cow parsley at the bank's edge. Like any nineteenth-century Tyneside shipwright in a stove-pipe hat, I had to work out how the vessel might be launched and steam raised. I also had to consider how to conclude matters after the steam trials. Although, on our farm, every machined piece of wood was (in adult reasoning) there for a purpose, a wheel-chock might nevertheless disappear for good from the cart shed and none be any the wiser or worse off. But one that reappeared in the guise of a toy boat, in some place of deliberate concealment, would require investigation by adults. I turned this over as I contemplated the dark pool. My eyes were drawn to the other bank facing us, because, out from under those dark alders, there protruded an enticing little jetty.

'Mind yourself. A fellow drownded where you are, one time.' I let my fear show.

'Arra, a good while ago, like.' Busty had had an even healthier respect for the Shanaun from the time when, last year, wading near here, he had cut open to the bone the heel of his foot on a broken stout-bottle.

Even by lying out full-length on the bank on our side, and reaching down with his longer arm than mine, Busty could not touch the surface of the water, still less place a model boat upon it. He pronounced that it would be necessary, after all, to approach the Dogs' Hole from the jetty on the other bank.

So we took a detour back the way we had come, onto the road, across the bridge and into the next county. We did not know through whose fields we were now approaching the river: we knew no one in these parts. We were in the demesne of people who were not our own. Unaccountably, for a boy who already had another life, if not an alter ego, in England, I had then the strong sense of a strange realm entered, my first archetypal exploration of a land not my own. But the colour of the earth on the naked cow-path underfoot seemed the same, the same cow parsley thrust up at us in the long grass, the hurdle-gates to the fields were as rickety as ours; when a Beetle passed us on the road, a driver saluted as one of ours would have, though the VW he drove had a different county plate. A green George V postbox in the hedgerow looked very like the one on the wall of Detta Hassett's bar in Tourmahinch, where I had posted Mother's letters to Daddy last year. It was a foreign country right enough, yet they did things the same there.

Although the detour took the best part of an hour, the last part across the fields from the other bank was easy and we found our way back to the Dogs' Hole by dead reckoning. We prospected the pool from the jetty.

Busty scooped up a boilerful of water in the cocoa tin. He remounted the boiler. Lowering the boat, he wedged her in a temporary haven behind a willow root and lit the burners.

Busty had not only brought matches but a packet of five Sweet Afton.

'How long have you been smoking?'

'Arra, I don't know.'

'PK smokes.'

'Don't I know it. He do be always at me for the cigs'.'

'Wouldn't he offer you one back'?'

'That lad wouldn't give his shit to the crows.'

Busty smoked the cigarette with hoarse little breaths. There was no delicacy, no play with smoke rings or the like. He flicked the butt in a wide arc out into the Dogs' Hole, where it fizzed out and drifted away slowly.

Below us, the steam had begun to jet out in fits and sputters from the ship's boiler. Busty dislodged her from the mooring, set the rudder and launched her into the pool. 'I'm going looking for a few trout', he whispered, indicating a spot thirty yards down-river where there was a little beach and there were many boulders in the water for the fish to hide behind. I watched his back as he moved off silently towards the spot. Again, I was aware of the quiet walk of his father about him, the un-self-conscious gait of the man who must spare his energy. He didn't want me near him as he fished, which suited me; thirty yards away he was company enough for me and I for him. I had affirmed myself with Busty; I had proved my idea with the steamboat; now nothing intruded or disturbed our quiet companionship; we lost ourselves and were thus fleetingly, but no less purely, happy.

When he finally took up his position, I could see Busty from time to time out of the corner of my eye in the patches of sunlight downstream, sitting in the water up to his waist. He had been wearing a boy's Sunday suit, one time belonging to his elder brother Hughie, the danger man; the jacket of it hung, pristine, above him over the water from a sprig of willow, the trousers, sodden, clung to his backside when he got up to stalk the trout.

The Dogs' Hole lost the sense of menace, and put on its own strange beauty, its calm, oily surface rippled only by the wake of my little steamer. All seemed sympathetic to me that day. I began to long for the moment later that evening when I would enter the kitchen by the green half-door, counting that my mother would be pleased to see me.

My father would have appreciated my workmanship and ingenuity, though his technical skills would have made the vessel more beautiful and efficient. Our boat must have a name. I thought of the merchantman he had sailed in the convoys, the SS *Irrawaddy*, or the *Western Warrior* which had borne him on his last journey here. In the photo-album in Curzon Street we had a postcard depicting the *Irrawaddy* at her launch on Clydebank; I had watched the *Western Warrior* dock at Comerford. I determined on the former name. In a surge of pride and daring, I resolved to show Mother my boat and tell her in whose honour I had christened it.

There was a stillness in the air and the scent of ripening barley across the flat calm on the surface of the Dog's Hole. So the second *Irrawaddy* made her second voyage without so much as a push from me. I reset her rudder then held her, cagily, because of the scalding jet of steam, until she was ready. She inched away from the jetty. At first she made slow headway but, with the burners now into their stride and the yellow flames licking up a couple of inches either side of the boiler and above it, a fair jet of steam issued from the blackened, cocoa-tin boiler. It sent the vessel in a wide curving periplus of the pool. Could my father but have seen her, the Small Ship *Irrawaddy* describing those wide ellipses, he would have been taken back; in my imaginings there that afternoon, Daddy spoke to me again of his days on the convoys and then, the most frightening experience of his war, his long voyage from Port Said to Bombay, when, night after long night, he had lain awake, with six hundred others in a hammock ten feet below the waterline, in submarine-threatened waters. Daddy, why were you spared, that year of 'forty-four? But not this year of 'fifty-seven? Daddy, come back. I peered far down, down into the blackness of The Dogs' Hole, as into, beyond, my own well of unhappiness; I...but the ice-cold, half-formed volition left me, the unspeakable sadness ebbed. Its backwash left me in my lost father's company again.

Talking to myself, I rehearsed his chat to me about the *Irrawaddy*, mimicking with savour his flat south London tones:

'A bit more rudder there, son.'

'Ok, Daddy. Ouch!'

'Mind - be careful, the boiler is hotter than a kettle...Why are you biting your nails so badly, sun-shine?' I pictured him gently taking my hand in his and spreading out my fingers. I saw the wedding ring on his finger. My mother wore it now, but he had promised it to me.

So began for me an hour's idyll. There I sat, strangely elated, in the company of my departed father in that land of lost content; within and without, outwith and inside me that dreamtime territory, whose last reaches I knew I was nearing. The breeze pushed sweetly through the leaf-canopy above and in front of me; the sun in the western half warmed my chest deliciously.

Into that long afternoon intruded only the dialogue of sounds from deep out of the landscape; Punch yapped far off at Dempseys; a mile to the west, the woollen-works lorry from Rossbeg double-declutched on our road before the hill to Kilcreggan. We had evicted a heron for the afternoon. It flapped low across the Hole, several times, its eye on me, out of a head pterodactyllic and primitive. Inches above the water, the swifts skimmed for midges. Out of the still air came the cries of cowmen and the hollering of the prize bull at Tize Court Farm. From afar, our purple mountain watched over all that gentle land, in its green and gold stages.

I doubted then that I would ever again gaze on vistas so lucent and beautiful; much though I might, afterwards, travel in the realms of gold; and thus, reader, it has been. I have visited four of the five continents and sat before many a fine view and noble prospect, but never again with the special, undimmed eyes and all-pervading imagination of a child.

The possibility came to me, the rumour, of wellbeing, even of joy - children's hearts are made for joy - and I wonder if I exaggerate in telling you that few moments of achievement in my later life have ever compared with the triumphal bliss that accompanied the launch of the *SS Irrawaddy* that summer afternoon on the Shanaun.

Busty crept up behind me and gave me a start. He had a string bag in his hand and held it up to my face; four trout gleamed in the net of it, with the dank smell of the river on them, black-eyed, shiny as laurel leaves, three-quarters russet, speckled in red.

'Will we go now?' he said. 'We needn't be going back to the bridge at all. Those Bishops' Stones are in it there below where I caught these. I got a look at them and I...'

'The stepping stones? Now you tell me! Why didn't we cross that way when we came here?'

'Well', said Busty, unsure of himself, 'because I heard of the stones alright, but, like, I never rightly knowed where they were. At school, Mr Barrett told us they were in it before the bridge was builded, that's for sure. They were put there for the pilgrims who used to come this way in their bare feet to the Bishops' tombs there in Grehans' field.' That Mr Barrett shared a sense of the history of these parts gave the schoolmaster something in common with me and, for a moment, I wanted to be on his side of the barricade. But he disliked my innocent father and the English. That was enough. Besides, he was wrong; the stones were prehistoric.

The crossing-stones traversed the Shanaun where she flowed wide and shallow, in a secluded, oxbow loop, downstream from where Busty had been fishing. I put down the Small Ship *Irrawaddy* for a moment and picked out a rust-coloured slate pebble at the water's edge. I flicked it across to the opposite bank. It flew true, not turning as it hopped on the water. It aquaplaned nicely for the last yard. Busty had never skimmed flat stones across water before and was fascinated.

There were nine of the Bishops' Stones, dry brown sandstones, height-matched. As we skipped across the Shanaun, I looked up and ahead to the west and to a perfect view of Slievegarriff above the broom and gorse on our side. How that mountain drew me and spoke to me: as she had once, to the travellers without number who had passed this way, living and partly living; I knew my pilgrim's crossing of these stones was a moment I would return to for its full meaning, a thing elemental and significant if only I could one day see it, find it, be it.

★

I had come to the end of my selective reading of the thirty or forty issues of *Sheepman of Ireland* and so had smuggled the heavy pack of magazines back up over the dyke to Deegans' in a spud sack. Apart from my encounters with the *Southern Express* at the kettle-window on some days after Vance and Grandfather had finished with it and with Robinson at night, I now had no other reading material with which to escape to the Morris Eight. I snooped incessantly in the bedrooms upstairs and the parlour and the blackened shelving behind the lintel of the hob for something in print that might thus far have eluded me. The parlour was out of bounds to us children and often locked. But not always. After dinner on Friday it was as cold as a Liverpool March afternoon. Accordingly, I was ordered by Aunt Feena out of the kitchen fug, with the smell of baking bread coming through from the Valor oven, and into the yard. As I passed the parlour door, I tried the brass handle. It yielded, so I slipped inside. The room was warmer than the kitchen, with the heat in the walls from the chimney breast. The parlour had the smell of the whole century about it, something between old railway compartment, empty sherry cask, convent wax polish, warm Bakelite and wireless valve, smoker's den.

The mantelshelf towards which I was drawn was exactly at eye-level to me. I noticed for the first time that Grandfather did, after all, possess a tobacco jar. It had been turned into a miniature barrel from, I believe, a piece of the mainmast of a tea-clipper and was guarded by two Staffordshire china dogs. Grandfather's addiction was to a Dublin black shag tobacco, Tiernan's Number 4 Full Strength, which he mostly bought, or sent me to Tourmahinch to buy, ready rubbed. Occasionally, he would use another of Tiernan's products, Number 17, which was a snuff. Sometimes he would produce a small block of the Number 4, bought in Rossbeg and hard as horn. He would cut slivers off it as if he were Dwyer the smith trimming one of Jellico's black hooves.

My eyes rested on a photograph, familiar to me from a copy we had in Curzon Street. The photo, a bamboo-framed window to the 'twenties, showed the Driscolls some time soon after Grandfather Thomas' wedding. He looked back into the parlour at me from a black-and-white farmyard somewhere, alongside his wife Maeve and the brother Joseph that had emigrated to Cheeseburg, Michigan. The young Vance I hardly recognised. I could identify the fifth member of the group, Nina, my grandfather's only sister; I was to meet her again, reader, at the end of that summer. The grandfather I knew now, in the flesh, had retained the same unusual softness of feature as in this wedding photograph. By contrast, his brother Vance's lineaments had grown sharp and angular, the nose and ears and jaw longer, the underlying profile of skull-and-jawbone having made its way to the surface of his features over the years.

The second photograph I saw, I already knew well from the print we had in Curzon Street. My father and mother stood outside the porch at St Camillus' in Tourmahinch, the day of their wedding. This was the picture I used to sneak down to contemplate in the front room in Curzon Street at night when, in the weeks after Daddy died, I feared I had lost the memory of his face.

A third portrait, in a white porcelain frame, showed a smiling, dark-haired young man in a hospital ward with the tubular frame of a bedstead at his shoulder. Christie, my late uncle, brother to Packie and Peggy and Feena, had died eight years ago of a blood disease before he was twenty-five. Christie Driscoll's abiding presence in that family was mediated to me chiefly through Peggy, and made a permanent impression on me: it was as if I had known him, though I was fourteen months old when he died. Grandfather Thomas paid his wife Maeve and son Christie visits in the parlour as others took flowers to gravesides. I suppose it was because the cemetery where the two lay together was a good way off from Three Crosses.

Opposite the mantelshelf stood a black oak dresser. I opened the lowest drawer and came upon a small cache of school texts. There were mathematical tomes, books on geography, a volume of Yeats, but I picked out *Deeds of the West-Britons* by Rev J M Deakin and hid this substantial work down the ample front of my red britches, balancing it delicately on the crotch. My thirst for print was about to be assuaged.

I pretended to saunter from the parlour, then out of the house and on up to the glade in the orchard, where the Morris Eight requiesced in peace. In the driving-seat, I drank in page after page of Deakin. He dealt mainly in the lore of Ireland and Wales, with excursions to Cornwall and to some of the legends of the Round Table that my father had first read to me in Curzon Street. Lancelot's betrayal of Arthur and subsequent repentance was a theme I could not banish from my mind. I found it hard, very hard, to encompass.

'By this time, Sir Lancelot had forsaken battles and become a priest. Taking up the body of the Queen, he buried it beside King Arthur's in one tomb.

'Within six weeks, Sir Lancelot, too, was dead. As they were burying him, there came to the forest two knights, Sir Ector and Sir Galahad, who for seven years had sought him through all the land.

'Lancelot du Lake,' said Sir Ector, as he bade farewell to his dead friend at the graveside, 'you were the best of knights ever to draw sword.' At these words, Beau Sir Galahad knelt and wept.'

Sir Ector's last words to Sir Lancelot both moved me and troubled me deeply. Ector forgave Lancelot. What right had Ector to forgive? Behold the perfidy of the adult world. And yet forgive he must, as Arthur surely had. Thereafter, reader, I luxuriated often in the pathos of that forest graveside scene, locating it, in my fantasy, in a familiar green clearing in the haggard at Driscolls' of Three Crosses, the surroundings, precisely, in which I sat, in the shell of Vance's one-time motorcar. Lancelot or Arthur? Arthur or Lancelot? My own Father, Roy Bennett, was it Lancelot that you were? Hero of heroes, did you betray us? Bozer you called me - Beau Sir Galahad. Arthur it was, that surely, you should have been. Roy. Leroy. Le Roi. The King. My king that died on me in February of 'fifty-seven.

Fifteen

Some Sunday people; Panloaf makes an offer.

It was Sunday and, in bed, in the darkness of the
landing, I had begun to hear the call of the bell from
Tourmahinch chapel across the fields. Downstairs the
house was silent; the fire unlit; the bread-oven cold.
Barefoot, I went down to the kitchen. I gave no scandal
in my knee-length nightgown recycled from one of the
men's shirts. I was deemed capable of performing my
own ablutions so I collected the soap towel and an
enamel basin from a little stand which was concealed
behind the kitchen door. These I took outside to the
rainwater butt. I struggled out of the nightshirt and
washed, stripped to the waist. I seemed to hear my father
speaking instructions to me over my shoulder, training
me in the techniques of cleanliness. I sluiced out the
bowl and the wash-water gurgled away, who knows
where, through a cement gully capped by a fat, blue slate.
The good weather was back and the rising sun began to
bless the land. I sat outside in the bright, warm angle

made by the porch with the kitchen wall and listened to the household stirring.

Breakfast on a Sunday was, indoors, hand-to-mouth. I was glad enough to sit outside, consuming simultaneously porridge and tea, both being thought equally good for us. In front of me on the churn-stand, Shep shared my collation, lapping up a panful of the latter beverage, milked and sugared, as good as any farmer. Not that our collie-dog did not enjoy porridge too. Again, as I have said, he was partial, for his dinner, to a platter of boiled potato peelings, cold, doused in sour milk.

Mother now had my three sisters in a row outside the house and was completing their toilet, the final touches being added with a face flannel soaked from the hissing brass tap of the rainwater butt. Each girl seemed a different-sized version of the next, their Sunday frocks covered by pink, double-breasted cardigans, which mother had knitted. She had purchased expensive, red-leather buttons for them at Bests near the railway station in Liverpool, to match their Sunday sandals.

We were to be the last to leave for chapel. Grandfather had long gone with Jellico and our trap to an early Mass in Rossbeg at St Egidius. This was the parish church from which Tourmahinch chapel, St Camillus, was served; you didn't know from week to week which priest would be sent. Feena and Peg had gone down to chapel in the Grehans' trap. Vance had taken his bicycle, the twenties' Sunbeam, which he would leave opposite the cemetery wall along with countless others belonging to the bachelors, young and old, in our parts. I had earlier caught a glimpse of Vance in his well-tailored Sunday suit and spotless fedora, as he straddled his bicycle to depart. What a distinguished figure he cut for us Driscolls, for a man of his age. Unlike Uncle Packie or Grandfather Thomas, Vance had something I later recognised as style.

I pulled the maroon gates shut behind our party and we set off Indian file down the left-hand verge of the road. My mother settled Kate in the folding pushchair and I led the way. Under the tunnel of horse-chestnuts we stepped it out, the morning wind sighing through the canopy. At the other end, in the sunlight towards the turn, we passed Dempsey's long fence and orchards on our left, and then the crossroads, where we bore right.

Some women who came down to mass wore widows' black in those days, woollen shawls with which they veiled their heads like nuns. Three of them from Coole walked sprightly, purposefully, a few yards in front of us.

'When shall we three met again, In thunder, lightning or in rain?' called out Lindie, who knew *Macbeth* from having been given *Lamb's Tales from Shakespeare* for Christmas. I permitted myself a guffaw just as two of the women turned their heads. Mother, looking stricken, called Lindie or me a gom, which did not sound positive. She hissed at my sister that it was a holy show that Lindie could not go down to mass without mortifying her own flesh and blood.

We did not speak to each other again, but our road hummed with voices and greetings and with the wheels of traps, as the families who lived further afield overtook us. In twenty minutes we had arrived in the village of Tourmahinch.

On one side of the road through the village was a high, grey wall, rendered and capped in slate, separating the church field from the road. Up against the wall waited the ponies and empty traps. At the end of the long file of these conveyances were parked four or five motorcars, all black but for a beige Humber as incongruous as a turtle-dove in a rookery.

We left our pushchair behind one of the short chapel buttresses and entered the church. My mother led the way, making Kate walk, so that she had a hand free to bless herself from the stoup.

Tourmahinch chapel was an architectural hybrid which could not have begun its life as a holy building. It had a porch with a gothic doorway, and a couple of Early English-style windows in the regular manner. It had a belfry. On the side facing away from Slievegarriff, it evinced more of the ancestry of a barn or a small mill, with four or five rectangular windows, bricked-up from within, their wrought-iron gratings and louvres left in place outside. It had a lawn, of a kind, on which stood stooks of grey hay from the summer before. There was no cemetery. Pathways through the sward led off into quiet corners if you were caught short during mass.

Within, the building had a mostly protestant feel about it, but for the sanctuary, where the red lamp glowed and candles shone. Elsewhere, there was little gilt or colour, no stained glass and the walls were devoid of picture or statuary, apart from the stations of the Cross, which were marked in a series of plain bas reliefs in moulded plaster. There was one altar at the end of a single nave. To the left was a side-aisle with a single row of pews facing an un-ornamented blank wall. A balustrade the length of the chapel separated this side-aisle which, during worship, was populated only by besuited menfolk. On the nave side of the balustrade sat the women and children, with some of the hardier fathers of families.

Mother led us down to the pew, third or fourth from the front, which she had shared with my father. Peg and Feena were already seated there. I sat next to Aunt Peg at the other end of the pew. Covering her face, so that those behind would not see her too friendly to me, Peggy whispered:

'Comport yourself, now, Bozer, and say your prayers. We have ours said.'

Perhaps I gave an impression I would ignore the injunction. I snuggled closer.

'Mind now, Bozer', she whispered again. 'Don't shame Mammy over-right the DBs.'

The Dyer Blasquets occasionally worshipped in our chapel and when they did so would occupy one of the front pews. The family were quality, being the owners of Rathmoven House and of the ample estate around it. Few people we knew had ever been in to the House, though it was barely two miles from Three Crosses. The postman from Rossbeg said there were palm trees as you went up the drive. In her youth, Peter Cody's mother, Agnes, had worked there for a good few years in their dairy, in the days before the creamery. She had left the

DBs suddenly, whether voluntarily or not was not entirely clear. I once heard Feena whisper it was scandalous. At the time, I took it that she, the best butter-maker in our parts, to leave Rathmoven was the scandal.

The younger son, Sam Blasquet, was the current head of the family, his elder brother Vernon having been captured at Singapore and having died in the war as a prisoner of the Japanese. Mrs Sam Dyer Blasquet was occasionally seen in the chapel and was reputed to be an American. Although the Blasquets were not farmers like us, (they were quality), they must have spent a good proportion of their days out of doors because they were all tanned almost to a foreign-looking hue. We knew that in other ways they lived differently from us. Not only were they thought to keep dogs inside their House but they would also take them out for special walks, as our next-door neighbours did in Liverpool. When it was the season, they hunted, not as we did, with snares or shotguns but in the grand manner, with friends from other parts, on horseback, as a sport. Then there was dress: Sam Blasquet did not wear a grey or navy suit to chapel, but came in tweeds. Again, their car, the Humber, was an unusual colour.

The other wealthy family in our parts were the Andersons, who did not come to our chapel. This was not because the Andersons were not quality (though, as Vance had once explained to me, they were not) but because they were protestants and worshipped in their own church on Sundays.

'Are the Andersons quality, too?'

'Ah, they're not, boy.'

'Why aren't they? Because they are protestants?'

'Not at all. Sure the quality is mostly protestant.'

'Well, why aren't they?'

'Too busy to be quality, boy. And you'd know by their talk and by the look of them. Any time I ever met an Anderson, whether Wesley or Phoebe or Charlie, they always had clean hands. But genuine quality would always have a bit of dirt under their nails.'

'Why?'

'That's the why.'

'Well, what work does a person do if he is quality?'

'Kilcreggan delved, And Rossbeg span, Rathmoven kept the gentleman', was all I could get from Vance by way of an answer.

I took an interest in the fingernails of the Dyer Blasquets two pews in front of us. They had their daughters, Joanna and Elspeth, with them. I craned and peered to get a line on any of them. The three women were in black gloves matching their mantillas. I missed my last opportunity when Sam got off his knees and sat back in the pew, waiting for the priest to come onto the sanctuary.

I have described Tourmahinch chapel as spartan in appearance for a catholic church, and so it was. Yet to the heightened and thirsting sensory awareness of a ten-year-old, it was the locus for all kinds of messages. There was the special sweet smell of the wax polish and the scent of clean linen in crisp alb, amice and surplice as the priest and servers swished past. Incense-clouds brought intriguing sensations to an olfactory system habituated to tobacco and wood smoke. An indefinable mystique of opulence hung there, enhanced by the gorgeous vestments on the person of the priest, Fr Haines, his jowls so close-shaven that they shone and the black hair of his head oiled and coifed like a film actor's.

Up to the pulpit went Father, between pine banisters lacquered the colour of marmalade. On this Sunday, the parting of the Red Sea had formed the basis of Fr Haines' observations from the pulpit, though whether it had been in the epistles or not I couldn't remember. Father's accent was not of our parts and I perhaps misheard him. The Egyptians, I recall from the sermon, suppurated on the one side. There were only twelve apostles but many desirables. Desirableship in general was open to every one of us present there that morning. And so on and so forth.

Jimmy Grehan had had an education at the monastery, and knew the first names of all the priests in Rossbeg. Outside the chapel after Mass he took hold of Fr Haines by his elbow. Haines had been a County hurler upcountry and avidly followed the game.

'Are you going with the Ganders a Thursday?' asked Jimmy.

'Were you listening to the sermon, boy?' countered Fr Haines.

'Ah, God, I was', said Jimmy.

'Quid tunc erat?'

Jimmy paused. 'Omnes drownderunt, Quod swimere non potuerunt.'

For that, Grehan got a dig in the ribs from Fr Haines.

'Ha ha, good morning, Father', said Sam Blasquet, taking his rightful place between the priest and Jimmy Grehan and offering his back to the latter. 'We're here until October', he said confidentially, not wanting any but Father to know his business. 'Come out to Rathmoven.' His accent struck me because it was that of the stranger, the hirsute tinker that Feena had fed at our porch. He headed towards the cemetery gate and the beige Humber, where his wife and girls were sitting.

Panloaf was standing foursquare at the porch holding out open wooden boxes by their cord-bound handles, in the manner of a juggler at the beginning of a routine. He had to take the second collection, which meant waiting till the last of the congregation left. In the meantime, he was conducting a conversation with my great-uncle.

Fr Haines put a hand on Panloaf's back and caught the eye of Vance, who stepped back tactfully out of earshot. Then he murmured to Panloaf: 'Go easy now, Michael, and don't be shaming the money out of the people.'

'Oh God, no, Father.'

'Good man.'

Father hurried on to his car and next mass. So on and so forth. Vance moved back so as to complete the conversation. Said Panloaf to Vance: 'I have the sow sick on me and they're a litter of grand little bonnivs. Ye could rear four above at Three Crosses and keep two for yourselves, why don't ye?'

Donald Madge

Sixteen

A donkey-ride of a kind, after which I overhear a conversation between Panloaf and his sister, but miss its full significance.

In the early afternoons, the adults sometimes took a short nap. On these occasions, my sisters and I were also constrained to repose and had to go upstairs, I to my angle on the dark landing where they had positioned my bed, an ex-Army portable construction in boxwood and hessian. But that afternoon, I yearned to slip away secretly from the sleeping household. My curiosity had been stimulated by Robinson Crusoe's constant talk of guns and by the fearsome Webley pistol Packie had shown me that Saturday. I had already made for myself a wooden rifle, which I will describe to you later. I had decided to head into the hill country with this weapon to round up and break in a mustang, casting Thady for the role. Thady was known neither to bite nor to kick; his treacherous half-brother, Richie, who looked identical to him, belonged to the Deegans and did both.

I wanted to share this adventure with someone and thought of Lindie at least as a companion; but she had had no part in the making of the gun and did not go in for cowboy lore; besides, she was napping with Beebie in Aunt Finola's bedroom, the one with the Great Exhibition wallpaper. It would be difficult to recruit her without giving the game away. So I retrieved my wooden gun from under my camp-bed and sneaked downstairs into the kitchen. The room was heavy with the scent of the soda-bread in the oven. As I entered the passageway leading to the green half-door, I caught the earlier redolence - as if archived there for me - of the boiled ham which had been brought out earlier for dinner. Then I was out.

If Thady wasn't working, he would spend his summer days at grass after he got back from the creamery each morning. There were two fields, the first halfway up, the other at the far end of our lane, where my quarry could be.

By 'our lane' I mean Driscolls' boreen. It wove through that land of youth where Ossian, son of Finn, once reigned for three hundred years; Driscolls' boreen was, is, the archetype of every road I have walked or ridden or driven since. I knew its stretches intimately, its humps and its bogs, its dusty, powdery reaches, its ruts, both wet and dry, its prospects out to Slievegarriff, or across fields of barley and of wheat, where the corncrake rasped, to Tourmahinch chapel or to the patterned quilt of spruces and telegraph pines in Kilcreggan woods. I knew its beeches and ashes, its overgrown slate stiles, its gates and the ruined ivy-covered habitations to which it once led. Driscolls' boreen we called it, but others would traverse it occasionally, with or without their livestock, the Deegans, the Grehans, the Brittans, the Reynoldses, Coonig the German. When I walked our lane, I could tell which of them had passed recently, from clues like discarded cigarette packets, or the fresh imprint of a wellington boot, or of Coonig's bicycle tyres.

Thady, it transpired, by elimination of the other possibility, had been quartered at the end of our lane, off up to the right in a far paddock which sloped upwards, quite steeply, to a wire fence before the ferns and conifers of Kilcreggan hill and wood. I trudged up through the two fields, the first boggy and very green with long grass, the second a hard, uneven hill field, patched with gorse and broom and hummocky with ants' nests. Thady had moved slightly so as to scrutinise me as I approached, and seemed neither pleased nor displeased at my arrival. I had brought a short cow-stick with me which I knew I must not wave at him. Again, so as not to alarm him, I was wearing my gun at my back by its strap.

'Come up, now.' It was Grandfather's phrase, signifying to Thady that he was to make himself available for some human purpose.

I followed my English instincts and patted and petted him for a few moments on the neck. He failed to appreciate these blandishments and walked along a few paces. He stopped. I took hold of a tuft of his mane and, hopping alongside as he moved off once more, I swung myself up onto his back. I hung on to his mane, gripped his fat little pot of a belly with my legs and got my balance.

'Go on, boy. Go on, you jennet.'

Thady walked on. He kept to the top border of the field where the furze and bracken began on the other side of the stake-and-wire fence. I had succeeded in roping and breaking in my mustang; now it was time to try him for speed. So I touched him in the flanks with my heels. He trotted; I retained my seat with difficulty.

Then I tapped him with the blackthorn stick, thinking I might get him to canter. The consequence was instantaneous: he bolted straight from the trot to a gallop. I was in panic. Headlong downhill he turned. I had no grip on him apart from on his mane. I was tossed like a pancake with every stride. I bit my tongue with the jolting. The dandelions and teasels and rushes, the broom, the hummocks and the couch-grass flashed by. We were through the bramble gap into the lower field in seconds. I braced myself. Then Thady threw me.

I half-came to my senses. I sat up but could not sustain the posture. My gun was intact. Back up into the top field, where I had first bestrode him, was Thady. A slow, insistent ache had set into my left arm. My middle finger hurt sharply and was strangely blue at the base. I lay back for many minutes, too concussed to move and bitterly wishing myself back on the landing in my Army camp-bed, with *Deeds of the West-Britons* or *Robinson Crusoe* at hand. My painful failure with Thady induced a deeper malaise of the kind Robinson had known.

'The anguish of my soul at my condition would break out upon me on a sudden, and my very heart would die within me, to think of the woods, the mountains, the desarts I was in; and how I was a prisoner, locked up with the eternal bars and bolts of the ocean, in an uninhabited wilderness, without redemption...'

After a while, I heard adult voices coming from the lane. I followed my instinct and struggled to my feet in time to hide under the lee of the hedge, at a point where I could peer through. Glory O'Donoghue was picking her way forward between the ruts on Driscolls' boreen, in the direction of our road and Three Crosses, with her brother, Panloaf.

Glory had Panloaf's block of a head with the same grey eyes. But her hair had once been dark, not fair, like his and she had a sallower skin, like a Latin. I could see that both she and her brother were dressed for visiting, Panloaf *à l'outrance*, in an Aran Island jersey ornate with Celtic motifs, though it was a warm afternoon. She was wearing a chocolate-brown suit and looked like one of my teachers from Pius the Twelfth. I somehow knew they were coming to us. On my side of the brambles, I moved noiselessly, like a trapper in the Alleghenies, to shadow them for the next stretch of the lane.

'Well, I never saw nor heard of her once in Rossbeg, never mind the Carlow Hotel', said Panloaf.

'Get away, boy', insisted Glory. "Twas in the bar there eying Brian Huntley she was, and she codding Tourmahinch with her talk of going to England or America. I'm telling you now.'

'I'd say 'tisn't drinking there she was, anyway, girl.'

Glory fell silent for a moment. I knew why. Glory was well able for a few bottles of stout or a sup or more of poteen at any time of the day.

'She'd be looking for your land, boy, and the father fierce at her to marry you. A Driscoll was always a land-grabber.'

'By Jesus, Driscoll could say the same of me, sure he could. Haven't Peg a quarter of that farm coming to her?'

'What age have you at all? Forty-two or forty-four, is it, Michael? Peggy Driscoll is eighteen. A little flibbertygibbet of a one that don't know her own mind. Only to make cow eyes at a grown man. I'll say no more.'

'Mind yourself, girl. With them good shoes you have.' I saw Panloaf give Glory a hand around the boggy stretch of lane by the whitethorn and the spring.

Glory had more to say, but on a different tack.

'Isn't Geraldine a fine cut of a girl and a good mother to those poor, fatherless yokes. She's a great worker and no mistake. With Bennett in his grave, the Lord have mercy on him, I'd say she will come home, with a few pounds from the insurance. Sure, she had no mass on going to England in the first place.'

Panloaf said nothing. Not knowing what to make of this, Glory continued: 'Sure Peg is a good poor creature, I suppose', as if rethinking her position again.

'Don't I know it? I'll be asking her, Glory. I'll be asking her any day now.'

You might wish to know how much I understood of this conversation there and then. Everything, I think, both on the surface and in the motives of the O'Donoghues. A certain sympathy in me for the pair jostled with dread at the thought that Panloaf's suit to

Peggy might prove successful. But the mood passed. I moved to other concerns; how I would explain the bruising on my arm and, worse, conceal the injury to my finger; I began to wonder what it was, wrapped neatly in newsprint from the *Southern Express*, that was in the string bag Glory was carrying. The speakers also passed on to other matters: the hiring of the reaper-and-binder they would need for their own harvest, a fortnight away, and whether Panloaf had struck the right bargain in cash and kind with its owner, Mr Wesley Anderson, of Tize Court.

Other snatches of conversation followed, borne back to me on the whispering summer air and between the deep sighs of the wind in the canopy above our lane. Did I hear this said?

'That fellow's not her child at all.'

'What?'

'Not at all.'

'Don't be talking now, girl. There could be any of the children to listen.'

Who was it that was not his mother's son? That afternoon, the question posed itself but without urgency. The information was not suitable for children's ears: what I knew then and know now of the world of adults did not fill me with confidence that it was suitable for adults either.

I let them walk on and, struggling with my bad arm and my gun over one of the new, red, tubular-steel gates, I slipped back onto the lane, out of sight behind them. I got back off the lane to our farm by way of the dyke and our orchard; when I sidled into the kitchen, I had not been missed. Glory and Panloaf were ensconced as guests under the hob facing my grandfather and my mother across the greying embers of the morning's fire.

Glory looked across at me: 'Hello, is it Adam you are? I have a present for ye.' Lindie and Beebie had not taken their eyes off Glory's package from the moment she walked in, but my sisters knew it could not be consigned until I was there.

Glory's present was a plain, cardboard box containing an assortment of penny toffee-bars in wax-paper wrappers. They were called Dublin's Best and came in three flavours: natural, strawberry and liquorice. I was well acquainted with the confections, since a penny was the usual tariff for a message run to Tourmahinch; Glory's gift was thus largesse indeed. Mother gently prised the box from me; I feared to resist in case my bad arm gave me away; she took out a bar each for us and kept the box on her lap, along with baby Kate, to secrete it away later.

Peg made the tea from the copper electric kettle and brought out some barmbrack from the press. I helped her and we went up into the parlour for the good porcelain tea-set. Glory's eyes followed us about our business. Panloaf had moved to seat himself at the dining-table, with his back to the company near the kettle-window, so as to look at the racing results in the *Southern*. When Peg came across he put his hand on her forearm. She caught the smell of his hair oil.

'Well, Peg.'

'Well, Michael.'

He: 'That's some class of a dress you have on you. Did you get it in Rossbeg?'

She: 'We didn't see Glory with a good while' (she dropped her voice); 'I heard she was troubled with the gout.'

He: 'Your father told me you got great marks in your Leaving Cert. there this summer.'

She: 'Will you take a cup of tea, Michael, now, and eat a bit of barmbrack?'

He: 'It's a beautiful day, Peg. Did you ever see such a beautiful evening?'

She: 'Are ye building over at Dunakielthy? I heard ye were building, Michael.'

He: 'Faith and I am, Peg. There you said it. I have a grand new kitchen with an Aga. And the light, too. They are putting in the light next week. A lovely kitchen, Peg, with a scullery.'

'Is Daddy there?' Aunt Peggy asked of us, turning her back to Panloaf. (He was not; after drinking his tea, Grandfather had gone out to our barn with Vance to sort the seed-potatoes. I remember this was a serious task and not one they would delegate to others, or ask me to help with. I think now it had something to do with a long folk-memory of the Famine).

'Only, Michael', she turned back and continued, 'he had a notion to ask you for another hundredweight of nuts, the same as before. Will you bring them up a Thursday, Michael?' (Last week, Vance had had to bring home unsold a couple of calves from the Rossbeg auction).

Seventeen

I meet the great Peter Cody at Tourmahinch and report on my encounter to Aunt Peggy.

On Tuesday morning, my aunts sent me to the shop for cigarettes. The shop, the creamery and the two bars were at Tourmahinch. Like Blanchardstown, Tourmahinch was a (longer) Irish mile and a half away down the road, maybe a mile across the fields. My aunts insisted I went the field way, on the pretext, selectively applied, that Addie wasn't allowed on the road yet, but the real reason was to forestall an encounter with my grandfather.

I got to the shop and noticed a fine pony, Diamond, in harness, up against the pebble-dashed wall of Hassetts' Bar. On the car Diamond was drawing were three silver milk-churns of the older, coal-scuttle shape, in the full sun. About to return the field way, with the contraband for Aunt Feena, I had my sandalled foot on the old slate stile set in the wall. Diamond clip-clopped up behind me, drawing the car and its three warm churns.

Peter Cody looked down at me from an immense height. I could see nothing of his face, with the sun shining strong over his shoulder. He wasn't wearing working clothes, but a gentleman's well-cut brown suit; the charisma of a hero came out of him. I wondered why this brooding Achilles should stop, remembering the look he had given me, outside our gate, the last time I had seen him. He jerked his head. 'Climb up there alongside me. Good man.' He gave me a hand as hard as saddle-leather. Instead of standing to drive, as he usually did, he sat down next to me on the sacking so as to be able to converse.

'How are you enjoying the holidays?' The fumes of stout on his breath came out powerfully with his aitches. But he had a pleasant voice and began to ruminate aloud about farmers' matters - who was cutting hay, who barley, and the bad price for milk. And then softly: 'Your daddy was English, is that right? And he died up there in Liverpool kind of sudden this year. You'd miss your Da, don't I know it...and he a good man to die so young.' He opened the wound again for me with his last remark and yet it was necessary. No one, not even Aunt Peg, had yet spoken to me in this way. Again the grief and pride welled up inside me in equal measure.

'The best are taken first", I murmured, not trusting myself to speak louder, a vessel brimming with emotion and liable to overflow. I stared up hard at sun-dappled Slievegarriff, now brown, now mauve, with the shadows of clouds chasing across her. A yellow wagtail ran along the road in front of the pony, then soared up into the blackthorns. Dempseys' fence came into view on the right of the road.

'If your Da was here', said Cody, 'he would be pleased to see what a fine strong lad you are.'

'Where he is now, he wouldn't want to come back.'

'By God, that was well said. You are a great man, so you are, Addie... and will your mammy come home with ye next year and live in Ireland?'

'I don't know.' I had not entertained the prospect that my mother might return with us to Three Crosses; yet to the sympathetic young hero who took an interest in me and shared my plight, it did not seem such a far-fetched idea. If we came back, would Peter Cody, newly and suddenly fatherless as I was, befriend me and guide me in the long years ahead when I must shoulder my father's responsibilities?

As we came up abreast of our gate, Peter said to me quickly: 'Your Aunt Peggy is a great girl. Do you think she'd go dancing with me?'

'No.'

'Why?'

'She says you're drinking your farm.'

★

'Now', said Peg, 'where's my young man? Bozer! Beau Sir!'

Where was I? At the top end of the Honey Meadow, the first of our fields off Driscolls' lane, bordering Deegans' paddock, where the apple trees and the hurley-ashes finished and there was a patch of sunny ground.

In this north-eastern corner of the field was an old well-shaft, with the grass growing thin around it. The well had belonged to another house that was once there; its stones had gone into building a stretch of the dyke between our farm and Deegans'. The well had been capped with a gigantic purple slate, oblong and the shape of a coffin lid, from the quarries above in Coole; Liam Deegan had the story from his late mother of the stone coming down by horse and four-wheeled wagon, during the first war, and seven women and a horse settling it over the mouth of the well because there weren't the men handy in them days.

I kicked off my wellingtons and lay out full-length on the capstone, scratching at it with a bent nail, brooding. Perhaps I was thinking that I must ask Liam about the house that had once been there.

'Where are you, boy?'

'What?'

I pulled myself up to a sitting position. The right side of my face felt flushed where I had caught the sun.

Peggy produced two toffee bars of the Dublin's Best variety and gave me the choice. At nineteen, she still had, figuratively, a child's sweet tooth and, literally, the dentition to cope with toffee. We gnawed at our bars. When she approached me, I had noticed Peggy carrying something I had not seen since the summer before. She put the blue velvet satchel into my lap and patted it. I slung the satchel from my navy elastic belt.

'It was good out of Pascal to keep this for you after he finding it in the hay-burrow last year. And you took your sandwiches in it to the National school last year, sure you did?'

I said nothing.

'Hang on to it now, for a souvenir, sure you will?'

'Mm.'

I watched her light a Craven A. She blew the smoke away as if it were an unwelcome distraction, transferred the cigarette to her left hand, then ran her right hand into the hair at the back of my head.

'Are you blond, or are you going dark? Or is it blue you are, Bozer?'

'You're a gas woman.'

'Don't be blue, now. Show me your finger.'

She looked at the swelling. Gently she manipulated my hand below the damaged middle finger without touching it. 'Is it still hurting? I'd say it is?'

'Yes.'

'Sure it is. You'll be better before you are married.'

'Peter Cody wants to marry you', said I.

'Bozer. You're a gas man, so you are.' It was partly my teeth, blackened with the liquorice toffee, that amused her.

'I know he does. He asked me if you would go dancing with him.'

'Is that a fact, boy?' she asked, although she knew it was.

'Do you like Peter Cody?'

'I do.'

'So do I.'

Peggy smoked on for a few moments, as we sat there on the edge of the capstone, our feet in the grass and shamrock and clover blossom of the orchard, Slievegarriff there, to draw our gaze out behind the thin screen of the whitethorns and alders. The mountain looked close and sharp in profile.

'Ye did great to save the bit of hay the other day, with the rain coming any time now, Bozer.'

'Yes.'

''Twasn't so great last year after the hay-saving when your Daddy and all gave out to you, over that burrow you made into the Kanturk, sure it wasn't?'

'No.'

'You were the apple of his eye, Bozer. Beau Sir. Where in the dickens did he get that name for you?'

'Beau Sir is Sir Galahad. In this book he read to me. *King Arthur and the Table Round.*'

'There was a child asphyxiated in the hay in County Leitrim, the other day. Did you know that, Bozer?'

I did. Secreted on the driving seat of the derelict Morris Eight, behind us in its little grove in our orchard, I had read the account in the *Southern*. A temporary rick of bales had settled, burying alive a little boy in a tunnel just like mine. In denial, I had tried to persuade myself that the newfangled bales were the problem, whereas a burrow in loose hay, as mine had been, was an inherently safer enterprise.

'Now Bozer, do you know that we are going to the seaside, Mammy, Lindie, Beebie, Kate, yourself and myself?'

'When?'

'Ah sure, that's the when.' She teased me. 'When Packie and Vance go to the Races. Ask them, why don't you?'

I suspect she was behind the whole plan. Peggy was always a peacemaker.

I have the blue satchel here in the house as I write. The sour-milk smell of it, that once nauseated me, is long gone from the bag but, fifty years on, reader, the odour of a refrigerator or a cheese shop immediately puts me in mind of blue velvet, Blanchardstown School, a womb-cum-tomb in a hay-barn and *When Did You Last See Your Father?*

Eighteen

To the seaside; a chance meeting with that gentleman of the road and a posthumous encounter with my father. Peggy.

It was a Thursday. We were in the navy-blue Ford Anglia van, on the way to the seaside at Skellymoher Strand, forty miles to the south-east and thus a two-hour expedition. Packie drove, flanked by Vance and my mother on the front seat. Katie was accommodated in the footwell under the dashboard, upon oilcloth cushions borrowed from the trap. She had to be prevented from fiddling with the handbrake, not because there was any danger of applying or releasing it (it did not work) but because she had trapped her fingers in it on the last outing and got a leprechaun's pinch. Vance and Packie, both in Sunday clothes, were going to the Races. Lindie, Beebie, Aunt Peggy and I sat on the floor in the back of the van, which was windowless, apart from a small porthole in each of the two rear doors.

'I need to go to the toilet', I said.

'You have a grand toilet there in the back. That's Grandaddy's pot. Make your river there like a good boy and the girls won't look, sure ye won't?' Packie was committed to the success of this sanitary arrangement as it had been his idea to bring the chamber-pot. Adult-sized, the vessel was only a quarter-full, yet the contents slopped around alarmingly. Despite the pressure in my bladder, I resolutely refused to use it. But the pain was becoming intolerable.

'Stop the van, now, Packie', said Peg.

Packie pulled over and lit up a cigarette. He inhaled a couple of times, deeply, then turned to me and said, exhaling tobacco fumes interestingly in a quivering blue mist:

'Go up there into the field behind that gate.'

'Behind the gate,

Said Pascal of late

A man with his river

Had right stand and deliver.'

The adults received this piece from Vance in a duly meditative frame of mind. Lindie and Beebie giggled.

With no handbrake, Packie needed to pull the van over where the road was level. He would have to keep the engine running because the Anglia was a devil to start when hot. The Lackendarraghs were up on the right; though not high, to be sure, mountains nonetheless to be proud of, with jagged sierra profiles and gentle foothills and lower slopes which inclined down almost to the edge of the road. Sheep, creatures we never saw in our parts above the Glas, grazed in the lower fields. I knew we were not far from a gulley my mother pointed out to me when we had traversed this road with Dad two summers ago. There was a cave in that gulley where, she told us, Eva Ban, the anchoress, had lived for forty years until after the War, talking mainly to herself and only in Irish or Latin.

Packie gave the Anglia a fraction of choke, to keep it ticking over, then came to the back of the van to release me by the rear doors. The girls squealed with delight when they got a good view of the sky and saw nothing but blue.

'We're near the sea!'

'The sea, the sea!' cried Kate.

I shinned over the gate and slipped out of sight of the road. I tore down my britches and pissed for all I was worth, the blessed stream arcing out and pattering down on the nettles.

'You have your Pearl with you, I perceive'; a languid voice, speaking in upper English, and sounding like Sam of the DBs, made itself heard behind me.

As I jumped and inadvertently sprayed myself, four thoughts went through my mind. I recognised the voice instantly. I guessed the speaker was there to visit the cave of the hermit Eva Ban. Thirdly, to disturb me at my immediate business, in the way he had, was not the behaviour of a gentleman. Lastly, I would have to rinse out my britches in seawater when we got to the strand.

'The sea, the sea', they heard the soldiers shout, passing on the joyful word.' continued the English tinker who had visited us for an alfresco dinner some Sundays ago. 'How she draws us all, like the Greeks of a time, on our journeys. How she insists. She draws me. But she is a treacherous mistress, Addie. Be wary of her this afternoon. You have your Pearl with you, I see.'

I couldn't make head or tail of his remarks about soldiers or Greeks but I knew about whom he was talking when he said Pearl.

'Yes', he said, 'your Aunt Margaret is a pearl by her nature. A pearl to be prized and protected. Look to her.'

'Goodbye', was all I could reply. He was resting a hand on the gate as I struggled across it, wanting to get away from him. I focused on the inch-long yellow fingernails, hoping he would not touch me. Then I ran to the van, without looking back.

'Have he his river made?' wondered Vance.

'What kept you?' asked Feena. 'Was it Eva Ban you met? Did she ask you up to the grotto for the sup of tea?'

In the gloom at the back of the van, no-one noticed my wet britches.

Packie drew up at the strand on the land side of a high brown concrete seawall. We children could not see the sea, so we looked up at the sky, mottled with clouds, trying to gauge which way the high winds would blow them and how many episodes of unbroken sunshine we would thus have, when we would feel warmth on our shoulders, as we bathed in the gelid Atlantic. Would the tide be coming in? We kept our questions to ourselves, sitting in silence as we had been bidden in the lee of the wall, enjoined not to distract the adults, while they unloaded the van. From high in that brindled sky there descended the drone of aircraft engines. I caught sight of a tiny, silver gnat in a patch of the blue, leaving shreds of a contrail. I knew my East from my West and guessed that it was bound for the United States.

'Catch this, Addie', said Mother, handing me a string bag with the sangwidges and flasks.

The rest of our beach luggage was distributed. It comprised little but towelling and clothing packed in shopping bags; neither Peggy nor my mother had brought a swimsuit, if they possessed one; their solitary concession to mid-twentieth century *rive-du-mer* culture was the grey-and-red Perfectone wireless set.

'We'll be taking our leave

Says Conor O'Keeffe.'

'Good luck, so', added Packie. Vance was in good form now that he was relieved of us, you could tell, because he rhymed again to Peggy:

'My dear niece, have you ever a cig?

High cockleorum, jig, jig, jig.'

'Will I light it for you?'

Peg produced a Craven A and lit it up for Vance in her own mouth. The men got back into the van. Back doors rattling, it whined into reverse, then ground its way, in first, back up the hill in the direction of the racecourse. The sun flashed out from behind the high cumulus and we yelped with the fun of it, scrambling over the wall ahead of Peggy and our mother, then down to the beach and the sea.

I do not know why Skellymoher Strand was the preferred destination for seaside outings. Some family connection, perhaps, a third or fourth cousin living there, I never got to the bottom of it. For all I know, there were many prettier beaches on that coast. The year before, in 'fifty-six, my father had borrowed the Anglia van to take us, driving on his British motorcycle licence as, he had maintained, one could in Ireland in those days.

The strand itself was like any other sweep of sand on a Celtic shore: long, wide, bare of kiosks or other public utilities, with a good wind whipping in from the ocean in the afternoon and, if you were a child, lifting the dry sand into your face. At the eastern end, where we were, the beach ended against a low, but sheer, outcrop of black rock, devoid of vegetation, which continued out to sea like a breakwater. There were no caves or rock pools. The western end of the strand was featureless, lost in the distant haze of spray from the breakers.

Ahead of you, to the south, no islands or headlands, no leisure craft, only sea, now green, now grey and, rarely, azure. That green was beautiful, but antipathetic to me, because it went with white horses and choppy ferry crossings and the *mal de mer* from which I inevitably suffered on the boat. At your back, above the high-tide mark, was a mile or so of old dunes, none very high, now colonised by sparrowgrass and rushes. Under one of these, my mother and aunt planted themselves, rolling up their summer printed-cotton frocks and lighting up their Craven As in an arcane huddle. Then they settled back to be vigilant over us and listen to the sigh and chatter of the incoming tide as it washed and purified every part of the beach.

Twenty yards from the adults, I sat on my haunches, with a dry towel over my shoulders, shivering slightly and digging a tunnel in the hard sand with my bare hands because Beebie and Lindie had both of the toy spades. I needed (and had obtained) a permission to enter the water when the sun next came out. The girls would not be allowed in the water alone, but in Liverpool at Pius the Twelfth, I had had school swimming lessons and had, the previous autumn, duly completed a length of the Pole Street Municipal Baths. I had been taken aback to learn, when I reported this feat to my father, that swimming was an accomplishment he had never managed, for all his wartime background in the Merchant Navy.

The sun switched on again. The beach lit up from grey to blond; the breakers rolled whiter and the sea blued. I ran down to the water.

Dashing through the surf, I suddenly and strangely discovered myself happy in the presence of my departed father, who had chased me as I scampered on this very beach last year. In those few moments, I was with him again and he with me as on that afternoon with Busty at the launch of the Small Ship *Irrawaddy* on the Shanaun. It came as a fleeting intimation that it did not matter that he was here no more, because he loved me from where he was. Rapture washed over me with the spume of the breakers. I knew then that Daddy wanted to pardon me for not being there in Curzon Street, for not turning up in time with the aspirins the day he died. His forgiveness engulfed me, again and again, with the sea that cleanses every thing. I waved to my mother and to Peggy, shrieking with delight. I plunged headfirst into a breaker, wrestling it, pulling out into its wake and swimming a few breast strokes with the sun on my back.

I waded over towards the rocky breakwater. Ten yards out in the verdicchio-white sea, beyond the outcrop, there was a black rock islet, three feet out of the water. That was the wreck of my ship and I, Robinson Crusoe, would swim to her.

'A little after noon I found the sea very calm and the tide ebbed so far out, that I could come within a quarter of a mile of the ship. I resolved if possible to get to it...you may be sure my first work was to search and to see what was spoiled and what was free.'

I struck out over the few intervening yards of water. As I neared the rock, I put my foot down and discovered I could not touch bottom. The sun went in. The sea coloured grey. I became aware of the bullying push of a swell and panic caught me. I abandoned course for the islet and struggled to make it to the outcrop. I regained my breast-stroke posture with difficulty, shipping seawater through my nose. The swell now seemed to toy with me, alive, monstrous. It dashed my bad elbow against the outcrop. I was deadly cold in the water now, losing control over my breathing. I dreaded letting my feet down or moving my arms to seek a grip on the viscid surface of the rock. I sensed, despairing, that the water was still too deep.

Within minutes of the ecstasy of dashing through the breakers, I lost hope of this life. I was on my way to my father, sooner than I could have expected. A wicked swell lifted me again and scraped me, half in paralysis, along the outcrop. I cracked my knee on something below me but the cold anaesthetised me to numbness. I was going to die in a pointless and banal accident.

Now the panic lifts and calm comes over me as I allow myself to be washed this way and that. Daddy is there to me, chuckling, in his open-necked brown holiday shirt. I love his slight tan, his beautiful dark hair, cut and slicked and handsome as mine can never be. The fear-paralysis of a moment ago - the fear-paralysis of my nightmares - leaves me. I want to be overwhelmed, to go where my father is.

But his voice, amid the muffled sound of other voices, comes to me through the soup-green underwater and spume; 'Go on home, son', Daddy is saying, 'Go on home.' There was sand under my feet. The swell had finished the murderous part of its sport with me, now it broke over my head like an over-friendly playmate.

My mother and aunt had moved down the dunes a few yards to be nearer the girls and, next to their excavations and sandcastle, they had spread out the towel which they shared with the Perfectone. Mother had the volume low and I couldn't hear what she was listening to.

'Sure, poor Bozer is half-drownded', said Peg. 'Come here till I dry you.'

She enveloped me in the towel and stroked the seawater off me. I caught the tobacco on her breath. Then she looked at me, half in merriment, half in concern, her forefinger under her bottom lip, her expression melding mysteriously for a few instants into an enquiring look my father would occasionally give me.

'Bozer, what's on you? Did you get a fright just now?' I looked away, unsettled, disconcerted by that look of my father's Peggy had given me, his presence glimpsed in her face.

'Full fathom five my father lies

Those are Pearl's, that were his eyes...'

My ears still rang with the muffled underwater voices. I had been spared for a reason, perhaps for a person as, once, in the War, in the Indian Ocean, my father had been spared for me. At Skellymoher, the thick green water had not closed irrevocably over my head. My terror had vanished. Daddy had come back to me in an enigmatic, mystical calm and I had begun to let go. In that calm, he sent me back. To know with exactitude why, I must await our next encounter. In the meantime, the story I give you is the one that runs best with what I learned and lived in my dreamtime and all the years since.

Nineteen

Peggy and Finola visit Panloaf; Finola announces a surprise.

'Arrah, Feena, we'll go over, the two of us.'

'What would I want over there in Dunakielthy, girl?
'Tisn't bonhams are on Michael's mind now at all.'

'We'll go for the crack.'

Panloaf O' Donoghue had four healthy bonhams he
couldn't rear and would give them to us. For our part, we
had a great sow which had farrowed a small litter of five
with a runt that wouldn't survive.

The division of labour on our farm meant that it was
largely Feena and Peg who superintended the chickens
and the pigs: Grandfather had therefore put it to them
after mass that they should pay a call at Panloaf's in
Dunakielthy, the next time they were on messages
nearby in Tourmahinch, to find out what ailed the sow
and cast an eye over the bonhams that Panloaf had in
mind for us. He didn't want them bringing in anything.

Balanced on the spout of the water-pump at the top of the yard, like a monkey on a stick, I watched my aunts as they busied themselves to leave. I did not accompany them to Dunakielthy that day and I may tell you later, reader, how, in that case, I am able to describe their outing. I watched them fold their raincoats to put on the bike-carriers. But they had not taken too much trouble: there was no need. Feena had a string bag on the handlebar with a gallon-full of our raspberries and a few pounds of Vance's carrots she had forked out of the kitchen-garden without asking him.

O'Donoghue's pigs, for some reason, were not in his outhouses, but at the end of a big, hummocky paddock adjoining the farm. The paddock was bisected by a double track, not more than a couple of hundred yards long, which led straight to their piggery. Behind the pig-house, the track continued for a mile or so through further pastures up the escarpment to another gate into Kilcreggan woods. It was a lonely road, leading to the quietest part of the woods, where Daddy and I had once seen a pine marten.

The O'Donoghues were not expecting the sisters, but no matter. Panloaf knew why they were there and said straight away that they would go over to the piggery in the trap, because he had the pony in harness ready.

'Arra, Michael', said Glory, 'let you and Peg go look at them bonnivs. What do Finola want going with ye? What have you there for me, Finola?'

Glory took the string bag from Feena and they went into the kitchen through a fine new door, painted cream, with a chromium letterbox.

'Stop there', said Panloaf to his dog, another collie like our Shep, but more of a tan colour and blessed with good hearing. The creature had trotted down to the piggery behind the trap. O'Donoghue's dog was unusual in that he had no name. He thus had to be referred to by means of a description, for example, the tan yoke from Dunakielthy or Panloaf's shep. Anonymity did not appear to have dented his affection for his master, nor, indeed, his *joie de vivre* in general.

The O'Donoghues' sow, at any rate the one in question, was on her side, asleep, with a clean farrow of seven blue-eyed piglets fidgeting around her but not sucking. At the other end of the stall lay the runt, which made eight. Peg and Panloaf studied the situation over the gate of the stall without going in to disturb, with Panloaf indicating the finer points of this or that bonham with his stick.

'Oh no, Peg, it isn't the metritis at all. Not at all. No more the mastitis. Grogan gave me a cream for that.'

'When was Grogan here, Michael?'

'A Tuesday, dear.'

'What did he diagnose for the sow?'

'He couldn't rightly say. But I wonder did the poor creature get a bit of a stroke? Nice little bonnivs, ain't they? Be telling your father, now, and I'll have four of them ready a Wednesday after the creamery, my dear.'

Peg knew what she would need to report to her father; she made her own guess why Panloaf had not summoned the vet a second time, but kept her counsel at this point. Panloaf helped her back up into the trap with a hand on the small of her back. She took her seat on the left and, closing the trap door behind him, Panloaf came across from his usual driving position to sit next to her.

'Well, now, Peg my dear, we'll have a little kiss here, now, before we go back.' He put his arm round Peg's shoulders. Peg blanched. She looked straight ahead.

'Drive on, Michael.'

'Only the one little kiss, now.'

He dropped the reins over the brass handrail and brought his right hand to bear over her left breast. His face was up against hers and she saw him old, prematurely so, with the capillaries out on his cheekbones and purses under his eyes and the pink of his scalp everywhere under the thinning, oiled crust of hair.

Peg stamped hard on the boards of the trap. The pony began to walk on. She knew she couldn't wrestle herself free of his embrace and stand up, because of the rocking of the trap on the uneven track, so with all the coldness she could muster, born perhaps of the good warnings she had had from the nuns, she told him:

'In the name of God take your hand off me, Mr O' Donoghue.'

Panloaf's left arm loosened somewhat but his right hand slithered down her front and lap to her knee.

'Take your feckin hand off of me, Mr O' Donoghue.'

She seized his hand by the wrist and moved it without difficulty to the handrail in front of them. As she did this, she was aware that Glory and Feena were outside the house in the line of sight a hundred yards away and that thus the moment was over.

'Drive on, Mr O' Donoghue. I'm real sorry. Truly I am.'

Panloaf now had both hands on the reins. 'Them are Friesians', said he, jabbing a finger towards three good-sized, sleek, black-and-white cows of a breed Peg had never seen before. He had them corralled in a muddy wired-off recinct of the pig paddock. 'Look at the teats on them. Great milkers.'

They clattered into the yard and up onto a flat, concrete pad that the O'Donoghues had just laid in front of the house. Glory was standing at the door of her new kitchen, where she had the tea ready. Without waiting for Panloaf, Peg slipped down from the trap and followed her inside.

On their way back from Dunakielthy to the turn, the sun behind them warmed the cyclists' backs, throwing their shadows down the road ahead. While waiting on the road outside the O'Donoghues' gate, Peggy had picked honeysuckle and foxglove and starry, pink, wild geraniums in the hedgerow, along with purple vetches and white stitchwort which she had carefully disentangled from the undergrowth. She had lined up the blooms on the handlebars of her bicycle, the stems gripped between the bars and the brake-rods. She looked as if she was transporting a window box and pedalled slowly, like an old-timer, with just enough pressure to stay upright, so as not to shake and damage the flowers. Feena had learned floral arrangement from the nuns at school and would display the flowers in the parlour.

'Panloaf has a bit of cash, alright', said Feena, pedalling abreast of Peggy and just keeping her balance at the low speed.

'He has, I'm sure.'

'Did you notice the good new china?'

'I did.'

'Glory told me she has a washing machine going into that kitchen any day now. Panloaf showed me the four fine iron straps cemented ready in the floor.'

'Four iron straps, is it?'

'Where did he get the cash, I wonder?' said Feena.

'Oh, sure, where indeed, girl.'

'He don't go betting, anyway. He's too cute for that.'

'Oh, he is.'

'What's at you, girl?' said Feena, after some moments.

Peggy flushed. At first she ignored the question and reported to Feena that the deal was done with the bonhams. But in her continuing confusion at Panloaf's behaviour, she could not but test her own feelings, try out her thoughts in words, so she went on:

'What do you think of Panloaf?'

'Arra, poor Panloaf - he's a harmless poor creature. Glory is an old fox of a one, though. Why?' Feena now had an inkling that something might have transpired down at the pig-house. To keep the dialogue going, she asked: 'Did you battle with him over the bonnivs? Did

Glory put him up to wanting to make a few extra shillings out of us?'

'He didn't fight me over the bonhams. 'Twas I fought him, girl. Fought him off after he touching me and drooling over me there in the trap.'

'What? Are you codding me?'

'Not a bit of it.'

'Will you tell Daddy?'

'No, girl, and no more will you.'

'Right so', said Feena. 'Sure we know where we stand now with that lad - that dirty old man, anyway. He can go to hell, so he can, where the best of quality goes.'

★

Aunt Finola had hold of me by the hand. In my free hand I held the beach spade with which I had been building dams and watercourses in the miniature swamp of mud and gravel at the road end of our front yard, by the spring water tap. Finola referred to this pastime as slobbering. It was evident to her that slobbering was destructive of character and she sometimes tried to get my mother to ban me from it. On this occasion, Feena ignored my activities and pointed to a fat spruce log in the kindling stack big enough for both of us.

'Sit down there, now, Adameen, until I tell you a thing.'

In her navy-blue cardigan and lipstick and black slacks she was as fresh and modern-looking as the mannequins I had seen in Treacy's of Comerford, where

Mother and I had bought my father his good woollen coat last year. Grandfather had no liking for the slacks or the lipstick. Then Aunt Finola (she could almost have been my Peg) produced a Dublin's Best for me in the liquorice flavour. We sat for a moment with our backs to the fuchsia hedge facing up into the yard. There was no one else in sight.

'That hen is looking lame', she said, pointing with the cigarette she was about to light at one of our two Rhode Island Reds, as the bird scratched and rootled in the damp sepia detritus of sawdust and spruce bark at our feet. Feena and Peg thought whites better layers. I thought the brown birds better lookers and they always appeared less scrawny. I didn't see anything lame about the unfortunate Rhode Islander in front of us, but Aunt Feena's remark might have been the death-knell for her. I sensed Feena's gaze transfer itself to me as I picked away at the wax-paper wrapping on my toffee bar.

'Know what this is?'

She held out her hand to me and I saw a gold ring, set with a small diamond.

'I'm engaged to be married. Now?' The last word was added to invite me to tell her what I thought.

'Peggy and Grandad will miss you when you leave Three Crosses.' I had none of the conventional responses. Trite formulae were not yet part of my vocabulary. It was, as it happened, the right thing to say.

'Oh I won't be far away at all.'

'Why?'

'Because I'll be Mrs Michael O'Donoghue of Dunakielthy.'

Mrs Panloaf! I was cute enough to realise that the soubriquet would no longer be acceptable.

'Does everyone know?'

'I didn't tell your sisters yet, Adameen.'

'Grandaddy?'

'To be sure. Sure Michael is after asking him.'

'I thought you would marry Jimmy Grehan.'

'Did you, Addie?'

'Yes; and won't he be disappointed?'

'Disappointed, Addie? Why would he?'

With the liquorice bar softening in my warm hand, I bit off another inch and was thus exonerated from an immediate rejoinder. What I asked myself was how she had broken her news to Jimmy.

Finola went on, looking down at her brand-new ring and the tiny seeds of fire, blue and pink and orange deep in the little stone: 'Michael is a well-respected man in these parts. I can count my blessings. He has a grand new kitchen built for me, with an Aga. I'll have Glory for my sister-in-law to help with the housework.'

In my boxwood camp-bed on the dim landing that night, I reviewed my feelings about Aunt Finola's betrothal. I began by being happy for Feena, hoping that Panloaf, Michael, had seen through to the truth about her, the truth that was bound up with her magical bardic gift. I knew somehow that Jimmy Grehan had seen and loved this in her. Needing to read, I forsook Robinson and immersed myself in my most recent borrowing from the parlour, *Deeds of the West-Britons*, until other thoughts supervened. Why, in the end, had Aunt Finola thrown over the admirable and open young Jimmy Grehan in favour of the cuter, foxier old farmer from Dunakielthy? Had I not heard Panloaf declare to his sister Gloria, on Driscolls' lane, the day Thady threw me, that his real interest was for my Aunt Peg? In default of Peggy, evidently Feena would do. Had Aunt Finola really informed Jimmy Grehan that his suit had been undermined, his place quietly taken by Panloaf? I wasn't so sure and surmised that Feena's head had been turned by the wily Glory and Michael between them with, doubtless, one or two subtle observations to her in regard to her younger suitor. This was how some behaved – even in the world of heroes:

'The wicked Morgan le Fay had a brother, Mordred, who was a false knight and a usurper. Soon he caused some letters to be written saying King Arthur had been killed in battle; and then he had himself crowned King at Canterbury. Also he went to Queen Guinevere and told her to make herself ready, for on a certain day he would marry her.'

Panloaf was, I decided, a usurper. It was another powerful substantive, like the word 'exile', that lodged itself within me, mining deep into the vein of my trust in the world of my seniors, spoiling the corn like the weevils did, as welcome as a Colorado beetle in a potato field, or a big, black-and-orange bumblebee.

Twenty

In the Honey Meadow, Aunt Peggy talks of history and of Peter Cody; in another of our fields, Grandfather Thomas talks of the same. A visitor to our farm. My mother gives me hope.

Peggy took us up a short reach of our lane, Driscolls' boreen, to the Honey Meadow. After the most recent tempest, the stretch had dried out and the walking was easy. So easy, that Lindie and Beebie had got away with wearing their good, red-leather sandals, which I had promised my mother to clean and polish on their return. We were in single file. I marched ahead, carrying the brown-paper package, kept by Packie for me, that I had received first from my father when Mother and I had taken the train to meet him off the *Western Warrior* in Comerford Dock last summer.

At the first bend, where the lane's trees thinned and the canopy lightened, was the gate to the Honey Meadow. The sky had cleared to azure; the sedative coo of woodpigeons, the chirrups of the warblers and linnets, in the whitethorns and hawthorns, gave way to sounds from ahead over the grain fields. A cockerel crew from

Dunakielthy. The swifts wheeled and screamed, skimming low. Peggy and Lindie stepped up to the gate. Beebie said 'Listen! That's Panloaf O'Donoghue winding his watch!' because that was what Daddy had told her when, at this same spot near the permanent spring, we had heard the call of the corncrake across the fields of grain, last year.

The eastern dyke of the Honey Meadow, our field, abutted our orchard and Deegans' home paddock. To keep matters complicated, everyone else still called our Honey Meadow Deegans' Old Field, because it was only ninety years since our neighbours of that name had ceded the use of it to us, the Driscolls. Then we got the title to it from the Land Commission.

We had given the field our own name because Grandfather had it let to, or had an arrangement with, a German fellow he called Coonig, from Rossbeg, who kept a few beehives there in the far corner. Coonig would occasionally be heard singing *lieder* I later came to recognise as Bavarian, as he pushed his bicycle, with a wicker box on the carrier, up our lane. If he didn't sing and if there was no breeze, the scent of a Manikin cigar would tinge the air in our yard and you would know Coonig had gone up to the Honey Meadow that day.

The Meadow was longer than it was wide in the direction of the wind which, in our parts, blew either easterly or westerly along the flanks of Kilcreggan hill. This made it the easiest of our fields from which to launch a kite. Yes, reader, the brown-paper package Packie had produced a week ago, the package that first came to Ireland with my father on the *Western Warrior* in 'fifty-six, contained a red, yellow and mauve Windsprite box-kite.

The kite lay on the grass, taut and ready for the air, a focus of fascination to me in an outdoor world where, hitherto, only God's flowers were red and yellow and mauve. The success of a primitive arrangement of cloth, wands and string, the romance of flight, the soaring and bucking of the kite, this tense, square flower of the air, the dramatic sweep of the line into invisibility - none of these held the least interest for Aunt Peggy, who took little part in the launch and glanced once or twice at the magical aerial machine as if it were an old crow.

At the top of the Honey Meadow, in the eastern corner and sheltered by a couple of Irish oaks, was the huge purple capstone slate, the shape of a coffin lid, sealing a disused well. On this stone Peggy elected to sit. She was in the bees' flight-path from the eastern hedgerow to the hives at the other end of the field; I watched her, as she tossed her head and flicked her hand at the occasional flier which mistook her, and her scent, for a flower.

Remembering what Daddy had taught them last year, the girls had brought along a few sheets of newspaper to fold and tie to the kite's tail as ballast, if the wind got too strong. There being only a gentle breeze, Lindie and I untied some of the existing hanks of paper. Daddy's knots were still as he had tied them and I nuzzled the little twists of last summer's *Southern Express* as if they might still bear the scent of him. I couldn't throw them away.

We launched the Windsprite. After it had been airborne for ten minutes, I started a new game Daddy had taught us, tearing scraps of newsprint and threading them onto the line. The breeze caught them and they edged their way up and up to reach the kite, by now several hundred yards from us. After half an hour, we had spooled out half of the line. Daddy had told us last year that it was a third of a mile long. A small spasm of anger jabbed at me: my father was needed here for this, to fly the Windsprite out to a third of a mile and see it dance over Dunakielthy Farm as he had promised. Daddy had left it all to me.

Peggy saw me looking at her. So she called me, from the slate where she sat, under the oak tree, with a couple of smart claps of the hand. The sound arrived across the meadow, out of synchronism with the action.

'Bozer! Bo-o-o-zer! Come here, I want you.'

The runs I had made to get the kite flying had tired me and the grass was long, in need of another cut for hay. I see myself now, in third person, as it were, trudging up the Honey Meadow to Aunt Peggy. I noticed, for the first time, what had been the gable-end of a house, incorporated into the dyke between the Meadow and Deegans' paddock. Peggy drew me like a magnet through that beautiful field, watching me, with her chin in her hand, as I skirted round the thistles and docks that were the final barrier in the corner. I sat next to her on the huge slate, our backs to the ruined wall. We looked west to Lindie and Beebie, to the kite, to the tin roof of Dunakielthy farmhouse and to Slievegariff.

'Was this a farm behind us?'

'It was.'

'Do you remember the people who lived here?'

'Indeed I don't, boy. They were people called Daverns in it before I was born. They went down to Cork, bag and baggage and took the boat to the United States. Your Mammy knows all about it. Be asking her. That dyke behind us is up with a good few years now. 'Twas builded with the stones out of the walls. Go up there now for yourself and look at them stones. There's plaster still on some of them. A hundred years ago they were maybe twelve or thirteen houses here, like. This part of the county was classified a congested district before the Rising.'

'I thought it was called Three Crosses because there were three houses together - us and the Deegans and the Brittans. Like three crosses on a map?'

'Arra, not at all. Fooleen! Sure aren't the Dempseys and the Reynoldses in Three Crosses too? And did you never go into the field to see those three crosses belonging to the old bishops?'

★

You will remember that Todd Davern has just married my niece Susie, Lindie's eldest. I went to the wedding in Connecticut last weekend, real-time. It was last Friday night before the wedding, when Todd looked at me over his whisky and said some of his forebears were from Three Crosses, County Toberenagh, that I disinterred from the dreamtime this whole dialogue with Peggy in the Honey Meadow. And many other conversations I have recounted in this story.

'I'm not allowed in the field with the three crosses. Because it belongs to Grehans and they keep bullocks in it.'

'Who told you that?'

'Peter Cody.'

'Arra, sure, the Grehans wouldn't mind if the field was empty. Not at all. But, em, when were you talking to Peter Cody?'

'On Tuesday. When he gave me a spin back from the creamery. I told you before.'

'From the creamery direct, like, or was it from

Hassetts'?'

'From the bar.'

'The poor fellow can no more stop himself drinking than fly in the moon. When he started the bad drinking, his mother Agnes would go down to Hassetts' with Jimmy Casey of Blanchardstown and Peter would be gone out of it. 'They would find him in the horrors in the back of the trap or maybe in the ditch, like, after they giving an hour or two looking for him. Know what 'in the horrors' means? You do, I'm sure, Bozer.'

'Drunk.'

'Senseless, boy. Day after day, God help him.' Peggy stopped talking and drew on her Craven A.

'Can I try your cigarette?'

'No. But if he met the right girl, he could maybe dry himself out. I couldn't be saying these things now to Daddy or Packie, do you know what I mean?'

'Yes.' I was thinking that if there was ever girl to offer hope to a reprobate, it was Peggy.

'I'm telling you now for a secret, Bozer.'

'Pad Dempsey said he's heading to drink himself and his mother into Ballinsaggart.'

'Is that a fact, Addie? Then, sure, Pad Dempsey's an ignorant boshthoon. Is all I can say.'

★

It was a few days later that I went off midmorning in the ass-and-car with Grandfather to our upper fields under Kilcreggan woods, to turn the hay.

Peg brought out the yellow vacuum flask and a few ham sangwidges wrapped in a tea-towel, in a string bag. I was permitted to harness Thady myself and backed the donkey between the skyward-pointing shafts. Grandad swung them down, settling the yoke-chain across the wooden saddle bridge and hitching the draw chains to the collar. We set off up our lane, to our fields, at a slow pace. We followed the fresh spoor of our eight cows, which had passed that way earlier after milking. Our unsprung, iron-rimmed wheels fitted the dried ruts exactly, but still we were jarred every foot of the way through the bare boards, and I had to hold down the sprongs, or pitchforks.

'You got a spin with Peter Cody a Tuesday. And what did he say to you?' asked Grandad.

Between jolts, I told him, omitting any talk of Peggy, because of what she had said to me in the Honey Meadow.

'Did you ask him about his suit? Be sure and never ask him about the suit. Did you ask him?'

'No. Why?'

'That's the why.'

'Why does he drink so much?'

'He's a hard drinker, altogether. But he used to be a fine cut of a young fellow.'

'Why did he become a hard drinker?'

'On account of his father Denny Cody dying the way I told you.'

'Does everyone become a hard drinker after their father dies suddenly, Grandad?' I said, with a heart-stopping premonition that my suffering might yet take a new direction; my father's pride and joy, I would yet run wild, the Colonial Boy; the last, vestigial rumour of my mother's and sisters' love for me to be washed away, *malgré moi*, in whiskey and stout.

'God help us, no, Addie.'

'Why did Peter, then?'

'Because poor Denny Cody wasn't a year in his grave when Peter went in to the priests and found out Denny wasn't his father at all. And Peter the last to know.'

'Who is his father?'

'Oh, he has a father right enough.'

'Well, who is his father?'

Grandad demurred.

'Never say this to a soul, Adam, boy, sure you won't?' I would not have, but what Grandfather entrusted to me was of little moment. 'His father is a powerful man altogether. He do be living not two miles from where we are standing.'

'And are those things Peter's crosses?' I wanted to know, remembering Peggy and Feena and their gossip at the gable-end bedroom window, weeks back, on the Tuesday morning after St Camillus' day.

'Two of them, anyway, to be sure.'

'Why, how many crosses has he?'

'Three, I'd say, like them bishops below in Grehans' field, heh, heh! And like the rest of us in the here and the now.' Grandad mused and hummed away at his private tune, 'dally dee, dally dah, dally dandy', tapping his pipe on the flat wooden mudguard.

While we talked, Thady had turned off the track into the hay field, following deep, dry ruts as if on a railway with the points for a siding set in that direction. Grandad took off bridle and bit and spancelled the donkey to a post in the hedge, where the grass was long but he couldn't get at the hay. Without bit and bridle, Thady had a curious naked look about the face, as my father used to without his glasses in the morning. We worked away, turning the long swathes of damp hay in the sun. High up the larks sang, tiny specks, sweetening that blue, blue sky. Frogs of every size and hue hopped away unsteadily as we turned the hay. A hare started and ran.

Grandad put my hand in the patch of grass where it had lain and I could still feel its body heat. Away on the road, we heard Busty's brother, Hughie Heaphy, come up from Blanchardstown, in his Standard Ten, crashing his two gears on our hill, on his way over to Coole.

Early next day, a Thursday, Mother went up to Kilcreggan with Grandad in the pony and trap, for paraffin-oil for the bread oven. Feena and Peg were still milking. I climbed up on top of the high gate-pier (an act forbidden) and sat to watch the farmers coming and going from the creamery. Panloaf the Usurper, too, went by, driving his horse and four-wheeler with some deliveries to make above in Kilcreggan or Coole. Then I recognised Diamond's brisk gait, and Peter Cody drove up smartly from the avenue. For some reason, he was no longer wearing the familiar, elegant brown suit. But he stood tall behind Diamond and had his usual panache. He pulled up at our gate, gave me a wink and leapt down, passing me Diamond's reins to hold. 'You're a great man, Addie' he said. 'Mind Diamond now for me, he's kind of nervy.' I brushed the seed off Diamond's back, where he had been drawing the hay-wagon the day before. Peter walked over to the arched doorway of our cowhouse and greeted my aunts. The girls looked up at his lithe silhouette in the doorway as he spoke:

'I have a grand bit of timber here would fix the bottom rail on the gate there for your father. You can be telling him I'll mend it after my dinner.'

'What timber is that?' said Peg, passing Peter the bucket of milk from under the cow and getting up from her stool.

'Deal, I think.'

She took back the frothing milk to filter it into the churn while Peter manhandled a great baulk of sweet-smelling pink timber, dropping it with a clonk onto the slate churn-stand beside her.

'Well now, ah, Peg, were you ever dancing at Sheehan's?'

'I was not.'

'Will you come with me a Sunday?'

'I'll hardly, Peter.'

Peg said it with a half-smile, clutching her milking overall around her as if the air had suddenly gone cold. But in the slight flush of her face, I saw the answer she had not given. And when she tossed her luxuriant black hair behind her shoulder and arched her eyebrow so exquisitely, I knew if I had been Peter I would have given up anything for her.

'Sure Peter Cody was in great form', I heard Feena say to Peg from the cow-house afterwards.

'He was', said Peg.

'And there was no drink on him, Peg.'

'I'm not so sure, girl. But he hadn't the suit', said Aunt Peggy.

★

Great-Uncle Vance had brought a parlour chair out by the porch and had lit up a Sweet Afton from a silver cigarette-case. It was the kind of touch of which only

Vance in our family was capable. My grandfather did not even possess a tobacco pouch but kept his supply in the packet in his hat. Vance must have been studying me.

'Geraldine!' He called across to my mother at the rainwater butt. I sensed I was to be the subject of whatever remark was coming and feared he was about to denounce some theft or other on my part.

'Are they something the matter with that child's arm?'

'What?' said my mother.

I assessed the situation for what I might have to reveal. By good fortune, Aunt Finola was not outside - she would be likely to see through any holding back on my part. Vance, I knew, would not get up from his chair and ask to look at my arm or finger.

'Is there something wrong with your arm, Addie? Come over to me.'

'I fell on it. It's not hurting now.'

'When did you fall on it?'

'The day the O'Donoghues came.'

'Move the arm. What happened your finger?'

'I bent it back when I fell. It was much more swollen yesterday.'

'Where did you fall?'

'In Haskins' field.'

'What were you doing in Haskins' field, Addie?'

'I went to see Thady.'

'Thady can shift for himself without you visiting.'

My mother took my bad arm and manipulated it briskly. Tears came to my eyes with the pain of it. I told her it was hurting less than two days ago. She appeared not to have taken in the swelling at the base of my finger. This had somewhat reduced since the day after my fall. Mother went on: ·

'I have a promise made to your father, the Lord have mercy on him, that I would take special care of you, Addie.'

I forgot the pain and began again to hope in my mother at this remark. 'Don't tell Vance', I whispered.

'I won't, boy. But don't go riding that old ass again, sure you won't?'

'No.'

'Is the finger hurting, boy?'

'No.' We both knew it was the kind of lie you were allowed.

'Well 'twill be better before you are married', she said, sending me on my way, but wanting, I thought and hoped, to embrace me like a son, the way she hugged her daughters Lindie and Beebie and Kate.

Twenty-One

In the apple-orchard, Peggy talks of family and of Peter Cody; she pines for him and I for her. A remark of Grandfather's on the road to Rossbeg.

'Bozer, would you ever ask Feena has she a cigarette?' Peg whispered to me that afternoon, when Grandfather had gone into the parlour.

When Grandad was alone in the parlour, he was not to be disturbed and could be there for an hour at a time with his portrait photographs, which he would take down from the mantelpiece and set out on the table. Grandad paid private visits to the parlour as others took flowers to gravesides. I suppose it was because the cemetery, where my late grandmother Maeve and their eldest son Christie lay together, was a good way off at Ballinsaggart.

'What was Christie like?' I had once asked Peggy.

'Christie was our life, boy, for the two years after he getting sick.'

My aunts and uncle generally didn't mind talking about those who had gone before but, with Christie, there was a barrier and all the Driscolls shared a love and a grief private from the rest of the world. Christie could do no wrong. *De mortuis nil nisi bonum*, I grant you, but on the rare occasions when I overheard his name mentioned between them, it seemed to go beyond speaking charitably of the dead; in his last failing months, I now see Christie had given, to each of them, something rich.

This afternoon, however, Grandfather Thomas had gone to his retreat because the parlour was also where he kept his own wireless for the sports commentaries. No women or children were allowed in when Grandad was following the racing because of the occasional intensity of his verbal reactions to the results. Though I never heard him swear in public. It would have been the scent of pipe-smoke from under the parlour door that had set Peggy thinking of cigarettes. I came back down from Feena's room concealing one.

Peggy led me out to the back of the house and beyond the lean-to hay-barn, into the apple-orchard where she and her sister would go for a smoke. We sat in a quiet corner under an ash tree and she lit up, balancing the cigarette between nails that seemed to me then as perfect as pearls. Pearl by nature she was, as the English tinker-prophet who had frightened me with his raptor's fingernails had twice told me: the day I came back from the walk to Kilcreggan Woods to find him dining *al fresco* outside the green half-door and, again, the day I met him in the field under the Lackendarraghs, on our way to the seaside. Peggy put her arm round me and stroked my face with a warm hand.

'Is Feena going to marry Jimmy?' I asked.

With what I already knew, it was a deceitful question, knowingly asked in the sly manner of an adult; I was hunting, again, for Peggy's intentions towards Peter Cody. What I hoped for from her was a place in her heart; if the die was cast, and she went with Peter, I yearned that they would find a space for me; that I would be something to them. But I was sorry the moment the question was out.

'Ask her yourself, boy, why don't you?'

Remorse and a sweet sadness washed over me then; I think I wept.

'Oh, now, now, Bozer. You're a great man. A great man to be looking after your mammy, so you are. Don't everyone say so? Did you get another spin up from Tourmahinch with Peter Cody? I'd say he finds you great company.'

At that point, I thought that if Peggy wanted to talk only about Peter, instead of talking about us, then I would have my own questions answered first, so I wiped my eyes and asked her straight 'Why did Grandad tell me I must never ask him about his suit?'

'It is his wedding suit, Bozer, which he has worn every morning these past five months. He was engaged to be married to the schoolmistress from the National school.'

'Great-Aunt Stacey's school? In Blanchardstown?'

'No, Ballindarragh. Everything was booked for the second of February and all the arrangements made. Only that, three days before the wedding, she went away. Peter got a telegram. The next thing was, he gave Moran the undertaker two pounds to drive round visiting every family on the list and cancelling the invitations.'

'Why did she leave him?'

'Well, now, you can be sure she never told him why. But I'd say it came from her family, when they made their enquiries about Peter's people.'

'And is she still in Ballindarragh?'

'Oh, no, she couldn't stay after that. Ah, sure, it wasn't all her fault. She was a young one from away up-country, not from these parts at all. But the worst cut was, 'tis said she knew who Peter's real father was before he did. Peter was destroyed with that.'

'And is that another cross of his?' I asked mercilessly, relieved that, for all the woes I had brought upon myself, this was not one I had to bear.

'Oh, to be sure', she said quietly. Then she gave me a long look, as if not just Peter, but I, too, were in her mind; she compressed her lips and turned them down at the edges, very grim altogether. It was a look whose meaning only came to me later.

If Peter Cody was not her future, then I longed for Aunt Peggy to tell me she would come and live in England and help look after Mum and us. My responsibility for my mother and sisters, during all the immeasurably long years of growing up ahead of me, seemed an impossible burden, without Peggy. I looked sideways at my aunt and saw her eyes big with tears and so I sat there, picking at the grass, while she smoked on in silence; each of us, it seemed, to deny ourself, or to be denied the one person in the whole world of whom we thought the most.

★

The opportunity of a visit to Rossbeg presented itself two days later, on the Monday. I have already revealed some of the meanings that the town had for me, in that world which I was soon to quit and never to leave. Rossbeg was seven miles from us, by either of two roads, the Blanchardstown or the Tourmahinch, it did not matter. Packie told me that the Blanchardstown road was an easier, more level, ride on a bicycle, but you arrived there by Tourmahinch in just the same time. The town stood on the banks of the Glas and had two crossing points - a modern construction in girders and a four-arched, grey granite medieval bridge. There was a castle and there were three or four churches, in particular St Egidius, where we would go on a feast day; the New Church it was called, though over a hundred years old. There was the one-horse railway station, too, its high-fenced steam-land demesne spellbinding. Spell-breaking too, was steam-land, because it was the portal to my other life out of the dreamtime. The Glas here was a substantial and dignified river, fit for salmon, fish that you could spot from the bridges. Rossbeg was not so far, maybe twenty miles upriver, from Comerford, where the seagoing ships docked and the Glas had become a grand, broad and stately stream, so wide as to be brown no longer but steel-grey, or even blue, as the mood took it.

'Will you take Addie, Daddy?' Peg pleaded to Grandfather Thomas. 'He's mad to go.'

'What's on him to go?'

'He could carry the messages for you.'

'I'll help anyway I can', I proposed.

'He'll help if he can,

All power to the man,

Says Judy McCann',

offered Vance, from the chimney hob, adjusting his denture with his tongue at the same time as he composed.

Grandfather shaved out of an enamel basin at the kitchen table. While he dried out his safety razor against the rust, I gave his Sunday boots a shine. We went up behind the house to call Jellico. He was grazing in a little recinct fenced off from the trees of the haggard. I was sent over to the hurdle gate and half walked it open, half yanked it, a few inches at a time. Because Jellico liked to pull the trap and could see Grandfather behind me in town apparel, which betokened a visit to Tourmahinch or Rossbeg, he came across at a trot. Jellico behaved the same of a Sunday, when the trap was used for chapel. That horse was well aware of the days of the week.

When set alongside the Deegans', our trap was the handsomer conveyance. With Jellico harnessed in, it sat back at a slight rake on its two, five-foot wheels, works of art in themselves. Deegans' trap, if anything, leaned forward, because the piebald Alice was only a pony. We didn't keep ours as smartly polished as the Deegans' vehicle. Even so, my eyes would linger on its beautiful shafts, shallow serpentines, impossibly slender for a diligence capable of carrying six people. Its proportions seemed natural for our road and the many roads like it, with their low walls and hedgerows. In it, we bowled along at a proper height, looking down on motorcars and taking in, perforce, the reek of oil and hot metal they exhaled, as they edged past beside and below us, alien creatures.

We harnessed Jellico. To save the fine wheels, Grandfather led him and the trap empty down through the stones of the yard. At the gates, mother bundled me into the vehicle, after Grandad, through the back door. I located myself up front with him, on the false-leather seat-cushions.

'Good luck now!'

'Good luck!'

The horse set off at a trot down the road towards the avenue and the turn. The trap's vulcanised tyres hummed on the road. I took in Jellico's power and beauty, half-mesmerised by the rhythmical working of his glossy and muscular hindquarters and the scent that came back from his body. I saw my first magpie, *rara avis* in our parts then, that afternoon. 'Fifty-seven was a bounteous summer; the blackberries well on their way, the hay-wagons loading in the fields, the fat quists, ahead of us on the road, so full of early barley they could hardly take to the air as we bowled up to them. It had been a good season for dragonflies and as we crossed Carty's Bridge we drove through a myriad of them, Jellico snorting and flicking his tail and mane. We took the Tourmahinch road for the hour's drive and all the traffic we met was the wool-processors' lorry with a greenish, putrid burden of waste destined for one of the deep shafts at Kilcreggan. Slievegarriff to our backs, we breasted a rise and the last stretch towards Rossbeg unfolded with fresh views to the distant river and the Lackendarraghs far beyond.

'When you were young, did you go to work in Rossbeg, like Packie, Grandad?'

'Why would I? Who would mind the farm?'

'Did you always live at Three Crosses?'

'I did.'

'On our farm?'

'My father before me was born in the Height bedchamber, boy.' (Because it had a high floor, Grandfather's bedroom had never had a planked ceiling fitted, so you looked up at the rafters and thatch. Grandfather pronounced height with a th at the end, by analogy with width and depth.) 'I was born there', he went on, 'in the same bed as my father. And your mother Geraldine came into this world in that exact bed and room. Now.'

The last word was spoken with emphasis, to express the pride and wonder of it all; so he looked to me for a response.

'What about your grandfather?'

"'Twasn't always our land and house. My father, the Lord have mercy on him, got the freehold from the commissioners after he a tenant with thirty years or more.' This point I came to understand later. Grandad passed me Jellico's reins, took off his hat and began to fill his pipe from the envelope of Tiernan's Number 4 he kept there.

'Did Granny come from our parts?'

'From Ballinsaggart road your grandmother came into Three Crosses and back out of Three Crosses, she went to bide in Ballinsaggart field. Do you know the meaning of that, Addie?'

I nodded. He meant the cemetery; Grandmother Maeve had died young. He took off his Sunday hat again and drew out, from the inner band, a small prayer-card. My grandmother's portrait photograph was printed there. It was only the second image of her that I had seen. Maeve Driscoll looked older than her thirty-seven years, baffled by the camera. I searched the bland features for temper and the toughness which I knew was there because Peggy had spoken of it. In vain.

'She came in to Three Crosses and took up her three crosses. And how was the meaning of that?'

I told him I knew. According to Grandfather, everyone got three sufferings. I could think of two of Maeve's. Grandfather put away Grandmother's picture, then looked across at me. 'Be sure now and be a good boy for your mammy; she loves you like a son.'

'She loves me like a son. Why *like* a son? I don't get you, Grandad. She's my mother.'

There was a silence from Grandad as we clip-clopped along. (And how was the meaning of that?) I waited.

'Oh to be sure', he sighed, 'God help us, Addie. Do your mammy be talking to you from time to time?'

The pipe fumes seemed to make Grandfather's eyes water. Tiernan's Tobacco was a plain, Dublin blend, bought loose at Hassetts'; down the years since, the aroma of tobacco, along with the scent of horseflesh, at a circus or a racecourse maybe, has always had the power to fix me instantly on the false-leather cushions in our black trap, that summer's day, fifty years gone, on the sunlit country road to Rossbeg with the shadows of clouds chasing across it, halfway from Slievegarriff to the Lackendarraghs.

The tears began to trickle down my cheeks, too. 'She doesn't talk to me like you or Daddy. When Daddy… She…doesn't…want me… like Lindie and Beebie and Kate. The way… the way she wants them.' The sky clouded over and Grandfather busied himself unfolding the tartan blanket for his legs against the chill. 'Ah, God help us. They are girls, Addie.'Tisn't the same between a mother and her daughters. When you'll be older, you'll understand.'

I did not understand then. Perhaps, reader, in my place, you might have understood. *Like* a son? *Like* a son? Those words had burned into me. I wanted to *be* someone's son. Somebody. I could be anybody. Whobody was I?

Twenty-Two

The road home from Rossbeg: Grandfather Thomas has more news for me.
My father: odi et amo.

In Rossbeg, Uncle Packie's services had been retained by the Main Street offices of the wool-processing plant which was the town's principal employer. Packie lived in a rooming-house above a fishing-tackle shop in one of the late-nineteenth-century, grey side-streets leading down from Main Street to the river and the quays. He could not receive us at his lodgings as he did not have the use of the room during the day. I do not know quite what his occupation was, but he had once told me he spent most of his day shuttling between the offices, the works and the warehouses, though there were some tasks at the mart in the afternoons. The mart was where Grandfather and I went. Packie met us in his working clothes - wellingtons and a brown, buttoned work-coat, like a vet's, with a collar and tie showing above the lapels.

Grandfather's business with Packie concerned, he told me at the time, livestock we might be sending to the mart in the autumn. (A conversation I heard a few days later, between Packie and my mother, modified this perception, giving inklings of coming change.) It turned out that his main purpose that afternoon was a visit to the solicitors in connection with his will.

At any rate, Grandfather Thomas and Uncle Packie left Jellico and the trap outside the mart office and decided to go to the Toberenagh Tearooms on the Main Street to talk. I was invited to stretch my legs in the direction of a sweetshop in the meantime. I walked part of the way with them to the teashop. There they parted with me and with two pence, on my promise to be back at the Tearooms when the Abbey clock struck the hour. In most children, there is no pain that sweets cannot assuage. I wanted to blot out the conversation I had had with Grandfather Thomas in the trap. I had reached the limit of my capacity to dwell on that searing remark 'she loves you *like* a son.' There were half a dozen shop windows to be investigated before I reached the confectioners' and, on the way there, I lost myself contemplating displays of enamelled hardware, smokers' perquisites and wireless sets.

'You, sir, how is your mother? A great deal better now, I'm sure.' The speaker blocked my way on the pavement outside Powers' The Premier Confectionery. Though hatless, he had on a grey, pepper-and-salt, double-breasted suit and a collar and tie. He stood too close to me and smelt of rubberised fabric and indigestion. When he brought his face down near to mine I could see the scurf on his faint eyebrows. 'And your Aunt Margaret? I was delighted when I heard she got honours in her Leaving Cert. and you, boy, are to tell her that.'

'Yes sir.' I was addressing George Barrett, the schoolmaster from Blanchardstown, the hater of the English (and therefore of me) and expert on the pilgrims' stones of the Shanaun. I stepped back, not wanting to catch his breath. Perhaps there had been no malice in his comment about my mother's choice of marriage-partner but, with my father the best of Englishmen that ever lived, I would never trust him. I noted yet another enquiry after Peg. Barrett belonged to that ubiquitous, pernicious minority of schoolteachers who dislike children, or perhaps boys; I would meet one or two more like him in the years to come.

'Sit up there now and guard the butter-box', said Grandad. The butter-box was a heavy piece of joinery, in weathered, grey beechwood, whose lid was hinged with a strip of bicycle tyre. Grandad had constructed it in his youth and never travelled without it. It kept the sun off the butter he brought home from the creamery.

'What's in it?'

'Look for yourself.'

'Ham! Is it for our tea?'

'Begor it is', said Grandad, letting Jellico slow to a walk on the long haul up the incline out of Rossbeg on the road back. 'Tisn't as good as our own, though, boy. I have a pig to kill a Monday week.'

For a while I sat with my back to Jellico, looking back down the winding road we had come, over the smoking chimneys of thatched farmhouses, at the huddles of buildings and streets strung out along the Glas. Across the river, the wool processors' waste-lorry was back at the works. Next to the factory stood the sheds where they stored the wool that came up from the Lackendarraghs to the south. Outside the town, again on the far bank, at the head of the old bridge, I saw the ruined castle of the Montallonds. Once a fine, Elizabethan manor, it was pillaged after The Breffni Montallond had tried to hold it against Cromwell. The Breffni, the last of the Montallonds, according to my mother, threw himself to his death from the parapets of the roof, when a stray musket ball took his wife. I took in the brown Glas at her low summer ebb and the second bridge in grey iron girders that was built after the Partition of Ireland. I heard the soft tolling of the six o'clock bell of the New Church with its rose window and bell-tower, striated in the Italian fashion with courses of brick and Connemara marble; I saw the protestant Abbey Church that was begun even before the Montallonds became masters in these lands. Such was Rossbeg.

The weather had brightened up again during the late afternoon and promised a pleasant drive home. We were on the quieter road back to Three Crosses. It took you the last few miles of the Great Vale from the Glas to our parts in the eastern foothills of Slievegarriff and Tourmahinch. The road out of the Vale would eventually become our road, that led up past our maroon gates in Three Crosses by way of the gap to Kilcreggan and Coole and points beyond, to the north.

With the respect due to Jellico's eighteen years, Grandad pulled him over for a few moments' rest, after we had breasted the top of the slope. I turned to contemplate the 'Garriff with Grandfather Thomas. Jellico's head went down to the grass of the verge. The cairn nipple on our grand mountain was sharp against the evening sky and her western flanks were doused in golden light. Grandfather got out of the trap and sat down on the verge ahead of the horse. He flicked his black briar pipe to the side of his mouth and held out his arms to me, as he had not done for a while now. Nine-year-old that I was, even so, I sat up on his lap, as uncomfortably for me as for him, knowing that he had something to say. I could see his bony knees through his trousers. What was in his mind? I sensed that he wanted to finish some business with me.

'When you'll come back to Three Crosses, Slievegarriff will be there alright, but, one summer, you mightn't see me no more.'

'Why?'

'Now', began Grandad, and paused to make sure he was on the right tack with me, 'because I could be gone back to Ballinsaggart after Maeve.'

I didn't respond, neither wanting to nor knowing how. So Grandad made the connection for me. 'Your father was a great man, so he was. A man to have been head of a family. Did your mammy ever tell you that?'

'I don't want you to go back to Ballinsaggart or to Heaven. Where Daddy is, when I wanted him here. At least, I have you.'

'God forgive me, little fellow, but I couldn't be easy in my mind not to be talking to you now about myself and yourself. When your mammy, that loves you like her own, married your father over in Tourmahinch, it was a grand day. Did you ever see the wedding picture in the parlour?'

'Yes', I said, shifting position on Grandad's lap.

'Mind my bad knee. Your uncle from England and your grandmother weren't in the picture at all, sure they weren't?'

'No.'

'And how was that, do you suppose?'

'They didn't want to come;'(I knew that well enough). 'They couldn't come.'

'Well now', (he took my hand and I had a premonition about what he would say) 'they wouldn't come, maybe because your poor, dear father was a married man before he marrying Geraldine.'

I sat very still as the words broke over me, not burning me this time, but washing something away and seeping down into my being. I knew more was coming. I braced myself for what Grandfather Thomas might say next.

'We never saw your father's first wife, Addie. But, we'll say, we knew they had a grand babby. A beautiful, tiny, baby boy called Adameen. Will you think of that, Addie? Adameen?'

'Stop it. Let me go!'

Grandfather Thomas was looking away again to the 'Garriff, our mountain that had been his daily horizon for nearly seventy years, to see would she give him peace of mind. He had released his embrace, but I could not move.

'Granddaddy, Granddaddy. It's not true. I am Mummy's. She loves me. I don't believe that story.'

'Adameen…'

'I'll never believe that story. I knew what you were going to say. Lies, Grandad. Why are you repeating them? Tell the truth and shame the devil.' I knew I was but making a noise, though I spoke in language adults would use. As we would say today, I could not process what I was hearing; I was in denial; I had nowhere to go.

'It isn't blaggarding you I am, God love you, Addie. You are Geraldine's boy, your mammy's boy, sure to God you are. 'Twas she adopted you, boy, to rear you, when your first mother could not, there in Liverpool.'

'It's a stupid story. Tell the truth and shame the devil', I blustered.

'My little Addie. My own dear grandson Adameen, that I took to myself the moment I set eyes on you, boy. Why would I be lying to you in the winter of my years, God help me. Oh God help me. Answer me, boy.' His voice was unfamiliar, cracking, breaking.

I had nothing to give.

'Well, the devil sweep you, anyway!' said Grandfather Thomas. He tipped the dottle from the pipe and produced a handkerchief which he applied to his eyes. 'Do you see Slievegarriff over there, the way she looks out over all the land and all types and all comers?

'Yes.'

'Will you show me your hand?'

'Alright.'

'Hold up your hand that way.'

It seemed partly a distracting game but, dismally and mechanically, I imitated his action, shading off Slievegarriff and the low, cloudy, western sunlight from my vision. Now I had no tears, only confusion, a fearful premonition fulfilled, anger. 'A fellow could put his hand up against the light and he wouldn't see Slievegarriff at all. He mightn't like her but she don't go away.'

'Can I put my hand down?'

'Why?'

'My arm aches.' It was the arm I had fallen on when Thady threw me. 'The fellow could…'

'He could, but a lad that was cute, would not be mad at what he couldn't change. He would look at it in the face. Faith he would.'

I had no tears and felt worse for it.

'Now show me your hand again.' He took my hand and brought it up to his neck. He ran my hand over the tanned skin of his neck and jaw. I thought it would feel like hide, but it was chamois and under it a hard swelling, a ball, something there like the feel of my own eyeball under the skin of the lid.

I took my hand away. 'What is it?'

'Well, now, Addie', Grandad stroked the lump in his turn, 'we'll say this, if it is a cancer, it could put me back soon enough in Ballinsaggart alongside of Maeve and

Christie, God love him. You were the spit of my boy Christie and he a baby. Faith you were.' Grandfather began to get to his feet. 'I took to you the minute I saw you, Addie, boy.'

★

When we drew in through the maroon gates, my mother, sisters and Feena were at the top of the yard, folding bedsheets outside the porch. Lindie and Beebie had their backs to us.

Grandad made an attempt to win a smile from me, winking as he put his finger to his lips. He moistened his forefinger and middle with spit and blew on them to make them cold. He touched the bare calf of Lindie's leg with the tip of the wet fingers, barking sharply like Punch from Dempseys'. My sister let out a yelp and leapt into Feena's arms.

That Grandfather Thomas's life was in danger was the rational expectation, yet - I cannot explain how I knew this - not the reality that would come to pass. I gave the part of our conversation relating to the lump in his neck little further thought. I did not believe Grandfather Thomas would be taken from me. Thus it transpired; for the tumour shrank, though it never disappeared, and he lived another fifteen years with only occasional recurrences of his other ailment, the bronchitis.

That night on the landing, under the thatch that kept out the night sounds from the yard and the fields, it was my departed father who shut out all other reflections. Peggy had put the bulb back into its socket for me and the light was on. Though I was two-thirds of the way through *Robinson Crusoe* and at the point where Crusoe and Friday have built and rigged a boat, I could not read on. I was drawn back to the first chapter, and to Robinson's dialogues with his father.

'*I observed the tears run down his face very plentifully, especially when he spoke of my brother who was killed; and that, he was so moved that he broke off the discourse, and told me his heart was so full he could say no more to me. I was sincerely affected with this discourse; as, indeed, who could be otherwise? And I resolved not to think of going abroad any more, but to settle at home according to my father's desire.*'

My own father's last desire? 'Daddy said he's waiting and don't be long.' Don't be long. What had possessed me to precipitate, as I undoubtedly had through my disobedience over the aspirins, the morning he died, my own and others' misery? What had I done? I put away *Robinson Crusoe* under the boxwood lattice of my army bed. I found a farmers' magazine I had forgotten to smuggle back to Deegans'. There was no peace there: an article on shepherding outlined the known techniques for rearing lambs rejected by the ewes.

That night, within the deep texture of guilt and of love for my father, anger had congealed into a hard little nodule of hatred. All mental pathways led back to him, whose glance, whose brilliantined hair, whose arched eyebrow, whose brown forearms, whose lithe body, whose way of cleaning his spectacles, whose contemplative stroking of his cheeks after he had shaved I remembered as facets of an especial excellence. *My* father, to whom I had thrilled when he called me by name, my father...with all the attributes of a hero, my father had yet concealed from me who I really was. A few hours earlier, Grandfather Thomas had proffered me a bitter chalice and an impossible test of my love and loyalty. Until that moment when I had sat on his lap at the verge of the road on the rise out of Rossbeg, I had been a son; now I must learn to be *like* one. I was baffled, and repelled, by this world of men and women of which I was not yet a part.

In the years to come, at night, in the hours of truth, I would seek out this knot of hatred within my love, teasing and picking at it with questioning, always beginning with 'why?' Why did you not tell me? To this day, in my sixtieth year, questions of any kind about motives, of the form 'why did you …?' whether directed to me or to someone else in my presence, bring out anxiety and the memory of pain. *Souffrir passe; l'avoir souffert jamais.* I wet the bed again that night. My mother quietly changed the sheets, keeping my shame to herself. My mother, did I say? Whose boy was I? I loved my father all the more strongly for the fact that the small seed of rage in me against him had germinated.

Twenty-Three

Death in the afternoon. Malice, cruelty, forgiveness.

The men were going to slaughter one of our home-reared bonhams, not (as it happened) one of those we had acquired from Panloaf. The condemned animal had escaped into the front yard while being led from his pen to the ash-tree gibbet near the mangold-grinder, behind the house. He was standing foursquare on the slate churn-stand, looking down at the maroon gates which barred him from the road. The bonham turned his head towards me and scrutinised me with his pink eyes. He was grown to a good size and I kept my distance. Only he and I were in the yard, until my mother came out from the house by the half-door.

The bonham suspected his hour had come and knew where the danger lay, so he ignored my mother and me. She took me gently by the wrist and led me back into the house. I extricated myself from her grip, once over the threshold, and sneaked back outside to watch. Packie and Liam Deegan came down from the outhouses behind the dairy. Vance followed but wouldn't be chasing. When Packie and Liam went across to the slate stand, the bonham skipped off and made a dash for the furthest corner of the yard, by the kindling-stack. He was cornered there and started to scream. I hoped his terror would be over quickly. Liam made a dive for him and battened on to his hind quarters like a rugby tackler, avoiding his jaws. The screaming reached a higher intensity. Vance came up with two hessian potato-sacks, from the dairy, to put over the victim's head, but warily, as he could not afford the loss of any more fingers.

There was a wrought-iron double gate, to the back of the house and to the outhouses, which the men never closed. On this occasion it was closed. Despite their robust attitude to creation and death's part in it, they even so kept us back from watching the slaying at close quarters. We were told white lies about the men being busy and not wanting us in their way. There was neither shame nor guilt, nor cruelty nor beauty in what they did to the bonham. But there was a touch of honour in the rich moment of the pig's passing. In those days, such occasions, like those of generation, birth and the high moments of religion, were for them who had come of age.

Peg came up behind us from the house. She leaned on the gate next to me. I hopped up onto the first bar to be nearer her level. She had been to Bridget Reynolds that morning. Bridget, like some barber of old, was known both to cut hair and to give injections (for rheumatism and for ringworm, chiefly), though no one knew what licence or sanction she had for the latter practice.

'What's at you?' said Peg, when she caught me looking at her hair, albeit she knew.

I wasn't sure whether I liked the new style. I tried to make my mind up before the next question. The smooth curve of Peggy's neck had been accentuated by the application of Bridget's scissors to the more wayward curls. I touched her hair. Perhaps it had been lacquered. It felt so different from my own lank and sweaty strands - my mane too long, now that I had no father to cut it.

'Bozer, will you leave be my poor bit of wool!' But her words belied her and took me back to the year before, the morning of my departure for Blanchardstown National School. Mother had pleaded urgently to Father as I stood in our porch, unhappily clutching the blue satchel. 'Roy, catch the brush, will you, and go at that child's hair? He has a head on him like a furze-bush. He'll have a show made of me with Aunt Stacey this morning.' How gently Daddy had restored order to my coiffure; then we had walked down to the maroon road-gate to meet my guide, Busty.

We could see the bonham, dangling on the gibbet by a cord from its back legs, with the curl gone out of its tail and the ribcage uncovered, at the end of the clean cut by which it had been eviscerated. Feena had the white enamel basin cradled to her apron as she stirred the blood, already lumpy, for the black puddings. On the spattered barley straw the blood rapidly darkened from scarlet to crimson. Near the creature's head was an aluminium gallon with some of the intestines in it, the colour of spilt milk. Our bonham, its eyes closed in death, seemed, nevertheless, to have a smile for us. It seemed to say: 'in the moment between two heartbeats, the path out of the forest opened; I have completed everything; your turn will come.'

Peg had a little vanity-mirror which she held away from me on the other side of her face, so as to see how Bridget's cut had turned out at the back. I guessed her thoughts were trickling in the direction my own were taking. 'Are you lonesome, Bozer?' she said, without turning. I would know what she meant.

'Yes.'

She didn't pressure me by looking back into my face and I was content to gaze at the luxuriant black curls of her hair and her beautiful neck, oblivious for those moments of my sisters and of the dark business around the bonham.

'Do you like my hair, Bozer?' she whispered, and I caught a glimpse of an eye on me in her mirror.

'Yes', I breathed, desperate for her not to turn and face me.

She snapped the mirror shut in its case and let out a tinkle of laughter. 'Good! But Bridget is a great one for the cutting, so she is. She cut hair there for a while for Harriet DB. Would you credit that? There will be a grand bit of ham now from that poor bonham. With a good bit of fat. Is there ever a bit of fat on you, Bozer? Wait till I see…sure, you're skin and bone and nothing else!' Her arm came round my waist for a moment to tickle me and draw me into her side.

Packie and Vance had their backs to the gate out of the wind and suddenly we heard the roar of the brass blowtorch opening up with the force of a minor explosion. Packie whisked the flame up and down over the cadaver and the miasma of singed bristles came down on the still air to me - the same scent as when I had burnt my eyebrows at the Dogs' Hole, playing with the burners on my steam boat, the Small Ship *Irrawaddy*.

'Go off now about your business, let ye', said Packie, looking across at us and turning down the blowlamp. 'Peggy, be minding them children.' Peggy gathered us around her and moved us back towards the house. Over our shoulders, we saw Vance manhandle the gate open for Feena to come through, with her basin of blood. 'On your way, now, with them children', said Vance to Peg. The high-handed manner to my aunt set me thinking how blind Packie and Vance sometimes seemed to her goodness. A Pearl before three swine.

Vance had the four trotters, crubeens, in his good hand. Formerly, the pig's trotters had always gone to Vance, the only Driscoll who would eat them. But then he lost half of his own crubeen to Hughie Heaphy's chainsaw; now he couldn't abide the look of them, so these were destined for the table of old Agius Reynolds.

*

We had three sources of water at Three Crosses Farm. There was a rainwater butt near the house for washing clothes. Outside the porch stood a cast-iron pump, painted green like the half-door, and, at the end of the yard, near the maroon road-gate, a good way from the porch and the half-door, there was a standpipe served, even in the 'fifties, by some kind of proto-plastic tubing which emerged, serpent-like, from the gravel and detritus at the bottom of the yard. Day and night, its tap spasmodically hissed and pissed, issuing spring-water, though with a metallic taste. This latter source served the cow-house for ablutions to their udders before and after the cows were milked and for rinsing the milking buckets. Uncle Packie was milking all eight cows that morning, which entailed a series of journeys to and from the standpipe.

I had the anger in me and I was idle. I began to bait Uncle Packie, each time he walked to the tap, with catcalls and chants. I employed some of the playground ditties I had learnt at Pius the Twelfth, while working in material of my own composition as well.

'Poor old Pascal

What a rascal!'

Out-Vancing Vance, but disdaining metre, I went on:

'The cows wouldn't let their milk down,

When they saw his ugly frown.'

I was aware, in my cruelty, that my uncle was a less dexterous milker than Feena or Peggy. Lindie and Beebie passed me on their way behind the house to their den under the horse-chestnuts. They had their dollies under their arms. Lindie told me to shut up.

Suddenly, Uncle Packie spun round, dropping his empty bucket with a clang and looking straight at me. What was it that I had said that tipped the balance? I don't remember. But I knew in an instant that I had over- applied the needle. It had found the nerve. The fear clutched at me. The brightness of my uncle's eyes and the black look of him unnerved me.

I ran, as I had never run, from the cow-house arch across the yard, leaping the logs at the edge of the kindling-stack, racing up the gravel to the green half-door in my dash to the captain's chair in the hob by the fire, before Packie laid a hand on me. We both knew violence was intended. With the temper on him, he might hit me much harder than he wanted. He would injure me or worse. The catcall phrase I had used - what in it had stung Packie? All this I seemed to be weighing up in those few seconds, as I pelted back to Grandad, hoping he was on his captain's chair.

He was. I crashed down on the tiles beside the chair under Grandad's stick arm. Had he not been there, I doubt my mother could have protected me.

'Ah Pascal, leave the child alone', said Grandad, half-irritated and half-interested.

'The devil is in him, looking crooked at me.' Uncle Packie came to a dead stop. 'And he busting laughing.'

I sat there under Grandad's arm, with a half-smile towards my uncle, pretending it was a game. But I had the palpitations in me and I would have looked white. There, in the semi-darkness under the hob, no-one could see. Mother, kneading the soda bread, looked across from the table and gave out to me for dashing into the kitchen so dangerously. She hadn't detected the real danger. Packie looked at me for a moment, his gorge down now. Then he turned away. Out he marched, his wellingtons squeaking on the tiled square round the fire.

I sneaked upstairs onto the landing to be on my own and dwell on the lesson learnt.

★

Gratuitous spite was to bite back at me, too, in the ebbing weeks of that summer. Joe Gandy walked down one morning through Three Crosses on his way to school. He had a hard face for a twelve-year-old. From my perch, on the top bar of the maroon gate looking out over our road, I caught his glance. His nose ran with a summer cold. His eyes were blue, bleary, bitter, red-rimmed. But he fixed me with two black pupils shrunk to tiny points in the sunlight. His mouse-coloured hair presented itself exactly as in the (hitherto, I had judged, rather improbable) Thomas Henry drawings of unkempt schoolboys in the *William* books I had taken to reading at home. Joe had all but passed our road gate when he said:

'How're you?'

'How're you?' said I.

'What have you on your back, boy?'

It was the gun I had made, out of a scrap of packing wood. I had ground up a chip of blue slate into a powder and mixed it with pig-fat to make a paint for the barrel. The *Sheepman of Ireland* had said that this was a paint-making technique employed by prehistoric cave-artists. My weapon had a bark-leather strap which I had cut from one of the ash saplings in the orchard. I had cured it with tea-liquor and finished the job with boot polish.

'What gun is that?'

'It's meant to be a Winchester.'

It wasn't of course, but because the description would have no meaning for Joe Gandy, I hoped it might deter further enquiry.

'Show me a look at it', said Joe.

'It's a model really.' I knew Joe Gandy wasn't interested in models.'

'Show the gun', said Joe.

The late-bell carilloned from the school a mile away down the Blanchardstown road, so I said: 'Are you sure you have you the time?'

'Show the gun', said Joe.

I unslung the weapon from my shoulder and handed it across the gate.

'Watch the trigger-guard. I haven't quite finished it.'

'Oh, yes', said Joe Gandy, putting down his satchel at the roadside for a moment.

He took my toy straight to his scab-shot right knee, paused and gave me a sly look. Then he snapped it to two pieces, wrapping them together with the bark strap and tossing them over the gate and into the kindling-stack for me to collect.

'The barrel was no fecking good', he explained, and I remember clutching at the remark as some kind of mitigation of his malice.

'Show the belt', he said, indicating my navy, elasticated, school belt. His own breeches were suspended from homemade braces.

'Show the belt.'

My mother called down to me from the green half-door.

Gandy jerked his satchel back up on his shoulder and strode on down towards the avenue, as if proving the gun for me had indeed been a great favour. I went back up to the yard to the dairy. I locked myself inside. I searched the gloom, eyes brim-full, for the tools and scrap-wood I would need to craft a new weapon.

★

Thpoth, as Vance had once called her when he had his teeth out, had five kittens and was mainly tortoiseshell. Partly because none of her markings could properly be described as a spot but also because Vance's lisped version of her name gave faint redolence of Ancient Egypt and its sacred cats, we children adopted the appellation. Thpoth lived on the Deegans' property, where she was rearing her offspring; her visits to our farm were infrequent, the more so after she had nearly been throttled by Lindie innocently picking her up by the neck when she was half-grown and Lindie was six.

Thpoth was not a fortunate cat. Unlike Zulu, the black tom, who was lazy and ate well, Thpoth was put upon and bony; she had at least two kinks in her tail from past entanglements with dogs or doors. She had a ragged right ear that looked as if it had been nibbled by caterpillars, like one of Vance's cabbages, but which Liam Deegan said she had got in an encounter with a stoat. Her cast of face gave her a slightly cross expression. But though she looked as if she might be temperamental or standoffish, it was shyness, really, and I always found Thpoth equable enough when she appeared in our front yard of a sunny afternoon, to warm her bones on the churn-stand. Then it was not difficult to get her to purr.

She let me stroke her a couple of times and I ran my hand down her knobbly spine to her hindquarters, which set her tail flicking and twitching with pleasure. Her eyes closed, her expression transmuted from crusty to seraphic, and she began to purr. As long as Lindie did not arrive, there was a good chance that Thpoth would sit there for a few more minutes. I considered slipping up to the dairy to fetch the cart. But if Lindie showed while I was away, Thpoth would vanish. So I scooped up Thpoth under one arm and carried her off to the dairy, in a dark corner of which, behind the bicycles, I had secreted the toy cart, with its new shafts. Vetting my surroundings carefully against the presence of adults, I slipped back out of the dairy with the miniature vehicle and its paraphernalia under the other arm and trotted off to a secluded part of the orchard. By now, Thpoth was bored with being carried and was wriggling.

I had anticipated some resistance from Thpoth when the moment came to secure her to the cart by means of the tackle I had prepared. In the event, she was quite obliging, allowing me to settle the bridge-strap of bark-leather across her back and fasten the baling-twine strapping around her chest. Throughout, she looked happy enough or, at least, no crustier than normal. But she was unwilling to do more than crouch there between the shafts with her chin on her front paws, looking straight ahead. She displayed not the least curiosity towards the cart behind her, nor towards the harness she was wearing. She appeared quite unconcerned. She would not, however, provide traction. A gentle hand shoving at her bottom made no difference. Pushing the cart itself from behind in an effort to jump-start Thpoth was an equally fruitless endeavour.

In order for both Thpoth and me to enjoy ourselves properly, she would have to be persuaded to draw the cart. So I stood up and tugged sharply at the cart from the front, over her head, using the long drawstring. This made Thpoth angry and she hissed at me. Intimidated, fearful that Thpoth would scrawb or even bite me if I bent down towards her, I took a step backwards. Thpoth promptly shot off and disappeared down the orchard, half out of the shafts, hissing and spitting, dragging the cart bouncing and sliding after her in a quite unsatisfactory manner. I followed ruefully in her wake. In our front yard, I soon caught up with the debris. I collected three wheels, an axle and a shaft, together with the remains of the cart. I put these precious resources into temporary storage under the kindling-stack near the maroon front gates.

*

Liam Deegan said to me of *Robinson Crusoe*: 'I think that must be a great book. I saw the film of it all right and I not much older than yourself. I have another book like it in the house by a fellow called Ballantyne. Any day now I'll find it and you'll have it to read for yourself.' We were sitting together on the churn-stand in Deegans' yard. I had let myself out by the maroon gates onto our road, walked up towards Kilcreggan and chanced on their road gates open. Liam had a tray with a fire-blackened aluminium pot of tea beside him, left out by his sister Josie.

Josie came out from their front door a moment later with two more cups and a plate of buttered barmbrack. 'I know you got your bite of breakfast, Addie', Josie said, 'but you could help out now with this bit of cake.' Her barmbrack was better than ours, I thought. The secret was that she put a dash of cinnamon in it, because that was the way Edward the retro-smiler, their priest brother in the States, liked it. He had brought her five years' supply of the spice on his last visit from Sacramento. The cinnamon was stored in a tea-caddy on the dressing-table in his room; it set me wondering into what kind of a person he had been turned by his exile. 'Father is coming home next year, please God', she said, as if reading my thoughts. We sipped at our tea.

We faced across towards their cow-house. Though more capacious, it was a much less imposing construction than ours, which was ashlar-built and had 1869 engraved in the keystone of its archway. The ill-fitting, grey-painted double-doors to theirs left a gap of a few inches under the lintel. This gave access to the swallows. 'Isn't it a miracle now, Addie, the way the same swallies come home every year from Africa?' I knew she wished her brother was also an annual visitor.

What was equally miraculous was the aerial accomplishment of these birds, (in retrospect, it was house martins they were), wheeling in the air above us and swooping, hurtling, through the gap over the doors, every few minutes, to the nest they had inside the cow-house.

'That swallies' nest is in it since I was a girl', Josie said, reading my thoughts again.

"Twouldn't be there now, boys, if we were in China', said Liam. 'They'd have soup made out of it by now, so they would.'

He looked at me slyly, I think to see if my stomach was turning. Liam was known in Three Crosses for his daily Paris oyster: he would feel in the nesting alcoves in that cowshed for a fresh hen's egg before his tea; this he would keep warm for an hour under his hat. Later, at the tea-table, his hat on his head in breach of custom, he would reach up, retrieve the egg, crack the shell in one hand and down the contents at a gulp. One evening in Deegans' kitchen last year Liam had put a warm fresh egg in front of me to see if I would follow suit. I had retched inwardly. 'Don't mind him, Addie', Mary had said. "Tis blaggarding you he is. Put it in your pocket there for Mammy to boil for your tea.'

'Come on, till we look at the rabbits', Josie said to me, as Liam drained his cup and picked up his sprong. We went by way of the house as she had to fetch a little milk and a bag of carrot-tops. I sat down in their chimney-corner on a springy, leather-finished car-seat like Vance's, next to the fire-blower. I noticed that they had a proper leather belt for their blower-wheel, rather than the adapted bicycle tyre which we used.

When Josie came back to the hob she asked me to carry the gallon with the milk. Then she showed me something else she had in her hand. I recognised the remains of the harness in bark-leather and baling twine which I had so carefully created for Thpoth.

'Addie, I found the poor red cat in our hay-barn in a bad way with this yoke round her feet and her neck.'

I blushed with the shame of it.

'I know you had the notion to get her to pull a little wagon for you. But that's not God's way with cats, sure it isn't? Some creatures He made as beasts of burden alright. But the poor Puss was made to catch rats and mice, so she was.'

'Is she alright?'

'Ah she is now', she said, and that was the end of it. The harness blazed up yellow for a few seconds when I put it on the fire, and Josie took me to look at the rabbits.

Twenty-Four

Peter Cody visits again. The Hunt Ball. The return of the native.

On Saturday, Peter Cody came up slowly from the front yard. My eyes sought for him to look at me as he passed, but on this occasion he had nothing for me. When he walked he had a habit of inclining his head to one side as if he always had to counterbalance a heavy pail. He wore a navy-and-scarlet check shirt close to his torso like a film cowboy, and went without braces because his trousers fitted at the waist. The sleeves of the shirt were furled midway up his brown forearms. Subconsciously, I rolled mine to the same position.

'Well, Peter', said Grandfather.

'Well, Thomas', said Peter Cody, offering Grandfather a Sweet Afton from the breast pocket of his shirt and taking one for himself from behind his ear. Grandfather resumed a conversation begun two mornings previously at the creamery.

'Well, now, we'll say, how many cows is Dempsey milking?'

'Eighteen, or maybe twenty. A good few, anyway.'

'Well, now, we'll say, did you see the machine going? And the milking-parlour. Is that what he calls it?'

'I did. 'Tis a wonder alright.'

'He put up th' old shed himself.' (Grandad referred to the new shed.) 'What did he give for the machines, I wonder?'

'Will I ask Grehan?'

'Ah, sure, no. It would be better to leave a leg on it, so it would. 'Tisn't that Jimmy wouldn't know, like. But he wouldn't want to be talking about Dempsey or his milking-machine. I'm telling you, he was scalded not to get the business off of Dempsey.'

That summer of impending change, Grandfather had seen a day coming when he would need to rear and milk more cows. With my aunts maybe marrying out of the farm and no knowing what my widowed mother's or even Packie's intentions were, he could not count on the labour in-house to hand-milk a bigger herd.

They walked off a few yards and spread out the mangold-sacks on the grass, up against the stone dyke between us and Deegans' paddock. They sat down to smoke at ease, looking down through their tobacco haze to Tourmahinch, its chapel, St Camillus' and the Lackendarraghs across the Vale fifteen miles beyond.

'Well, Peggy', Peter called out at length.

'How're you, Peter?'

She had, in the meantime, taken in how Peter was and indeed everything about him, out of the corner of her eye; she had been caught slightly as she would not have wished to be by Peter's visit, flushed with the hard labour of turning the crank of the mangold-grinder for Grandfather. The men were watching her while she threw the last of the mangolds for the cows into the cast-iron hopper, two at a time.

Peter stopped smoking and got to his feet. He went down to the mangold-grinder and took over the handle while Peggy switched buckets. Feena came up to collect the last one, brimming with yellow chips. She said nothing to Peter. Perhaps they had already spoken at the gate. Feena, not unfriendly, took me by the wrist and directed me back to the front yard, now that my work was done. But I loitered, fascinated by Peter, the suffering, handsome young hero who had offered me something like friendship.

Thady sensed that the last of the load was off the cart so, looking to get out of harness, he walked on; Grandfather got up and followed the vehicle down the slope of the back yard to the lean-to, where the carts were kept out of the rain. I heard Peter say: 'Peggy! Peggy, will you come down to Comerford with me in September?'

'Why would I?'

'I hadn't right to ask you to Sheehans that time, Peggy. You are above that place.'

'Comerford? Is it the Hunt Ball you are asking me to?'

'I have the ticket bought.'

'And if I said no to you, Peter?'

'I'll stay at home for myself, so I will, Peggy. I won't bother you again. And I'll make you a present of the ticket for you to give to anyone you please.'

'If I went with you', her eyes followed the creaking ass-and-car, 'Daddy will ask how you will get me home.'

'Tony Drennan, sure.' Tony drove one of the two motor-taxis in Rossbeg. Such a conveyance represented real luxury, if not decadence.

★

In consenting to go to the Hunt Ball with Peter in eight weeks' time, Peggy was consenting to walk out with him and no other in the intervening period; which was why Peter drove down from Coole in his late father's trap and appeared at our gate the next Friday evening.

Lindie and Beebie were being washed for bed and I had not yet been called in for my own ablutions. *Robinson Crusoe* awaited me on my landing; in the meantime, I had my second wooden gun with me and stood on the top bar of the maroon gates. The gates became my ironwood stockade, all that protected me in the cave of my solitary existence from the dangers of the island at large. I was presenting my piece against the leader of a native war-party. The canoe by which they invaded my island and my peace of mind was, in my fantasy, moored in the miniature swamp down our road at the entrance to Reynolds' lane. Diamond, in the shafts of the Codys' trap, trotted downhill from the direction of Kilcreggan and Coole. As he approached, he slowed to the walk and drew up. In the east, the heavens were fast blackening, with a low dark blanket of cloud south to north over half the sky, like a pall, but flaring bright along its ragged front, where the sun struck at it from Slievegarriff behind us. I could make out Peter wearing a good brown chalkstripe suit, with a white shirt open at the collar and an English peaked cap of a cut you didn't see on a farmer in those days.

'Well, Addie, how're you? Show the gun.' He put my rifle to his shoulder with the panache of a marksman and picked off a coyote. He looked again along the barrel and pretended to try the weapon for balance.

'That's some class of a gun, alright. With a strap and all. You had right to make a holster for it.'

'Tomorrow I might.'

He passed me up my weapon.

'Will you guard the Deadwood Stage for me, Addie, until I go up and speak to your Aunt Peggy.'

I got down and unbarred the gate. Peter, in his good shoes, hopped across the puddles at the foot of the gate and then crunched on up the gravel of the front yard to the green half-door. Feena came out from the kitchen to the door like a barmaid and offered him the sup of tea out of a Royal Worcester cup and saucer. He took it standing outside the porch of our house, while she went back inside to drink hers. Peter set his cup and saucer down carefully to one side on the concrete plinth of the porch. As he straightened himself up slowly, Peggy, who had appeared at the door, watched him intently. I caught, in those seconds, a fraction of the meaning he had for her; a tide of happiness for them both swept over me, but also, and contemporaneously, I luxuriated in melancholy and foreboding.

'Let me sit up in the trap behind Diamond.'

'Another time, pet', said Peggy.

Unlike ours, the Codys' trap was fitted with carriage lamps. Fine lamps, but not so beautiful as one of Packie's treasures which I coveted, the *King of the Road* acetylene-carbide bicycle-lamp. Diamond drew away. I ran out on the road behind the trap for a few yards, lest Peggy and Peter drive out of my world utterly and into one of their own, where there would be no further use nor meaning for me. I called after them: 'It's dangerous! Light the lamps, light the lamps...'

After a second or two, as if he had heard me and listened, Peter pulled Diamond over, before they reached the avenue where Dempseys' long orchard fence began. I suppose he got out his cigarette-lighter. I saw the flickers and then the yellow glow of the candles lit.

Diamond jogged off again down the road and towards the avenue, with the red spy-lights of the lamps glowing and jiggling to his clip-clop, as the silhouette of the trap and its occupants played tricks with my straining eyes and melted into the blackness under the trees.

★

'Josie told me', said Peggy, 'that Father Ed was coming home for a month. Did you know that?'

'What?' said my mother.

'Tis next year he's coming, girl.'

'Tis next week, girl.'

'What's bringing him back out of California?'

'He has a wedding. A big wedding upcountry in County Dublin. An American girl, I'm thinking.'

Father Ed appeared at Deegans' half-door with a sister on each side of him. I think he came home on the aeroplane. He gave me a wave. I was mildly shocked to see the top half of him in a red-and-gold open-necked Hawaiian shirt. He was shorter than Liam, bald and tanned. Another kind of hobo, Father Ed was an exile in a cause. He had been eighteen years in the States, first as an Army chaplain and now a parish priest. He had been home for the summer on three occasions in that time. But he wrote two or three times a week. And how he wrote. Josie kept his letters in ribboned bundles like love-letters, in heavy cardboard Kalamazoo boxes at the bottom of their kitchen-press. It was her practice to read out a week's worth after tea of a Sunday to Liam and Mary and they would tell her what to reply. Then the three of them would kneel down for their prayers.

Mary was more reclusive than Josie. She was deeply shy but shared her sister's sweetness of nature. She was one of the pious women of the parish and, when not working the farm, would often be over at the chapel, to which she had keys. She was the organiser and animator of the Legion of Mary in Tourmahinch and plucked up the courage once to tell me she wanted me for the Legion when I was older: I could join in Liverpool and come out with her on her rounds when I was home for the summer at Three Crosses. As we spoke, she half-turned from me when her eyes caught mine looking at her hare-lip.

I had once heard my mother say in a whisper about the priests that it was the best of the Irish priesthood that went away from Ireland on the missions; any from the quality or others with money in their families would study at home for the diocese.

'Lookit, you hadn't right to be saying those things, now, Geraldine', said Peggy.

'What's the harm in what I said, Peg? Sure I wouldn't be saying it, girl, if it wasn't for Josie herself telling me.'

Father Ed was sombre that afternoon. I learned, at tea that evening, it was because, earlier in the day, he had given the last rites to two men killed in a road accident at the cross of Lissarma, where the road west from Tourmahinch met the highway to Dublin.

'Oh God, 'twas a fierce smash.'

'I think they were foreign tourists coming down from Dublin in some class of a motor-van. They were one of them killed in it, anyway.'

'God help us.'

'Ah, 'tis desperate. And Willie Sheehan wasn't thirty. The wife and the babby are in the Sancta Corona and it's a poor lookout for the two of them.'

'Would he be a Sheehan of Glenpaudie?'

'Arra no, but a first cousin, alright. She is a Delahunty.'

'Know where the Guards found one of the wheels off of the motor-van?'

'Where?'

'In the convent garden at Smith's Turn, with the Presentation Sisters wondering how it came there.'

'That's half a mile from Lissarma, girl. Go away out of that.'

'I'm telling you now, without the word of a lie.'

It was not an unusual conversation. Road accidents were neither rare, nor taken for granted in those days; they were a chastening manifestation of the new world arriving and their detail was always reported at table. *Et in Arcadia ego.*

Twenty-Five

*A tragedy on the road home from Tourmahinch. A funeral at Ballinsaggart
and where it left me.*

Peter Cody mended the left-side bottom-rail of the
maroon gate on the Wednesday. He finished the job with
a coat of red paint, a near match, on the new timberwork
and afterwards went in for his tea in the parlour with
Grandfather Thomas, to talk about milking machines.

On the Thursday, Vance (unusually) sent me down
to Tourmahinch on a message, brushing away, for that
purpose, Aunt Finola's prohibition on my being out on
the road unaccompanied, but, as a precaution, instructing
me to take the short route through the fields as soon as I
reached the first gate. So, before I got to the turn after the
avenue, I cut through Grehans' field, with the granite
Celtic crosses standing in their own precinct, guarded by
a spear-topped iron railing. The grass grew high inside,
like in an old graveyard. It was said that the spot had once
been the site of an oratory as well as the tomb of the
three bishops, though nothing else remained.

Beyond Slievegarriff, the weather looked set for another change and a chiller wind blew down from the Coole valley to the north. In the fields, though the sun still shone, the cows were on the move towards the sheltered corners. I came out on the road again at Tourmahinch, by way of the slate stile, and went up through the village, past Hassetts' bar. I didn't like to look in through the coffee-coloured open doors. I knew that, if I caught their eye, Detta or Maudie or their customers would call me inside and make me give an account of myself. I went to get the cigarettes at Cullen's where Dad used to take us for ice-creams. Gabbie Cullen would cut them off the block in front of us, moistening her thumb on her tongue to pick up each wafer. As I entered, there was music I recognised. Aunt Feena's magical voice came out at me from the back of the shop, its trills and cadences winging out over the chords of the melodion, almost unnerving me with their beauty. As Gabbie was getting Vance's cigarettes, Peter Cody appeared. He put a hand round my shoulder and bought me a twopenny bar of toffee. Then Panloaf spoke up from out of the gloom at the back of the shop. The Usurper had been sitting with Feena as she sang and played.

'I have a bit of white pudding here for your Grandfather Thomas.'

'I'll give it to him, Mr O'Donoghue',' I said.

'Oh no. He might kind of forget. Give it to your Aunt Margaret to cook for him and be sure and tell her you got it from Michael, now, won't you?'

'Are you coming, Adam',' Peter said to me, 'I'll give you a spin home.' As we drove past Hassetts', I glanced in, and the regulars, close-packed in the semidarkness, looked back at me from behind the glint of their bottles of stout.

Peter noticed my curiosity and said: 'I don't go in there anymore.'

'Do you go to Crealeys', then, instead?'

'By God I'm done of the drink. If it isn't too late.'

We looked up at Slievegarriff. Little of the summit was visible. The rainclouds swept across the lower slopes, brushing the tips of the conifers. But we still had the sun on the road and on our faces as Diamond, the chains of his tackle jingling, kept up a good pace in front of us. Just before the blind turn below Three Crosses, we heard Hughie Heaphy coming down fast from Coole in his motorcar. Peter pulled Diamond over and halted there with one wheel on the verge. 'Easy, now, Diamond.' At that point, Heaphy, still unseen, gave a shocking blast on his car horn, close at hand.

Of the accident, I still have a sequence of razor-sharp memories. Diamond reared up above us between the shafts and I felt the churns topple. The horse slithered and slewed the cart out into the middle of the road. Then Heaphy's headlamp seemed to be coming up at my face. I blacked out. The next thing I felt was terror of the fern-fronds brushing my face, as I came to. I saw the smashed wheel of the cart and Diamond on his haunches, bucking and struggling to stand. I saw the bluish, spreading lake of milk on the road, and I half-suffocated with the sweet smell of it.

Then I saw poor Peter Cody, lying below the low mossy granite wall over which I had been thrown: his body still, the life gone out of him, his eyes open, the hair on the back of his head all matting in blood. There was Hughie, sitting sideways in the driver's seat of the Standard, feet on the road, fingers in his red hair, repeating: 'Tis drunk he was, for sure...', a lie which I knew would be found out against him.

'Oh Mother of God, the child, Bozer...' I heard the familiar voice, but Peggy was in shock, strange-looking. Later, Grandad told me that Panloaf heard the car-horn and the crash from a good quarter of a mile away in Cullen's shop. It was Jimmy Grehan, in the Vauxhall, who drove back up to Coole for Doctor Gilbank, alerting my mother and sisters at Brittans' as he passed. Peggy had heard the crash from Three Crosses and had run down to the turn with the bread dough still sticking to her hands.

★

And that is how I came to take part in a second funeral in 'fifty-seven, and visit Ballinsaggart cemetery before ever I expected to, there to contemplate two more graves and crosses, one shared by Grandmother Maeve and Uncle Christie and another, the great, damp hole fresh-dug for Peter Cody, alongside Denny's, his stepfather's, grave.

★

That graveyard at Ballinsaggart stood up against the mountain wall, the last tended ground before Slievegarriff's vast wastes of bracken and heather. After the interment, a hundred mourners dispersed on the sward between the tombs and the gravel pathways, in knots of four or five. I separated from my mother and the family party, in order to pelt Busty Heaphy with green jade chippings which I had secreted in my pockets. He returned my fire with a nonchalance that suggested he was unaware of his brother Hughie's predicament in custody at the Barracks. The buzz of talk there in the cemetery went on for a good hour, before kith and kin turned their backs to Slievegarriff and drifted out of the wicket gate towards their cars and traps. 'Poor Agnes Cody, God help her', said everyone. She travelled back to the house, at the head of the cortege, in a Triumph limousine belonging to the Andersons of Tize Court.

Grandfather Thomas, standing just outside the wicket gate so as to smoke his pipe with propriety, said to Aunt Feena: ''Tis strange. Old Panloaf seemed very mournful altogether and yet I never knew him give Peter Cody the time of day...' Feena said: 'Sure, I think 'twas talking to Peggy that he somehow felt the loss.'

In that late summer, the broken half-call of the cuckoo sounded below in Ballinsaggart woods. The cuckoo could no longer sing its song properly; it sat in some high, well-shaded nest, unwelcome through no fault of its own; it had no place there, with its two or three siblings that were not, in any case, siblings; worse, it would bring those fledglings disaster.

★

On account of the funeral, dinner was served at teatime that evening in Three Crosses. The men had gone over to Codys' for the reception and came in at six, still in their funeral suits. They blessed themselves and placed their Sunday hats on the table next to their dinner-plates where you would put a side-plate. There were fried rashers as well as bacon boiled with cabbage. The tea, made and drawn at the hob, was placed in the centre of the table. I remember the cutlery: Sheffield steel or plate with rat-tailed forks and spoons and ivory-handled knives with blades honed like razors to half their former width. Uncle Vance and Grandad sipped from their saucers, though Packie, I noticed, like a modern, or an Englishman, imbibed from the teacup.

The conversation turned on who had gone up to Codys' with Agnes Cody in the Andersons' car after the interment.

'Was it poor Shoogie Mackie there cooking with Mairead Cody?'

'It was. By God, the creature got shook-looking.'

'She did. 'Twas good out of her to help Mairead and Agnes in their hour of need.'

'Well', said Packie, 'Shoogie didn't last long in Panloaf's employ.'

''Twasn't Panloaf hired her, boy. It was Glory', said Grandad.

'Shoogie is better off out of Dunakielthy farm and that's a fact.'

'Sure, Glory would be too cute to pay her. Only give her pocket-money, that's all.'

Mrs Mackie was a black-shawled widow living in a council house in Tourmahinch with her brother Eamonn, the parish bell-ringer. She was called Sugar or Shoogie because she was thought to keep a gallon of molasses by her hob and to be in the habit of bringing the fire on with a ladleful of the sugar from time to time as necessary. Where she got the molasses in those pre-silage days nobody knows.

'Shoogie is cute enough too. 'Twasn't on account of the money she left, I heard.'

''Twas Glory gave her the marching orders.'

'And how was that?'

'Well I heard Glory told Shoogie boil cabbage to go with some pig's tongue for the tea one evening.'

'Well?'

'Glory had messages in Hassetts' and, with one thing and another, she gave the whole afternoon there over a few glasses of stout.'

'When your one went to cut the cabbage didn't she find it covered in shelegabookies.'

'What harm? Don't the French people eat them yokes?'

'Oh they do, but poor Shoogie couldn't bear to look at them, don't mind pull them off the leaves.'

'Your one left the cabbage in the ground and gathered a bag of dandelion leaves instead. She boiled up a good pound of them on the new Aga for Glory's tea.'

'Get away.'

'I'm telling you now, Glory ate her 'nough of the dandelions with the bit of tongue that evening. With the few bottles of stout she was after drinking, sure she was none the wiser. Only, that night she had a misfortune there in the bed. She couldn't make out what happened her at all, at all.'

'She did, so.'

'Did the English tinker go above to the Codys?'

'He did, I believe.'

'Was there a tinker at the funeral?'

'The old fellow, the Englishman with the pipe and the long hair and the long nails and the knapsack, that do be here every summer. Sure, Adam, you saw him in the chapel, didn't you?'

In the chapel I had seen him: the hobo, tinker-prophet, with his warnings, who knew about me and had frightened me behind the gate in the Lackendarraghs, the day we went to the sea. But I had hardly given him a thought, except to wonder what business of his it was to sit in the row behind Agnes Cody and to exchange private words with her, before the priest came in to bless the coffin.

In Ballinsaggart chapel, that day, there came adrift the frail evanescent mental construction I had begun to stretch like a healing web over the wound of my earlier bereavement. The vision of a safe haven elsewhere during the coming long years, into which, with Peter Cody, I might have sailed from my island, proved baseless fabric. What of the good purpose that might have been served by our common loss of a father, our common affection for Peg? Peter, my Achilles, the lithe, dark champion whose return to the battlefield and last aristeia with Peggy had been so poignant, so promising, so brief. My Lancelot. The future was torn away, lost. Peter Cody was no more; gone, in that year of 'fifty-seven; one, so young, among countless others; I had not thought death had undone so many.

Twenty-Six

Private conversations in the final days at Three Crosses. PK Reynolds tells me something about myself.

The final days of our sojourn in Three Crosses passed very quickly. At the end and edge of my dreamtime, Peggy withdrew a great deal to her room, with Feena and with my mother. Busty Heaphy made no more visits, though before we left I was to see him again by chance. Lindie and Beebie and Kate played with the Brittan girls. None in the family sought me out, though, at table, all acknowledged it was a mercy me to have got up off of the road without a scratch after the accident. I was thought happier to be pursuing my own reflections.

In the early mornings, I heard the aunts in the kitchen below pounding the dough or plying the flat-iron, whispering to each other so as not to awaken Vance. The fire was lit in the parlour those evenings, under the monochrome gaze of Great-Uncle Joseph of Cheeseburg, Michigan, of Grandmother Maeve Driscoll and of Uncle Christie that died when I was fourteen months old; the sup of poteen was brought up to the room from out of a black recess in the chimney-hob in the kitchen; between all the living Driscolls of Three Crosses - Geraldine, Feena, Peggy, Packie, Vance and Thomas, there ensued late conversations of whose content I remained in ignorance. I finished *Deeds of the West-Britons* in long, night-time sessions in my army bed on the landing, the hearth cold and the kitchen silent below me.

★

Provided I walked purposefully and gave signals that I had a job for him, Shep was willing to follow me. He was a farmer's dog and denied his company to dawdlers and to the leisured or idle. On the last Wednesday, in my loneliness, I had inveigled him for company into my den in the orchard in the shell of the Morris Eight. I sat with my arm round him, picking burrs out of his coat, moodily rasping the Morris's brake-handle up and down in its mounting, in a way that would soon have irritated any other companion but the stone-deaf animal beside me. My thoughts meandered towards the Liverpool to which I would soon return, as if to exile. But Three Crosses was exile, too, a dream-place where I no longer belonged, from whose beauties I had, by my own disobedience, expelled myself.

Liverpool - Paul Sinkiewicz had been in Miss Pargeter's class with me at Pius the Twelfth. He had a reputation as the class catapultist. One of the weapons (which he regularly concealed in his bottle-green gaberdine school-coat) had a pouch the size of a small purse. Charged with gravel, and used surreptitiously among the elms in Swindles Park, near the school, it could deliver a satisfying blast into the canopy and, sure enough, a few leaves would flutter down. But no starlings or sparrows had fallen lifeless at our feet (as we had secretly and cruelly hoped). I later heard that Paul had graduated to airguns when he had gone on to the secondary modern. I had been told by my mother to stay away from him then.

Paul had told me he favoured Sod Medley's for his supplies of catapult-elastic. Sod sold long skeins of model aircraft rubber-band, which was the material Paul rated most highly. If you asked for catapult-elastic in a toy shop, Paul maintained, you were sold an expensive and inferior product. I had avoided Medley's Toys on Marksfield High Street since the distraction with the train-set on the morning of my run for aspirins for my father, the morning he died. Because the shop had been the occasion of the disobedience which had ruined me and from which so much had followed, I had, in fact, imagined myself denying Medley's Toys my patronage forever. But I was weak and needs must for a ten-year-old. Somehow, I formed a resolution never to look at his train-set display again; this proved easy to keep: the enchantment of that wheeled cosmos in miniature had gone and has never returned.

'Thank you Mr Medley', I had said clutching the packet he had made up with sixpence-worth of propeller rubber. 'Mr Medley', I called him. It was said he did not mind being called 'Sod' to his face even by his boyish clientele. But you had to be prepared to be addressed by an obscene soubriquet in return. Paul once told me what his was. Retailing Paul's nickname to my mother earned me a slap across the back of my legs. I later found out what it meant. The propeller rubber had travelled with me from Curzon Street to Three Crosses.

In the shell of Vance's motorcar, I repeated Paul's obscene nickname to my companion, Shep, trying it out in my mouth. Lip-reading me, the dog showed no interest and eventually I let him out through the boot, shot home the Morris handbrake, and reached for *Robinson Crusoe*, where many truths and many truth-fantasies lay.

'Here was also an infinite number of fowls of many kinds; some which I had seen, and some which I had not seen of before - and many of them very good meat - but such as I knew not the names of… I could have shot as many as I pleased, but was very sparing of my powder and shot…'

Game abounded on my island. Every now and then I would hear the flock of thirty or forty half-grown Christmas turkeys that Reynoldses were rearing. These exotics, which I had never seen at close quarters live and in the flesh, filled a useful play role as the unknown fauna on my island. The turkeys were housed birds but would occasionally be outside, foraging without apparent supervision on Reynoldses' boreen (their house, unlike those of the other farmers in Three Crosses, was set well back off our road). I assumed that the birds knew our road was dangerous. In my boy's heart, the fun, the crack, would be to stalk them and blast them with road chippings from my catapult; I factored in neither cruelty nor consequences.

I used the serrated bread-knife to cut out a suitable handle for the catapult from a bit of ash in the kindling stack. The pouch would have to be fashioned from a scrap of boot-leather. The bark-leather which I could produce by stripping saplings in the orchard would not have the necessary resilience.

I had regained possession from Peggy of this blue satchel which I have in front of me, real-time, as I write. It had come into my life the summer of 'fifty-six, the year before, carrying my copybook and soda-bread sangwidges to Blanchardstown National School. Now an accoutrement for a sylvan hunter rather than for a scholar, it would serve as holster for the catapult with a compartment that could be filled with ammunition.

I loitered by the kindling stack with an eye to scaling our maroon gates, which were barred and tied shut. Mother was at the top of the yard, washing dishes at the soft-water rain-butt. I could hear my sisters' voices from behind the house, chanting playground rhymes to the patter of the rubber balls they were juggling against the smooth back wall of the dairy.

'What's your name?

Butter and Cream.

Where're you from?

Ballinamon.

Who's your Da?

Willie McGrath.

Where was he born?

The Mountains of Mourne.

Who's your Ma?

I'll ask my Da…'

On went the litany-like chant and the deft juggling.

Who's your Ma? I looked longingly at my mother Geraldine, moved by her industry and her stoicism; instinct impelled me to distract her now from her platters, to hug her, to murmur to her in the embrace the question: 'Whose son am I?' By a contrary instinct, I feared to trespass, as I had on the second day of the holidays, the afternoon of Daniel Brittan's christening. Geraldine had been unwilling to speak to me then of my godmother, if I had one, the day Mrs Brittan showed us the photographs of babby Daniel; why should she now reveal what she knew of my birth-mother? I ran the risk, not merely of addling her poor head by pressing with my questions, but of alienating any prospect that she might come to love me in her own way, as Peggy had promised me she would. *I'll ask my Da*: By my disobedience, had I not thrown away that key to my identity?

I scaled the gate and dropped noiselessly into our road. I became Gene Autry, mounted on an imaginary, piebald, Apache pony with a fat belly like Thady's. I galloped down the crown of the road towards the shaded entrance to Reynoldses' lane on the right, where the low, granite wall, green-tinged with algal growth, broke for a few yards and the hawthorns and blackthorns forced themselves up between its stones. A quagmire had formed at the mouth of the lane. Having waded my pony across this Rio Grande, I became Crusoe again and set myself to discover what manner of fowl my island might provide for my sustenance. Reynolds' turkeys were out in force; mawkish, ugly birds I thought them, especially the whites. I looked around me. I unbuckled my blue satchel. I took out the catapult and charged it with the birdshot I had gathered at the roadside. I went down on one knee and took careful aim into the centre of the gaggle.

'Hey, boy! Hey, boy!'

I panicked but held fire, then dropped most of the road-chippings out of the sling of the weapon, in my confusion. Some of the birds took fright, too, at the shout and forayed up into the higher branches of the hedges. The youthful voice, just broken, had been close at hand, yet I could see no-one. Then a green conker-shell landed at my feet.

PK, the only son of the family, whom we rarely saw, had, after all, been keeping an eye on the birds. He was sitting in a tree branch which arced across Reynolds's boreen, thus stationing himself between the turkeys and our road. He had an eye out for some of the local dogs too, especially Punch, the guardian of Dempseys' apple orchards on the next farm down our road.

'Them are weer (he meant our) turkeys. They kind of remind me of a flock of ostriches.' The thought had crossed my mind, too: the half-grown birds had that gangly look about them.

'Why are they called turkeys?' he went on, toying with me. 'They had right to be called mexicos.'

PK had been pointed out to me at a distance last year at the National School in Blanchardstown by Busty as the cleverest boy in the place. He was also bigger than I was and had no reason to be well-disposed towards me at that moment.

'No, because they're American.'

'Mexican.'

'American. I've seen a picture of one in a book called *Audubon's Birds of America*.'

'I never heard of that. What is it that you have in your hand?'

'Nothing.' I transferred the weapon quickly to the pocket of my britches then began to shake the blue satchel with its road-chippings, like maraccas, to throw him off the scent.

'Show me a look at the sling, will you?'

I had been disarmed of my Winchester by Joe Gandy. I wasn't going to hand PK the catapult and be relieved permanently of that weapon. If he were to threaten force, I had the chance of escape while he dropped down from his perch. Again, to chase me, he would have to abandon the turkeys. But I calculated he might risk that and still collar me before I made it back to our maroon gates. Therefore I decided to change the subject of conversation.

'I have to get back now. I've got sums to do for school.'

'For school in England, is it? That's a show. I never do homework.'

As I look back, I see this was a lie. It was the first of many times I was to hear and believe (to my own competitive disadvantage) similar protestations from clever classmates. Busty had told me PK was streets ahead of his fellow-pupils in the National school. He was thus unlike his peers and, yet, he wanted to be like them; every good boy deserves favour.

I thought to provoke him, to distract him from turning the conversation back to my catapult and Reynoldses' turkeys, so I said, foolhardy:

'More fool you.'

It was a mistake. PK did not repay the offence by telling me he would report me to his father for my intended attack on their livestock. Instead, he swung his legs slowly from his roost high above me and spoke down to me:

'Do you know what a bastard is?' At first, I believed he was merely vaunting his wide reading.

'A blaggard', I said.

'No.'

'A caffler.'

'No.'

'A culshie fellow.'

'No.'

'An omadhaun.' (Peggy had once addressed me as such: I had inferred from the context that the term meant some class of an idiot.)

'No.'

'A bonham. Or a bullock?'

'Not at all.'

'What is it, so?'

'A bastard is a lad that don't know who his own father is.'

'So?'

'People say you're a bastard, Addie Bennett, so they do. But maybe you didn't know?'

The moment is as of yesterday. I remember the way he continued to swing his legs from the knee slowly and deliberately in the air fifteen feet above and ahead of me. I remember the dry green ordure on the soles of his wellingtons and the clean, white half-adult legs of him between his short britches and his wellingtons. The look of those legs, thin and etiolated, I had attributed, (*post hoc ergo propter hoc*), to PK's wearing long trousers before it was time. I remember the puzzled, muted burbling of the flock of turkeys behind him on Reynoldses' lane; the very birds knew the enormity of what PK had said. I remember the sickness churning in me and his black hair, barber-cut. I remember my blood cold with the ineffable sadness on me and his few tiny dark freckles and his mouth half-open with the trace of a smile. I remember.

★

So, that afternoon, PK Reynolds joined the English tinker, my mother Geraldine, the rest of the Driscolls and the world-at-large that knew more about who I was and to whom I belonged, than I did myself. PK was the native-American who, having found out his adversary's name while concealing his own, now possessed part of his identity and wielded power over him. My sense of thraldom to some fearful presence had emerged before, in the images of my recurrent cauchemar - the thing, the small dark cloud in the playground at Pius Twelfth that watched me and closed with me to engulf me. The second dream, which I described earlier, of my half-nakedness at school, made my humiliation explicit.

There was a third, much less terrible, more portentous dream, from the last nights of that summer under Slievegarriff, sparked perhaps by a feature on Arjuna and Krishna in the *Southern Express*.

I am bedizened as an Indian prince. I stand in the huge court of an eastern palace on the banks of the Glas in red brick and pink stone, windowless except for a high clerestory from whose rows of unglazed windows I am observed by countless jostling onlookers. I observe myself as if disembodied or in a gigantic mirror. I am sumptuously attired in a shimmering suit, all gold and green, smothered with jewels. My turban is carried in front of me on a scarlet cushion by my real-life tormentor, Joe Gandy, in an altar-server's soutane. Behind me my retinue proceeds, as gaudily attired as I am. My classmates from Pius Twelfth; Paul Sinkiewicz. Great-Aunt Stacey on the arm of Winston Churchill, who melts into Mahatma Gandhi and walks barelegged below his black frock-coat. I am full-grown, tall; my eyes dark, made up with kohl. My hair is black, as I have always wanted it, in my dreams, falling rich over my brow, brilliantined like Rhett Butler's in *Gone With the Wind*.

Liam Deegan in Hindu apparel, his brother, Father Ed in his Hawaiian shirt and Uncle Packie bearing a golden carbide lamp, are my advisers. From the far corners of the court come my female suitors, with their retainers, in groups. My counsellors whisper into my ear that, though there are twelve potential brides, there is a presumption that I must choose my Aunt Peggy, while being seen to give a fair hearing to all. I worry that I may not recognise Peggy, that the other contenders may appear in her guise and deceive me. I see only four or five of the candidates in this dream: each is lovelier than the last, each could be Aunt Peggy, under the diaphanous veils and powder and rouge. I am fascinated, torn, confused; I awake.

★

My mother Geraldine took my sisters up to the Brittans' after dinner on the Thursday. The men were out. With Peggy and Feena in the house, in one of the last, deep conversations upstairs, I could be left at home at Driscolls'. I did not protest too much. When I heard Feena begin to play the blue melodion, I went upstairs to listen, wondering whether they would call me in to join them. In the gloom of the landing, however, I saw their bedroom door shut. I tiptoed away. Both Peggy and Feena were singing *The Wild Colonial Boy* and, if I could not be with them, I preferred to be out of earshot.

I gave much of the afternoon to *Deeds of the West-Britons*, the volume by the Rev Deakin which I had withdrawn without authorisation from the collection in the parlour sideboard. I went back for comfort, in my bastardy, to the tale of Galahad, the Good Knight whom I had learned to adulate at my father's feet, during his patient readings to me, after work, in the tiny drawing-room in Curzon Street, while my mother prepared the tea.

'The shield which I give thee,' said the White Knight, 'will confound thy enemies, smite thee as they may with their blows.' So he gave to Beau Sir Galahad the shield that had been wrought by Joseph of Arimathea. Sir Galahad and his squire rode through a forest and came to a hermitage where dwelt all alone a saintly woman who had retired from the world.'

★

On our road, I stepped onto the grass verge under the fuchsia hedge. My back was to our gates. My mind was partly on the shield wrought by Joseph of Arimathea and partly on my mother's and sisters' imminent return down the hill from Kilcreggan and the Brittans'. Six weeks ago, I had stood on this spot to meet my mother on the first day of the holidays. Then she had come up from Cullen's dairy on her bicycle, bringing the cheese in a brown-paper parcel on the carrier. I had not thought she had wanted me then. Perhaps she had started to miss me now, in these days after the crash in which she might have lost me, when she had spent so many hours apart with my aunts. I pictured her longing for me this afternoon. In a moment, when she rounded the bend on the road above she would see me waiting out for her and I would seek out love in her face.

But it was not my mother, Geraldine, and Lindie and Beebie and Kate that I encountered at the maroon gates that Thursday. Below me on the road, from the direction of the avenue, the forms of Joe Gandy, PK Reynolds and Busty Heaphy took shape from under the trees. They were heading up our road to Kilcreggan and a few minutes later came level with me.

Busty Heaphy, my companion of the early weeks, himself in long trousers now, like PK, looked at me with a half-smile. In what followed, he never said a word. It was not his silence then that I came to resent; it was hard for him. His brother Hughie bore responsibility for the accident in which I had barely escaped injury and Peter Cody had lost his life. But I took it as a betrayal that Busty was in company with the other two. I wished to hurt Gandy, and PK, too, if possible. I didn't care how.

'You broke my gun, you fecking idiot', I greeted Joe Gandy as he drew abreast.

'Mind your gob, you sir', Gandy sneered. He put up a finger at me like a schoolteacher, the watery eyes of him glittering with malice.

'Mind now, Addie. Joe is only...' said PK. I knew from his tone and from the very way he stood there that PK was wanting to do some good at this point. But I said:

'You go mind your fecking turkeys, PK.' And yet I could sympathise with PK. All he was guilty of, in one sense, was to have called me a bastard for trespassing on Reynolds' lane with intent to harass his family's livestock.

The gorge had risen in me at the sneer on Gandy's face. I stepped down from the verge. We squared up and pushed each other, once each. I no longer feared those insolent pale-blue eyes with their hard little pupils. Nor was I in awe of his bigger, stockier frame. It would have been too easy for me to hit him. Did I see a shadow of fear cross his face? How would I strike him? With an open-handed slap across his face leaving a good red mark on him? Or with a good punch of my fist in the mouth, splitting his lip and bringing on a nosebleed? He could retaliate as he saw fit, for all I cared. He could kill me. I saw myself dead on our road, like Peter Cody.

Something, or someone, stayed my hand; my rage vanished. Was it the strains of distant music from Feena's bedroom in the house behind? Simple cowardice, you say? What does it matter? It was not courage. I had my shield; smite me as my enemies might, with their blows, I was beyond caring about the consequences. PK walked on up towards Kilcreggan; Busty and Gandy followed.

Twenty-Seven

The last day in Eden and final revelation there.

I have spoken of Stacey, the headmistress of Blanchardstown National school; my other great-aunt was Nina, Ninnie, Grandfather Thomas' sole surviving sister. She lived about eight miles west of Three Crosses, above Ballinsaggart where the cemetery was, on the lower slopes of the 'Garriff. From the high window of the organ-loft in Tourmahinch chapel, provided the weather was fine, the white speck of her house could be descried on the line between the woods and hill pastures and the mauve bulk of the mountain proper. Ninnie was a farmer's widow with five grown boys.

Great-Aunt Nina's was a household of laughter, the trigger for which, both in Ninnie and her sons, was not merely what most people would find comic but any occurrence outside the routine. Ninnie's farm on the 'Garriff, a mile up from Ballinsaggart, was so isolated that they saw very little of the rest of the world. Did they only laugh in company? I have sometimes wondered in the years since. 'I nearly died laughing', I would hear Ninnie say. But she was ninety-eight when she passed away. Laughter was good medicine for her boys, too, with all five in good health and working into their late seventies in this twenty-first century.

Ballinsaggart took an hour to reach by bicycle from Three Crosses. Peggy and Feena were in the habit of regular visits to Nina at Ballinsaggart and, in these latter days of her widowhood and with the arthritis she had in her wrists and knuckles, they would do an hour's dusting or washing for her. But today, presently, Feena was going over to Dunakielthy to call on Michael O'Donoghue (Panloaf was a soubriquet now forbidden to us in her presence). So when Peggy came down from her room and announced her intention to go alone to see Ninnie, I saw my chance and begged my mother to be allowed to go. It was August 30th, 1957, a Friday, our last full day in Three Crosses.

'Arra go on, Geraldine', said Peg, 'he's well able to ride your bicycle.'

'The roads, girl. Will he stick close to you, Peg? I'd be worried for the roads.'

'He'll be good as gold', said Peg.

Said Feena: 'Maybe he could weed a drill or two of spuds for Ninnie. He'd be handy for that. Isn't that right, Addie?'

After Tourmahinch, the first four or five miles of the back road towards Slievegarriff and Ballinsaggart were dead flat. Then there was a half-mile climb up through the wooded gap of Glenpaudie till you reached the junction with the Dublin road. After a mile or two on this fast, empty road, with Slievegarriff above you in full magnificent view, you took a right turn up through the last of the good land to Ballinsaggart. There was a further steep climb out of Ballinsaggart for the said mile up a grey, gravelled track to Ninnie's.

At Tourmahinch, Peggy pulled up her bicycle before Hassetts' and whispered to me to go in for a couple of twopenny ices.

'Keep yourself to yourself, Bozer', she said, 'and don't be telling Detta your business.'

On the level road west out of Tourmahinch, we bowled along with little expenditure of energy. Peg rode outside, to my right, freewheeling for long stretches so as to let me keep up. We left the chapel and creamery behind us. With the saddle down on Mother's Rudge, I could just about remain seated to pedal. The day was neither warm nor cold, though a cross-wind blew down from the north-west, the first of the autumn winds that had begun to blow the day Peter Cody was killed at the turn. But I remember the beginning of this Friday journey as the prospect of paradise regained.

Grandfather Thomas and Geraldine, my mother, were steeped in the history and the lore of our parts. When she and my father Roy had been out and about, Geraldine would tell him her stories of the Fir Bolg, or the hermit of Killinunty; stories of Fionn's women, Cuchulainn, Eva Ban, and of the abbeys of True Cross and Clarepoint, the Three Crosses and the Rock of Munster.

By contrast, Peg, Packie and Vance liked to know who owned and walked the land now. When I was out with any of the latter, they could not pass a gate on a country road for a radius of twenty miles around Three Crosses, but they knew or wished to know to whom it belonged, the acreage of the field it guarded and what it would be growing or rearing this year and next.

'Those two fields are belonging to Brittans', said Aunt Peggy, nodding as we passed a hurdle gate on the left.

'The Brittans our neighbours?'

'Arra, no, boy. Brittans of Ballinavoca, second cousins. They had barley in them last year. They do be talking about planting beet down on this land, but sure the water isn't in it and I wonder will they ever? Did you see the old mill in the field by Carty's bridge? 'Tis Brittans of Three Crosses owns that, alright. PK's grandfather got it. They had it let for a good while to the Delahuntys of Castle East. There's a Delahunty one married to a Drennan lad in this farm up here on the right.'

Peg yarned away as we ticked along in top gear on our bicycles. When she had run out of local detail or had, perhaps, tired of me as an ignorant and uncomprehending interlocutor, she began to sing in Irish. It was an old song, an exile's lament, she had learned in the convent. I found the English for it many years later.

'Ancient Slievegarriff, O mistress of men

Fionn and Cuchulainn walked thee

In thy vales fain would I meet them again

Alanna, the day I turned from her

I left my soul with her

'Fold of the fox and the hare and the grouse

O mountain dark as a storm-cloud

Breast of my childhood and mother of men

Alanna, the day I turned from her

Bewitched, my soul, by her

'Here the clouds darken, my eyes strain to see

Alanna, your child's face is dim to me

But bright is the sun on Croke Garriff's hill

For this is the day I turn to her

I left my soul there.'

With the exquisiteness of the tune and the plangent voice that insinuated itself into my very being, a melancholy as chill as the shaded side of Slievegarriff came over me, a profound romantic sadness for what would never be mine. Had Great-Uncle Joseph hummed this lament, he who looked out at me in monochrome from the frame of his picture in the parlour, with eyes as soft as Grandfather's? Great-Uncle Joseph, for whom the sands of time had run out in Cheeseburg, Michigan and for whom what had once been his would never be so again.

Peggy stopped singing. 'Have you the sheroose, Bozer?' I said no; nothing was upsetting me.

'Don't you like me to sing?'

'Yes. I want you to sing, but I can't bear it when you do.'

'What is it with you then, Bozer? Is it the blues? The blues on you?'

It was too much and I began to cry. The deep truth was that I thought my heart would break without Peggy in Liverpool. The words I managed to get out in response, between my sobs, were: 'I'm going home tomorrow.'

'The summertime blues. Be a brave boy now; you have your mammy and your sisters to help.'

'You had a mammy. I have no mammy. Grandad told me.'

She braked gently and stopped in the road. I brought the Rudge to a halt with a judder. Smiling and sad, Peg rested her elbows on the handlebars and looked right into me, body and soul. She thought out for a few moments what she would say.

'Oh now, Bozer. Geraldine is your new mammy and she loves you in her own way. She has to rear you, boy, as if you were her own flesh and blood, with all the joy and the suffering.'

She was careful, almost detached in what she said, calculating, as I later realised, thus to stem the tide of my sadness and hopelessness. Trust Aunt Peg though I did, at the time I was sharply aware this last utterance was a contrivance, a composition, and I doubted her in that moment. I had come too far since the trauma of Grandad's revelation, on the road back from Rossbeg, that I was not my mother's son.

After that day, what had also embedded itself and hardened within me was the notion that Geraldine did not love me: I never eradicated that perception, not that summer of 'fifty-seven, nor the next, not in forty years; worse, I assumed I was not innocent in this hopeless state of affairs. Mother loved her own children and would do her duty by me for my father's sake. I was owed the love the way you owe money, like the promise on the back of a green, English pound note. It could not be helped. I must be alone, an exile and wild.

Yet responsibility for my mother and sisters was what I, in my turn, owed. With Daddy gone, through my own negligence, I had to support, to provide, to atone. I might, one day, have shared in Aunt Peg's life with Peter Cody. The romance of that had both appealed and appalled. Peter had had the hero about him that I had wanted for Peggy. Like me, he had suffered and his suffering was like mine, so he qualified as her suitor. Because I had lived, vicariously, his tribulations, I had hoped in him. And I had hoped that, though Peg would have had to put Peter before all others, I would not fade out of her life. Now she would find another; though the newcomer might not be a Usurper, a Sir Mordred, like Michael Panloaf O'Donoghue, he would not be a White Knight or a hero, a Peter Cody, nor would he have anything in common with me.

My composure had partly returned. 'She doesn't love me. Not the way she loves my sisters. Not like Daddy did.'

'Well, do you know what?' said Peggy, hooking back with her foot the off-side pedal and preparing to make off again, 'I think you're a smasher of a lad. Honest to God.'

I told her that that was fine and had she decided I was a smasher the day I broke the axle on Kate's pram on our way back home from Kilcreggan woods?

'Oh ho, you're a gas man, now, Bozer, so you are. Come here, I want you.' She leaned across to me without dismounting, put a fondie from her lips onto her three middle fingers and stroked them across my cheek.

We set off again, cycling abreast. I sensed Aunt Peg looking across at me more frequently than before we had stopped. Now we were on the haul up to the fork of Lissarma, at which we would turn south on the main highway. This was a lonely, wooded road, full of the scent of pine, between dark, high, ivied banks with the spathes of cuckoo-pints spiking out, and deadly nightshade. Happiness came back in the kingdom of imagination. I was Sir Galahad, Peggy my squire. We rode through this forest at the bidding of le Roy Arthur, my father, in quest of Ninnie, the saintly woman who had retired to a hermitage.

Beyond the trees in the sunlight at the top of the rise we saw the sweep and curve of the Dublin road in front of us.

'Are you tired, Bozer?'

'Just need to get my breath back.'

'Mind now, sure you will? This is a fierce dangerous road.'

Peggy stopped for a moment at the fork, as I thought, to rest for a moment and take in the quiet grandeur of the panorama to the south and the might of Slievegarriff now close at hand and facing us. Behind us was the dark and mysterious beauty of the scented glen up which we had toiled.

But then she pointed out fresh tyre-marks and gouges in the new surface of the road. She told me, though I already knew, how Willie Sheehan and a Dutch tourist had lost their lives there.

We stood there for some minutes, our minds on the other road accident, the accident that had so changed both of us. We blessed ourselves and bore south on the main road, freewheeling for many minutes around the long, gradual curve and glad to be in the sun again. After a couple of hundred yards we passed the entrance to the convent on our left. It was, or had been, a slate-roofed, grey, Irish-Georgian manor, the only building on that side of the road for a mile or two. It sat sweetly in a demesne hedged by honeysuckle and fuchsia with a deciduous wood at its back after fields that had once perhaps been parkland. The Sisters even kept a few deer, which we glimpsed as we passed. It was through their open, black- and-gold gates and onto their lawn that the renegade road-wheel from the fatal crash had trundled and bounced. *Et in Arcadia.*

The convent at Smiths' Turn provided one kind of Irish past. As we neared Ninnie's, another was on offer. We had left the main road and cycled up through Ballinsaggart. Too young to sweat at the armpit and groin, I chafed and started to flush in the sun. The last mile took us up an unmade road to the last house before the gate onto the mountain. The fields around Ninnie's, stony and rush-infested, were, even so, full of interesting depressions and mounds along with the four ivy-covered gable-ends - all that was left - of a couple of dwelling-houses. Nina's home was the only surviving edifice in a famine village.

That visit to Great-Aunt Ninnie's on eastern Slievegarriff was the closest I had ever come to the vast, massy breast to which every field and lane seemed oriented in that land I once inhabited in my dreamtime and which, in turn, has inhabited me. The 'Garriff was the summit and summation of it all, her whims and moods and clouds and sun-patches and the promise of beaten paths up through the heather were the whims and moods of the people of our parts. As we wheeled our cycles into Nina's yard between two whitewashed boulders end-capping the drystone wall, I glanced up the last few yards of the track, and beyond to the mountain, half-knowing even then, that the scene I encompassed would never leave me. I saw the last gate before the 'Garriff, rusting under powder-blue paint, and I saw the bold, bare body and massive sweep of her beyond, up and up to pile upon pile of clouds in that heavenly sky. One day, not today, I would step through that last gate onto the mountain.

Great-Aunt Ninnie was at the door when we arrived. She wore a grey cotton suit with a St Brigid's cross brooch of silver and bog-oak on the lapel, and a cream blouse. In fact, in the years I knew her, I never saw her in her working clothes. Like her brother Vance, when she wanted to show it, she had style.

'Well Glory be to God, ha haha!'

'Well, Ninnie.'

'I knew 'twas you, Peggy, and, ha haha, is it Adameen you have there with you? Look at the long pants on him! What age have he? What brings you over to Ballinsaggart, little man?'

'I took a figary', I said, reckoning my use of the Hibernian would add to the general gaiety. (In English: I acted on a whim.)

'Will you listen to the Englishman? He took a figary! Don't he have the gift of the gab?' said Nina, her voice ascending to falsetto and then shimmering into a further peal of giggles.

'Ninnie', said Peg, 'you're in the best of form.'

'Sure I am: but with poor Daddy gone a twelvemonth now, the Lord have mercy on him, I don't be laughing no more', chuckled Ninnie and burst into renewed giggles. 'Oh, God help us!' She regained composure: 'don't be standing there with yeer mouths open to catch flies. Come in, let ye.'

We went up into Nina's parlour rather than into her kitchen, though it can hardly have been in my honour. The feel of the room was very like that of our own parlour at Three Crosses, but for the absence of a wireless-set in the far window. As in ours, the ceiling was in white-distempered pine planking. The walls were papered in an ancient design of floral sprays on a buff ground, the windows curtainless except for nets. Nina had a family of three Staffordshire china dogs on the mantelpiece just as we did, over a cast-iron fireplace, and a couple of pewter candlesticks. There was a small, silver-framed photo-portrait of her late husband, Paddy, next to a picture of Eamonn Dev, the President of Ireland. Ninnie saw me looking at Paddy and was reminded to produce three small obituary cards printed with postage-stamp-sized copies of the same portrait.

'I have these kept for ye all at Three Crosses with a good while, Peggy.'

Peggy put them into her purse then went out of the parlour unbidden, to do some chore or other for Nina. I didn't mind being left with Ninnie. Like her brother, my grandfather Thomas, she was easy to be with. My great-aunt told me to pull up my parlour chair to the table, like a good man. She sat down slowly with her arthritis, giggling ruefully with the pain of it, then opened a leather-bound picture-album that was already on the table next to the Bible. 'Now', she said, turning the first page, 'that's our wedding day. Look at the fine head of hair Patrick had then, the Lord have mercy on him. Faith and 'tis to the shearers I used be sending him every month after we were married.' I saw something of my Aunt Peggy's features in the young Ninnie: the thick, wavy hair, the darker tint to the skin under her eyes, the squarish cast of face and small Driscoll ears. She, a Driscoll, had been a beauty too, dark-haired like Aunt Peg.

Peggy came back into the parlour with the tea-tray, creaking over the polished black floor-boards.

'I have beds to air, Peggy.'

'Come on, so, Ninnie, till we strip them. Mind the photographs, now, Addie, with the tea you are drinking.'

They closed the door behind them. I flipped over the heavy pages of the album, slipping back the grease-proof paper. In this section there were contact prints, half the size of a postcard, four to a page. I recognised some of the subjects. Not one of them took a good photograph, peering at the amateur cameraman, fiercely or wan, as the mood took them. The adults stood, subdued, in their everyday clothes with their livestock or machinery, the children in rows, oldest to youngest, against their cottage walls. All had once looked at the birdie and said 'cheese', but none looked relaxed. That adjective was not part of the language we talked in those days, in our parts, unless, I suppose, we were quality.

Then I saw the picture of my father. It was a head-and-shoulders studio portrait, subtly backlit, postcard size. My father had had many smiles for many occasions and I knew this one immediately. Daddy was young in the picture, but not so young, perhaps about thirty. There was another face.

Its owner smiled straight out at the camera from behind my father's right shoulder. Her head was tilted and turned slightly towards Daddy's so that their cheeks touched. Her bare arms were crossed casually in front of his chest. She was, I think, wearing a dark frock. The frock, if such it was, had a white, out-turned collar which partly covered a necklace of dark, irregularly-shaped beads. The young woman was blonde, with her hair done up in the gamine fashion. She looked at me with eyes which were my eyes. Her nose was long, not too long, with the suspicion of a bridge, the nose and the bridge I would have. I did not have the small, Driscoll ears; neither did this young woman, I could see, her hair gripped back behind her right ear, with its ample lobe adorned by an earring set with a dark stone. I knew *this woman was my mother*.

The effect of the picture on me was as if I had been struck with a bludgeon. It was as much as I could do not to let out a long, primitive wail, a call, from deep within my child's being. My body shook. I was weakened. What hit me was physical, like a hunger pang, but an emptiness that could not be filled. I went dry at the mouth - a thirst I would never slake.

That moment of my final discovery, final dissolution, has never left me. I was not destined to see the picture again and yet I have seen it, almost daily, these fifty years. Was *this woman* already my mother when the picture was taken? I was angry not to know; angry with my not-mother Geraldine, angry with the father I venerated, for taking this part of me to the grave with him, leaving me with a pack for my journey tomorrow and forever, that, for his sake, I wanted to shoulder, but which was too heavy to bear.

*

My mother Geraldine and we were booked on a Dublin-Holyhead night sailing. With the windy, autumnal weather, we feared a gale at sea and a bad crossing. Aunt Peggy prepared flasks and sandwiches for our journey. As the evening began to darken, Peggy brought me to the road, by the hand, to look out down the avenue for Tony Drennan's Wolseley. 'Will you be lonesome for me, Bozer?' she whispered.

'I will surely, Peggy', I croaked. She straightened out my parting and held my face in her scented hands, the pearl-like nails all bitten down. She wiped out the tears from the corners of my eyes with her thumbs. 'Well now, don't be sad any more. I'm coming over to ye all in October.'

'Will you stay with us?'

'Why wouldn't I? Sure I'll be starting at the nursing there in Liverpool.' In her trench coat and headscarf, Geraldine came up behind us and I read her face. She narrowed her eyes as once she used to, in the days when she might have loved me, in a prelude to a smile. I detected there confirmation of Peggy's news. Even before Geraldine spoke, I began to believe, to my pure delight, that my future was transformed.

I knelt on the morocco-leather rear seat of the Wolseley with my sisters, as we waved our goodbyes through the rear window to the little group of family and neighbours clustered at the maroon gates in the fading light. Peggy stood a little apart, smiling, hand raised. I knew she was waving for me and I nurtured a fierce, unutterable, private joy. I turned to face frontwards and settled into the leather. On my right, the sun set in a blaze over Slievegarriff, its last rays lighting up for a second all the chromework of the fascia and kindling a glow on the horn button. Then the black Wolseley purred away towards the three crosses and the turn.

The wind swept through the chestnuts and the oaks of the darkening avenue, as we passed, whirling the green and gold leaves from the first fall into eddies and dunes in the ditches. The autumn wind blew, that evening, at the end of the dreamtime which is before my eyes now; the time of interments and disinterments: the unearthing of questions and mysteries; the burials of my father and of Peter Cody in those last days and the loss of an Eden where once we had dwelt; gone with the wind.

Twenty-Eight

October 1957 to August 1976.

'There's just something to draw to the mother's attention. The metacarpal on the middle finger of the right hand', said the Hungarian lady doctor with gold teeth, 'was fractured some months ago and has set out of true. I'm astonished the mother didn't notice anything at the time. It shouldn't affect', she paused to check my name on the file, 'Bennett's ability to participate in school life.'

The headmistress, Mrs Frowstie, wrote this down and addressed me, in the polite third person: 'But he has kept up well with his handwriting, hasn't he?'

'You must remember what happened to this finger, Bennett ', the doctor persisted. 'Don't you? Did you show it to your mother?'

I told her I couldn't remember precisely but I had been playing with a friend called Thady at the time.

At her desk, Mrs Frowstie reviewed her notes while I lowered my trousers and the doctor checked my testicles.

'Sink-wits!' A nurse came into the headmistress' office escorting Paul Sinkiewicz, who was next for the drop. The nurse collected my file; I was medically fit for my transfer to the grammar school.

★

The next month, October, Aunt Peggy was due in Liverpool. She had written to Geraldine to say that, for the first sixth months, she would be required to live in a hostel a long way from Curzon Street. Thus she visited us at 44 only once before the Christmas holiday; she told us then that she might move in with us at Easter. But the hope, with which the summer of 'fifty-seven had ended, foundered on the realities of Liverpool and of bread-and-butter. From the Easter of 'fifty-eight, Aunt Peggy would be obliged to live in at the hospital, in order to complete her training. I found this out when she came to bring us a fresh turkey two days before Christmas, as she was due to take the boat home. Aunt Peggy broke her news to me in my bedroom as we sat on the edge of my bed, her arm round me.

'Sure, won't I be coming every week to see you all, and that's a fact, now, with Mammy working, and all the cleaning and cooking? And Feena coming too, now, before the summer? Will you be lonesome for me?'

Peggy went away that evening. The bright jewel I had clutched at in the Wolseley, the evening we left Three Crosses, slipped from my grasp again. I remember she left a medical textbook in the hall. I read the pathologies of the diseases and studied the coloured lithographs, aghast for her. After Christmas, Peg brought chocolate for my sisters and books for me on the evening she stayed over. After Easter, as she studied for her SRN badge, she wrote that she might need to change hospital and thus it proved. She moved to Carlisle. Geraldine sat down to write to her, two or three times a week, at the same time as she wrote to Three Crosses. She allowed me and Lindie to put in sheets of our own. When Geraldine got Peggy's replies, she would sit down by the fireplace in Daddy's old chair with the pineapple finials and read extracts to us.

'I wrote to Packie on Sunday to tell him to mind Daddy and Vance with the milking on account of the brucellosis. By the way thank you for sending on the Southern. No doubt yourself saw they had diphtheria in Blanchardstown after some of the farmers ditching. Was it the Delahuntys of Ballindarragh, I wonder?

Geraldine please on no account have worries about Derrick Fowles. He is a delightful man and very calm and considerate to me. He has a good post with a building society.

Be sure now and place all your trust in Our Lord God and his Holy Mother,

I remain

Your devoted sister

Margaret

I shepherded my own sisters to and from school most days in my last months at Pius the Twelfth and never lost them in the park again; I polished the family's shoes each morning; I overcame my infantile dislike of the vacuum-cleaner and learned to use it; I shopped for the family; in short, I took seriously the imperative, the encouragement, offered to me by the adults of Three Crosses, to be a great man now and look after my mother Geraldine and my sisters.

★

Geraldine was to remarry, in 'sixty-two. Robert da Souza, a native of Goa, was a male nurse (as they used to be called), with many brothers and sisters, two of them in this country, who took Geraldine to their hearts. After leaving a seminary in India during the war, Robert had emigrated at the time of Partition and qualified here. My mother, my adoptive mother, was fortunate in her choice. It was a long marriage; Geraldine and my stepfather died four years ago, as I write real-time, within eight months of each other.

Bob (as I was permitted to call him) spoke English well, but in a smiling drawl, in tones which I can only describe as out of acoustic focus, which made it difficult for the listener to separate words. He could have perfected his elocution and eliminated his accent, had he chosen. But he had reached a level with which he was happy and he did not bother to improve. I never discovered what his bedside manner was like and it often occurred to me that he would have made a better surgeon than the nurse he was. Focus and precision, along with dexterity, were part of his make-up, despite what I have just said about his verbal skills. He was a collector of clocks and old watches. On nights when he couldn't sleep, he would dismantle and service our wristwatches in the kitchen in the small hours. We would find them, correct to the second, on the mantelpiece the next morning. Lindie and Beebie and Kate took the da Souza surname. Geraldine and Bob elected that I remain a Bennett after my father. I did not speculate on their motives at the time. For family allowances and, years later, university applications, my identity was problematic.

Problematic... What I could not share with Geraldine or Bob or my sisters was private memory of my father. That, as you see, I have carried for myself down the years. When it was necessary for my mother to talk of that part of the past, I noticed that good-hearted Bob would be present; but, like and respect him though I did, I could never swallow the fact that he, through his private, adult, knowledge of what had gone before, owned another part of me. My father Roy's physical legacy to me had comprised the yellow-and-red Windsprite box-kite, the horn-handled penknife and the book of Arthurian legends. But those, now lost, artefacts only stood as symbols for his true and deep bequest to me: the mystery of who he was, who my mother was, and the dull, corroding pain of a daily interrogative: who was I?

When Bob came into our lives I could no longer, in the nature of things, be the precocious man of the family. Father-like, his hand would come across my shoulders; I appreciated the family good-night kisses he introduced, the opening offer to me of the fresh crust of the bread at teatime, the smart Raleigh - blue, not black - that I had always wanted on my fourteenth birthday; the conspiratorial sympathy on the arrival of the school report and the glossing over of the critical comment ('Adam is his own worst enemy... Adam's lack of concentration... incessant daydreaming... he is distracting others...'); the National Savings Certificates on my birthdays; the suppers thoughtfully left out for me after Youth Club. Yet, driven from Eden, I did not belong in Curzon Street, or in the new house at the end of Ackerley Park. On the surface, all was as it should have been. Because Geraldine needed him to, Bob gave what he could: he could not give what I needed.

In our recomposed family we all knew, I think, that I was biding my time until I would be independent: flying the nest, leaving home, were phrases that held no terrors. There was little unkindness between us; there was, in fact, as much serenity as adolescence permits; there was a sort of love, but it did not abate the tides of rage and guilt in me which I could not understand, nor diminish my conviction of incompleteness and failed personhood. We gently grew apart in the home they had done their best to build for us.

*

I threw myself into my studies at the grammar school? I did not. The appetite, the drive for disciplined study failed me time and again. If I studied and progressed at all, it was as a matter of compliance on the one hand and of the good offices and long patience of the school on the other. I immersed myself in books, any books I could get my hands on. I read almost any poetry. I was drawn to the classical languages and, in some parts of that field, was not without ambition, but without the illness should attend it. Physics met some deep need in me. The subject was not merely difficult, it was hard, too, nailed down to that world of matter which, like the hellish black rocks at Skellymoher Strand, obtruded, without compromise, into the sea of dreams in which I lived.

I made no enduring friendships at the grammar school, though I was deeply envious of those who had. I thought of myself as an outsider and a misfit.

'He was his parents' only son, his father's pride and joy

And dearly did that father love the wild colonial boy.

At the age of sixteen years he left his native home

Across the sea to Australia he took a mind to roam

To rob the wealthy squatters there, their houses to destroy

A terror to the public was the wild colonial boy.'

Aunt Finola's ballad resonated down the years with the truth about me: I was, I thought, the only son of my father, who had loved me, and of the beautiful woman whose picture I had seen, once, in Ninnie's parlour on the second last day of the dreamtime, in the last cottage farmhouse of the famine village above Ballinsaggart. My wildness must be inevitable, prefigured for me in those lines.

Other classmates were keener, brighter, far worthier: a case in point was my identical peer, (we shared the same birthday), Foster. After one lesson in Latin scansion, Foster could read off a hexameter immediately. So he was called to the front of the class to sight-read fifteen or twenty lines from the first Aeneid.

'En Priamus. sunt hic etiam sua praemia laudi

Sunt lacrimae rerum et mentem mortalia tangunt.'

'Look at Priam; here, too, you see virtue get its reward. Here are the tears of things; the dead-seeming past that goes straight to the heart.'

Foster declaimed faultlessly; the rest of us sniggered. We knew he didn't want to stand in front of the class, because his toes were showing out of the front of his socks and shoes. Pov Foster got a first at Oxford. The last I heard of him was that he became an MP.

Some masters singled me out as worthwhile, and a friendly gesture or a genial look in the eye has stayed with me a lifetime; one or two took it upon themselves to dislike me, as Barrett of Blanchardstown had done, and to let their disdain show with a curl of the lip. I suspected that they warned their pupil favourites to avoid my company in and out of school. On my visits to the home of Paul Sinkiewicz (though he and I were at different schools), I fancied I read this message of unwelcome on his father's countenance. Sinkiewicz senior, however, a blimpish-looking clone of an RAF officer, at least made an effort to talk to me in his heavily-accented English: what did I think of the Soviet Union, he continually asked me, and seemed pleased by my responses. If *persona non grata*, I was, at least, persona chez Paul.

My delinquency inside the grammar school, when detected, was punished by canings (three minor and one major) in the years I was there. Outside academe, I took to crime in three forms: vandalism, drunken aggression - I was banned from two boys' clubs for having been constantly in the thick of fights - and occasional thieving: stealing comestibles from corner shops; pilfering cigarettes, drink and petty cash from clubs and from public houses. I was a solitary operator and too clever to be caught. I nevertheless carried scars from some of the fights I took part in. When I was fifteen, I was stabbed twice in the side with a flick-knife, to the hilt, but (by some miracle) not critically. I successfully concealed the two wicked little slits in the skin above my left hip, along with most of my other cuts and contusions, from both Robert and Geraldine, as once I had hidden from her the damage to my arm and finger, the day Thady threw me, in Haskin's field, under Kilcreggan woods.

In the eight years from that summer at Three Crosses to the end of my schooling, I had one more letter from Busty Heaphy. He made no mention of Peter Cody's death, (which his brother Hughie had caused), nor of Hughie's fate at the hands of the law. Geraldine made periodic trips home, either alone or with Katie while the latter was still at Pius the Twelfth. One of Bob's sisters would move in for a week to look after him, me and my elder sisters. Neither Vance nor Grandfather Thomas nor Uncle Packie ever visited us in Curzon Street, nor at the new house on a small estate, Ackerley Park, in the same area of the city, to which we removed in 'sixty-two.

One summer evening, in that year, 'sixty-two, I was walking home with three or four packets of cigarettes in my pockets, along with the apparatus (a miniature, barbed harpoon I had developed from a dart), which I had used to steal them from behind a grille at a church club after a dance. A group called the Silver Beatles had played there the season before. As I negotiated a dark ginnel on my way back to Ackerley Park, the silhouette of a policeman under a streetlight appeared a few yards ahead. I turned and ran. He gave chase. I thought I had shaken him off and I slipped home, where I concealed the results of my larceny and spent several hours in fear of a knock at the door that night.

To have been publicly exposed as the juvenile delinquent I was would have meant failure, in my own terms, in the task of trust I had received from Peggy and Grandfather Thomas at Three Crosses, to be a great man for Geraldine and my sisters. Daddy would have wanted me to be true to that commission: it was the reason why he had sent me home, the day I heard his voice under the sea at Skellymoher Strand, the day of my near-drowning. Despite the tiny bubbles of hatred that effervesced within my love for him, for the way he had left me, I must not let him down. Nor, further, did I wish to court expulsion from school, largely because of the confidence in me displayed by Pettigrew, the Physics master. Pettigrew had part-breathed, part-drummed his subject into me. He little knew, while he was alive, from what a future he had also helped to save me; I foreswore further crime.

Once my university future was settled, my mother and I attained a serenity of a sort; in the six months I spent at home, after leaving the grammar school in 'sixty-six, before I went away the following year, we considered each other anew; she talked to me over the dough-bowl (Bob liked soda bread) about her eldest brother Christie, eighteen years dead and the secret joy and sadness, cross and crown, of the Driscolls. Geraldine told me in a valedictory way that I had been as good a son to her as Christie had been to his mother, Maeve, and that she would miss me. These words, though I could not bring myself to believe them, seemed to offer prospect of the intimacy and forgiveness I had long craved, craved since the days of the dreamtime. But too much had not passed between us. Geraldine could not share with me a word of her life with Roy my father, *our* life; I believe she also knew, somehow, the full story of my criminal undertakings outside of school and our home, not speaking of them to spare both herself and me.

★

An undergraduate now, I luxuriated in a loneliness of my own making, forming occasional acquaintanceships rather than, like everyone else, circles of friends. One girl I was introduced to described me as nice but queer - we would say weird today. The comment came back to me through my first-year lab partner, Bez Peate, a northerner like me. Bez was hardly normal himself - prematurely middle-aged, I thought, with an academic stoop and absent-minded enough to attend his lectures in carpet slippers.

As you see, I permitted myself to feel censorious about Bez; I also judged, and found wanting, the social groups to which most of my undergraduate acquaintances belonged. I was unbothered that I must have appeared to them, at best, an aloof and spiky oddity. Notwithstanding my isolation, (Crusoe-like, I would go for days without speaking to others), I was as adept as everyone else at acquiring and coming to terms with the hypocrisies and concealed agendas of adults.

Not all my perceptions were flawed, however, and you may find this paradoxical: I can remember no feelings except gratitude for what England and my grammar school and university education had done for me. This was not, I discovered, how matters were seen by some of the other grammarians and many of the public schoolboys alike, whom I encountered. I am as weary as you, of harrowing accounts by the rich, the important and the well-connected, of how they were let down in life by their privileged educations and only attained the pre-eminence due to them, against all the odds, by virtue of a lifetime of struggle in the teeth of such disadvantage.

★

The call of the summer of 'fifty-seven, by then eight long years in my past, made itself all the more poignant in the new university world. On crisp October and November mornings, it was to the Faculty Library for Humanities that I often repaired, rather than to the labs or the Natural Science Library. Hawthorn Passage, a brick-walled alleyway and a short cut to the Humanities Library, became Driscolls' lane from my dreamtime; the coppered-green dome of the Library, behind the lime trees at the end of the passage, was Slievegarriff. In its mahogany chart-room, with the geologists and antiquarians shooting me odd glances over their National Health spectacles, I pored over nineteenth-century Ordnance Survey maps of Coole and Kilcreggan.

I knew that those maps represented a landscape of my past from which I had been cast out. Meandering in capillary threads over the green-and-orange hatching were the happy highways where I had gone and would not come again. Every tiny curve, every symbol for a dwelling, every bunching of the contour lines was a locus from which, like Odysseus over his sacrificial trench, in the *Book of the Dead*, I summoned up apparitions of Vance and PK, Busty and Packie, Feena, Cody, Grandfather and, the queen of all visions, my Aunt Peggy. So much had been played out and prefigured that summer in those places. In the longing for my father and the unrequited questioning in the stillness of the nights, I would come back again and again to the reaches east of Slievegarriff: metaphysical realities for me as much as points in time and place. In dwelling so intensely on and in those few square miles in the lee of Kilcreggan and the 'Garriff, I was, of course, seeking a way back, not only to the now-veiled world of the South Riding of the county Toberenagh, but to the veiled being that was Adam Bennett.

*

In that case, you ask, why did I not return to Three Crosses to visit? Last Friday night, real-time, at the Morningwood Country Club near Hartford, Connecticut, Todd Davern, the night before he married my niece Beebie's daughter Susie, asked me the same question. My only answer is a trite formula: the time was not right. Todd understood me. He told me he had majored in Greek Literature. Susie had thought of Greece for their honeymoon. But he wasn't ready to visit the country today. He feared to lose something; he could not say what.

*

After two years, I took and passed the first part of my degree examinations in Physics. I began negotiations, as you could in those days, to change to English Literature for my last year. In the event, I stayed with Natural Sciences. My deep reason for wanting to change was, of course, rooted in the life I had shared with my father and later, all too briefly, with my nineteen-year-old aunt, Peggy, at the end of my dreamtime: Malory's *Mort d'Arthur*, you see, was a special subject for Part Two in English that year. Only connect.

I sat my Finals in the June of 'sixty-nine. I stayed on in digs for another week in order to attend a Graduation Ball. My partner would be a historian, also a third year, Dolly Denstanley. Our eyes had met across the mahogany tables of the green-domed Humanities Faculty Library, during one of my forays there in the first year. I had piloted my own ship for three years, slowly moving apart from Geraldine, Robert and my sisters. I had not seen my adoptive parents for six months when I graduated; I had spent less and less of my vacation time at home, living in the south. After a spell as a trainee librarian, I joined a London publisher.

I came very close to returning to Three Crosses in 'seventy-two, when my grandfather, Thomas Driscoll, died in the Height bedchamber at Three Crosses. In my own bed in south London, I raged for him at first against the dying of the light. But then I remembered that a lad that was cute would not be mad at what he couldn't change. He would look at it in the face. Faith he would. Mine happened to be a hospital bed; I can at least claim that appendicitis stopped me saying my farewell to him in Ballinsaggart.

When I was twenty-seven, Dolly Denstanley and I broke off our engagement. At twenty-eight, I was sent on my first working trip to the capital of the world, New York City.

Twenty-Nine

August in New York and a conversation long overdue. October in Wales
and a further resolution.

New York City surprised me by being as I expected it
to be. It was famous for being famous. It was the land of
the *Midnight Cowboy* and of half-a-dozen more films I
had seen. I was more New-York-savvy when I got to
Penn Central than Joe Buck had been, as he stepped off
that Greyhound bus. Hoardings near the station said
Einstein on the Beach was opening at the Met in
November. Einstein was one physicist who had entered
my heroes' gallery at university. Albert stood there with
Merlin, Arthur, Achilles. Albert's equation had summed
up New York City: energy, masses, Times Square, the
speed of light. I was taken by private affluence and
shaken by public squalor in Manhattan, Brooklyn and the
Bronx. I disliked late summer in Central Park exactly as I
knew I would, the way New Yorkers did, for whom
August was the cruellest month, breeding rats out of the
dead metropolitan tenements nearby on Eighth Avenue.

For me, New York was about to mix memory with desire.

Eventually the heatwave broke, and tepid rain power-showered down, without warning. Subway stations on Manhattan sucked in the pedestrians in their thousands. An A-train, jammed with steaming passengers, screeched into Franklin Avenue between Manhattan and Queens.

I had a seat. A short, bald, middle-aged guy, one in a thousand, did not. He had his back to me and was sweating into a plain, grey shirt. Was there a touch of the clerical about him? He barely kept his balance, peering at station billboards out of dirty carriage windows as if through grease-proof paper. He held his head slightly inclined to one side. I saw two fleshy seams where his head met his neck; two folds, two laughter-lines where he had last seemed to smile at me out of the back of his head as we jogged to chapel under the horse-chestnuts of the avenue below Three Crosses in the trap, behind Alice, the piebald pony, one Sunday long ago in my dreamtime.

What I wrote just now is that he was one in a thousand. One in a billion is what I meant. This was the priest, the exile, Ed Deegan of Three Crosses, Rossbeg, Toberenagh, Ireland. I got up and tapped him on the shoulder. It was three o'clock in the afternoon of Tuesday 30 August, 1976, nineteen years to the day from my bidding goodbye to Three Crosses.

On Wednesday, we sat at the dark end of a deli on 42nd Street, next-door to Vandamm's Theater, lunching on pastrami sandwiches and grits. Father Ed cut his food like an American now and sat hunched over it, hairless forearms on the formica, cradling the melamine plate. He looked across from time to time at me. Twenty years evaporated under the glow of the table lamp. In the play of his features, I kept glimpsing his sisters Josie and Mary Deegan and Liam his brother, our neighbours at Three Crosses, once upon a time.

Ed still had the Hibernian parlance from our parts, overlaid attractively with the tones of the West Coast where he had spent so much of his life. That day in the diner on 42nd Street, he was dressed the way I remembered him on his vacation at Three Crosses in 'fifty-seven. It was probably the same Hawaiian holiday shirt. Navy trousers and open-toed sandals. Jesus boots.

'I am in New York for the next few years, anyway', said Ed.

'Nearer home.'

'To be sure', he said.

'When did you last see your sisters? And Liam?'

'Three years gone, this fall. But I'm going home to marry Daniel Brittan in October. I have to stop in London first. I'm renting a car. Why don't you come over with me?

'Babby Daniel? He can't be twenty. I remember the day of his christening.' I had my reason for remembering: Daniel had a godmother.

'I recall you well from that summer, Adam. You lived in your own world up there in Three Crosses, didn't you?'

'I suppose I did. I must have been an enigma to you.'

'When you were happy, no. Oftentimes you were as happy as a sandboy. Josie told me all about you.'

'I was happy…' I murmured, trying out the sentence for its sound and meaning.

'Until your Pa died, yeah? The same year Daniel Brittan was christened. You lost it. You were one sad, sad little guy. We could do nothing for you.'

I had the sensation that I was choking. It was exquisitely painful for me to get the next words out. I tried hard to keep control of what I was saying. It did not work.

'I was to blame for Dad dying. Can't let it go, Ed. My whole life is such a waste. Since he went. My mother blamed me.'

'Come on', he said.

I tried to mask the full extent of the turmoil his probing had caused, by avoiding a silence. I went on: 'I know she did. I read it across from my own feelings. She had to. She couldn't help herself, I wasn't her son. It was that he died without squaring things with me. He just went away, out of it, leaving me all the responsibility and I was angry with him.'

'Want to know what I think, Adam? You're gonna carry that stuff in that bag with you to the grave. But stop fighting it. Then you can go deal with it.'

'I think of my father all the time. It's so deep. I hate and I love. Why that should be, you may perhaps ask?'

'No; it's allowed.'

'I wish, I wished he had taken me with him, Ed. I had three close calls that summer at Three Crosses. Was I trying to catch up with Dad?'

'One of them was the day you nearly got killed alongside Peter Cody at the turn? That right?'

The emotion surged within me again, threatening to cut me off. But I had to speak. 'I play it in my head like a film, that accident. I've never said this to anyone else.'

'For you it was like losing an elder brother, right? You were both after losing your fathers.'

Tears tracked down over my cheek bones. I wondered if Ed could see them. I wept, silently, in the shadows, out of the embers of rage and of a deep and dreadful emptiness. 'And because we', I said, 'because he... was in the dark about who his real father was. I'm still angry about it, Ed. For everybody else to know...' from the deep recesses in me the thoughts came, forming words and sequences against my will; 'as if they owned a part of you without your permission. Why should they? How dare they? Why did my father let it happen? I keep suppressing it all, Ed. Peter was a kind of hero for me. I was glad my Aunt Peggy loved him.'

'Yeah.' Ed paused for a long minute. 'I always thought what a good-looking fellow he was.'

'Who? My father?'

'Him too. I meant Peter Cody.'

'After he was jilted, though, Peter found out who he really was. Aunt Peggy told me, long ago. Grandfather

Thomas knew - he said his father was a local man - but he never told me who.'

'His father was local and then again, not so local', said Ed.

'You know as well?'

'Peter's father was a Dyer Blasquet, the younger brother of Sam of the DBs of Rathmoven House. His mother, that you know, Agnes Cody, was a Delahunty of Castle East, working at Rathmoven as a butter-maker.'

Peter Cody a Dyer Blasquet. And he to have known it before he died. The truth might one day set me free, too.

'The DBs',' Ed went on, 'are long gone from Rathmoven House. Long gone. Now Sam, do you remember Sam, he took the roof off of the big house because he wouldn't pay the rates on it. It is a shell now, like Carty's Mill, fit only for bulldozing and that's all. His wife couldn't bring the furniture out of Ireland back here to the States as she wanted so it all went for auction in Dublin. By the vanload, boy. They were four days shifting it.'

'I remember Sam. Came to Tourmahinch chapel once or twice in a beige Humber.'

'He's still alive and in his nineties.' We ordered coffee.

'You're not so bad-looking yourself', said Ed. 'Are you going with anyone? Dating?'

I told him about Dolly and me.

'Well, what'll you do now, Adam? Did you ever think of the priesthood?' I had come down from the high, dreadful plateau where the talk of my father and the accident had taken me. I gave Ed a shallow rejoinder. I said the careers master at my Protestant grammar school had not mentioned it as an option. After a pause: 'What's it like, being a priest?' I said.

'Hell and Heaven, like anything else. This isn't a great time for me. I'd sooner be back in Sacramento, boy. And I don't want to be going back to Ireland for the wedding.'

'Why?'

'Arra.'

'Where is Daniel's wedding?'

'In St Camillus' Chapel at Tourmahinch, boy. Oh, 'tis a godsend to me to meet you like this, Adam.' Ed was looking across at me with a sixty-five-year-old's hope and vulnerability, the way Grandfather Thomas had sometimes done. Somehow, an image from my boyhood reading in the dreamtime seeped through into my consciousness. It shaped itself into a scene from *Robinson Crusoe*.

'It now remained that the captain and I should enquire into one another's circumstances. I began first and told him my whole history, which he heard with amazement. And, indeed, as my story is a whole collection of wonders, it affected him deeply. But when he reflected from thence upon himself, and how I seemed to have been preserved there on purpose to save his life, the tears ran down his face, and he could not speak a word more.'

A whole collection of wonders. A collection of wonderings. I continued my story when we met again for dinner at Fr Ed's institute in Queens. On the Friday, I took an evening TWA flight back to London. Ed was depending on me to come to Ireland with him, I understand now. The why of that, however, is for another narrative. It was on that first day of September that I saw the Brittans' coming occasion was the occasion coming for me to make my journey.

★

October arrived, prematurely grey. The red-and-black 1100 automatic purred west, at a steady forty-five, up and down the long, straightened Welsh roads that now filleted the countryside.

'I'm bored with the freeway', said Ed, pulling over into a lay-by and fishing for the AA book. 'We got plenty of time before the boat. Will we take the back roads from here on?'

We broke our journey again, to eat, at a hamlet in west Wales. The Post Office, with its red Morris GPO van parked outside, sold food. On the same plot as the Post Office stood Watlerton Rural Life Museum, housed in a First-World-War munitions hut, freshly painted in olive green. It is no longer there in Watlerton, but it was the nineteen-seventies' ancestor of a thousand twenty-first-century interpretative centres. Ed paid Mrs Adam, the postmistress, fifty new pence entrance money.

'He's an Adam', said Ed, indicating me.

'My husband will be along directly to open up for you', said the postmistress, 'he's an Adam too, twice over', she laughed like my Great-Aunt Ninnie, 'Adam Adam.'

'My middle name is Adam', said Ed, to make it clear we all shared the same problem.

We sat in the 1100 and sucked on our ice-creams till Adam Adam appeared. He turned up in a grey BMC Riley pickup full of wire milk-crates in the back. The Adams did a bit of everything.

'By here', he said, unlocking the door of the Rural Life Museum and leaving us to our own devices. We stepped inside and stood in front of a four-wheeled, horse-drawn butcher's van. It had been cleaned but not restored. The navy paintwork bore the knocks and chips of daily use. The vehicle had gone out of service in the late forties.

'Remember Panloaf O' Donoghue's four-wheeler?' I said.

'I do, indeed. It was belonging to the railway. He bought it from the stationmaster in Rossbeg. He never kept it long because it was the hell of a thing to drive the poor horse up to Coole hauling a half a ton of nuts.' He changed subject and asked me about my future.

'I can't see a pattern ahead. Maybe I've got to feel it before I see it.' Yeats' fierce romanticism was on my mind at the time. 'Did you ever read Yeats?'

'He that sings a lasting song

Thinks in the marrow-bone.'

Astride a 'twenties delivery tricycle was a tailor's dummy, done up in a baker's outfit. Amongst the accoutrements displayed on a hay-bale next to the tricycle, was a Lucas *King of the Road* carbide lamp.

I had spoken in a neutral way of feelings a moment ago. Now I was awash again with primitive emotion; in that nickel-silver and japanned work of art, with its great, jewel-like eye of a lens, coalesced all my complicated feelings for Packie and Peggy and Feena, alongside the rawness of the first cut, the deepest, into my soul when Daddy died, the cut that had never healed.

'Which year, exactly, did they pull down our house at Three Crosses?'

'Four years ago, after your grandfather Thomas dying. Why?'

'What happened to the carbide lamp?'

'Carbide lamp? You got me there.'

'It was an old bicycle lamp, identical to that one. It belonged to Packie Driscoll.'

'A bicycle lamp, right. Packie was in the States when they took the roof off the house. I don't think he has gotten back to Three Crosses since your grandfather died.'

'Ah, yes', I said. 'There was a gun, too.'

'A gun, too, says you!'

I lapsed into silence. Who got them, the lamp and the gun? Ed looked at me once or twice the way people do when they think you need help. My yearning for those artefacts was obsessional, in the marrowbone. The tears of things.

★

'Who's coming to the wedding?' I wanted to know. We had left Watlerton Rural Life Museum behind and were weaving our way in third gear through the back roads towards Port David. Blizzards of autumn leaves whisked up behind us until the land became open and treeless, as we neared the sea.

'The world and his wife.'

'Peggy?'

'Peggy?'

'My aunt, Margaret Fowles?'

'Hardly. I heard she was out of touch with the family. Your aunt Feena O'Donoghue writes to her. Isn't Peggy married and living in Bishop's Stortford?'

I pretended to sleep as the last miles slipped by, reliving the past which waited in front of me. There had been mystery about Peggy's marriage to Derrick Fowles; the preliminaries for it had involved, for me, a number of long evenings in charge at 44 Curzon Street, reading Palgrave's *Golden Treasury* and listening to Radio Luxembourg with my sisters, while my mother visited Peggy in her digs on the other side of the city, returning by taxi at midnight or later. I had not been party or witness to the deliberations. Of the Driscolls, only my mother Geraldine and Aunt Feena had attended the wedding. After their marriage and a bare six months after setting up home in Drogsden, Derrick and Aunt Peggy Fowles had moved to the South of England.

When Peggy had gone away with Derrick, I had endeavoured to imagine her changed utterly and belonging now to the land of my lost content which I was destined never to regain. But on days and nights in the years of my adolescence and youth, she often insinuated herself into my dreams. In one recurring image, she would be looking at me over the top of a book she was reading to me, as if she were my father Roy, as if to tell me the affection she had given me in the dreamtime had been something he wanted, a continuation of his love for me.

My mind took me back to another female face, one I had seen for the only time at my father's funeral, framed in a headscarf, her slight form in a belted, camel winter coat. This was Greta, the woman from the foundry where my father had worked. Because of my indisposition and consequent sequestration by headmistress Frowstie at my father's funeral, Greta and I had not encountered each other that day. Was the dimpled infant with golden curls showing from under her bonnet, whom Greta had brought to church in the pushchair, my sister or half-sister? I could not banish the insistent question. Was my father, my hero, le Roy that loved Beau Sir, loved us all and wanted only the best for us, capable of this infamy - to father another child, not only on this woman, bodily, but on my mother Geraldine who was not my mother and, finally, on me? That question remains, real-time. Another, I reflected, would be much easier to settle and I resolved to make the necessary searches. Was Greta my godmother, the godmother of whom Geraldine would not speak because I had addled her poor head, the day of the Brittan baptism in July 'fifty-seven?

Who brought me into this world? Where and who was I in it? The blood-catechism took me back, finally, to

Great-Aunt Ninnie's and to the picture there for me to find in the album in her parlour above Ballinsaggart. A blonde woman with a dark necklace and earrings, cheek-to- cheek with my young father, looked at me out of a face like mine, a face she had given me. My mother.

I pretended to wake up. We had five miles left to Port David.

'Where is Great-Uncle Vance Driscoll now? Is he on his own?'

'I'd say so, Adam. But I don't rightly know where.'

Ed fell silent and the long conversation about the 'fifties dreamtime that had begun the month before, in New York, came to an end, as the 1100 whined down the last steep hill to the harbour. A conversation full of sound and fury; perhaps I have been an idiot to tell the tale. I see now, real-time, so many streaks of sense and meaning. For too long the philosophers have tried to change the world. The point is to interpret it.

When we embarked at Port David the wind was brisk, the sea was green and the boat rocked gently but ominously in the harbour at her moorings. Beyond the breakwater, the white horses galloped. The swell slapped like a boisterous lecher at the base of the lighthouse. I knew the crossing would upset me; travel medication would make no difference. I said nothing to Ed. Sixty miles west, beyond the horizon, across the mystical green whale-road, the families would be on the strand at Skellymoher as Peggy and Geraldine, Lindie, Beebie, Kate and I had been: they, like us, once upon a time, staring out to sea over half-consumed bottles of Corona and ham-and-tomato sangwidges.

Thirty

A wedding; I return to Three Crosses; finis.

Tourmahinch Chapel had grown smaller but had otherwise changed little in the twenty years. Shoogie Mackie's brother Noddie still tolled the single bell, but with what seemed more urgency, on a wedding day. The cracked stonework of the coaming over the porch, the slate roof with its slight sag, the slate-capped buttresses - all was as I needed it to be. There had never been a straight line in the building: in that respect, at least, it stood comparison with the Parthenon of Athens, spartan though it was in others. Only the strange, blind side of the chapel, where the altar-boys would go to relieve themselves, looked different in 'seventy-six, ablaze with wisteria.

I sat at a single prie-dieu which had been wedged into a space on the left, between the balustrade separating nave from aisle and the pulpit. It was a poor vantage-point from which I only caught glimpses of the bride and groom, and saw little of the other guests. When the time came, I heard Ed, as if disembodied, preach from almost overhead. After the wedding mass, though I had intended to reintroduce myself during the photographs to those who would know me, my courage failed me. I slipped out of the churchyard to await Ed by the 1100, which we had parked at the end of a line of cars, a good way out of the village, towards Slievegarriff. On my mother Geraldine's black Rudge bicycle, I had last travelled this road the day Aunt Peggy had taken me to Great-Aunt Ninnie's.

By the time I had pedalled the road of return from Ninnie's mountainside farm at Ballinsaggart, it had become the road of no return; I was in possession of an indelible, black-and-white mental image, the face of the woman who had borne me, the final truth that had made my undoing complete. Geraldine's, but not my mother's, Rudge had brought me back to Tourmahinch and Three Crosses.

Ed was held up in the churchyard. So I got a ride to the reception in Rossbeg from a first cousin of the PK Reynolds of Three Crosses who had explained to me when I was ten that I was a bastard. The First Cousin lived up in Coole and was a great friend of the Heaphys. Mercifully, he knew little of the Driscolls, or of me. He apparently drew no connection between me, Hughie Heaphy and the accident at the blind turn on our road in which Peter Cody had died. He wanted, in any case, to talk about the troubles in the North and I obliged him with a few non-controversial remarks.

The Toberenagh Tearooms, or Hotel, it was now called, was our venue. The restaurant and bar still opened directly onto the pavement of Main Street, Rossbeg and the signage and livery of the place was still black and gold. I had separated from the First Cousin and had arrived too early. Rather than attract attention in the lobby when Mr and Mrs Daniel Brittan, the newlyweds and any panjandrums arrived, I took a glass of champagne and walked through to the terrace at the back, to muster courage for the coming encounters.

Beyond the stone terrace was a sloping rear garden, which would have looked down a hundred yards towards the Glas, had not the brick warehouses at the quayside blocked off most of the view. Because of the sweep of the Main Street and its shops at my back and on my right, I could not see Mount Slievegarriff in the west, except, I fancied, her peak and cairn, unless my eyes deceived me, behind the campanile of the New Church. Ahead of me, on the other side of the river, the Great Vale ended. Above the piered, stone bridge on the road up and out of Rossbeg towards the coast, I saw a new house or two.

'Enjoying the view?' asked the Hotel owner and master of ceremonies. I fancy he was the old rocker, Pad Dempsey, that Aunt Feena had once fancied, and made a mental note to ask Ed about him. Was he still playing in a showband in Comerford? 'Wait until I loan you a binocular.' He came out of an office in a moment with a pair of Zeisses in a leather case and I put down my champagne. I opened the case and slid out, from their scarlet snug, those binoculars, bible-black, serious, massy, glossy. The oil in the focusing spindle had taken in the scent of the leather. The instrument sat perfectly in the hand, a tactile feast. Its eyepieces turned with the same buttery smoothness as had the knobs and switches of my laboratory oscilloscopes or, further back, the knurled faux-ivory dials on Mother Geraldine's Perfectone portable wireless of old. The Zeisses reminded me of Uncle Packie's black Raleigh and its Lucas *King of the Road* carbide lamp. I would, I resolved, have a Lucas lamp or, at least, a pair of Zeisses of my own, before I was thirty.

I scanned the new bungaloid cottages on the road to Comerford and beyond; I picked out glimpses of the river sparkling behind the warehouse windows; I focused on the restoration work on the battlements of Montallond Castle, from which The Breffni had plunged to his death; I panned out over the rooftops to the summit of Slievegarriff, on whose rounded flanks I had neither trespassed nor trodden, for all that she had watched over us, summer after summer, in the dreamtime. With the field-glasses, I saw for the first time her naked nipple - the cairn, clear and sharp. I think, reader, this was the point during my visit at which I found myself able to decide to go back to the site of our house, the Driscoll farmstead at Three Crosses. I had still to face encounters at the wedding reception: Geraldine and Robert, perhaps, who might be surprised to see me. Feena and Michael Panloaf? Would Feena be playing the melodion later in the evening? Peggy and Derrick? The Codys? The other Deegans? And, without ever a cod now, whobody else?

'Ain't he the spit of his father, though, Daddy?' I heard from behind me, and turned, with as much poise as I could muster, to see who it was that remembered both me and Daddy. But the dowager, who was talking behind her hand to her husband, was looking at someone else to whom to attribute salivary honour. Why, in any case, should I have expected to be recognised? It was nineteen years, I was a dark-haired young man, not a blond boy; these people whom I had once thought mine, if they had ever been, were so no longer. They, not I, were the heirs to this place; my first disobedience, that morning of the aspirins at Curzon Street in February 1957 and its catastrophic sequels, had long ago denied me a way back to the lanes, hills, meadows and mountain of my Eden. After my return to Three Crosses, I would climb my mountain and there I would leave my mark, planting on her cairn a slate pebble from the Shanaun.

I sauntered on down to the end of the garden with the Zeisses in one hand and my drink in the other. I sat down in a little arbour under a ragstone wall. It might once have been a privy, no matter: now it had a manicured, English feel about it, with its fresh paint in bottle-green, guelder roses trained against the boards of its sides. The rest of the guests were beginning to show. I watched some of them through the field-glasses as they drifted out onto the top terrace. Most of the men stayed inside at the bar. The women brought their drinks outside. I trained the Zeisses on their faces. The older mothers, with the joys and pains of their families written in their faces, their hair drawn back in buns, or cut short, dead and un-dyed; they wore flowered blouses under plain suits. Did I hear Mr Hughie and Mrs Poppy Heaphy of Coole announced by Pad Dempsey, the master of ceremonies? The First Cousin who had given me the lift to the Hotel had mentioned that Busty Heaphy was gone to Dublin for the summer.

A group of young women, friends of the bride, I imagined, sipped at each other's drinks and practised their school-leavers' reminiscences, looking down at the Glas behind me. They were well-to-do. One wore a hairband like a tiara and carried a handbag that glittered with sequins or jewels. I was sure she was an Anderson of Tize Court. The sceptred race, the form divine. With the look of money went a touch of the flirt and, hatless for a moment as she rearranged her hair behind her right ear, she incarnated for an instant that image of my own birth-mother I had seen once in Great-Aunt Nina's album and daily thereafter.

The sun came out to light the centre of the garden and I put down the binoculars. In a minute or two, I would go up and see with whom I had been positioned at table. I was a singleton: Ed would be sitting with the bride and groom.

I looked up again at the french windows to the terrace and saw a woman in her late thirties, standing with her face in profile. She looked to her right, her right elbow cupped in the palm of her left hand. The jewelled, Tize Court heiress and her companions to her left were eclipsed. It was Aunt Peggy. What every virtue, every grace, Peggy, all were thine.

Had Peggy seen me, recognised me in the chapel? I supposed she had no idea I was to be there. I felt suddenly weak. Too much was about to surface and I doubted my ability to handle myself publicly, if I approached her now. She would have Derrick with her. I would ask Ed to reintroduce us during the meal. I fitted the Zeisses back into their case, as a hand into a glove.

Though the pleasure of the instrument in my hand had scored with me again, my mood had changed. I headed back up the slope of the garden. For all my twenty-eight years, I was suddenly tired, slow, low. My innards still ached from the retching on the boat yesterday. My courage went. I could not join the reception yet. I wanted to be elsewhere for a few hours. To sleep, perhaps to dream. I was locked out.

★

The Drennans still had a taxi business in Main Street, though they now ran Datsuns. I asked Drennan *fils*, (he told me his name was Jaxie, but I couldn't bring myself to address him as such), to drop me at the turn between Tourmahinch and Three Crosses. It was where Hughie Heaphy's Standard had hit Diamond the pony and capsized the milk-car, throwing me onto our road and killing Peter Cody. I would walk up past Dempseys' long fence and orchards, then under the horse-chestnut tunnel and on up to our maroon gates. We took a long time getting there, following a combine for a mile - a great, high, blood-red behemoth with a farmer-pilot atop, sat in a control module like some Skylab astronaut.

On the left, I passed the three ancient crosses in the bishops' tomb that had once been an oratory. Reynoldses' farm came up on the right, but their house was now hidden from the road by twenty years' growth of trees. Their driveway, where I had planned to catapult at turkeys, was newly-surfaced like a county road. So they had prospered. I passed our Kanturk barn on the left. I remembered two spans; now there were four, every one full with someone's hay-bales. Then I came to our entrance. The fuchsia hedge remained. The gates were still in position, in their original paint, with Peter Cody's mended bottom rail visible.

But Three Crosses farmhouse was history; not even the gable ends with their sash windows had survived. What had been the dairy outhouse was now a long outcrop of boulders at the top of the yard. A black-and-white rooster stood on one of these and watched me. An ancient fear returned and I gave him a wide berth. The cast-iron pump still stood. The old cow-house, 1869, the best-built in our parts, with its date over the arch, still stood. The gap, where our house had been, opened up a prospect and a short cut to the haggard. I stepped bodily through the ghost of the house, across the hearth-tiles where Grandfather Thomas's captain's chair had stood, through a few square yards of grass that had been Vance's bed-sitting-room. I came to the glade, to the rusted-out shell of the Morris Eight where I had sat in the company of Man Friday and Morgan le Fay, of Lancelot and Lamorak, Crusoe and Cuchulain. The metal wreck, a monochrome brown now, inside and out, had meanings for someone else, too: the grass around it had been flattened by recent footsteps.

I was drawn back through the haggard to the front yard and the open maroon gates. I stepped out into our road, unchallenged, and turned into the entrance to our lane, Driscoll's boreen, where, in summer, our Herefords and Red Polls would pass, twice heavy, twice light, four times a day. The lane had not changed much, except to be darker and narrower. It bore the ruts, not of the cartwheel, into which I had fitted my red Sunday sandals walking here with Daddy in the dreamtime, but of the patterned tyres of the tractors I could hear growling in the fields, Allis-Chalmers, Fordson and Fergie. I walked on up for a hundred yards, skirting our orchard and its dyke, passing Deegans' home paddock. I left the lane when I came to the Honey Meadow. The field was being grazed by a few Friesian heifers. I ignored them and followed one of their paths from the gate up to the north-eastern corner of the mead, where there were the remains of another dwelling, once lived in by people of the name Davern.

The old well in the Honey Meadow had belonged to the Daverns' house. Now, like Daverns', our own house, Driscolls', was no more. Seventy years back, the well had been capped with a giant slate hauled down from Kilcreggan by seven women. Time had shrunk the huge coffin-lid shape that I remembered, but it was still an impressive piece of rock, primal, a twentieth-century menhir.

Twenty years ago, of an afternoon, I had stripped off my shirt, lain out on the smooth slab in my burgundy britches and scratched away at the stone, with the half of a quartz pebble I had smashed for the purpose with a couple of blows of the pein-hammer. Half-dormant there, under the afternoon sun, I used to dream of myself as some caveman, wanting to leave my mark on the stone, in the twentieth century, with my graffito-work. Sometimes it rained, the drops hitting the sun-warm stone first and vanishing into it: then, as the stone soaked and darkened, its grain came out, in strange magical meandering washes and striations. Now I sat on its edge, rough-grained and fissiparous, like a gigantic bitten fingernail, with my back to what had been our dwelling

Donald Madge

at Three Crosses and the timeless apple-trees in our orchard that had outlived it.

Here, in the Honey Meadow, I had played in my father's last summer; here, in the following year, I had passed on to my sisters the lore of the Windsprite box-kite that he had taught me; here I had avoided the humming menace in the far corner of the meadow, where old Coonig had kept his beechwood hives. The German had chosen his field well. Long gone were the hives, but bees aplenty remained; I sat alone in the bee-loud glade.

Westward I looked and the land was bright where the Deegans had cleared and sold a few of the great horse-chestnuts at the far end of the next field. Therewith opened up a new prospect to Mount Slievegarriff. The old order had changed, yielding place to new. This was a landscape now for others, other children, other persons yet to form themselves in its ways and contours, and I must embrace its passing; God fulfils himself in many ways, lest one good custom should corrupt the world. I had sipped heaven there, as others would. Combine harvesters, Ford Zephyrs and Honda 50s, black-and-white cows would be the stuff and furniture of their dreamtime as reapers-and-binders, ponies and traps, carbide lamps, Standards and Morris Eights had been of mine.

For half an hour, the images of those summers of 'fifty-six and 'fifty-seven passed again before my eyes; my story there to grasp at, to capture, as if through a glass, darkly. As I write this, real-time, at sixty years of age, one does not have that long to wait for final revelation.

*

Behind me, I was aware of a woman in the Honey Meadow making her way up the cowpath. The footfall was careful, quiet. 'Bozer!' The chime of the voice did not fail me, 'were you lonesome for me?'

Peggy took off her raincoat and revealed the outfit I had seen her in earlier that day, a navy barathea jacket, white blouse, pearls, a Trussardi bag and a beige, pleated skirt. She arranged the raincoat and sat down on it at the other end of the capstone, where she had last sat with me, nineteen years ago. Our eyes met. Mine drew her momentarily into the whole of my being, then I looked away.

'I saw you', I said, 'at the Tearooms. I didn't catch you then. I didn't feel like lunch. But I'm going back this evening for the hooley. Of course you knew the house was gone? Where's Derrick?'

'Derrick? The house - ah, sure, Adam - all gone...' She broke off into a bell-like laugh, as if she was about to toy with me, but it was not that. I thought later she was wary, taking stock. 'You have your father's voice, Adam.' Her own voice was what it had always been. She had not changed so much for me as I had for her. Every virtue, every grace remained.

She fixed me then with a long look. She shook me utterly, quickening my pulse again. I could not meet her gaze. She took off the pressure, turning her head away towards Dunakielthy and Slievegariff. Then my eyes sought out her face in profile and the lips which I would kiss before the afternoon was out.

'Where's Vance now?' I asked.

'He came out of the Sancta Corona a fortnight ago and now he's in the nursing-home in Rossbeg, boy. St Brede's. Doing great. I was in to see him yesterday.'

I was almost dissolved by her goodness. As I had been over those short summers as a boy.

'I thought that when I knew you weren't my real aunt any more I would never get over it.'

'Oh, now, Adam. I heard great reports about you.'

'Let me say it, Peggy. I was trying to cope but it was so different for me. Lindie and Beebie and Kate - they all came through well. And so did I, I suppose. You move on, people tell you. But you never move on. You take it with you. You build on. Another layer, develop another crust. What's left under the crust? That's the thing.'

'Oh, I never forgot you, boy',' said Peggy simply. 'Do you remember Coonig and his beehives up there in that corner?'

'I do.'

'Do you know what happened him, Bozer? Do there be anyone still call you Bozer?'

'No. Go on.'

'He was sent back to Germany, so he was. They kept him in Rossbeg Barracks for a few weeks then I believe they put him in prison in Munich.'

'I can't get - I think about Peter Cody always, Peggy. After Dad, he was my hero. He was lost like me, trying to find a way back.'

'He was so.'

'Father Ed told me Peter Cody's real father was the younger brother of Sam Dyer Blasquet. It happened when Agnes was working at Rathmoven House. Did you know that?'

'I did. But 'twas Denny Cody that put the roof over Peter's head and Agnes'. He reared Peter, the Lord have mercy on the both of them.'

Peggy opened her bag. She took out her purse and unfolded in front of me an obituary from the London Telegraph, cut out to about A4. I felt as if I had seen the obit and photo before. The accompanying portrait was of an insouciant young man in military uniform. Now I saw the picture with new eyes. He was so like Peter Cody, but there was someone else there. Peggy's eyes met mine. 'Remember him? You met him.'

'Of course, but it can't be Peter.'

'No; it's Reggie Blasquet, his real father.'

'And - '

'You met him. This was Peter's father, Reggie Blasquet, the old gentleman tinker from the quality, with the long, yellow nails.'

It was so; now I drew out, in memory, something of the young officer's smirk in the face of the English hobo, as, nineteen years before, he had jumped me making my river, when Packie had released me, after stopping the Anglia van near Eva Ban's, on the road to Skellymoher Strand.

'*After the War, he returned to the enthusiasms of his youth and in particular to the history and lore of the counties of Comerford and Toberenagh. The family seat was Rathmoven House near Rossbeg. In his later years, he spent his summers in travel and research in southern Ireland, where he acquired a reputation for eccentricity.*

'*Dyer Blasquet was the author of* Fields Martial *(1949), on the military experiences which led to his later pacifism and* The Rock of Kings *(1953), on the pre-Norman history of the southern counties, as well as of a number of collections of poems, privately published.*'

Peggy opened her bag to put away the purse and newspaper clipping. Immediately, I saw there, in the Trussardi bag, the 'thirty-nine Morris Eight handbrake release that started me on this tale. She blushed, then laughed.

★

We sat in the Meadow for another hour. The afternoon was mild, the autumn slower to come this year than in England and Wales. The sun moved west towards the 'Garriff and Dunakielthy. Peggy was staying over there with Panloaf and Feena or, should I say, with Michael and Finola O'Donoghue, the owners of Dunakielthy Farm.

'Derrick?' I said.

'I told you. Gone.'

'Why?'

'I left him, boy. 'Tis five years now.'

'You left him?'

'After he hit me. Then I found he was married before.'

'Divorced?'

'No, boy. 'Twasn't the church I had to contend with, but the police. Mr Derrick Fowles was a bigamist.'

★

We turned, so as to keep the sun out of our eyes. With the house demolished, from where we sat on the slate slab, we could see across east to Mickeleen hill bathed in October light and to the treetops that marked the course of the Shanaun in the valley below. When I asked Peg about the Morris handbrake release she had in her bag, she told me it was for Vance, whose car the Morris Eight had been. Then she said that, perhaps, she had really meant it for me.

So, reader, the brake-release became my souvenir of the day of Daniel Brittan's wedding; which is why, real-time, it sits in the passport drawer of the bureau in front of me. Next to it, in the same drawer, I have put a souvenir from Saturday's wedding in Hartford, a pair of American robins in hickory-wood, personally presented to me by the newly-weds Todd and Susie - Lindie's eldest and my niece - Davern. Todd had been engrossed when, in the loggia at the Country Club, the night before his wedding, I described the remains in the Honey Meadow of a well with a gigantic capstone and of a house once dwelt in by men and women with his surname. One wedding sets in train thoughts of another.

We talked on, Peggy and I, of the past in front of us, of realities, rumours and fables, our words sometimes heavy with the truth, sometimes skipping along the surface in the general direction of the deep flow, like the ducks and drakes I had played, with flat, brown slate pebbles on the Shanaun with Busty, so many years ago. She spoke to me of her childhood, her fractured experiences, of Christie, too, her eldest brother who had died with the leukaemia in 'forty-nine; she said things I cannot reveal even here, but that they measured the depth of the well of her love. I told Peggy my story, the story whose evolution within me I, an exile, a castaway, a prodigal without return, a stranger to myself and to the good, had so long and so deeply feared.

She understood. And what did I understand then? What I grasped was the truth of her struggles and suffering. I grasped, too, the hand she slipped into mine as we negotiated the briars before the last slate stile. Her face, a lover's now, looked up into mine; I had, at last, hope of return to a world I had betrayed in that summer of 1957 and thereafter. Here was my responsibility. Here I had to be a great man now. I understood. The dreamtime was recapitulated, recovered, restored to me, in those moments, after the wasteland of the last twenty years. The scent of lily of the valley and the sight of her pearls spoke to me. That I would love Peggy was written in the truths of childhood.

'We must visit Vance this evening in St Brigid's, Adam. Then we could go back to the reception for the crack. There'll be a hop this evening and Feena playing.'

'Said Great-Uncle Vance

Looking askance

Are ye going to a dance?'

'Arra, stop, the poor creature is still at the rhyming and he ninety-six. I said I'd go in to see him before they give him his bit of supper.'

'Vancey's supper? Do you know what that means,

A plate of boiled cabbage and a pair of crubeens.'

Peggy laughed and laughed. 'Oh God help us!'

'Coming with me?' I said.

'It seems that I am, Adam.' She brought her face up to mine. Then she placed a fondie, loose, light and long upon my lips.

The End